TO APPRECIATE THIS BOOK TO THE FULLEST, PLEASE VISIT THE WEBSITE: bobvillarreal.com, AND EXPERIENCE WHAT THE AUTHOR CALLS "READ (THE BOOK) AND VIEW (THE SITE): A NEW AND EXCITING WAY TO ENJOY A BOOK." CONTENT INCLUDES PHOTOS ARRANGED BY THE PARTS OF EACH LETTER, GOOGLE EARTH TOURS FOR THE PARTS, PAINTINGS BY LOUIS S. GLANZMAN (COURTESY OF NATIONAL GEOGRAPHIC), THE LETTERS OF PEDRO DE VALDIVIA TO KING DON PHILLIP OF SPAIN (FOR VOLUME II), AND SEVERAL MOVIES TAKEN BY THE AUTHOR OF MUCH OF THE GROUND OVER WHICH THE EXPEDITIONS TRAVELED.

BOOKS BY BOB VILLARREAL

CLAWING FOR THE STARS; A SOLO
CLIMBER IN THE HIGHEST ANDES

THE ADVENTURE CHRONICLES OF PEDRO
DE MERIDA, VOLUME I: ALMAGRO

THE ADVENTURE CHRONICLES OF *CONQUISTADOR* PEDRO DE MÉRIDA

TRAVELS TO ANCIENT CHILE IN THE YEARS OF OUR LORD, 1535-1537, WITH DIEGO DE ALMAGRO (VOLUME I), 1540-1554, WITH PEDRO DE VALDIVIA (VOLUME II), AND 1524-1550, WITH FRANCISCO PIZARRO AND THE SUBSEQUENT SPANISH CIVIL WARS (VOLUME III); BEING ACCOUNTS OF THOSE JOURNEYS TO THE FARTHEST MOST REGIONS OF THE INCA EMPIRE, AS RELATED TO HIS MOST CATHOLIC MAJESTY, KING DON PHILIP II, OUR MOST SOVEREIGN RULER

As recounted by himself, Pedro de Mérida, a Chile *Conquistador*

BY

BOB VILLARREAL

PRESENTED IN THREE VOLUMES,
OF WHICH THIS IS

VOLUME 2: VALDIVIA

Copyright © 2019 Bob Villarreal.

All rights reserved. No part of this book may be used or reproduced by any means, graphic, electronic, or mechanical, including photocopying, recording, taping or by any information storage retrieval system without the written permission of the author except in the case of brief quotations embodied in critical articles and reviews.

This is a work of fiction. All of the characters, names, incidents, organizations, and dialogue in this novel are either the products of the author's imagination or are used fictitiously.

Abbott Press books may be ordered through booksellers or by contacting:

Abbott Press
1663 Liberty Drive
Bloomington, IN 47403
www.abbottpress.com
Phone: 1 (866) 697-5310

Because of the dynamic nature of the Internet, any web addresses or links contained in this book may have changed since publication and may no longer be valid. The views expressed in this work are solely those of the author and do not necessarily reflect the views of the publisher, and the publisher hereby disclaims any responsibility for them.

Any people depicted in stock imagery provided by Getty Images are models, and such images are being used for illustrative purposes only. Certain stock imagery © Getty Images.

ISBN: 978-1-4582-2253-4 (sc)
ISBN: 978-1-4582-2252-7 (hc)
ISBN: 978-1-4582-2251-0 (e)

Library of Congress Control Number: 2019915989

Print information available on the last page.

Abbott Press rev. date: 11/08/2019

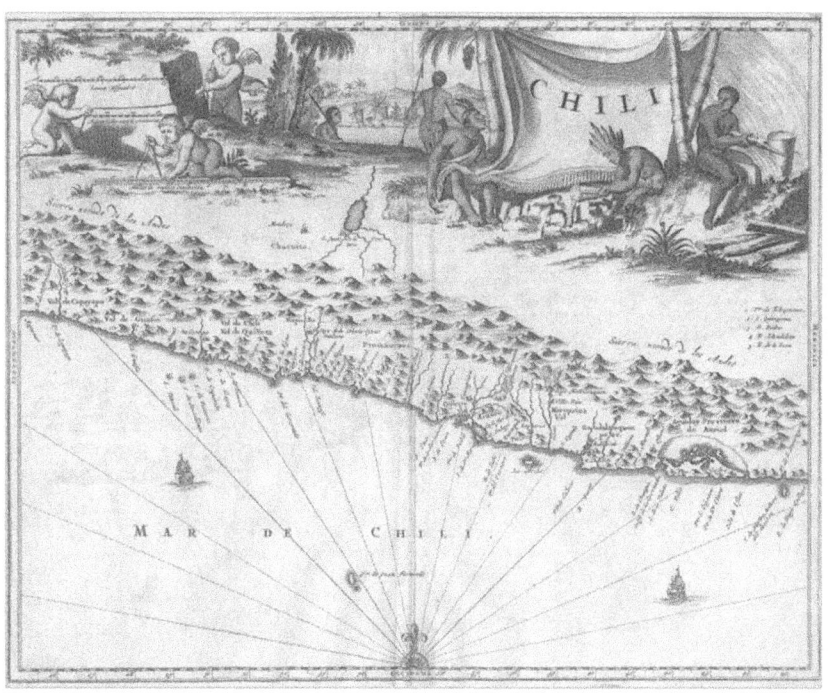

Antique print map of "Chili," by Arnoldus Montanus, published in Amsterdam by Jacob van Meurs in 1671. In the Public Domain. R. Villarreal Collection.

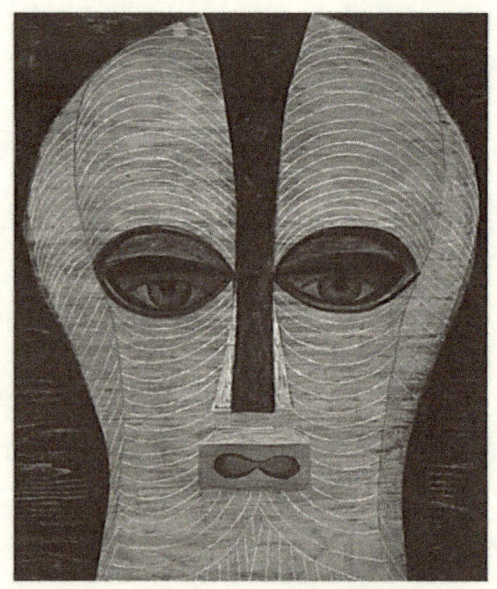

A Mapuche warrior stares from his dark jungle hiding place as he waits for unsuspecting Christians. Artist: Robert Shore. Copyright permission by MBI, Inc. 9/24/18.

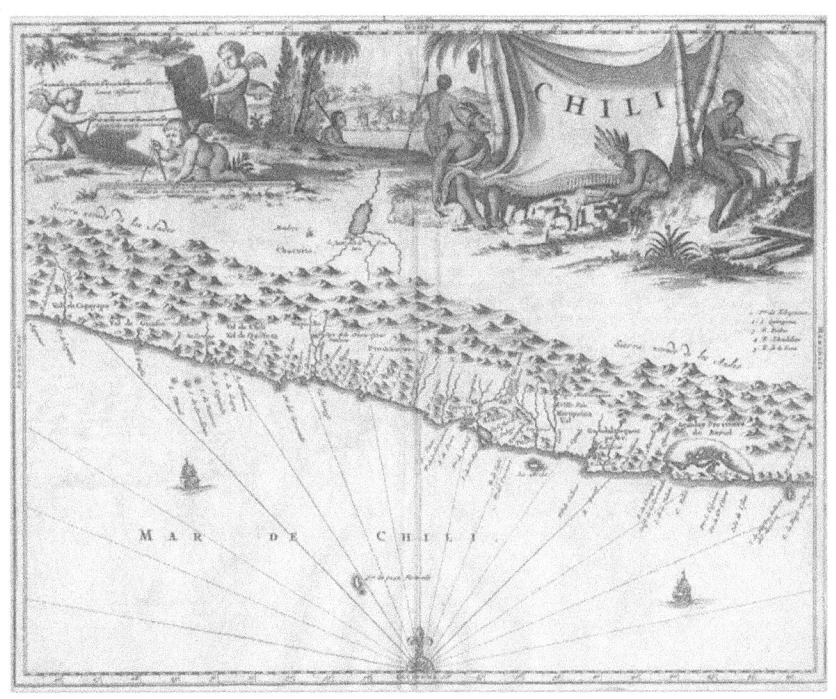

Antique print map of "Chili," by Arnoldus Montanus, published in Amsterdam by Jacob van Meurs in 1671. In the Public Domain. R. Villarreal Collection.

A Mapuche warrior stares from his dark jungle hiding place as he waits for unsuspecting Christians. Artist: Robert Shore. Copyright permission by MBI, Inc. 9/24/18.

PROLOGUE

A date known to most in the Western World is 1492, when the discovery of the Americas by Columbus closed out the Middle Ages and set the stage for the modern history of the New World. As a result, the people of Spain felt themselves a chosen nation and one destined for momentous events. The new lands offered an outlet for the ambitions of men frustrated by the exhaustion of their country and the endemic poverty that had plagued it for generations. The enthusiasm of these adventure seekers soon focused upon the discovery, conquest, and settlement of the new, unknown lands. Many military expeditions of but a few hundred men sent forth by the King left Spain for the new territories and swept to the farthest-most borders of the Americas in only several decades. Many of these men sought large returns on the investment of their time and money in such risky undertakings. Gold most of them desired, of course, but equally important were landed estates worked by peasant natives who would extract the soil's bounty for them. These new lords wished to enjoy their possessions, like the manor nobles at home in their olden land, and pass them on to their heirs in future generations. During these momentous times, one of these adventurers, Pedro de Mérida, became a *conquistador* and chronicler of the New World, one who would leave a vibrant record of his travels in Chile and Peru for us.

He tells his story in nine letters to King Phillip II, historical narratives here broken into three volumes. In the first three of Volume I, de Mérida tells of the Diego de Almagro Expedition to Chile in 1535 to 1537 and the return to Peru, a distance of more than 3,500 miles. In the fourth, fifth, and sixth letters of Volume II, he recounts his adventures with the Pedro de Valdivia Expedition to conquer Chile during the years 1540 to 1554. De Mérida's correspondences comprise the only formal record of the Almagro and Valdivia journeys composed by a member of the expeditions, and they help fill the historical void. Impressed by the first two volumes, the King asked de Mérida to tell of the Conquest of the Incas begun by the Spanish under Francisco Pizarro in 1524 and the following disruptive years that saw civil war amongst the conquerors. Thus, we have Volume III.

As for the times our narrator lived in, life was exciting in the sixteenth century Spanish domain, since it appeared to hold more possibilities for European man than ever before in its history. It was now apparent that the inhabitable earth was a larger place than previously understood. This abrupt extension of horizons to unheard of physical dimensions was paired now with a sense of destiny that Spain was the designated representative of God to Christianize the globe. Were not the discoveries of Columbus obvious proofs of the special approval of Divine Providence? Every Spaniard must have thought himself exceptional in the eyes of the Lord, and thus felt his people to be the chosen race of the Almighty. This thinking unleashed a vibrant national energy and vigorously inspired the fervent imagination of young men. And to be young during this period in Spain was to believe in the heretofore impossible. An enlarged world brimmed with probabilities of adventure and riches in which the most improbable dreams and hopes of fame and fortune might come true.

De Mérida maintains a strict concentration upon the new lands of Chile and Peru, and this focus fuses his life with the stunning epic of the Conquest of the New World. Fortunately for the reader, he is often present when dramatic events take place, is close to the leaders when they make decisions, and shares their successes and failures. With a realism and intensity born of one who actually lived what he tells of, he transmits to his pages descriptions of the swathes of land never before seen by European man and the many happenings, including numerous detailed battle scenes that occurred during his travels. Also, the old soldier offers the reader countless memorable portraits of the major participants in these world changing events. But he gives surprisingly few details concerning his own life. We do know that he almost became a Franciscan monk, but set that pursuit aside for the journey to the new-found lands. He says nothing of his parents, but we may assume that they were surely of at least the middle class, for he had the somewhat uncommon ability to read and write. Moreover, he often reveals a moral sense of character, a good amount of learning, and an education in horse riding and the use of the sword. All of these indicate some level of education.

We must assume that de Mérida took thorough notes of his exploits and recorded the names of all those he associated with, the places he visited, and the things he saw. For how else to explain his letters written to King Philip many years after the events of which he tells? His writing style is direct and without pretension. While he occasionally registers his personal reactions to an event or person, he ordinarily tells his stories without inserting his own value judgments. While the work has the feel of a novel with its spontaneous recitation of adventures, detailed battlefield descriptions, energetic anecdotes, and the engrossing dialogues of the historical characters, it is still history as recounted by a horse soldier who suffered the pain of several wounds, endured hunger, the fear and tribulations of personal combat, the tension of campaigning in strange lands against antagonists of enormous numbers, the continual confrontation of the unknown, and his eventual crippling by a warrior's arrow to his ankle.

Despite hardships, one may surmise that our chronicler, a product of the Spanish desire for adventure, rather welcomed most of the discomfort, for he never complains or gives notice of his dissatisfaction. As he says on numerous occasions, he was seeking adventure. As it transpired, he found it, and in abundance.

As a final note, the author has traveled some seventy percent of the routes followed by the expeditions and is able therefore to convey his understanding of the terrain and people encountered in de Mérida's telling of things.

Bob Villarreal

TABLE OF CONTENTS

VOLUME 2: VALDIVIA

PROLOGUE...vii

THE FOURTH LETTER

PART AA.   THE STORY TO BE TOLD; WE LEAVE THE SACRED CITY FOR THE FARTHEST MOST REACHES OF *NUEVA ESTREMADURA*..1

PART BB.   THE PASSAGE BEGINS; WE CAMP AT THE RAQCH'I COMPLEX; A SUDDEN DEATH AMONG US..................................18

PART CC.   OUR WAY TO PUTRE AND THE VILLAGES AND PEOPLE ALONG THE WAY..26

PART DD.   OUR ENTRY INTO PUTRE AND WHAT TRANSPIRED THERE; CAPTAIN VILLAGRAN AND SEVENTY MEN JOIN US FROM TACNA...34

PART EE.	WE BEGIN OUR PASSAGE OVER THE AVENUE OF THE VOLCÁNS; OUR HUNT OF THE *SURI*, OR LESSER RHEA	43
PART FF.	OUR JOURNEY DOWN THE AVENUE CONTINUES; DOŇA INÉS USES AN ARQUEBUS TO SHOOT GUANACO	55
PART GG.	CHIU-CHIU AND CALAMA, AND WHAT TRANSPIRED THERE; OUR FIRST ENCOUNTER WITH SANCHO DE HOZ; WE MEET AGAIN, HUAMANPALLPA, THE *DESERT CACIQUE*	63
PART HH-II.	OUR PASSAGE TO ATACAMA AND THE DIVERS HAPPENINGS ALONG THE WAY; WE ARE JOINED BY CAPTAINS RODRIGO DE QUIROGA, FRANCISCO DE AGUIRRE, AND THE TWENTY-FIVE MEN WITH THEM	78
PART JJ.	OUR MARCH SOUTH TOWARDS THE DISTANT COPAYAPU; A STRANGE SICKNESS ATTACKS MANY OF US; OUR CAPTAIN NAMES A NEARBY PEAK, "DOŇA INÉS"	85
PART KK.	OUR APPROACH TO COPAYAPU	95
PART LL.	OUR TIME IN COPAYAPU AND WHAT HAPPENED THERE; ANOTHER ENCOUNTER WITH THE LOUT, SANCHO DE HOZ	 100
PART MM.	OUR DEPARTURE FROM COPAYAPU AND THE JOURNEY SOUTH TO PAPUDO; THE EXECUTION OF JUAN RUÍZ	114

THE FIFTH LETTER

PART NN. THE EXIT FROM PAPUDO; THE MARCH TO THE RÍO MAPOCHO; THE GREAT BATTLE OF THE HUELÉN AND THE FOUNDING OF SANTIAGO *DEL NUEVA EXTREMADURA* 127

PART OO. CONSTRUCTION OF SANTIAGO *DEL NUEVA EXTREMADURA*; THE FORMATION OF OUR *CABILDO*; ANOTHER ENCOUNTER WITH THE INCA *TOQUI*; THE EVENTS AT MARGA MARGA; LOCATING VALPARAÍSO HARBOR 143

PART PP. CONFRONTING THE CONSPIRATORS AGAINST CAPTAIN VALDIVIA; HIS ACCEPTANCE OF THE GOVERNORSHIP; A GOLD DISTRIBUTION; THE DESTRUCTION OF OUR CAPITAL CITY AND THE BEHEADINGS OF SEVEN *CACIQUES* 157

PART QQ. OUR CROPS FAIL OUR NEEDS; THE MAPUCHE CONTINUE THEIR RAIDS; DE MONROY, DE MIRANDA, AND FOUR OTHERS LEAVE FOR PERU; A SURPRISE SHIP ARRIVAL; THE RETURN OF DE MONROY AND DE MIRANDA 170

PART RR. DISTRIBUTION OF OUR LAND; MOVES AGAINST THE MAPUCHE TO THE SOUTH; RE-DIRECTION OF THE FIGHTING NORTH; MICHIMALONGO AND THE BATTLE OF LIMARI IN THE NORTH 180

PART SS.   A VISIT TO THE SITE OF VILLANUEVA DE LA SERENA; MY MARRIAGE TO PILCA HUACA, THE INCA PRINCESS AND *CACIQUA*; THE LA SERENA FOUNDING; THE VOYAGE OF EXPLORATION TO THE SOUTH AS RECORDED BY PASTENE IN HIS JOURNAL; MICHIMALONGO BECOMES A FRIEND 193

PART TT.   DE MONROY SENT A SECOND TIME TO THE CITY OF KINGS TO HIRE MEN; THE KILLING FIELDS OF QUILACURA; WE REACH THE BIO-BIO AT PENCO AND RETURN TO SANTIAGO TOWN; PASTENE RETURNS, WITHOUT DE MONROY; GOVERNOR VALDIVIA LEAVES FOR PERU TO FIGHT GONZALO PIZARRO; DE HOZ FINALLY MEETS HIS DESERVED FATE 215

PART UU.   SANTIAGO DEFENSES STRENGTHENED; VICEROY LA GASCA APPROVES VALDIVIA AS GOVERNOR OF THE PROVINCE OF CHILE; THE VICEROY'S LEGAL CASE AGAINST OUR GOVERNOR; HE REACHES VALPARAÍSO STATION AND HEARS OF THE DESTRUCTION OF LA SERENA; THE SEPARATION FROM INÉS DE SUÁREZ; HER MARRIAGE TO RODRIGO DE QUIROGA..232

THE SIXTH LETTER

PART VV.   SKIRMISH AT THE RÌO NIVEQUETEN; BATTLE OF THE ANDALIÉN; THE BATTLE OF FORTRESS PENCO; VALDIVIA ORDERS THE HANDS AND NOSES OF THE CAPTIVES CUT OFF 245

PART WW.   THE FOUNDING OF CONCEPCIÓN DE MARÍA PURÍSIMA DEL NUEVO EXTREMO; MY BRIEF RETURN TO SANTIAGO; MEETING MY NEWBORN SON, VICENTE; VALDIVIA'S MAPUCHE 'PAGE,' LAUTARO; THE FOUNDING OF LA IMPERIAL 265

PART XX.   THE CLASH IN THE MARIQUINA VALLEY; THE FOUNDING OF VALDIVIA TOWN; A TERRIBLE SHAKING OF THE EARTH FOLLOWED BY FLOODING WATERS FROM THE SEA; VILLAGRAN RETURNS FROM PERU WITH 200 MEN; THE FOUNDING OF VILLARRICA AND ARAUCO 278

PART YY.   THE RETURN TO SANTIAGO TOWN; WE ADOPT OUR DAUGHTER, INÉS; MICHIMALONGO RETIRES; LAUTARO ESCAPES AND IS REPLACED BY AGUSTINILLO 288

PART ZZ.   THE GOVERNOR'S UNPOPULAR DECISION TO ESTABLISH MORE FORTS; THE FOUNDING OF FORTS TUCAPEL, PURÉN, AND LOS CONFINES; DE MÉRIDA SUFFERS A CRIPPLING WOUND; EVENTS PRESAGING A TRAGEDY; THE FATED BATTLE OF TUCAPEL 297

THE AFTERMATH; THE CLOSE OF THE CHILE
ADVENTURES 314

APPENDICES

APPENDIX A 321
APPENDIX B 326
APPENDIX C 327
APPENDIX D 329
APPENDIX E 331
APPENDIX F 332
BIBLIOGRAPHY FOR VOLUME II 345

THE FOURTH LETTER

Written to the King by Pedro de Mérida from Santiago
del Nueva Extremadura on November 12, 1566.

PART AA

THE STORY TO BE TOLD; WE LEAVE THE SACRED CITY FOR THE FARTHEST MOST REACHES OF *NUEVA ESTREMADURA*

1

Once more, Your Majesty, I take stylus in hand to relate **further adventures** in the fabled land of *Nuevo Extremo, Nueva Estremadura*, or Chile,[1] with Captain Pedro de Valdivia, as I promised to do in this, my Fourth Letter. In this and the correspondences following, I present an honest and authentic narrative of the things that transpired during my years with Captain Valdivia, as I did with the letters to Your Grace concerning my time with Captain Almagro. I wrote and will write them from the notes I kept at the time of the events as they happened and thus follow closely the facts in every particular.

With that as preliminary to my relation, Sire, I should now recount, in as brief a space as possible so as to avoid prolixity, what transpired once the Almagro Expedition left Arequipa after the battle there and traveled

---

[1] Valdivia uses all three names in his letters to the King to identify Chile and so does de Mérida. See "Historical Sources" on the site.

to Cusco in 1537. Captain Almagro intended to break the blockade by Manco Inca of the Pizarros[2] and our countrymen. On the way to Cusco, Indians attacked our force in the village of Calca[3] on April 4, 1537. We were able to repulse them rather readily, although I sustained a spear wound high on my right thigh. This became infected in the following days and I found myself in a great deal of pain and unable to walk. Father Molina[4] tended me in a way that saved my life, and I shall remain indebted to him always.

As a result of my wound and my intentions not to fight my countrymen, I missed the battles that saw Captain Almagro lift the siege. For various reasons, he soon thereafter engaged in a feud with the Pizarros over the control of Cusco. He won a first victory, only to have the Pizarrists later triumph at the battle of Las Salinas,[5] the fight that claimed the lives of several of those on the Almagro Expedition, including Lieutenant Castilla. During these days, Hernando Pizarro located a small warehouse with numerous rooms near the city's western boundary and bestowed it upon Father, so that he might open his Hospital for Natives there. And there I remained for several months, cared for by Father and his native physicians.

One afternoon, Father Molina visited with a woman, who introduced herself as Inés de Suárez. When she inquired about my injury and recovery, I could tell she had knowledge of medicine. As it transpired, Father had instructed her in the care of the sick and wounded since she planned to accompany Captain Valdivia on his expedition to Chile and would serve as the medical assistant. Surprised and pleased, I told her of my desire to return there and indicated an interest in the Captain's plans. We talked also of other matters and I discovered she had been born in Extremadura, my birth place also. She asked about my guiding

---

[2] For the events of these tumultuous times, see The Adventure Chronicles, Volume III: Pizarro.
[3] Calca lies some fifteen miles north from Cusco in the Sacred Valley of the Incas.
[4] (1494–1580). This is the priest friend of de Mérida on the Almagro Expedition. Please see Volume I: Almagro.
[5] April, 1538.

duties with Captain Almagro and commented a few times that I would be an important member of the expedition, but that remained a matter for Captain Valdivia to decide.

Two days later, the lady returned, on this occasion with Captain Valdivia, now Francisco Pizarro's second in command, a man extremely mild-mannered and unassuming. The three of us spent a memorable time together and discussed numerous subjects, including the region of our birthplace, Extremadura. And our conversation was rich with the distinct accent of Extremaduran Spanish.[6] The Captain said he was born in Villanueva La Serena[7] in 1497. Inés began life in Plasencia, 145 miles north of La Serena, in 1507. And I started mine in Mérida, sixty-five miles west of La Serena, in 1505. So we were neighbors, although we had never met, in the most special of places in all of Spain.[8] At one point, the Captain asked if my sympathies might lie still with the Almagrists. I answered that my injury and my desire not to shed the blood of a Spanish brother had prevented me from participating in any of the battles against the Pizarrists. I added that my sole interest now was a return to the land I had fallen in love with and there begin a new life. This was of the most importance to me and I thought of little else.

The Captain stroked his beard with his thumb and forefinger, a habit we witnessed often in the coming years and a sign he was deep in thought. Within moments, he rose from his chair, smiled broadly, stretched out both his hands and gripped mine firmly.

"Pedro," he said, "I have the ability to judge a man's character quickly and have never been wrong about such things, and you are an honorable man. I know this from our conversation, those men from the Almagro

---

[6] Only a Spanish linguist could explain how it differs from other Spanish accents.
[7] In several more years, Valdivia will found and name a scenic city by the sea, La Serena.
[8] Estremadurans throughout the centuries have always held themselves in high regard, despite the impoverished nature of their land. The difficult conditions there caused many young men, and women, to depart for the Americas to seek their fortune in the 16th and 17th centuries.

Expedition who have talked about you, and from your birthplace. It is right that we forget the troubles here in Peru and strike out for a new life in a new land, one I call *Nueva Estremadura* in celebration of our homeland. I want you to join us and lead the guiding contingent, composed of men you select. I shall also offer you the position of First Lieutenant, a promotion in recognition of your skills, your abilities, and your importance to our expedition."[9]

But first, he said, I must recover my health, to which I responded I had regained it the moment our conversation began!

"And what of the slight limp you have as a result of your injury? You mentioned it to Lady Inés when she visited and I notice it now. Are you able to ride a horse without pain or discomfort? You know better than I the distances we must travel."

"I assure you, Sir, I have already mounted a horse and proceeded at a slow walk with no difficulty. Soon I will try a trot and after that a full gallop. When I feel ready for your personal approval of my skills, I shall approach you for evaluation."

"Very well, Pedro. I need your guiding skills to make our journey a success."

Captain Valdivia rose then from his chair, as did Lady Inés, shook my hand warmly once more, and Inés offered hers too as they departed.

After this meeting with the Captain and Inés, my loyal and enduring friend, Vicente Montesinos, visited me and Father Molina in mid-day, and we recalled our journey together with Almagro to Chile. The adventures on that passage had provided a turning point in our lives. For Vicente, it was the determination to return there and find a suitable town to settle down in and begin an occupation, what that might be he did not mind. For

---

[9] Captain Almagro had promoted de Mérida to Second Lieutenant for his exploits at the Battle of Huasco. See Part P of the Second Letter in, <u>Volume I: Almagro</u>.

Father Molina, it caused the inspiration to found the Hospital for Natives. For me, the beauty of the land in the central lowlands of Chile produced a desire for a new beginning, a place to start the next chapter of my life.

Vicente at one point remarked that upon our return to Cusco he had made the decision to stay out of the battles with the Pizarros, since he detested a fight with his countrymen, just as I. Quite by happenstance, he became friends with Captain Alvar Gómez de Almagro, the brother of our recently departed Captain Almagro,[10] a man of the same sentiments who declined to participate in the continuing battles among the Spanish. Fired by the stories of the Chile adventure told by his brother, he wished to go to that land. Alvar Gómez spoke to Captain Valdivia about his aspirations and found himself warmly welcomed by him. When he introduced Vicente, who told of his intention also to return there, it gratified Captain Valdivia to gain such a valuable member of the Almagro command, for Montesinos was well-known for his accomplishments on the field of battle as well as his intelligence off it.

Another frequent visitor with Vicente was Juan de la Torre, our friend from our Extremaduran homeland. He preceded us to Peru by eight years, having served under Pizarro's command in the initial expedition to locate the Inca in 1524. A Pizarro loyalist, the Governor designated him the first mayor of Arequipa[11] soon after we left for Chile with Valdivia. I shall rely upon him for information concerning events in Peru during my absence to Chile in my future letters to Your Honor.[12]

Before I commence the telling of our journey, Exalted Excellency, I should mention that Captain Valdivia authored five letters to Your Majesty through the years 1545 1552.[13] In none of them does he tell of our year's

---

[10] Diego de Almagro was executed by the Pizarros in July, 1538. De Mérida tells more of the particulars of his death in, The Adventure Chronicles, Volume III: Pizarro.

[11] (1500-1590). He was appointed mayor in August, 1540. De la Torre devoted his life to Peruvian municipal duties.

[12] These letters are contained in, The Adventure Chronicles, Volume III: Pizarro.

[13] As mentioned above, these five letters appear on the web site under "Historical Sources."

march from Cusco to Chile. When I read his letter of 1545, doing so at his request, I remarked upon the omission. He replied forthrightly that the events had transpired five years previously and no longer had relevance to his and our situation in the new land. Nevertheless, now that he has passed from this life, it is my intention to tell of events that occurred that our Captain did not record, as well as enhance those he did, on the journey to the site of our capital city as well as incidents in the years after in *Nuevo Extremo*.

And now, I shall begin. Upon recovery from my thigh wound, and after convincing our Captain my riding skills were unaffected by it, we began our journey on the main plaza in Cusco, the sacred city of the Inca Empire, on Monday, January 15, 1540.[14] A High Mass celebrated in the small Church of the Assumption of the Virgin[15] on this day marked our departure for the fabled land of Chile. The celebrants, Father Cristoval de Molina and Father Jacopo Suarez, had accompanied our Almagro Expedition, and the Captain thought it fitting they bid us farewell. They did so in a solemn yet joyful manner as we Christians, as the Captain preferred to call us, sang sacred hymns complemented by Indian flutes and drums, the players directed by Father Molina. Two hundred Indians of those to accompany us also attended this mass, a testament to the success of our priests in converting natives to our Holy Faith.

Governor Francisco Pizarro, who had granted the land of Chile to Captain Valdivia, amid controversy I shall address at the appropriate time, was there to see us off as we began wending our way from the city at the hour of Sext.[16] And at his side stood our friend Prince Paullu, now the chief Inca, put in power to replace Manco Inca, initially by Captain Almagro and, after the Captain's execution, by Pizarro.[17] The Dominican Bishop of Cusco, the honorable Bishop Vicente Valverde, stood next to Prince

---

[14] Neither Valdivia nor historians give an exact date in January for departure.
[15] This church no doubt was the predecessor to today's Basilica of the Assumption of the Virgin that sits on Cusco's main square.
[16] Please see Appendix E for the Canonical Hours.
[17] Almagro placed Paullu Inca on the throne in 1537. After the Captain's death, Pizarro allowed Paullu to remain in power. He stayed as the head Inca until his death in 1549.

Paullu.[18] Those of us from the previous Almagro Expedition were happy to see the last, we hoped, of Francisco Pizarro. At the arrival in Cusco of the gold shipment we had let pass on the march south with Almagro to the great mountains, he ordered it held for his own plans. The gold we had thought must come to us upon returning, Pizarro used instead to finance building projects in Cusco and the City of Kings.[19] This provided a disappointment to all of us whom Captain Almagro had promised to reward for our Chilean duty, but such are the actions of some men and their excessive grasping for wealth. We Almagro men kept this discontent amongst ourselves since Captain Valdivia and Pizarro remained close friends.

It turned cold and wet, but the weather failed to damp my happiness at our departure and my eagerness to tread a new path in life, a path I had no idea ultimately where it might lead. By the afternoon, we moved through a small village and camped that first night near its southern border. Our order of march on this day came to characterize our daily journeys in the coming months. My guiding team of Ayar, my loyal and dependable guide from the Almagro Expedition days, Lope de Ayala,[20] an able young man of flushed complexion assigned me by our Captain, and I, led the procession. Ayar's desire to accompany the expedition arose from his hope of guiding and equipping merchants and traders among the established villages of *Nueva Estremadura*. His brother, Hanco, had decided to stay in Peru and guide local merchants to Arequipa and Tacna before one day joining Ayar in Chile. Then came our Christian horse soldiers, headed by the brother of our departed Captain Almagro,[21] Capt. Alvar Gómez de

---

[18] Bishop Valverde served as the first Bishop of Cusco from 1537-1541.
[19] Within several years, the Spanish renamed the city, Lima.
[20] (1520-?). This man appears on the list of expedition members by Errazuriz, Crescente. History of Chile: Pedro de Valdivia, published by Imprenta Cervantes, Santiago de Chile, 1911-1912, but otherwise is lost to history as to what became of him. The names of all the expedition members noted in this letter come from the Errazuris book. See Appendix A for a partial list.
[21] Captain Almagro and his followers were defeated by the Pizarrists at the Battle of Las Salinas in April, 1538, and was condemned to death soon thereafter.

Almagro, our *maestre de campo*,²² with his chief lieutenant, Pedro Gómez de Benito,²³ at his side. My friend Lieutenant Vicente Montesinos, and Alvar Gómez's son, Juan Gómez de Almagro,²⁴ followed behind. In sum, our number was twenty-seven men.

I must interject here that the honorable Captain Valdivia, in his first letter to Your Catholic Majesty, says, "I raised up to one hundred and fifty men with whom I came to these lands, all of us on the way going through great toil." Some read this to mean we started from Cusco with that number of men. That is a misinterpretation of what the Captain intended to convey. He meant that when we reached the site of the new village of Santiago de *Nuevo Extremo*, we totaled one hundred and fifty. When we left the sacred city, though, our numbers were those as I have stated,²⁵ the others having come to us while on the march. The Cusco men were mounted and ten of them had ridden with the Almagro Expedition.²⁶

Returning to our order of march, after the guide team, the Indian farmers and llama *arrieros* followed, 950 in number,²⁷ including about 250 women, along with 2,000 load-bearing llamas and our pack-horses. Another Almagro Expedition compatriot and close friend of Paullu Inca, the resolute Ancohualla, had recruited these natives at the behest of both Paullu and Captain Valdivia and now led them on the journey,

---

22 This was a chief of staff role that assisted the Captain General, in this case Capt. Valdivia. It was created by King Carlos V (King Philip's father) in 1534.
23 (1492-1567). This man was another Extremaduran, born in Badajoz.
24 (?-1569). Juan Gómez was to fill many important positions in the years ahead.
25 As noted, Valdivia says in his First Letter that he arrived at the site of Santiago with 150 men. However, documents have come to light over the last 100 years that show some joined the expedition on the way. There is disagreement as to how many left Cusco; some say as few as seven, others more than fifty. Now we have de Mérida's number, the twenty-seven he mentions above. See Ida Stevenson Weldon Vernon, <u>Pedro de Valdivia: Conquistador of Chile</u>, University of Austin Press, 1946, p. 49-52. She agrees with him.
26 Historians do not cite how many Almagro veterans accompanied Valdivia, but this number of men indicates that others wanted to begin a new life in Chile, just like de Mérida and Montesinos.
27 Weldon Vernon cites the number as "....1,000 more or less....", but offers no historical citation. We now have de Mérida's figure.

along with his three *caciques*. He required of his people that they be farmers, raisers of livestock, and colonizers of a new land. We became friends with them, since we all would farm the land together. Anco had joined us, while declining an offer from Inca Paullu of a high post at his court, because he wished to be close to the land and live as a common Indian rather than as a man of the nobility. Both the Captain and Paullu thought him the right man to lead the Peruvian natives to Chile. Our Captain had an enduring admiration and respect for Ancohualla, as I shall make clear over the coming months and years of my relation to Your Majesty.

As to the movement of our goods and provisions, the heavily loaded llamas carried different kinds of fruit and vegetable seeds, salt, coops of chickens, two small pigs, two goats, hoes, spades, other farming tools, two large bags of blue beads for trading,[28] a bellows and blacksmithing tools, and, heaviest weight of all, a supply of iron horse shoes carried by the packhorses. Included too were food stores for us all: dried fish, dried llama meat, or *charqui*, dried fruits and vegetables, *papas, quinua, chuño, maize*, beans, squash, salt, and so on. Hernando Vallejo[29] and Bernal Martinez[30] accompanied this large group. Next appeared our scrivener, Luis de Cartagena.[31] His was the important task of preparing official documents recording the founding of villages, the awarding of land grants, and other papers required by the authorities in the City of Kings and Spain. Since paper was now available in Peru, he had received enough to replace the old parchment he used formerly. An additional duty required him to note each day's date, a task he discharged by consulting a copy of the Liturgical Calendar, so kindly provided us by Father Suarez. The Captain also appointed de Cartagena as our food provisioner, with the responsibility to keep our food stores replenished, a most vital duty. Following rode Inés de

---

[28] These beads were of sodalite, known as the "Inca's stone." The Almagro Expedition had used them as well.
[29] (?-1553) He would be a casualty at the Battle of Tucapel.
[30] (1508-?) He became a minor government figure in Santiago in the 1560's.
[31] (1513-1561).

Suárez,[32] our Captain's woman, astride her white horse and leading several pack animals carrying medical supplies and other indispensables of the expedition. I shall write more of this remarkable woman throughout our time in Chile. And with her rode Captain Valdivia, with a small statue of our Blessed Mother strapped around the horn of his saddle pommel.[33] He had the Virgin Mother with him at all times.

I should say more here than I have already about our leader, Your Majesty, because he proved himself a man of great distinction, both during his early years in Spain and his later years in Peru and Chile. Ever since his youth, he had trained himself to work with his hands, follow a sober mode of living, and condition his body so that it remained as strong as it was healthy. He took study at university as an *abogado* in civil affairs and demonstrated his ability in such subjects by the formation of *cabildos*[34] for each village he founded in Chile.

The Captain differed from other *conquistadores*, Majesty, in that he had engaged in a military career from his earliest years, and was well educated. He fought in Flanders in 1520 for Your Father, as well as in Italy in the Italian Wars. My lasting memory of him is the use of his raised clenched right fist to acknowledge and approve a deed well done, a gesture he had acquired while campaigning in Italy.[35] As the years passed, the gravity and dignity of his character revealed themselves to those who had dealt with him, and marked him out as a man qualified superbly for employment in great affairs and positions of leadership. In 1534, the Spanish army sent

---

[32] One of the most memorable women in the conquest of the Americas, Suárez was born in Plasencia, Extremadura, Spain in 1507. She came in 1537 to search for her husband Juan de Mélaga, who had left Spain to serve in the New World with the Pizarro brothers. She searched for him in several countries until she discovered that he had died at sea. She arrived in Lima in 1539, applied for and was granted, as the widow of a Spanish soldier, a small plot of land in Cusco and rights to several Indians to farm and maintain it. Shortly after this, she became the mistress of Valdivia. See Vicuña, Alejandro, <u>Inés de Suárez</u>.

[33] As noted by Diaz Mesa, <u>Leyendas y Episodios Chilenos</u>.

[34] These were Spanish municipal governing bodies.

[35] The rich meanings of hand gestures continue to define Italian expression. In fact, the upraised clenched fist has this same connotation today.

him to Peru to serve under Francisco Pizarro, who recognized his abilities and appointed him his second in command and after, awarded him the lands of Chile. He did not rise to this level of honor by lacking discipline, Sire, but rose to it by possessing it.

In battles with the Indians, all knew him as a formidable fighter, who stood his ground and confronted his opponents with a threatening expression, as he believed such an appearance, accompanied by a loud and menacing war-cry, frequently frightens the enemy even more than Toledo steel. He displayed this behavior at the battle of Las Salinas, at which the forces of Pizarro overwhelmed those of Almagro, captured, and afterwards executed him, as I shall relate in my future letters to Your Grace. He possessed, too, a pious nature, for he kept a small statue of the Virgin Mary close to hand, as I have said. At mass, his remained the loudest voice to give expression to the hymns we sang and the prayers we recited. On the march and when dismounted, he dropped occasionally to one knee, folded his hands in a sign of prayer, and recited words known but to him. I will take other opportunities in the coming months and years, Excellency, to describe this man and his notable accomplishments.

To return to my relation, as for priests on our expedition, we had none. Those in Cusco wished to remain and continue their work converting the Indians there and in the rest of Peru to our Holy Faith. This gave me pause, since all of us wished to attend mass and worship Our Lord Jesus Christ in the difficult days ahead. As a measure of his concern, our Captain had sent a letter of petition to the Church authorities in the City of Kings, asking that priests come with us so as to bring more of God's creatures in the new land of Chile to our Holy Faith. As a result of this request, several joined us in the ensuing months and years.

As to the route we would follow, I must state that the Captain was most open to a different one than Captain Almagro had taken. He welcomed the advice of Lieutenant Montesinos, Ancohualla, Ayar, and me, that the best course would be to march to Putre, the small town we had passed on the way to Tacna, and from there proceed south through Copayapu and then down to Papudo. He needed little convincing in this regard, since we knew the terrain, and so he decided on this itinerary early in our planning.

I should indicate here, Sire, that in the days before departing, the Captain had asked that I explain the route to all the men. To fulfill his request, I collected information from Ayar, Ancohualla, Montesinos, and other Almagro veterans, and prepared the following description of our journey. I quote the information precisely, since the document remains in my possession, as written by our scrivener, de Cartagena, at the time. I gave copies of it to the men, even those who could not read, and read its contents aloud when Captain Valdivia called us together a week prior to departure. Ayar, Ancohualla, and his *caciques*, attended as well. The Captain interjected his own comments of clarification at certain points in the reading and we both answered questions as they arose. This is the document in its entirety.

FOR HIS EXCELLENCY CAPTAIN PEDRO DE VALDIVIA, HIS OFFICERS, AND THE MEN OF THE EXPEDITION TO *NUEVO EXTREMO* FOR THE SETTLEMENT OF THAT LAND AND ITS DECLARATION AS A PROVINCE OF THE KINGDOM OF SPAIN.

Gentlemen, about the march to *Nueva Estremadura*, our Captain's intention is to explore the land south and east from the village of Papudo in central Chile for the founding of a capital city. In 1536, Captain Almagro dispatched a lieutenant in search of gold in that area.[36] He returned instead with accounts of farm lands rich with a soil that permitted the natives to grow crops of fruits and vegetables several times a year. Captain Valdivia feels this location might be the ideal site to establish our city.

Concerning the first half of our journey, there are three segments. The first is the passage from Cusco to Puno/Llave to Putre, the second from Putre to Atacama, and the third from Atacama to Copayapu. I shall address our travels south from Copayapu when we reach that town in a

---

[36] This was Lieutenant Alvarado. See Part R of the Second Letter.

few more months. It is fortunate we have as our guide, Ayar, who helped lead the Almagro Expedition through Chile. Some of you here remember this man from those days and know of his complete reliability. Before assisting Captain Almagro, he spent several years guiding trade caravans with his friend, Hanco, and their fathers, from Calama to Arequipa and Cusco. He wishes to do the same someday among the villages in the new land.

The initial part of our march, we Almagro men have no knowledge of, since from Putre we traveled to Tacna and afterward on towards Arequipa and not directly from Putre to Cusco. But Ayar has traveled this land before, and his special knowledge will see us through this initial portion of our journey. The second part is from Putre to Chiu-Chiu, Calama, and Atacama, over the Avenue of the Volcáns, a land of smoking mountains that appear all along the route; one will be in sight every day. Much of the journey follows the Río Loa for divers weeks; the terrain is high in elevation and the weather cool. In Calama, the Captain will meet Huaman, the local ruler of the surrounding land and towns, a man known by those of us on the Almagro Expedition as the *Desert Cacique*. Captain Almagro granted him authority to rule this part of Chile if he became a Christian and ruled according to Spanish custom. The Captain, however, did not send a priest to him because of the chaos in Cusco when we returned there. We shall see what his present circumstances are. The third stage is from Atacama to Copayapu, a passage through lands like that on the Avenue of the Volcáns.

The following identifies several of the landmarks and towns we pass on the march to Copayapu. The dates of departure and arrival are approximate, since unknown difficulties may present themselves and alter these estimates.[37] The walking rate of the llama, eight to ten miles a day, determines the speed at which we travel.

---

[37] As it happens, there were many events along the way that altered these dates. In fact, they entered Copayapu on August 19, more than a month behind the schedule. But, this did not cause any problems for Valdivia or the expedition.

Departure Landmark or Town	Arrival Landmark or Town
Cusco, January 15, 1540	Puno/Llave/Titicaca, February 13
Puno/Llave/Titicaca, February 15	Putre, March 17
Putre, March 24	Salar de Huasco, April 19
Salar de Huasco, April 20	Chiu-Chiu, May 8
Chiu-Chiu, May 9	Calama, May 12
Calama, May 13	Atacama, May 23
Atacama, May 26	Cerro Llullaillaco, June 15
Cerro Llullaillaco, June 18	Copayapu, July 15

Water Availability

With the fortunate addition of Ayar as our guide, finding sources of water on the initial part of our trip to Putre should not pose a problem, as most of the time we follow the Río Llave. From Putre, those of us from the Almagro Expedition know the locations of lagunas, *estanques*, and streams all the way to Copayapu. Two areas that may offer difficulty will be between Calama and Atacama, and the approach to Copayapu. We shall fill and carry *poros*[38] on these occasions, if necessary.

Temperature and Altitude

The march to Puno is over ground higher than Cusco, with the temperatures quite cool. Puno and the laguna they call Titicaca, however, are higher still and initially may cause sickness.[39] Occasional storms will present themselves. Most of the land between Puno/Llave and Putre is higher than Puno.[40] We can obtain relief, as the Indians do, by chewing the coca leaf constantly. The temperatures will be cool during the day and

---

[38] As mentioned previously, these are gourds used for water storage.

[39] Puno, with today's population of 150,000, sits at 12,600 feet, while Cusco is at 11,000 feet.

[40] The altitude of the land between Puno and Putre ranges from 12,800 feet to 13,800 feet.

cold at night. This will be true also on the Avenue of the Volcáns, from Putre to Chiu-Chiu; likewise the journey from Atacama to Copayapu, so each man must possess warm clothes. Occasional severe storms, with rain and snow, are always a possibility, although usually the snow melts after the sun rises. The temperatures will be higher in the few villages we pass through, as the elevations are lower. Additionally, the air is exceptionally dry with little moisture in it around the towns of Calama and Atacama.

Roads

We plan to follow the Inca road between Cusco and Puno. The few roads we encounter after that lie in Chiu-Chiu, Calama, and Atacama. They become more common again when we draw close to Copayapu and then proceed south towards the pasture lands of Chile, where our Captain shall choose property for our settlements.

Forage for the Animals

Ichu grass shall remain the staple for the llamas and our horses and be available the entire way, as was the case with the Almagro journey. The water sources we encounter have other grasses on their shores that can serve as additional fodder.

Food Stores

We must stock substantial amounts of llama and guanaco *charqui* and large stores of dried fish. Dried fish, *quinua*, dried and fresh fruits and vegetables, *charqui, chuño, papas* and other assorted foodstuffs are available here in Cusco, and farther on in Puno and Llave. Putre offers a variety of goods for the next section of the passage. Furthermore, groups of guanaco should be common south from that town. When we have the need, we will surround a herd, gradually close the circle, and kill them as they try to escape, as we did with Almagro. North of Chiu-Chiu, we encounter the Río Loa, with fish, ducks, and water enough to meet our needs. Chiu-Chiu, Calama, and Atacama have meat, fish, fruits, and vegetables, and we shall restore our supplies at these towns for the march to Copayapu.

Seeds and Animals for our New Land

As we found on the Almagro Expedition, the natives of Chile are accomplished farmers and harvest several kinds of fruits and vegetables. And they are efficient at directing water from rivers and lakes to their crop lands by the means of channels and aqueducts. As Ancohualla has told me, the men of the Inca armies who invaded Chile years ago taught this to them, for they were farmers as well as soldiers. To increase the variety of crops they now cultivate, we have seeds of *maize*, squash, beans, guavas, chirimoya, pears, avocado, yucca, oca, pumpkin, peppers, and asparagus. As for animals, we are taking fifteen chickens,[41] two small pigs, and two goats.

Temperament of the Natives

The natives south of Cusco and down to Puno should present no problems for us since those around Andahuaylillas, where the Almagro Expedition encountered numerous warriors, have accepted us in their land and are now peaceful. The rest of the three parts of our march to Copayapu should also lack native threats. Our Captain insists we stay vigilant, however, whenever we are near Indian settlements. And we must remember ours is not a military invasion of Chile. Yes, we shall fight when attacked. Our intent, nonetheless, is to establish peace with the people

---

[41] The thinking was, until recently, that the Spanish introduced chickens to South America. In 2007, however, an international research team reported that it had found "the first unequivocal evidence for a pre-European introduction of chickens to South America," or presumably anywhere in the New World. The researchers said that bones buried on the South American coast were from chickens that lived between 1304 and 1424. A DNA analysis linked the remains to the Polynesian islands.

and farm the new lands with their help. This will lead to the foundation of villages that will grow in the coming years.

Terremotos

We did not encounter a *terremoto* years ago on our march south from Copayapu and our passage back north, until we experienced one in Tacna. We now know they happen often, especially close to the coastal regions. There is little we can do about such an occurrence except to endure it by prayer.

More men for the Expedition

Lieutenant Montesinos and Captain Pero Gómez intend to leave our march at Putre and ride to Tacna to meet the men, led by the honorable Francisco de Villagran,[42] there awaiting word from the Captain as to when and where to join our expedition. The information we have is that fifty to sixty men, all mounted, including several priests, will increase our current numbers.

Such comprised the content of my report. I closed by saying Ayar and I would brief the Captain and Ancohualla each afternoon about what we might expect on the coming day's march.

---

[42] (1511-1563). Valdivia mentions Villagran several times in his letters to the King.

PART BB

THE PASSAGE BEGINS; WE CAMP AT THE RAQCH'I COMPLEX; A SUDDEN DEATH AMONG US

18

    *L*et us leave this, Your Majesty, and return to our journey. Two days out from Cusco, we passed through the village of Andahuaylillas, the site of a battle with natives in the hills outside the town on the Almagro Expedition. Nothing happened on this occasion as the Indians now tolerated us in their land. Here, we departed from the course south we had taken with Captain Almagro, which led towards the eastern shore of Lago Titicaca. Our direction would be southwest, to the western shores of that laguna. Two new men rode up late that day, Juan Almonacid[43] and Captain Pedro de Miranda,[44] at the point where the water of an irrigation canal fell over small stone escarpments carved out of the rock by Inca builders. We now numbered twenty-nine. Captain Valdivia appointed Captain de Miranda as the officer in charge of making and breaking our encampments every day,

---

[43] (1518-1592).
[44] (1517-1573). We shall hear more about this man in this and in the coming letters.

since he had experience in laying them out, and asked Juan Gómez de Almagro to designate men to perform the necessary tasks at de Miranda's direction.

That evening, Captain Valdivia called us all together as he wished to make known the rules that would govern our behavior in future months. Every month, he repeated their reading. He proclaimed the following, and bound us all to observe them under pain of prosecution by the Captain himself as the final judge and imposer of punishment. They deserve disclosure as they set forth the governance of our behavior and I quote from the document de Cartagena scribed at the time.

Gentlemen:

First, our primary purposes in Chile are to farm the land together with our Indians and found villages and towns. Our second is to spread the word of our Lord and Master, Jesus Christ. I shall recruit priests to see to this. Furthermore, should we find gold objects or deposits, we may possess them, but must never ravage the people or the land in search of them.

Second, should any man blaspheme Our Lord Jesus Christ, Our Lady, the Holy Apostles, or any other saints, he must suffer severe punishment, determined by me.

Third, no Christian shall mistreat the Indians with us, nor take anything away from them, because they are our friends and are with us to settle *Nuevo Extremo*. In addition, any man who attacks natives along our way, unless they have attacked us, shall incur severe punishment as decided by me. That being said, be friendly, yet know how to kill any Indian you meet.

Fourth, any man who leaves our camp at night or departs from the march, without the permission of the *maestre de campo*, will suffer twenty lashings with rope whips.

Fifth, any man who foments rebellion against the leaders of the expedition by encouraging desertion, causes others harm or injury, will suffer death by hanging.

Sixth, all men must possess good armor, such as a neck guard, a morrión,[45] leggings, and a shield.

Seventh, we shall arm ourselves with the Toledo[46] sword and the long lance.[47]

Eighth, when in lands occupied by menacing natives, no man will sleep unless he is fully armed and shod with his footwear, so we might be at the ready to defend ourselves against attack.

Ninth, when amongst the high mountains, all must wear their clothes at night and lie with sandals so as to prevent freezing of hands and feet.

Tenth, any man who sleeps on guard duty or leaves his post shall suffer death by hanging. So too the punishment for any man who goes from one camp to another without permission from his Captain.

Eleventh, anyone who deserts his men and Captain in battle will be drawn and quartered for his cowardice. So too the punishment for any man who kills a fellow soldier out of malice.[48]

Twelfth, any man who deters our force from effecting the peaceful colonizing of the land shall be subject to prosecution for insurrection against our purpose.

Such were the directives Captain Valdivia gave us, Your Honor. One may know from them that our leader was an honorable man who understood

---

[45] The morrión was the open metal helmet worn by Spanish soldiers.
[46] As mentioned previously, this refers to the steel makers of Toledo, Spain. They made the best swords and knifes for centuries. The swords were three feet long and sharp on both sides.
[47] Their lances were long wooden spears with iron or steel points on the ends, used to devastating effect on masses of native foot soldiers.
[48] They carried out this gruesome sentence in different ways. Sometimes, they hanged, beheaded, and then chopped the victim into four pieces. More often, they tied ropes to the four extremities and fastened the other rope end to the pommel horns of four horses. Upon command, the animals raced forward and pulled the body apart.

The Adventure Chronicles of *Conquistador* Pedro de Mérida. VOLUME 2, VALDIVIA

how to order the actions of men, since he knew it is true about human nature that men loathe those who do not enforce discipline, and respect those who allow them no compromises.

And now, I shall take up again the telling of our passage south. In several days, while following the Río Villkanota, and traveling on an Inca road of well-fitted stones, we came to a deserted site with buildings and structures that had importance. The Captain sent word forward to stop for midday refreshment here and listen to Ancohualla tell the meaning of this place. When we had dismounted, Anco joined us riding the young mare given him by the Captain as a mark of his rank and authority among the Indians. He began by saying that this location, called Raqch'i,[49] served as a control point on the road between Cusco and the towns in the south, such as Puno. A three mile perimeter wall encircled the Inca buildings. On the other side of this wall, an enclosure with eight rectangular structures around a bright courtyard served to welcome travelers, with lodging for the people and stables for llamas. Anco explained further that different parts served different functions: one to house troops, others to conduct religious festivities, still more to store food and supplies. The irrigated terraces on the hillsides testified to the agricultural richness here. A warm spring fed water to a pool for cleansing the body. And a large temple,[50] obviously for religious rites, completed the scene before us.[51]

PHOTOS: See images of Raqch'i, 4AA-DD.8-.14, on the website.

When Ancohualla had finished speaking, my men and I joined Gómez de Almagro, his son, Juan, and Montesinos for a brief respite and ate whatever we carried in our pommel bags. Gómez removed his morrión, draped his right leg over the pommel horn of his saddle, and had something to eat while we discoursed on the wonders of the buildings and temples. Vicente had found the small melon he was eating rotten, so he threw it out in front of our position. Within moments, an immense shadow passed above our

---

[49] This place is a protected archeological site today.
[50] This is the Temple of Viracocha.
[51] The Spanish tore down most of the buildings in late 1540, soon after Valdivia and his men passed through.

heads as a huge condor swooped down and grabbed the discarded piece. This spooked the horse of Gómez, and it reared up, thrashing its front legs as it did so, and threw him to the ground, the right side of his head striking a boulder of considerable size. Montesinos and Juan Gómez de Almagro ran to him quickly, with me close behind. Blood oozed from his mouth, right ear, and nose. As we tried to stop the bleeding with my spare shirt, Inés de Suárez rode up with a horse carrying medical supplies.[52] She now took matters into her own hands.

She seemed an angel of mercy as she cradled his head in her arms and tried to stop the bleeding with a cloth bandage. She talked with soft and soothing words, almost singing, telling him to stay strong, to call upon Our Lord Jesus for mercy, and stay with us, for we needed his strength and companionship. She did this for awhile, but then stopped. Placing his head gently on the ground and covering his face with a small cloth, she said sadly, "He is gone. May our Blessed Savior show him mercy in His kingdom."

22   The Captain had watched all that transpired and now came forward, knelt at the side of Gómez, placed a small crucifix on his chest along with the small statue of the Blessed Virgin, and held his right hand in his own as he led us in a heartfelt prayer for our fallen comrade. I looked at Montesinos and Juan Gómez and saw the anguish in their faces, for one had lost a friend, the other his father.

Late that day, our Captain named Pedro Gómez de Benito our new *maestre de campo*. He met with all the men and put forth a proposition. Inés de Suárez had distinguished herself this day, he said, as an important participant in our venture, and his proposal recognized this by now referring to her as Doña, Doña[53] Inés. All acknowledged her importance to us and all agreed to address her thus, as it seemed most fitting we do so. De Benito informed Valdivia and Doña Inés of our wishes and they were

---

[52] Weldon Vernon in <u>Pedro de Valdivia,</u> mentions that Almagro fell from his horse, but does not mention the cause. She also notes the medical attentiveness of Inés de Suárez.

[53] This title was a mark of esteem for a person of personal distinction.

most pleased to accept her new title. At our meal that night, she thanked us with a graciousness that confirmed the rightness of our decision.

Here, it may be worthy of remark about the Captain's lady, Inés de Suárez. He called her his *criada*,[54] but we all knew her as his *mujer*. This remained a scandalous partnership to a few, yet failed to deter their relationship in the least, as there had been a precedent for it in Mexico a number of years before.[55] She had come to the Americas in 1537, at the age of thirty, to look for her husband, Juan de Mélaga, who had left Spain for the New World with the Pizarro brothers. After months of continuous searching in numerous countries and after learning of his death in Guatemala, she arrived in the City of Kings in 1538 and shortly thereafter met Captain Valdivia.

Hers was a beguiling presence, for she possessed the bluest eyes, and had the habit of winking with the left to those around her when she was of good cheer. Her laugh became quick and high pitched when she found things amusing, and this was infectious, since it caused those close by to engage in the fun of whatever the cause of her merriment. She could conduct herself in a lofty manner on occasion, and change everything quickly with a bit of impishness. Swift to anger, she became impatient with those she found hesitant or incapable of making a decision. Not surprisingly, she was fast to action, realizing swiftness leads to success. This evidenced itself through the years, and I shall relate as accurately as possible those occurrences that transpired. Then too, she displayed behavior at times commonly ascribed to men, and when exhibited by a woman might be called vicious and barbarous by some.

She possessed a large heart, one predetermined to gentleness and loving care for the sick and wounded. Indeed, this trait is the predominant memory I have of her, and I shall tell about incidents of her caring for the sick in future years. She learned her medical skills from Father Molina, as I have said, by studying under him and the Indian medical men he

---

[54] The Spanish name for a maid.
[55] This reference is to Hernán Cortés and his native woman mistress, Doña Marina, who lived with him during the conquest of the Aztecs and even bore him a son. De Mérida is discreet in not mentioning their names.

employed. As to her physical presentation, her beauty was not completely without similarity among women and not of the kind to astound others. Her simple presence, though, caused unfailing fascination. Her mannerisms, combined with the persuasive charm of her conversation and the aura she projected of herself in the company of others, did possess a considerable capability to stimulate those around her. The sound of her voice was distinctive and charming, for it rose and fell in irregular fashion, mesmerizing those listening to her. This, coupled with occasional hand and arm movements to make or emphasize a point, made it difficult to take one's eyes away from her when she was speaking, even for a moment. She owned a marked ability with languages, easily learning to master new sounds and words, which meant she rarely needed a translator, even when we found ourselves amongst the Mapuche later in our journey, when their different dialects proved confusing. In sum, her physical presence and comportment offered that of a captivating woman and I shall write further of her in the ensuing years.

To return to the death of our friend, Sire, the subsequent day in a heavy, damp mist, we buried Alvar Gómez de Almagro in a grove outside the Raqch'i complex and placed a covering of heavy stones over the grave. His son, Juan Gómez, spoke movingly about his life and the respect he had for his father. The Captain then led us in prayer that our friend might find eternal peace with our Lord. Such was the wish of us all for him.

We spent the rest of the day in reflection and preparation for departure on the new morning. At the hour of None, four men rode into our encampment and announced they wished to ride with us to Chile. After they met with Captain Valdivia and received his approval, he introduced them. They were Francisco de Galdames,[56] Juan Gallego,[57] Antón Hidalgo,[58] and Manuel Anaya.[59] With the passing of Captain Almagro,

---

[56] (1508-1558).

[57] This man's name appears on the list mentioned previously, but without a date of death.

[58] (1512-1577). See, <u>Declaratión de Bautista Ventura, Juan Gallego, and Antón Hidalgo</u> in J.T. Medina, <u>Documentos inéditos Para La Historia de Chile</u>.

[59] (1513-?).

The Adventure Chronicles of *Conquistador* Pedro de Mérida. VOLUME 2, VALDIVIA

we totaled now thirty-two in number. Our Captain read them his rules of conduct and assigned them daily tasks to support the expedition, like those the rest of us had. The day after, January 23, we resumed our passage south in the order now familiar to all. Although it was the middle of summer, the air was cool and occasional breezes made it seem even colder.[60]

The next town of size we entered was Hullaqa,[61] on February 7. Ayar had told us on the journey that the townspeople here were skilled at weaving wool clothing, which we would need in Puno, and especially on our march to Putre and beyond. We made camp outside the town and used the blue beads to purchase warm clothes for the upcoming weeks. Anco led us about the market district, which offered all types of sewn goods. There were socks of all sizes and different colors. This was true as well of sweaters, pants, blankets, hats, shawls, dresses, shirts, indeed, anything needed by the body for warmth and comfort. And the colors. Blues, greens, yellows, reds, purples, oranges, all had their places in the market through which we walked. I asked Anco how they colored all the things before us. He answered by saying that when they wanted to dye something a particular color, they were quite particular about the natural color of the material, which must be white or light brown. They then used a secret process to prepare things to take the dye before they dipped the cloth into it. And the color of anything soaked in this manner remained always, and the dye stayed bright ever after. But if they started out with dark wool or did not use the correct process, the color looked unpleasing.

25

---

[60] The air temperature is also a function of altitude. Here, on the way south, the elevation varies between 12,400 and 12,900 feet.
[61] This is the *Quechua* name for today's city of Juliaca, with a population of 225,000. It is called "The Windy City" because of the stiff winds that frequent the area. Additionally, it is known as "Sock City" and "Knitting City" because of its production of wool socks, sweaters, and other clothing, all of bright colors. It sits at an elevation of 12,549 feet.

PART CC

OUR WAY TO PUTRE AND THE VILLAGES AND PEOPLE ALONG THE WAY

26

We left this settlement after two days and in three approached a small, unremarkable village called Puno.[62] Three days after, we entered the community of Llave,[63] where a river of the identical name entered the great Laguna Titicaca. Ancohualla told us that the third Inca army to invade Chile passed through here on its march to Putre, and this is the way we would follow. On February 17, with the Río Llave on our left, and south, we marched west amidst a barren landscape. I noticed, as I had years before, that the flat desert land presented itself with opposites. For here appeared these vast spaces, occasionally populated by small, colorful desert flowers, that gave the brown earth a texture all its own. To some men, this terrain seemed unexciting. But I saw beauty here resembling that which we had seen before on our travels through Chile. It felt good to be back again.

---

[62] With a population today of close to 150,000 inhabitants, Puno is an important agricultural and livestock region on the western shores of Lake Titicaca. At 12,556 feet, it is quite cool the year round.

[63] Llave is thirty-three miles south from Puno and has 58,000 inhabitants.

The Adventure Chronicles of *Conquistador* Pedro de Mérida. VOLUME 2, VALDIVIA

PHOTOS: Images of the towns and landscape through which they passed are in 4AA-DD.13-.31.

In two days more, we stopped by a small settlement on the river.[64] Only a few people lived here, but they seemed friendly and of good cheer. Vicente had told us the night before he intended to start a daily fishing contest among the men, just as Diegito had done on our passage on the Avenue of the Volcáns, and it began in earnest when Captain de Miranda and his men finished laying out our campsite. Those who participated did so with laughing and shouting, while those watching from shore cheered on their favorites. Vicente and Ayar had invited the villagers to watch these strange visitors splash and play in their river, and they too laughed with the rest of us. When the merriment came to a close, Montesinos motioned to the natives and, in a show of friendship, bestowed half of the catch upon them, which caused wide smiles and bows of gratefulness. The Captain and Doña Inés had watched from the very beginning, laughing with the rest of us. And this gesture of kindliness towards the villagers pleased Valdivia a great deal, to the extent that he called to Montesinos and thrust his right fist in the air in appreciation, as was his wont. At the evening meal, Captain Valdivia congratulated my friend for his friendliness towards the natives. "It seems to me that the Lieutenant has shown us how we must behave in this land, gentlemen. The natives must see us as friendly and never as combatants coming after their land and crops."

We moved on towards a village Ayar called Cachuma.[65] When we came to it in two days, the few villagers waved to us as we passed through to a campsite for the night. Vicente conducted a fishing contest and again made part of our catch available to the townspeople, which produced smiles all around. *Ichu* grass remained plentiful, and the llamas and horses ate their fill.

I should relate here, Your Highness, an event of great importance, for both Christian and Indian members of the expedition. It happened in this manner.

---

[64] This must have been Siraya, at 12,800 feet. It is still a small settlement today, as one may see on the site.

[65] This is another small community on the way to Putre with fewer than 500 inhabitants. Its elevation is 13,050 feet.

Doña Inés knew of the large contingent of men to join us at Putre and had requested from the Captain someone who might work with her to meet our resulting medical needs. She planned to teach this person all she had learned so that they could assist her as needed. She had a concern too about attending the Indians, as Ancohualla had asked her recently if she might help those providing for the medical needs of his people. He had a suggestion as to who this might be and La Doña mentioned this to the Captain.

In response, Valdivia talked with Anco, who proposed that a young Indian woman of his acquaintance might fulfill our Doña's needs and his. It happened that this lady was the daughter of Inca royalty in Cusco, who were friends of Anco. He had promised them he would care for her in the new land, keep her from harm, and make certain she found a suitable husband. She joined the expedition because she wished to begin a new life in the land of Chile, as both we Christians and the Indians wanted to do. She was a hard worker, said Ancohualla, despite her royal background, and she should serve well as a medical assistant to Doña Inés in caring for the Indians. Valdivia discussed the issue with La Doña, who said she knew the woman Anco had in mind. This Inca princess, for such she was, had approached La Doña one day when she was administering to a sick Indian, and asked if she might help, to which Doña Inés assented readily. It happened this young woman had an uncle who cared for the medical needs of the Inca, his household, and those of other Inca royalty. She had asked him to teach her the skills of the physician, since her nature inclined to caring for the physical needs of those around her. He agreed, and such became the beginning of her acquiring Inca medical skills.[66]

---

66 When the Incas needed medical help, priests usually performed healing rites to cure them. Their physicians had an understanding of the medicinal properties of herbs and plants as well. The bark of one tree, for example, produced quinine, which they used to cure cramps, chills, and many other ailments. They used the leaves of the coca plant to numb people who were in pain. And they had a drug, called *curare,* that they extracted from a tropical vine. This drug caused a patient to lose feeling temporarily in a particular part of the body or to lose consciousness, which facilitated amputation and even brain trepanning. If Pilca Huaca had a basic understanding of these drugs and procedures, in addition to knowledge of prayers and incantations, she was well suited for the physician's role.

So it delighted Doña Inés that it was this woman whom Anco put forth, and she was gratified at the prospect of having an aide to assist her. She suggested to the Captain that the Indian woman could help her as her lady-in-waiting of sorts, and aid in the care of both Indian and Christian patients. This Valdivia proposed to Ancohualla, who said it would be important to the young woman and the entire expedition for her to help in this way. Anco asked the Inca lady about this, and she accepted the offer from La Doña and the Captain most happily. From this moment on, Doña Inés and this Indian woman treated the sick before we began our journey each day, La Doña for the Christians and the Inca lady for the Indians.

Briefly, I should say more about her, as I had seen her on occasion with Doña Inés. Her name was Pilca Huaca,[67] the name of a wife of the Inca Huayna Capac, who had ruled the Inca Nation years before.[68] Short in stature and of an uncommon beauty, similar to the women in Cusco, she was different in appearance from other Indians in that her skin appeared more light in color than brown and her eyes a dark blue, like our Doña's.[69] The times I had seen her so far it seemed her nature always to be in a good humor. Where others saw hardship, she saw opportunity. And I never observed her angry or upset with those around her. Instead, her countenance seemed disposed towards cheerfulness. Yes, she displayed sorrow at the injuries of those she treated. These shows of emotion, however, departed quickly. As a sign of her continual good nature, she hummed Indian tunes frequently, which sounded warmly melodious to those near her. I shall tell more of this woman, Majesty, as our journey continues.

---

[67] She was addressed always with the two names, much like our use of Betty Sue or Mary Jo.

[68] (1493-1527). Inca women of the upper class often named their daughters after prominent women of the past.

[69] This was not uncommon. Pedro Pizarro in his *Relacion*, p. 471, says, "The people of this kingdom of Peru were white, swarthy in color, and the Lords and Ladies whiter than Spaniards. I saw an Indian woman and child who would not stand out among white blonds." As for blue eyes, golden Inca death masks, with blue eyes, have been unearthed in several parts of Peru. One such is from Sipán.

In the days after leaving Cachuma, it became colder in the daytime and always at night, even now, in the summer months. The clothing we had acquired in Hullaqa proved its worth, as Ayar had said it would. One day, we passed a small settlement with a number of huts, and I remarked upon what must be the cruel nature of life here.[70] Ayar responded that the people moved to Puno when the cold became too harsh. Perhaps that time had not yet come, for we saw a few villagers at work and moving about. When Valdivia ordered a halt at a distance outside town, the weather had warmed somewhat.

I should tell, Majesty, of our relations with the Indians who accompanied us on the journey and camped but a short distance away from us each evening. We treated them as kindred spirits, as they wished for new lives and opportunities in *Nueva Estremadura*, just as we did. The Captain encouraged us to make friends with them, as we would all be planting crops and tending livestock when we found a suitable site for our capital city. The afternoons proved best for this, when our tents were up, our horses groomed, and we had occasion to relax. Valdivia served as our example, since he talked frequently with Ancohualla and his *caciques* about sundry topics. Ayar made friends with a number of natives and brought them to visit with Montesinos, Lope de Ayala, Juan de Almagro, and me. And Doña Inés had conversations regularly with Pilca Huaca and several of the other Indian women.

A common interest involved taking part in games with our Indian friends. Sometimes, these were Inca pastimes. On other occasions, we offered our own entertainment. As an example of an Indian activity, a favorite, approximating our draughts, they played on a board with sixty-four dark and light colored squares. Players began with twelve pieces, blue beads for one participant, small stones for the other. These the contestants positioned on the dark squares, opposite one another, leaving the middle rows empty. The players moved their pieces diagonally, and never backwards, with the object to capture the other competitor's stones. There are further details, Sire, but these should suffice here.[71] Prizes,

---

[70] This settlement is today's Mazo Cruz, at an elevation of 13,100 feet.

[71] Draughts, or checkers, as we call it, has been played in some form for several thousand years.

decided on before the game's start, were awarded the winners. Games such as this allowed both the Indians and us Christians to see the other man in a different light and situation, other than the riding and walking of our every day journeys. Occasionally, Indian musicians, with flutes and stringed instruments, walked about and provided entertainment.

After more days on the march, we reached a small village called Capazo.[72] Ayar rode ahead to assess the nature of things. He returned after awhile and said we must bypass this place, as the villagers complained of headaches and fevers. This we did, staying well clear. A slight breeze here moved above the free and open land; where the sky was blue, it had a hazy and languid nature about it. The sun warmed us, and as we rode slowly along over the limitless desert ground, our horses seemed in good, even playful, spirits. Then, black heads of thunderclouds rose fast above the northern horizon, and the deep rumbling of far-off thunder began rolling across the sand. When I looked up, the entire sky had become darkly cloaked, and the desert to our front assumed a purple color beneath the blackening sky. Abruptly, from the thickest part of the clouds, a flash leapt out, and quivered again and again down to the land. At the same time came a long, rolling peal of thunder, followed by a cool wind with the suggestion of snow. I indentified a site quickly and we waited until the others rode in before making camp. We finished as a light snow began falling. It lasted a short while, but it had become much colder as a result.

Moving on, one bleak, cold day, at a settlement Ayar called Visviri,[73] we stopped for refreshment. Lieutenant Montesinos called to me and pointed south. "There are the two mountains outside Putre!"[74] Indeed they were, as Ayar and I confirmed. When our Captain came up with Doña Inés, the sight gladdened them. He called to the men and shared with them the important goal now within sight and within our grasp. Later, we

---

[72] Another small encampment, with 1,300 souls today. It sits at 14,400 feet. There have been modern instances in the winter when women and children here leave for Putre in the west, where it is warmer.
[73] This small community today numbers some 350 people, at 13,500 feet.
[74] As noted in the Third Letter, this is the double-summited peak Taapaca.

made camp by a fast moving stream. The men caught fish here, and we celebrated our nearness to Putre with the large catch and a festive meal.

In two more days, now traveling south, we happened on an Inca *pukará*, like those we had seen on the journey north from Copayapu.[75] This one remained in good condition, with double parallel walls around a complex composed of structures with circular walls and stone floors. Ayar explained more about it after Ancohualla and Valdivia arrived. Among other things, the first Inca army sent to invade Chile years before had used food in this fortress put there by the local natives.[76]

In the days after leaving the *pukará*, we encountered *bofedales* and small *estanques* frequently, with small villages and settlements among them. The people here were friendly, and we waved and smiled as we passed them in the fields, as did Ancohualla and our Indians. In the late afternoons, we visited occasionally while de Cartagena used our blue beads to barter for fish, *charqui*, and a variety of vegetables. A large variety of birds in this region helped increase our food stores. On a day with the scent of rain in the air, at a location along a low ridge, we saw in the distance two snow capped mountains of great beauty. Ayar called them "the brothers," since they resided so close together and in appearance seemed to resemble each other.[77] Here, Ayar made it known that we were five days from Putre. Captain Valdivia reminded our *maestre de campo*, Gómez de Benito, and Lieutenant Montesinos that once there, they would ride to Tacna, meet the new men, and return with them. Ancohualla and one of his *caciques*, Yumalla by name, would ride with them.[78] Vicente said it should be two and a half days to the town from Putre so we could expect them back in about a week.

---

[75] These were the *pukarás* of Catarpe near Atacama and Lasana outside Chiu-Chiu in the south.

[76] This is the *Pukará de Copaquilla*, at 13,650 feet. It was restored by students at the University of Tarapaca in 1979.

[77] These are the dormant strato-volcanoes Pomerape (20,610 feet) and Parinacota (20,827 feet). They are known as the "Payachatas", or fraternal twins in *Aymara*.

[78] Yumalla is a peasant name and has no *Quechua* or *Aymara* meaning.

After three days, we rode into a dry water channel that looked like a road. And near this riverbed appeared a sight I had seen last on the Avenue of the Volcáns. *Géisers.* Several shot bursts of white steam into the air from the hot pools of water that bubbled to the surface from beneath the high mountain now close by.[79] We awaited Valdivia's arrival. When he rode in and saw the wonderful sight before us, he signaled we should stay here for the night. There were enough warm pools and streams for Christians and Indians alike, and the waters provided enjoyment into the late evening.

---

[79] This must be the Jurasi thermal basin and springs which lie some six miles to the east of Putre. There are no active geysers today, but the thermal hot springs are a favorite with tourists. The mountain referred to is Taapaca, 19,230 feet, which sits to the east of Putre.

PART DD

OUR ENTRY INTO PUTRE AND WHAT TRANSPIRED THERE; CAPTAIN VILLAGRAN AND SEVENTY MEN JOIN US FROM TACNA

ate the following morning, at the request of our Captain, I sent de Almagro and Ayar ahead to notify the town *cacique* of our approach. They returned, and reported the townspeople looked forward to our arrival. A short distance from the village,[80] the Captain ordered a halt as he and Ancohualla wished to receive the *cacique* before entering the town. Presently, a most pleasant man with an engaging smile appeared, alone, with no entourage. He bowed to both Captain Valdivia and Ancohualla and Anco translated the man's welcome to us. His townspeople, he said, would have food and drink ready on the morrow. This, Valdivia replied, suited us since the day's march had been a tiring affair. At the town chief's departure, we made camp. It was March 22, five days later than planned. Vicente,

---

[80] Captain Almagro avoided Putre and bypassed it, as recounted in the Third Letter, because he thought it and its surroundings offered good terrain for an ambush by Inca warriors. The town lies at 11,600 feet.

Gómez de Benito, and Ancohualla and his *cacique*, prepared to depart on the morrow for their ride to Tacna to welcome the new men.

At daybreak, the four men left, leading five pack horses apiece to haul provisions back to us. At mid-day, we visited the village and partook of the foodstuffs offered by the natives. Our Indians ate and strolled about as well. Doña Inés and Pilca Huaca conversed with the women they met, while others of us accompanied Valdivia about the main square and saluted the men there. We smiled often and conducted ourselves in a most friendly manner.

Later, before assembling for the late day meal, I found the Captain sitting on a rock by his tent. He had summoned me to discuss an important activity he wished performed. He appeared deep in thought, for he stroked his beard with thumb and forefinger, as was his inclination. He was pleased, he said, about the welcome earlier in the village, since again we had shown people in this new land we came in peace rather than with a desire to dominate or rule by force of arms. Yet, he worried about how long this behavior might remain thus, for he felt someday there must be fearful bloodshed in confrontations with the Indians. He hoped this might not be so, but that we must accept it notwithstanding. Although calm times passed for the present, Your Majesty, eventually his worries would prove to be correct. Our conversation changed to the matter about which he had called upon me. He asked that I take de Cartagena, and whomever else I wanted, and visit the nearby settlements to barter and trade for food for the coming march down the Avenue of Volcáns. "And seek out *poros* for every man, Pedro. You and the other Almagro men have assured me water should be plentiful. I want to be ready if it is not, however." I assured him I should do so. "And remember," he continued. "Tomorrow is our Lady's Day.[81] I wish we had a priest to say mass in honor of our Blessed Lady."

On the morrow after our morning refreshment, we assembled and recited prayers to our Blessed Virgin Mary, as it was her day. Our Captain knelt on one knee as he held his statue of Our Lady overhead. Yes, we preferred

---

[81] The Blessed Virgin's day of the Annunciation, celebrated on March 25.

a priest and mass, but true feelings from the heart at times don't need such things to find sincere expression. Afterwards, I set out with my small band and fifteen pack horses and llamas to seek provisions from the close by settlements and farms. De Cartagena, de Almagro, de Ayala, Ayar, and his Indian friends, Rimac[82] and Paucar,[83] and I continued with this for some time and it made for a successful undertaking. The wetlands between the *pukará* and the two mountains in the south provided the richest farmlands. And the settlements there bartered eagerly with us. We found *poros*, as Valdivia had requested, and a large variety of fruits, vegetables, dried fish, *chuño*, *quinua*, *maize*, *charqui*, salt, and hot peppers. The *maize* pleased our Indians, Rimac told us, as they could begin the process of making their drink of *chicha* with it.

On Tuesday, April 2, eight days after our men had left for Tacna, Captain Valdivia expressed concern about their whereabouts. He asked if I might ride with him to see if we could see dust or movement from the direction of their return. We had been in the saddle only until mid-morning when he yelled that he saw dust in the air to the northwest. Valdivia withdrew his spyglass from his saddle pouch and focused it upon the distant scene. Within moments he shouted that it was our men coming towards us. Soon, a large number of men and horses became apparent, moving at a walk. When they came closer, I recognized Vicente in front, with Gómez de Benito to his left. They saw us, broke into a round trot, and waved. When they were within hailing distance, Captain Valdivia shouted out a welcome and held his right fist in the air. They saluted in return and rode up to us quickly. We dismounted and walked towards them, shouting our welcome and thankfulness at their arrival. Vicente and Gómez dismounted and we gripped their hands in salutation. Presently, a man of notable distinction, made apparent by his walk and bearing, came forward and called out to Valdivia, who moved hurriedly to him. They embraced each other, laughed, and smiled. This man, the distinguished Francisco de Villagran[84] and a friend of the Captain's, had served with him as a

---

[82] *Quechua* for "eloquent."
[83] This is *Quechua* for "very refined."
[84] We will hear more of this Captain throughout the coming years.

young man in several battles of the Italian Wars.[85] He had left Cusco promising to locate additional men for the Chile journey as he traveled to Arequipa and Tacna. And he had kept his promise, as we learned, for a total of seventy[86] men accompanied him, including four priests. We totaled now 102 men in number.

Among the new men, I recognized fifteen friends from the Almagro days and offered my hand in welcome. The coming weeks would allow us to find out more from these men about events of the intervening three years. I sought out Ancohualla and found him conversing with his *cacique*, Yumalla, near their ten pack horses, all with large sacks of provisions on their backs. It had been a successful journey, he said, and remarked that they had acquired much of what they wanted. I told him of our provisioning with Rimac and Paucar among the settlements in the region, and he expressed great satisfaction with this.

Later that day, when the new men had set up their tents and tended their horses, Ayar and I looked for Vicente Montesinos to learn of the happenings in Tacna and its efforts to recover from the earthquake we experienced there in 1537. We found him sitting with the Captain and others, listening to Captain Villagran and a number of his men tell of the events in and around Arequipa before they rode to Tacna, there to await word from us about our location. Vicente and our Captain motioned us to come forward, and we did so. After introductions, Villagran continued his telling of things. When they entered Arequipa, he said, the people there were friendly and welcoming because of the deaths of the *cacique* brothers, Huanca and Thonapa. These were the Indian leaders we killed at the battle at Fortress Arequipa years before. Their stay turned unpleasant, however, for a volcán directly east of the town rained down cinders for

---

[85] These wars were a series of conflicts from 1494 to 1559 that involved, at various times, many of the city-states of Italy, the Papal States, and most of the major states of Western Europe (France, Spain, the Holy Roman Empire, England, and Scotland).

[86] Weldon Vernon corroborates De Mérida's figure. However, she offers no historical citation in support of it.

many days.[87] They fell in such quantity they obscured some parts with a yard of dust, in others two. Fields of *maize* and wheat were buried, large trees withered, and most of the flocks died for want of pasture. The ashes that fell covered the land around the town for ninety miles. One day they found 500 llamas and guanaco dead in one place, and ducks and birds lay all about in others. Houses fell in from the weight on their roofs, while a number were saved by the diligence of their owners, who removed the cinders as they fell. The falling powder obscured the sun occasionally, and this caused the people to use candles in the middle of the day. Captain Villagran led his men out and on towards Tacna because Arequipa had become unlivable for the present.

He went on to say that after departing from Cusco he had enlisted two captains, Francisco de Aguirre[88] and Rodrigo de Quiroga,[89] to meet us at Atacama with men they would recruit while riding south from Laguna Titicaca, through Tarija and Tupiza. They said they expected to be at Atacama the beginning of June and planned to wait there until they should hear from us. Apprised of all this, the Captain gripped the hand of Villagran and thanked him with great effusiveness.

The talk changed to the town of Tacna, where they waited for days until Montesinos and de Benito arrived to lead them to Putre. Vicente mentioned our brief stay there with the Almagro Expedition and the terrible *terremoto* that had struck when we were a few miles out of town. Homes and buildings had been destroyed, Villagran said, although few people were killed. Building new homes now had become the main activity of the townspeople and someday things should return to normal. The Great *Qhatu*[90] was one of the first structures restored, and Vicente

---

[87] This was Volcán El Misti (19,101 feet). Volcanologists, who study these matters, believe it erupted in 1540 or 1541. De Mérida has clarified the date for us.

[88] (1507-1581). Valdivia mentions de Aguirre in his Letter 1. He will hold several important posts in the years to come.

[89] (1512-1580). De Quiroga will also hold important administrative jobs in the new land.

[90] This was the large outdoor market mentioned in The Adventure Chronicles, Volume I.

had led the men through it so all might see the wonderful things we saw there years ago.

Juan Bohón,[91] a deep voiced man, told of the cock fights[92] they saw in Arequipa. Two owners put their birds in a small ring and let them fight, until the injury of one so badly it could no longer continue or the death of either. Indians attended these fights and yelled loudly to encourage the cock of their liking. In certain matches, the owners attached sharp metal spurs to the feet of the birds. This made for bloody encounters the crowds appreciated even more.

Alonzo de Monroy,[93] whom I had known briefly in Cusco and remained friends with in the coming years, related that all the men had brought foodstuffs with them, and this caused a shout of thanks from de Cartagena. He planned to add them to what our men had returned with and what we had acquired in the surrounding settlements.

Pedro Cisternas[94] said he had an arquebus, the sole man so armed. I commented it might become useful should we need to kill guanaco to increase our meat supplies. He became excited about this and said he had already killed three of them outside Tacna and eagerly should do so again whenever requested. Something he had learned, he told us, was that the bullet is so large[95] he aimed at the legs or the head of the animal rather than at other parts of the body. This saved the good pieces of meat from damage from the bullet.

Pedro de Gamboa, who had lost his left eye in a battle with Indians in Peru and wore a black patch over it, introduced himself as an architect of cities and demonstrated in the sand before him how he planned to lay out

---

[91] (?–1549). Valdivia mentions Bohón in his Letter I to the King.

[92] Cockfighting dates back 6,000 years to the time of the Persian Empire. It is still popular in Arequipa.

[93] (?-1545). Valdivia refers to de Monroy in his Letters I and III and de Mérida will elaborate on his exploits in his Fifth Letter.

[94] (1505-1590). This Cisternas enjoyed a colorful history in the early days of Chile, and de Mérida will relate some of this in his letters.

[95] An arquebus bullet ranged in size from .60 to .80 caliber.

new towns, given the chance to do so.[96] Valdivia took notice immediately, and I saw the two together later, discussing matters. As it turned out, Sire, this man and Captain de Miranda, who possessed this talent as well, presented drawings eventually of the new capital city for the Captain's approval. I anticipate my story, however.

Our conversation at an end, Valdivia asked Gómez de Benito to gather all the men at his tent before the evening meal, as he wished to introduce our new priests. When we had assembled, each of them said a few words in greeting. They were Fathers Juan de Cabrera,[97] Juan Lobo,[98] Diego Perez,[99] and Rodrigo González Marmolejo,[100] all of the Dominican order. They had brought wine with them, which meant we could attend mass again. It happened in addition that Father Lobo possessed medical skills, and he offered to assist attending the sick whenever called upon. This pleased our Doña Inés and Pilca Huaca a great deal. On the new day, the priests passed among us and blessed all with holy water. Subsequently, Father Marmolejo[101] said mass, our first such celebration in months. Later, Captain Valdivia read the new men his rules governing our behavior and I read the route description for the journey to Copayapu.

I must tell Your Highness that one of those who came from Tacna with Captain Villagran proved a man with a unique talent, as he made us laugh and put us in a pleasant mood. By name, Rodrigo Hidalgo,[102] he was no relation to Antón Hidalgo, who had joined us in early February, but they became friends quickly. Newly arrived in Peru from Spain in 1539 seeking adventure, Rodrigo hoped for a new life in Chile and joined

---

[96] (1512-1552). De Gamboa, in fact, did lose an eye in a fight with Peru natives.
[97] This priest appears on the Errazuriz list but is otherwise lost to history. See Appendix A.
[98] Valdivia in his Letter I mentions this priest to the King.
[99] Referenced by Valdivia in the same letter and is on the Errazuriz list.
[100] (1487-1564). Valdivia respected this priest a great deal and mentions him several times in his letters. He was to become the first bishop of Chile, although he passed away before assuming that office.
[101] Father Marmolejo and the other priests were Dominicans, as de Mérida says, as were Fathers Molina and Suarez on the Almagro Expedition.
[102] (1516–1576).

Villagran at Tacna. By some happenstance, Valdivia had learned Hidalgo, who looked half his age of forty years, had a playful nature when the times needed levity and the Captain had asked him what sorts of entertainment he provided. The two spent a short time in conversation, and Valdivia remarked afterwards that Hidalgo offered to entertain us and our Indians occasionally. And when we came to a town or village, he planned to perform for the townspeople, in particular the women and children. The Captain thought this might help relieve fear among them that we came to do harm.

The day following was market day in town and farmers and their families brought their produce to the village for bartering with the townspeople. This presented an ideal moment for Hidalgo and, at Valdivia's request, he took full advantage. He announced his presence with a small flute with which he played low, deep notes, and high, shrill ones as well. When a crowd had gathered around him, enough to cause him to stop and give a performance, they witnessed what I shall now describe. He carried with him a court jester's hat, with three projections of cloth that sprang out in different directions. Each one was of a different color, with a bell sewn to its tip. When he put it on his head and shook it, the hat alone caused the natives to laugh and clap.

PHOTOS: Please see photo 4AA-DD.31 for what Hidalgo may have looked like.

Next, he juggled fruits, vegetables, whatever caught his fancy. He kept several of these in the air at one time, such a number that the villagers began to laugh and cheer loudly at his skill in doing so. Then, at the end, when all the items fell to earth and he began acting as though he was crying, the crowd began to moan and groan in sympathy. When all appeared quite morose, he sprang up suddenly and, with a large smile, resumed his flute playing, at which the crowd clapped and laughed once more.

Then, to continue the merriment, he waved to a young Indian woman in the crowd to come forward. She did so eagerly, and when she was quite close, Hidalgo began twisting his face into different shapes, sizes, and expressions, each funnier than the previous one. As he did this, he rolled his eyes in ways that seemed impossible for the average man. These brought loud laughs, especially from another young lady who laughed so hard she turned red in the face.

That over, he asked the first woman to remain with him. He produced a flat piece of metal from his pocket, positioned it in his left hand, closed it, and raised both above his head so all could see them. At this, he asked of her, with his eyes and head movements, which hand contained the metal piece. She chose the left hand. He opened it, but no coin appeared there. He dropped his arms, reached behind her left ear, and pulled the coin forward.[103] A shout of amazement arose from the crowd, and they clapped, yelled their approval, and called Hidalgo, *qamchu, qamchu*. I walked over to Ancohualla, who laughed and clapped, and asked what the word meant. A funny person in *Quechua*, who makes people laugh, he said. From that point on, we addressed Hidalgo as *Qamchu*, instead of jester, and he enjoyed his new name a great deal. At the conclusion of these festivities, Valdivia addressed us and said we had made friends of the villagers this day and we must seek to do the same in the other towns we would enter. Rodrigo Hidalgo had become our Emissary of Merriment, he said with a laugh, and should serve us well in the land of *Nueva Estremadura*.

---

[103] Yes, this modern-day magic trick goes back through the centuries.

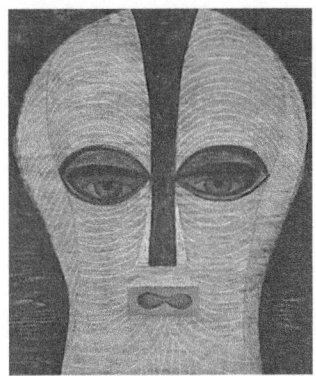

PART EE

WE BEGIN OUR PASSAGE OVER THE AVENUE OF THE VOLCÁNS;[104] OUR HUNT OF THE *SURI*, OR LESSER RHEA

43

*F*ollowing more than a week of preparations for our journey southward, Majesty, our Captain proclaimed we would leave in two days. We did so on April 12, after a mass said by Father Marmolejo, two weeks behind our original schedule, although this caused little concern to the Captain or any of us. We now had a different order of march. My guiding team of Ayar, Lope de Ayala, and me, rode out front and led the procession, as before. Behind us were Gómez de Benito, Lieutenant Vicente Montesinos, and Juan Gómez de Almagro. With this group rode Captain Villagran, second in command as appointed by Valdivia and equal in rank with Gómez de Benito, still our *maestre de campo* and now third in command. Captain Valdivia consulted with them daily. After these came our men, all in good humor. The prospect of going to a new land brought smiles to all our faces. Then rode Valdivia, accompanied by Doña Inés, and behind was Ancohualla at the

---

[104] Photos and images of peaks on the Avenue are in the Part W, Third Letter images section on the site.

head of the Indian contingent. Next came the llamas, the pack animals, and llama dung gatherers. Finally, de Cartagena, Hernando Vallejo, and Bernal Martinez, formed our rear guard and came last.

IMAGES: See 4EE-GG.1-.19 for images on the Avenue.

On this comfortable autumn day, we waved to the Putre villagers and moved southeast slowly, towards the Smoking Volcán we remembered from the Almagro days.[105] We followed a small stream at the bottom of a valley whose walls rose above us. It felt good to be in the saddle again, as Vicente had said at our morning meal. Late in the day, my men and I mounted a slight rise and stopped, as this appeared good ground for a campsite this night. As I whistled in a low, contemplative way to myself, we sat still in our saddles and looked back at the mile-long procession of Christians, Indians, and animals, as it moved towards us in an inexorable manner. It had an aspect of inevitability about it, for it bore all our hopes and aspirations for new lives and new beginnings in our new world.

44   I should say something here, Sire, about two of our new priests. Father Juan Lobo was a tall man, taller than Father Suarez on the Almagro Expedition. He stood six feet, six inches, much higher than the rest of us. And because of his stature, his saddle had fittings of long flaps to accommodate his extended legs. When a man stands higher than those around him, he invites the presumption of knowledge and other attributes from those of lesser heights even though this is not always the truth. In the matter of Father Lobo, however, it was the truth, and his size, in company with his religious calling, made him a compelling man worthy of respect.

He possessed medical skills as well, as I have said. Before arriving in the New World, he served as a priest at the Cathedral of Seville. His duties included tending the needs of the sick, and teaching the Spanish language to young people in the city. Wishing to use his abilities, Doña Inés asked that he help her by tending our sick troops and assisting Pilca Huaca

---

[105]   As mentioned in, <u>The Adventure Chronicles, Volume I</u>, this is today's Guallatiri, one of the highest active volcanoes in South America at 19,918 feet.

in caring for ill Indians. He assented readily. He said, moreover, that he intended saying weekly mass for the Christian Indians with us and another priest would help him. This pleased La Doña. She also requested further assistance from him by asking that he help her educate Pilca Huaca in our language. She had been trying this herself, she said, but Father's skills in instruction should cause a larger success. Again, Father Lobo consented to do so quite happily.

As for his personal mannerisms, he spoke in a low voice, without excitement, and this gave a sense of gravity and weight to all he said. He granted himself moments of lightness, however, when matters became humorous, although soon he reverted to a calm and steadfast outward demeanor. A few found this perplexing, but I welcomed it as the right conduct of a man of God. I trusted him at once, and that trust remained the basis of our friendship during all the coming years. In total, Father Lobo presented himself as a man of considerable substance, physically, intellectually, and spiritually.

Father's friend to help him with the Indians was Father Juan de Cabrera. They had become close when they met in Arequipa, since both wished to bring the word of Christ to the Indians. Indeed, Father de Cabrera saw this as his single purpose in life, the reason for his stay here on earth. When Father Lobo told him of his talk with our Doña and that he had offered Father de Cabrera to help with instruction of the Indians in our Faith, Father was delighted. When Doña Inés informed the Captain of the desires of these two priests, he called them for discussion with Ancohualla present to learn of their activities with the Indians. As it happened, Anco had been thinking about the Church's teachings ever since the last days of the Almagro Expedition, when Father Molina had engaged him in conversations about our Faith. The proceedings went well, and thereafter the priests walked amongst the natives daily, visiting, discussing, and proselytizing. It did not surprise us, Excellency, that in the coming months, divers Indians came to embrace our Holy Faith.

Nevertheless, to return to Father de Cabrera. His hair was bright silver, uncommon for a man his age. This lent a great deal of distinction to his every action and utterance, since they seemed those of a wise and knowing man, and they were. In addition, he possessed a gift most found comforting. If he were discussing with someone a subject troubling to that person, he put his right hand frequently on the shoulder of the one talking, and this provided a sense of his understanding and commiseration. This made him a favorite with the Indians as he moved among them, as his nearness provided a sense of friendliness and trust. And he possessed a musical nature that the Indian music makers called forth, for he requested they play at his masses on Our Lord's Day, and they did so. This provided more to see and hear at these celebrations, and more Indians attended them.

I must return to our journey, Your Honor, for after four days on our passage, with the days cooler and the nights colder, the Smoking Volcán rose in the distant east, steam rising from its topmost heights, the drifting white and grey smoke resembling our battle flags flying before the wind. On Thursday, April 18, we made camp near the swift stream where Diegito and his friends on the Almagro journey had made us laugh with their failed attempts to capture vicuña.[106] We Almagro men told others of what happened, and even now it brought smiles. The animals still roamed in abundance here, since we saw them often in the near distance.[107] Neither our men nor the Indians tried to capture them, as the creatures proved too quick and crafty.

Within days, a stream met the river we followed and made the point of their juncture pleasant as an encampment,[108] with abundant *ichu* grass to please our animals. And it happened here, Majesty, that a most extraordinary, but sad, event occurred. As we began erecting our tents, Juan Gómez exclaimed upon two small dust clouds in the south. Both

---

[106] The expedition is now on the royal road of the Inca. It entered Chile from Bolivia through what is now the international border crossing of Tambo Quemado on the Bolivian side and Chungara on the Chilean, It stretches all the way to the Araucanian territory in southern Chile.

[107] The area the expedition has entered is the large vicuña reserve maintained today by the Chilean Government, as mentioned in Volume I.

[108] The Expedition had been following the Río Chusjavida. The Río Lauca meets it here.

moved slowly east, with a separation between them of almost a mile. They prompted Ayar to study them closely; then he whistled to Rimac and Paucar in the Indian camp, pointed to the nearby clouds, signaled to them with his arms and hands, and shouted something I did not quite understand.

Now other men had arrived, Vicente among them. Interested in the proceedings, they asked about the strange nature of the dust clouds in the distance. Just then Ayar's friends ran up, clutching their *ayllos*,[109] what we call *bolas*, resembling those Diegito and his friends had used on the vicuña hunt years before. Ayar explained what we saw: a number of large, flightless birds called *suri*. He reminded me that he had mentioned these *suri* when we passed through here on the Almagro Expedition, although we saw none on that day.[110] Their meat is quite flavorful and we could supplement our food stores if we wished to hunt them, he said. I looked at Vicente and, with a shrug of my shoulders, gave him a look of, "Why not?" He understood forthwith and strode towards me with a large smile on his face.

PHOTOS: See 4EE-GG.2 for a photo of the Lesser Rhea.

Valdivia had now come up and asked for a report. Vicente replied that since these birds could provide fresh and dried meat, he thought it worth the while to hunt them. Our Captain waved to Ancohualla, so that he might participate. When he joined us, with Yumalla, Valdivia apprised them of our proposed adventure. He said it would require a number of horsemen and suggested we include the Almagro men who had participated in the guanaco hunt several years before. He appointed

---

[109] This is the device consisting of three stone balls connected by a rope that is thrown about the feet of the hunted animal.

[110] These are the lesser rhea, or Darwin's rhea, found at several locations in South America, including here where the Expedition has made camp. They stand up to five feet tall and can weigh sixty pounds. A rhea on the run can reach up to 40 mph. Their meat is especially tasty, but it must be cooked quickly, otherwise it loses its flavor. Their feathers are used for dusters and their skin for cloaks and outer garments. The hunt took place near the strato-volcano, Arintica, 18,363 feet.

Montesinos as the "Master of Horse"[111] for the hunt and made available all the horse soldiers he required.

Ayar observed that since the birds can run faster than a horse, we must drive them towards the banks of the stream in the east, which they would hesitate to enter.[112] There the killing could begin. He went on to say that capturing them with *ayllos* might be difficult, as it had been with the vicuña, and perhaps a better tactic might be to use our swords to sever their heads from their long necks. This seemed a preferable tactic to us. Yumalla, who had indicated his desire to participate, said he planned to use the *ayllo*, as he knew nothing about sword handling.

Word of the hunt spread quickly, and presently sixteen men made themselves available, including Yumalla, Juan Gallego, Francisco de Galdames, and Juan Almonacid, among others, half of whom had participated in the guanaco kill in the Almagro days. Vicente gathered everyone together and made known his plan. We were to arrange ourselves in two parallel columns spaced twenty yards apart. At Vicente's command, we would advance and then, at his second command, tighten the distance between us as we drew closer to our prey. When the *suri* found themselves at the water's edge with no means of escape, we would take the moment to strike.

By now, both camps had come forth to see about the commotion and learn more concerning our undertaking. There arose much excitement when the purpose became known, with laughing, clapping, and singing by all in excited expectation. Ancohualla, the Captain, and Doña Inés urged us on with happy shouts of encouragement quickly taken up by all. Lieutenant Montesinos placed us in the two files and rode at the rear, so all could hear his commands. He put me as the rightmost forward horseman, with Yumalla, armed with an *ayllo*, as the leftmost. These served as important locations since Yumalla and I had to execute Vicente's orders expertly or the columns might become distorted. This gave me pause, as Yumalla did

---

[111] The reader may recall that Lieutenant Castilla served as the "Master of Horse" in the guanaco hunt near Llullaillaco in Volume I.

[112] The expedition has left the Río Lauca and now is following the Río Paquisa.

not possess a good horseman's skills. He had asked Montesinos to ride in the forward position, however, and received his permission to do so.

At Vicente's order, we proceeded forward at a trot and moved towards the two flocks of birds that were growing closer together. With little dust now, we could see them quite clearly. Their large size and long necks surprised me. Those thin shafts proved perfect for the sword! As to their movements, they did not rush in a straight line, but back and forth, changing direction from left to right and right to left very rapidly. Now we rode at a canter and then at full gallop. The *suri* reached the river and, as they did so, my position was at the right of the flock, now crowded together as one, and composed of almost sixty birds. As we closed on them, Vicente slowed us first to a canter, then a trot, and ordered us to close up the files. Yumalla turned in my direction and I his. The men shortened the distance between them to ten yards so the birds found themselves trapped between the water and our advancing half circle.

"They are ours, men," shouted Montesinos. "You may take them as you wish, and quickly!"

The killing now commenced with vigor. Our Toledo steel sliced through the *suri* necks as though they were ripe fruit. Even without their heads, though, they still ran about for several moments, this way and that, with blood spurting from their headless bodies before finally collapsing. In a short period, I had slashed the necks of four of the animals; the other men were successful too and soon bodies covered the ground. At the instant I spotted another for a kill, a loud cry from Montesinos startled us. "That is enough, men. Withdraw! Withdraw!" The man closest to me, de Galdames, shouted an emphatic monosyllable and, looking up, I saw the reason for his vulgar exclamation. Vicente was riding off to the northeast, away from us, and urging his horse on at great speed with his whip. This surprised me, until I heard two men to my right, Bohón and Gallego, shout that a man appeared down, with his horse dragging him at a gallop. They pointed in Vicente's direction and we saw him chasing a horse whose rider did not sit atop it but at an angle to its right side with his foot still in the stirrup. As we watched, the horse slowed and

Montesinos drew alongside and stopped it with a pull of its bridle. We all left off our killing task and rode out to identify the unfortunate man. Before I could learn his identity, a horseman riding ahead of me yelled that it was Yumalla! Before we reached the scene, Doña Inés had galloped in with her medicine bag to assist Montesinos in freeing the man's leg from the stirrup. It was a bloody sight, for he bled from his head and entire upper body, since he had struck several rocks and stones. Valdivia and Ancohualla rode up as Vicente removed his coat and folded it under Yumalla's head. Our Doña felt his chest gently for the beat of his heart, then raised her head slowly to Anco. "He is dead, my friend."

"I saw how it happened," murmured Montesinos. "He leaned to the right and down to try throwing his *ayllo*. But he lost his balance and fell to the side, with his foot caught in the stirrup."

Ancohualla came to Yumalla's side, knelt down, held the man's hands, and closed his eyes for a short time. Then he rose slowly, removed his cloak, and draped it over his friend's body. "Let us leave him here. We shall bury him tonight." A quiet melancholy settled over our two camps as we remembered Ancohualla's *cacique*. I had not known him well, but the Indians held him in high esteem. Anco and his men buried him that night, right where he lay.

Early the subsequent morning amidst the sadness, Valdivia and Anco met to discuss a course of action. They agreed that plucking the *suri*, skinning them, and carving the meat, presented the immediate tasks to perform. After that the drying process could begin. In sum, we needed three days. To lead the required tasks, the Captain put Lieutenant de Cartagena in charge of our men and Anco chose one of his new *caciques*, Tupa,[113] to lead the Indians. As it turned out, we had killed a total of forty-two birds. Montesinos and Tupa also led efforts to fish the river nearby to increase our supplies of dried fish. This meant Vicente and his friends could indulge themselves with their fish catching game again. During these meat and fish preparation days, those who wished to visit Yumalla's grave to pay their respects did so. There were no Inca priests

---

[113] This man was named after Tupa Inca, who reigned 1471-1493.

among the Indians and, even though Yumalla was not a Christian, both Father Lobo and de Cabrera said prayers for him at the burial site. The Captain and Ancohualla attended; so too Doña Inés and Pilca Huaca, Tupa, an additional new *cacique* named Huayna,[114] Captains Villagran and de Benito, Indians who had converted to our Faith, and others who had still to do so.

Having offered our farewells, Ayar, Juan Gómez, and I, relaxed that afternoon by observing the Indians pluck the *suri*, skin them, and carve the meat. We watched one Indian in particular, who performed the skinning and carving tasks skillfully with a sharp knife given him by one of de Cartagena's men. Once others had removed all the bird's feathers, they passed the carcass to him. He positioned it on its back and began dressing it until it lay, bare and shiny, with its legs in the air. Afterwards, he thrust the knife point into the skin stretched tight over the stomach. The blood gushed out and onto his hands, a thing he enjoyed. I say this because it brought forth a large smile and a sharp yell of satisfaction and triumph. Next, he pulled out the guts and, after locating the liver and kidneys the Indians value for their soups, threw the rest into the desert. Then he cut the bird in half, lengthwise, and afterward proceeded to carve chunks off, placing them in two piles, one for our meals during the impending nights, the other for those who prepared the meat for drying and *charqui*.

Late that day, the *suri* meat was ready for our eating pleasure. Ayar told us it must be cooked with haste, otherwise it might dry out rapidly. The taste was pleasing, and we ate our fill. De Cartagena said the bird's flesh dried readily and the *charqui* would provide pleasure. We found this to be so in the approaching weeks.

When the days of meat and fish preparation ended,[115] we set off for Chiu-Chiu, Calama, and Atacama. At mid-day, Montesinos came forward to ride and converse, as often was his habit. On this occasion, he remarked

---

[114] No doubt they named this man after Inca Huayna Ccapac.
[115] The meat drying process went on for several more days as they continued the journey south. The surrounding air's aridity helped a good deal, as this is the Atacama Desert, the driest in the world.

upon our upcoming meeting with Huaman, the *Desert Cacique* of Calama and the other towns in the vicinity. He recalled that Captain Almagro had offered Huaman the governorship of the territories he governed if he studied the tenets of the Catholic Faith, learned the Spanish language, and remained friends with the Spanish people who traveled to this land. This Huaman had promised to do.

"And yet, Vicente, as you know, Captain Almagro became so distracted by events in Peru on our return that he never sent priests or teachers to educate Huaman and his people."

Montesinos went on to observe that Father de Cabrera might be perfect to provide the spiritual needs of Huaman and his Indians. He had already made it known to us, he said, that it was his calling from the Christ to bring others to Him. And, remarked Vicente, he possessed the ability to teach others our language. We agreed we would talk to Father when our camp was up and the horses cared for.

We chose a camp area by thermal pools on a wide salar with numerous *estanques* on its surface.[116] Late that day, Montesinos and I visited Father de Cabrera and told him of the *Desert Cacique*, his agreement with Almagro, and Huaman's special needs as a result of it. At this, Father expressed profound excitement, raised his eyes heavenward, and made the sign of the cross. I told him as well about the High Priest of the High Mountains, Anta-Aclla Picchu, and his meeting with Father Molina on the Almagro Expedition. That encounter revealed that the Inca religion shared some of the truths of our Holy Faith. Sire, perhaps Your Highness recalls that I included the record of the discussion between these two holy men as an addendum to the Third Letter.[117]

Father de Cabrera posed various questions and asked if Father Lobo might join us. When he did so and heard about the needs of Huaman, to learn our

---

[116] They have just passed Arintica, so this must be the thermal waters of Polloquere, which lie on the Salar de Surire. The salar takes its name from the large number of *suri* in the vicinity.

[117] See <u>Volume I: Almagro</u>, Appendix B for an account of this meeting.

Faith and our language, Father Lobo observed, "Father, this is your destiny!" And when I said that Huaman had studied in Cusco to become an Inca high priest and possessed a religious nature, this produced more enthusiasm. We all smiled in high spirits, for here was the first man of our expedition who might realize his dream of starting a new life in this new land.

Father Lobo, however, offered an observation pertaining to the Captain. He must approve of Huaman, it seemed to Father. If he withheld his approval, he would not leave Father de Cabrera with him. This seemed a worthy observation. Montesinos and I assured him, however, that we intended to meet with Valdivia and tell him of Father de Cabrera's heartfelt aspiration to bring more natives to our Faith. In addition, we planned to talk further about the *Desert Cacique*, his unique abilities, and his desire to fulfill the promises made to Captain Almagro. We did so in the evening, before our meal, with Doña Inés present. She expressed great interest in Father's desire to convert the Indians and said Our Lord had sent him for this very purpose. Captain Valdivia agreed with this and summoned the two priests. When they arrived, he told them of our discussion and said it had been three years since Captain Almagro had passed this way and we knew not whether Huaman remained still of a like mind. He preferred to meet with him first, with Vicente and me in attendance, and afterward decide what to do. As for Father de Cabrera's request to attend as well, the Captain gave his enthusiastic approval. He went on to reveal that a promise he made to Francisco Pizarro, when he awarded him the land of Chile, was to bring many natives to the Faith, a pledge he sealed with his word. "You shall help me keep my vow, Father," said Valdivia. "And that is important to me." And so this matter rested, awaiting our meeting with Huaman.

On the coming day, at our rest for refreshment, dark clouds, which had formed in the east over the mountains, began moving towards us. I sent Ayar back to consult with the Captain, since it looked as though a fierce storm threatened to break at any moment. He returned quickly with orders to set camp without delay. Most had their tents up before the heavy sounds of thunder shook the darkened land. Shortly thereafter, brilliant flashes of light flew to earth like steel sword thrusts from on high. We could tell a few of them hit near our encampment since the noise they made upon striking the earth sounded close by. Presently, the flashes of light left off, and shrieking winds blew the taste of rain and snow across the salar's water and sand.

That night, heavy rains fell from the heavens and struck against our tent walls. Eventually, they left off, replaced by a strange silence. The loud beating of snow followed, as the storm attained the height of its fury. Sometimes, we had to hit the walls from inside, otherwise we should have found ourselves buried beneath the white, cold burden. Before the sun's rise, the tempest moved away, and we found it an occasion of peacefulness for fitful sleep. Later, we saw the results of the tumultuous night. Large mounds of snow lay all about, most nestled against the tents. I will decline to go on longer at this, Excellency, and shall say that while we lost one horse and two llamas struck by the shafts of light, there were no injuries or deaths among us, thanks be to our precious Savior. Doña Inés and Pilca Huaca went from tent to tent asking after our health. Valdivia ordered a day of rest after the hardships of the night, and our priests said masses of thanksgiving that all survived safe and well.

This day we did not give completely to pondering the difficulties of the night, Your Highness, since who should appear amongst us, complete in costume and blowing his flute with great gaiety seeking to lighten our mood, but Rodrigo Hidalgo, our *qamchu*. And now he had an assistant, Paucar, a friend of Ayar's. Hidalgo performed his tricks and games, which produced much laughter and clapping. Paucar, being new at this, provided more laughter, principally for the Indians. He did things such as sing, jump high in the air, and walk on his toes. Although we Christians never quite understood all of it, his antics made a large number of Indians double over with laughter. This became particularly true when he walked on his toe tips, as he wobbled for a distance with his legs buckled and bent, then jumped high into the air and flipped backwards while doing so. This brought appreciative claps from us as well, as it required a good deal of skill to perform such a feat. After this day of merriment, all were ready to resume our journey. And this we did on the morrow, the storm now only a distant recollection.

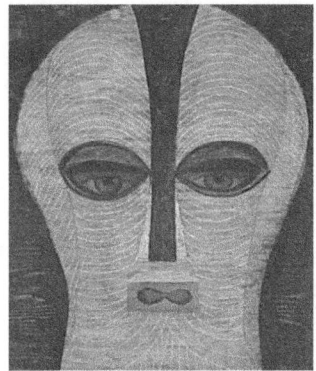

PART FF

OUR JOURNEY DOWN THE AVENUE CONTINUES; DOÑA INÉS USES AN ARQUEBUS TO SHOOT GUANACO

55

For some time, our daily journeys remained unremarkable. Vicuña we saw, guanaco also, as they grazed on patches of brush and *ichu* grass. Streams and lagunas were nearby always, just as Ayar, Vicente, and I, remembered them from the Almagro days. Montesinos remained adept at recalling the locations of *bofedales* along our route of march, and reminded us when we were a day or two from one. We came upon one that lay southwest from a faintly smoking volcán, and our Captain ordered a rest near it for two days. The two lagunas close by provided fresh fish for eating and more for drying.[118] In addition, there lived numerous birds of all sizes about their shores, as well as flamingoes on their surfaces, the wonderful birds we last saw years before on our journey through this land.

---

[118] The volcano referred to is Isluga (18,208 feet), which the Almagro Expedition passed years earlier. The two lagunas are Parinacota and Arabilla.

It was here that I first heard of discontent among the Indians. Ayar's friend, Paucar, came late in the day to play a game of shoes and, resting afterwards, we commented upon subjects of interest in casual conversation. Paucar made it known Ancohualla had disciplined one of the men recently by standing him in front of all the natives and telling them of his transgressions. This was an uncommon action for Anco, he said, and observed that he thought it ought to have the proper effect. Neither Ayar nor I felt compelled to inquire about this further.

The new day provided a surprise for us all, as events came about completely without equal on our journey so far. At the end of our morning repast, Pedro Cisternas, the arquebus man and now called the "gunner" by Valdivia, hailed those of us near his tent at the hour of Terce and asked if we might assist in the shooting of some guanaco. At this, Doña Inés strode forward from the Captain's tent carrying the arquebus! She announced she wanted a number of men to accompany her and Cisternas on a guanaco shoot. Seeing a woman hold a large and heavy gun even a strong man had difficulty in handling prompted me to look towards Vicente with a smile and nod that a woman of this sort one encountered but rarely.[119]

Montesinos and I stepped forward forthwith, followed by Hernando Vallejo and Juan Gómez, both with wide smiles, and then others who had participated in the *suri* hunt. All were in good cheer, expecting something novel. We were not disappointed for very long. It became apparent quickly that La Doña had planned things carefully and knew exactly what she wanted us to do. We would approach the guanaco we could see in the distance by the laguna, about 100 yards away, and move slowly to avoid scaring them. She said she had noticed over the last days that when we passed them they ran from us infrequently, unless we came too close or else made a run at them on horseback. We must position ourselves gradually, she said, so as not to disturb the animals, in two lines perpendicular to the laguna, with her and Cisternas at the top end center. Once in position, we horse soldiers should face one another and hold our

---

[119] An arquebus of this era was a muzzle loader, weighed 12-14 pounds, fired a .69 to .80 caliber round, and had a range of 120 yards.

places, as the guanaco would deem us a natural barrier to their escape, the laguna being the other, as they remained hesitant to enter it. Thus, we had them bounded in an enclosure of three walls. Your Excellency, I have included a drawing of our deployment for Your perusal.[120] If the guanaco began running, they would do so towards Doña Inés and Cisternas, and those horsemen closest to those two must ride towards each other and seal off the enclosed space. Our Doña explained further that as the guanaco grazed on the laguna's shore, Cisternas would load the arquebus, position the fork rest to steady its barrel, and then she would aim and fire. This might frighten the animals and they all would run, she said, as the sound was akin to an explosion, even though they stood at a distance. She did not know what they might do, but that we should soon find out.

Such was the plan. While it seemed rather unorthodox, it did have the aspect of disciplined thinking and thus promised possible success. We now took our positions. Vallejo and Juan Gómez were the two lead horsemen of the columns, one on the right and the other on the left. Montesinos and I were the last in either line and would close the enclosed space should it be necessary. Forty or more guanaco grazed now at the laguna's edge, and so both files moved forward in column at an unhurried walk. Doña Inés proved correct in her assessment that, if we moved deliberately and without noise or sudden movement, the guanaco might fail to take notice and remain where they stood.[121] When Vallejo and de Almagro had attained the water's shore without surprising the animals, the men in both columns stopped and turned inwards. Everyone was now in position. In the meantime, a large crowd of our natives and countrymen had gathered to watch the proceedings. They remained quiet and as still as possible for fear of disturbing the animals.

IMAGES: 4EE-GG.8 shows an arquebusier using a rifle fork. 4EE-GG.9 is a drawing of how the men lined up in support of Doña Inés.

---

[120] See Appendix B for a depiction of this formation.
[121] The author noted this behavior of the guanaco on his many climbing trips across the Atacama Desert to and from high Andean peaks. See <u>Clawing for the Stars</u>.

Montesinos and I had the opportunity to watch La Doña and the "gunner" work with each other. First, she pressed small balls of cloth in both ears. At her command, Cisternas put the fork in the ground and proceeded to load the arquebus. This took time, during which Doña Inés gestured to me. "The Captain taught me everything about the arquebus while in Cusco," she said. "Let's see how well I learned!"[122] She said this with that wink of her left eye that told of her good mood and a laugh that said she found things amusing. With the preparations complete, Cisternas brought the gun to Doña Inés. She placed it in the fork, put the butt end to her shoulder, and took aim down the field. Cisternas raised the small bowl he carried that contained live embers from burning llama dung and awaited her order. After brief moments, she let out, "Light it!" At this, he lit the match clamped at the end of the serpentine, or curved lever, and touched her shoulder; all was ready. She pulled the trigger slowly, the serpentine dropped down, the match ignited the priming powder, and this set off the main charge. Fire flashed from the end of the barrel, causing a thunderous report, and an animal fell in the distance. Surprisingly, the other guanaco acted as if nothing had happened, bothered neither by the noise of the blast nor by the fallen animal in their midst. I looked at Bohón, on horse to the left of Montesinos, with an expression of astonishment. In the meanwhile, Cisternas and La Doña prepared for a new shot. It produced a result like the first, a second dead guanaco and the herd still feeding on *ichu* grass. And so it continued until the seventh shot, when Cisternas declared himself out of powder for an eighth. At this, Doña Inés yelled and signaled for all of us to join her. When we did so, she thanked us and asked Vallejo to tell de Cartagena and Tupa, the provisioners, their work of skinning and butchering could commence. "And tell de Cartagena our share is three animals and Tupa's is four."

The crowd welcomed us back, led by the Captain, who greeted his *mujer* with a flourish of his right arm and a deep bow. Loud huzzahs arose for La Doña, and rightfully so. She had put on a performance of great skill, Sire. Later that day, the shooting demonstration provided the topic of

---

[122] As footnoted previously, Valdivia won early fame as a young commander in the Italian wars of 1522-1525. The arquebus played an important role in several of the battles, so the Captain must have had a working knowledge of its operation.

most interest around the campfires. Vallejo and Juan Gómez had the nearest view of how things occurred, as they had been at the head of the columns and therefore positioned on the shore line close by the animals. Vallejo said the firing of the gun was not that loud, and this was de Almagro's observation as well. As to why a falling guanaco did not alert the others that things seemed amiss, neither had an answer. Vicente did, however. He thought the animals had never experienced such events before and so misunderstood what was happening to them. In addition, our horse soldiers, he said, kept steady throughout the entire time, and this provided a further signal to the guanaco that nothing threatened them.

That evening, Valdivia declared a further day of rest so the provisioners might have more time to prepare the meat. We spent the day, Our Lord's Day, attending mass and singing hymns, grooming our horses, indulging in games, and resting for the days to come. Ayar noted that on the morrow we would camp at the *géiser* we had encountered with Captain Almagro and we might see it blow skyward.[123] Later, we enjoyed fresh guanaco meat at our evening repast.

Late on the new day, we made camp close by the *géiser*. As we had experienced with Almagro, there was no set time for it to send hot water skyward, so those close to it yelled out when they thought it was about to do so. Valdivia and Doña Inés found themselves fascinated by the water displays, so much so the Captain asked Father Marmolejo to christen it the "Sacred Fountain of our Lady." And so Father did.

The coming days of our journey remained unremarkable and absent excitement. But one incident proved notable, Your Honor, since Valdivia referred to matters that would one day find expression in the new land. It happened at the daily afternoon report that Ayar and I made to the Captain. On hearing that we were close to herds of alpaca at the place called Huasco, he nodded in acknowledgement, while his gaze looked past us at a scene of more interest.

---

[123] This is the Puchuldiza *géiser* mentioned in the Third Letter of Volume I.

"Look, Pedro." I turned in the direction of his extended right arm and there nearby sat Father Lobo, with Ancohualla, his *caciques*, Tupa and Huayna, and Pilca Huaca. There were two other natives included, Paucar and Rimac, Ayar's friends.

"That is the future of our Indians in the new land. Father began teaching Pilca Huaca our language, at Doña's request, and I asked Ancohualla and his men to participate too."

"I thought there had been an improvement in Ancohualla's speech, even though he knows some of our language." I said. "Now I know the cause of it."

"This shall serve a larger purpose, Pedro. For I wish the Indians to help us govern in the towns we found. To do so, they must know our language, how to speak and write it."

Doña Inés, sitting close by, added to this. "We have asked de Cartagena to train them how to write. He will begin this tomorrow. And Pilca Huaca is learning to speak very well, certainly more so with Father as her teacher than with me!"

Ancohualla turned towards us briefly. The Captain, noticing him, gave his clenched fist thrust upwards, as was his habit.

Valdivia turned his eyes upon me. "Pedro, I wish to speak to you about something of importance, the building of towns and the supervision of them by *cabildos*. I plan to speak with Captain Villagran about you. You are an intelligent man, honest and forthright. The Captain gained experience in municipal affairs before coming to the New World by serving on town *cabildos*, including that of León.[124] I have asked him to take a few men into his confidence concerning the administration of town affairs, and you will be included. I need men like you, so learn well, as I expect much from you. We will talk more of this in the future." He reached for my hand and clasped it firmly. I must say, Your Majesty, that the Captain's special notice of me, as fit to help govern a new town, took

---

[124] The *cabildo* is an administrative council that governed a Spanish municipality.

me by surprise, for he had said nothing prior to reveal his intentions. I tell this, Sire, so You may know the talent of this man, as he had the ability to see and plan for things in the future, something not granted all men.

We arrived at the region called Huasco on Thursday, May 16. Alpaca roamed there in abundance, as we Almagro men recalled from our previous visit. Ancohualla had told Valdivia these animals were unfit to eat but highly prized for their fur. As we had warm clothes enough, the Captain ordered no harm to come to them. A day and a half later, we came to an area known to certain of us, although in an unpleasant manner, as it was the vicinity of horse soldier Mejia's untimely fate on the Almagro expedition.[125] When we had received permission from Valdivia, several of us accompanied Father Perez to the grave site for brief prayers. I had known the man by sight, but had never conversed with him, as Vicente had. Fortunately, the grave remained undisturbed, and still lay within a small rock and sand alcove on the slopes of the nearby volcán.[126]

As Father intoned prayers for the departed, black thunderclouds rose rapidly in the east and moved quickly past the northern slopes of the mountain and directly towards us. No more than a brief time passed before the heavens above became densely shrouded, and at that instant a bright flash struck the earth a short distance from us, followed by a rolling peal of thunder. Father made a hastened sign of the cross, followed by the exclamation, "Let us go, men. We must ride for it!" The entire party broke into a full gallop and rode to our camp. We arrived as flakes of snow began to fall, leaped from our horses, tore off the saddles, hobbled the animals, and entered our tents just as the winds blew with such ferocity that torrents of snow flew horizontally across the land. Down it came in heavy amounts, until the clouds lifted as swiftly as they had descended, and shortly the sun began its descent towards the horizon.

On the new day, much before the earliest rays of the sun began to brighten the eastern edges of the sky, a low, distant rumble awoke us. Ayar said it

---

[125] This area is the Salar de Coposa. See Part W of <u>The Adventure Chronicles, Volume I.</u>
[126] This is the stratovolcano Irruputuncu, 16,939 feet.

signaled the mountain coming awake. When I looked out the tent door, a faint, golden glow appeared at the top of it that alternately waxed and waned, like the well-lit campfire that burns brightly, begins to fade as it consumes its fuel, yet later springs to life when more is added. Others exclaimed upon the sight and sound. De Almagro said this land seemed enchanted; by what, he said, remained unclear. His was not a comment of fear, but of wonderment.

Later on this morning, Our Lord's Day, we devoted to masses said by our priests; I chose to attend the one for our Indians. Both Fathers Lobo and de Cabrera held services for them, as many Indians now attended. The native music at Father Cabrera's appealed to me, and so I took my place among other Christians present. My eyes wandered, and I saw Pilca Huaca in the row of Indians closest to the proceedings. This caused me to reflect upon the changes that she had experienced during the short period of our journey. She was learning more medical skills from la Doña, studying how to speak and write our language, and acquiring an appreciation for our religion. Indeed, these were large changes in the life of any of us. I wondered what it all might mean for her one day.

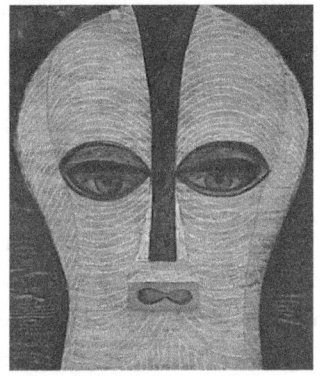

PART GG

CHIU-CHIU AND CALAMA, AND WHAT TRANSPIRED THERE; OUR FIRST ENCOUNTER WITH SANCHO DE HOZ; WE MEET AGAIN, HUAMANPALLPA, THE *DESERT CACIQUE*

*A*fter two days, we crested a slight rise and before us in the distance rose the two volcáns that give birth to the Río Loa, the river we would follow for several more days.[127] The long valley of the river stretched far to the south. We drew rein and, gathering together, sat looking down on the vast land we were about to traverse. It made an arresting sight, remarkable to the imagination, as the single stream of water found itself bounded on the east by volcán after volcán. Its features of grandeur were the vast extents, the solitude, the wilderness, the tall mountains that set a majestic tone for the entire scene. And mile after mile, the river coursed through land as flat as a frozen laguna. Here and there the river forked into tributaries, and an

---

[127] These are the peaks Miño (18,568 feet) and Aucanchilca (20,262 feet).

occasional *bofedal* rose in the distance reminiscent of a green island, and these relieved the monotony of the desert.

IMAGES: Please see 4EE-GG.16-.19 for images of the terrain the expedition travelled.

From our position, we could see no living thing moving across the land, yet we knew there were, lizards, guanaco, birds, and *tinamou*;[128] these did live along the river's banks, and they and more would sustain us in the approaching weeks. Before those behind my guiding group rode up, I had the thought, Sire, that in this new land we would prosper by the strength of our arms and the courage in our hearts. We all knew that we had strength and steadfastness. All we needed was to attain the location of our capital city and there begin our new lives. As we looked out upon the scene before us, we could hardly wait to do so.

Miles still lay ahead before we should enter Chiu-Chiu; the ground we trod remained flat, or mostly so. Sometimes it glared in the sun, an expanse of warm, bare sand; sometimes it lay beneath large sections of *ichu* grass that dimmed the sun's light. The hills and mountains in the east changed often as the wild and fantastic forms of the volcáns joined with the lesser peaks. And in the west, on the other side of the Loa, the almost level monotony of the desert remained unbroken as far as one could see. The Pacific lay out of sight, but surely the sand only ended there.[129]

One cold day, with the distant threat of a storm upon us, Ayar observed that we stood three days from Chiu-Chiu, and this prompted a thought about the *cacique* there, Auqui, and, farther on, Huaman in Calama. I stopped my horse, motioned my men forward, and awaited Montesinos to arrive. When he did so, I asked him if he had any thoughts about what action we might suggest to the Captain.

---

[128] This is the Chilean partridge.

[129] De Mérida is correct with this observation. From their location, there is nothing of note but dry desert all the way to the Pacific coast more than 100 miles away.

"Well, I think we should send Ancohualla ahead to Chiu-Chiu and find out the situation, and see if Auqui and Huaman are still the *caciques*."

"My thought exactly, Vicente."

During our time for relaxation in the afternoon, we found Valdivia and Ancohualla discussing matters of importance, but not so significant as to exclude us from their conversation. We gave voice to our thoughts, and both men, after discussing the particulars, approved of such action, with Anco quite eager to go, saying he wanted to see Auqui again and learn about Huaman. He said he would leave on the morrow and take his new *cacique*, Rimac, with him. Tupa and Huayna would be in charge until his return. The Captain asked Anco also to tell Auqui he should inform Huaman that Valdivia comes to honor Captain Almagro's treaty with him and his promise to send a priest.[130]

Valdivia then summoned Ayar, as well as Villagran and de Benito. He was excited about what he wished to discuss and made it known without delay. He said Captain Villagran had reminded him that Francisco de Aguirre, Rodrigo de Quiroga and the men they recruited, would be awaiting us in Atacama the beginning of June. And since today was the second day of that month, he wished to ride to the town, welcome the new men, and greet them warmly. They had come from Tupiza, a journey of several days to the east.[131] I turned to Ayar and asked if we might bypass Chiu-Chiu and Calama and ride directly to Atacama. He replied we could, by a way he knew, and instead of needing twelve days we should require only three, if we used pack horses to carry our stores instead of llamas. Our Captain, pleased at this, smiled and declared, "Men, we ride at tomorrow's first light. Villagran, you are in charge until our return."

Sire, I must digress and tell of a most despicable man, Pedro Sancho de Hoz, for soon he shall appear upon the scene. He enlisted in Governor

---

[130] See Part W of the Third Letter, Volume I.
[131] These men had traveled south from Cusco, past Lago Poopó, to the town of Tupiza. The Almagro Expedition passed through the village on its way south to Tucma, in 1535.

Francisco Pizarro's forces early in the conquest of Peru. I remember him since he joined Pizarro in 1531, along with Vicente Montesinos, before my arrival in 1532. When Pizarro's personal secretary, Xeres, returned to Spain in early 1533 because of a broken leg, he appointed de Hoz to replace him.[132] By deceitfulness, lying, and cheating, the new secretary made himself out to be more than he was. He claimed to possess a large fortune, but this was a lie. He managed to have written for him false documents purported to be from Your Father, the most beloved Charles V, granting him permission to conquer and colonize all lands to the south of Peru. Pizarro, with the help of his associates, discovered the falseness of these claims and decided to award *Nuevo Extremo* to Valdivia instead of de Hoz. Thus took hold in the breast of de Hoz a deep hatred for Captain Valdivia.

He attracted a few men inclined against Valdivia. I believe this came about because the Captain remained unaware others might have doubts about his authority in the new lands, so he was slow to recognize the extent of the de Hoz threat. As an aside, Sire, an affair such as this never happened to Captain Almagro, at least in the years I knew and served him. He demanded instant respect by his outward demeanor, for it was threatening to most. It was clear to me that if the Captain had a man like de Hoz in his command suspected of treachery against him, he would have exposed him straight away, made him to confess, and hanged him forthwith from the nearest tree.

As to the man's personal characteristics, he had the nose of a ferret, and stood less than five feet in height. When standing and talking with others, he had to bend his head backwards to carry on a conversation. He engaged in aggressive behavior towards a few of us with loud words and looks of disdain for those who refused to believe as he did. As to a constant habit, he spat regularly and often. At first I thought this because of an overabundance of saliva. Others thought it a show of contempt towards those men or events he found detestable. I now believe the latter is the truth. In addition, he had the eyes of a weasel and looked often to the left, right, and forward when agitated. These eye movements and the constant

---

[132] Such is confirmed by Weldon Vernon.

grin on his face caused most men to deem these traits as indications of dishonesty and deceit and he had few friends as a result, except those inclined to treachery. Such is the portrait Your Highness needs in order to understand better what I am now to relate.[133]

Of course, our expedition left Cusco without de Hoz. Our Captain despised him and knew his claims to *Nuevo Extremo* to be false and all of a fancy. This man resolved, nonetheless, to find us on the march with his friends, who remained convinced de Hoz should be the rightful heir to the southern lands. He intended to kill Valdivia and proclaim himself the ruler of this part of the New World. And they did find the expedition here, a few days from Chiu-Chiu, as we found out afterwards from our Doña and Villagran. It happened the night after Valdivia, Ayar, Vicente, and I, left for Atacama to welcome the new men, those recruited by the aforementioned de Aguirre and de Quiroga. De Hoz and two men entered the camp unseen late at night. He approached the Captain's tent, reached inside to feel for his body, and found La Doña's instead! She screamed, grabbed a sword, and woke the camp, including Villagran and Gómez de Benito, with her shouts and oaths. De Benito arrived first. Doña Inez, holding her sword ready for action, yelled questions as to who the intruder might be, what his intentions were, why he and his companions had sharp knives in their belts, and other such questions. Outside the tent, and with the light of late burning camp fires illuminating the scene, all could see our Doña eager to give battle. She clutched a nine inch stiletto in her left hand and held her sword menacingly in her right. A grim smile upon her face, said de Benito later, made her look as though she was about to enjoy herself.

Campfire light then revealed the intruder. "I remember you from Cusco, de Hoz! I am unsure of your purpose here, but should you come close to me again, you scurrilous dog, I shall plunge this dagger straight to your throat and my sword right through your heart!"

De Benito told me she spat this out with such vituperation that no one doubted she would make good on her threat in an instant. By now,

---

[133] Weldon Vernon and others provide an unflattering portrait of de Hoz, but de Mérida's is blistering.

Villagran had arrived on the scene. Recognizing evil intentions afoot, he ordered our men to hold the intruders and, going up to de Hoz, put his large hands on the blackguard's shirt collars, lifted him a full foot off the ground, and held him there before throwing him down at his feet. He said he knew de Hoz as a false man who wished the Captain harm, and he intended to recommend to Valdivia on his return that he should hang him for attempted murder. To this the accused professed his innocence and asked for fair treatment and a fair trial as any innocent man falsely accused would receive. The Captain let out a contemptuous laugh in response.

That night, after matters had calmed and de Hoz and his followers had been confined and watched closely by our soldiers, Villagran directed Gómez de Benito to rise before dawn on the new day, ride to Atacama with Juan Gómez de Almagro to inform the Captain of the recent events involving de Hoz, and ask him to return at once to mete out punishment. I stood with Valdivia when de Benito and Juan Gómez rode in and listened as they related the incident of several nights prior. The Captain stroked his beard with thumb and forefinger slowly as he listened to this strange tale the men had to tell. When they ended, Valdivia uttered an oath of vile contempt for de Hoz and ordered the captains and new men we had just met, twenty-five of them, to remain in Atacama and wait for the expedition, since he had urgent business to attend to. We left for our camp north of Chiu-Chiu after the most basic of preparations.

In two and a half days we drew near our encampment, and who came out to meet us on horseback but Sancho de Hoz! When he and his men rode up with their guards, we all had our swords drawn. They dismounted and bowed low to Valdivia, de Hoz agitated and remorseful, for he begged the Captain's mercy, calling all a mistake and a misunderstanding. Villagran arrived and shouted that none of them deserved leniency. Valdivia waited a moment and presently had us sheathe our swords. He sat on his horse and said nothing, merely staring with disdain at de Hoz groveling before him.

"I shall take up the issue of your punishment at another time, de Hoz. If I were to decide your fate now, you and your accomplices should hang this instant."

With that, he waved us forward, and we entered camp shortly thereafter. A downcast de Hoz and his wayward partners presently entered our encampment under guard and returned to their solitary area, there to endure the shouts of disdain and looks of disgust by our men. As a punishment for de Hoz, Doña Inés and de Benito convinced the Captain to make him ride with a saddle less than comfortable, one that had been on the back of a pack animal, as it proved unsuitable for a rider. While it had most of the particulars common to such a necessity, it lacked a seat, which had been stripped off to serve some other purpose. Convinced of this as a fitting minor punishment for his despicable behavior, Valdivia commanded the lout to ride with it the remainder of our journey, or until it caused discomfort to the horse. The subsequent morning, de Hoz mounted his new saddle. We knew it was a most painful experience, since he winced over and over again as he rode. Doña Inés laughed and yelled a coarse reference to what he should feel between his legs at the end of the day's passage and how much he deserved it.

The Captain appointed Captain de Miranda and four soldiers to guard de Hoz and his men day and night. De Miranda convinced Valdivia they should never be allowed to ride their horses, except for de Hoz and his painful saddle, since this might increase the possibility of their escape. Rather, they should walk behind the llamas and help collect their dung for our fires! This pleased Valdivia. And it delighted Doña Inés that de Hoz would continue to suffer daily in the saddle. And there I shall leave this for now, Excellency, until events cause a return to these tawdry affairs at a future instance.[134]

Since I have spent time to discuss the de Hoz matter and de Benito's involvement, Your Honor, I must interrupt my relation and tell more of the honorable and steadfast gentleman, Gómez de Benito, for Your Excellency has every right to hold this man in honor, as he has been Your and Your Father's steadfast servant these many years. Born in Badajoz,

---

[134] De Mérida's telling of the incidents related to Sancho de Hoz and the encounter in Chiu-Chiu are similar to several declarations of witnesses in J. T. Medina, Collection of Unpublished Documents Concerning the History of Chile, 1888-1902, including the Declaration of Inés de Suárez in the same publication.

Extremadura, a short distance from the birthplaces of our Captain, our Doña, and me, he was the most battle-hardened of Valdivia's captains and the most accomplished cavalry officer among them as well. He delighted in the telling of his adventures with Hernán Cortés and the battles they fought against the mighty Aztecs. The most vivid account he related dealt with the fall of Montezuma and the destruction of the city in Lago Texcoco, Tenochtitlán, in August 1521. Many an evening on our journey, men eager to hear of the Spanish exploits in New Spain surrounded his campfire, and he never disappointed us. The most requested topic for his telling was the march down the great Causeway towards Mexico, with great towers and buildings rising from the waters of the lakes and all built of stonework. Juan Gómez once asked the old Captain if the things he saw and described to us were not a dream. "So they seemed to us, Gómez. So they seemed to us." Vicente remarked one evening to the Captain he thought that never again in history would there be found other lands such as he had seen. "Surely not, Vicente. And all the wonders that we then witnessed today are all vanished and lost, never again to find a re-creation." [135]

As for other particulars, his was an infectious personality. He always seemed to be smiling, as this was the way he viewed the world, and it drew others to him. This is not to say he saw all things as humorous, since they were not. And whether engaged in light-hearted conversation among friends or thoroughly involved in the complex dangers of battlefield exigencies, his pleasant expression remained unchanged. He stayed a pillar of constancy to his troops and remained calm in all situations, since he had seen and experienced most things on a field of battle. He made a unique sound when he spoke, the result of a blow to his mouth during the fighting and destruction of Tenochtitlán. The clout left a slight scar on his upper lip, and words with an "s" and "z" caused sounds distinct to him and to him alone when he spoke. He remained a faithful servant of Valdivia, who rewarded his experience and integrity with government

---

[135] The story of the conquest of the Aztecs, as told by Bernal Díaz de Castillo in his <u>The True History of the Conquest of New Spain</u>, is an unforgettable telling of the Conquest by one of its participants.

positions of importance in our new capital. Such is my memory of the esteemed Gómez de Benito.

While we were with the Captain in Atacama, Ancohualla and Rimac had returned from their ride to Chiu-Chiu, there to assess the situations of Auqui and Huaman in Calama. As matters stood, both men were well. So too was Urco, Huaman's chief counselor. Auqui said he intended to go to Calama and alert the *Desert Cacique* of our coming, and that his assistant, Pato,[136] would welcome us to Chiu-Chiu. There was unpleasant news, however. Anta-Aclla Picchu, the High Priest of the High Mountains, had entered the afterlife two years before. He had died of his age, said Auqui. I remembered this holy man with a great deal of admiration and respect. Though he was not a member of our Faith, I must hold that throughout the ages Christ has had a special place for men like him.

In the succeeding days on the passage to Chiu-Chiu, Vicente and I, at the Captain's request, provided more information about Huaman to him, Villagran, and Father de Cabrera. They asked several questions and, after hearing our responses, Valdivia pronounced himself eager to meet with him. "Gentlemen." he intoned, "I had my differences with Almagro, as you know. Still, I recall a conversation with Francisco Pizarro in which he made reference to Almagro's ability to choose wisely those he took into his confidence, like Montesinos and de Mérida here. And I say if Almagro trusted and admired this man, it is my inclination to do so in similar manner. This assumes, of course, Huaman is still of the same mind and intentions as three years ago."

Father said that he was enthusiastic about what we had discussed regarding Huaman, as he seemed a man of deep faith, although inclined towards the Inca religion. This last did not deter Father. "I feel I know the way to his heart and mind even though I have yet to meet him. I may say this because we share a deep interest in the religious life. Although he never became a high priest, he intended to do so had not the death of his parents caused a change in his calling. As for the people, I have learned to discern the inner feelings of the Indian while here in the new land, and

---

[136] This was a peasant name with no Inca association.

I believe I can bring many of them to know our Christ. May Our Lord grant me this blessing!"

The Captain nodded his approval as he replied to Father. "Father, we are of equal mind about the *Cacique*. I must be truthful, though, in what I am about to say. If you decide to stay, you shall be alone here for months, for my highest priority must be to bring farmers, priests, workers, and soldiers from Peru by sea to populate the capital city of *Nueva Estremadura*. But I will tell you this. And do not doubt me, for I have honorable men here who will hear my promise and hold me to it. I shall petition the honorable Bishop Vicente Valverde in Cusco to send a priest to you within a year of founding our new city. My feeling now is that this should occur in early 1541, so I shall convey my request in 1542 or 1543." He looked around at the rest of us with a sober expression full of intention. He rose and took Father's hands in his, as a testament to his promise. Father de Cabrera fell silent for a brief time, but he had a large smile on his face notwithstanding, for Valdivia's words had found their mark. He invited us to kneel and put his right hand upon the head of the Captain. "O blessed Lord, we ask that you watch over your devoted servant, Captain Valdivia, as he prepares to found and populate new cities that shall redound to your glory forever."

Such was our preparation for meeting the *Desert Cacique*. I shall now continue my relation, Noble Excellency. When we reached Chiu-Chiu,[137] indeed, Pato and a small number of townspeople came to meet my guiding band as we drew up. He was an Indian with a history here, since he and Ayar grasped hands in a show of friendship, as they had last met when we passed through the town years before. When Valdivia and Ancohualla arrived, Pato bowed, and declared the town ready to greet us on the morrow and it would be an honor for the villagers to do so. The subsequent day, we and some of our Indians walked through the town; Hidalgo and Paucar performed for the people, causing much good cheer. Villagers led us to long tables at one side of the main street and

---

[137] Today's San Francisco de Chiu-Chiu lies at 8,284 feet and has a population of 300 people. Tourists visit on feast days. However, most of the population left the town several years ago when effluent from the Chuquicamata copper mine contaminated the nearby Loa River.

offered us small sweet cakes and cups of fermented juice, refreshments most appreciated. Our Indians also partook of the offerings, and all had a pleasant day following numerous weeks in the desert.

On the day after, we set off to the west towards Calama with our friend, the Río Loa, on our right. The warmer temperatures were welcome, since we had left the cold, higher elevations on the Avenue of the Volcáns days before. Late on June 15, the town appeared in the distance, its features altered by the warmth of the air, since it seemed to shimmer as the dying rays of the sun's light brightened a seemingly endless expanse of desert lands.[138] Captain Valdivia arrived and announced this place would be our camp for the night. He then summoned Ancohualla and asked that he and Rimac ride forward and alert Huaman of our arrival next day.

On the subsequent mid-day, the Captain led us forward, with Villagran close behind, Father de Cabrera and me riding next. Valdivia wore an elegant black cloak with threads of thin gold laced through it, a noteworthy remark upon how important he held this encounter. Before long, we discerned an entourage of three figures in the distance, followed by other Indians. The Captain turned and waved me forward. When I joined him, he said he recognized Ancohualla, a royal figure at his left who must be the *Desert Cacique*, and an additional man. I confirmed Huaman as the central figure and identified the dignified Urco as the third man, the *Cacique's* counselor.

We dismounted, and Huaman came forward dressed as when Captain Almagro met with him. He wore small gold plugs in his ears, a mark of Inca nobility that testified to his youthful days spent in Cusco studying for the Inca priesthood. Knotted cords wrapped round his head secured a headpiece, which signified his aristocratic blood line as well. And yet his clothes remained those of the humblest of his subjects. A white tunic, dust colored pants, and ordinary sandals of llama hide appeared so unremarkable they made him seem like a common Indian.

---

[138] Calama sits at 7,400 feet and has a population of 148,000 souls. Most of the jobs are with nearby mines, especially Chuquicamata.

PAINTING: Please see P3.2 for a rendering of Huaman's headdress.

When he drew up to the Captain, he knelt on one knee and addressed him as most honorable "Sinchi." Valdivia looked to Anco and asked the meaning of this name, and learned that it bestowed great honor, for it was the first name of the second Inca ruler, Sinchi Roca Inca,[139] and meant "valorous, generous Inca." This pleased Captain Valdivia greatly. He spread open his black cloak, grasped Huaman's hand, and drew him upwards to his feet, an extraordinary gesture in itself. As Valdivia and Huaman exchanged pleasantries, Urco gestured to all to follow him. As we proceeded forward, large numbers of the town's residents, young and old, strolled through the streets. Most smiled and some even waved in welcome as we passed among them towards a quiet section for discussions among Huaman, our Captain, Captain Villagran, Father de Cabrera, Father Lobo, Urco, Auqui, and Ancohualla. The rest of us stayed a distance apart to await orders. Montesinos and I could tell the day was going well, since the participants smiled and laughed occasionally. There were serious times among them, to be sure, for there were important topics under discussion. After a time, Valdivia gestured to de Cartagena to come with his writing materials. Soon after, he called the rest of us to draw closer.

"Gentlemen, I wish to declare that I have appointed Huamanpallpa, the *Desert Cacique*, as my personal representative in this territory, until I send someone in the future to administer it with him. He has pledged to learn our language and our Holy Faith, and I know he will do so, for he is a man of honor and a man of his word. And he has welcomed Father de Cabrera to help in both of these endeavors. I have had recorded all we have discussed and agreed to and I shall now sign it before you. When we establish a port near our capital city, I shall send it to our King as a record of how I am administering this land for His Majesty."

Ancohualla translated this for Huaman, who smiled and nodded in appreciation at the Captain's words. Having signed the document, Valdivia pulled forth from his neck a silver crucifix hanging from a cord

---

[139] This Inca ruler reigned from c. 1230 to c. 1260.

with our Lord's likeness fastened upon it. He draped it about Huaman's neck and rested it there. This brought a stir of approval from us, as it presented a most significant show of trust and camaraderie.

"This is a testament, Huaman, to our friendship and confidence in one another. May this always remain so."

"Most honored Sinchi, you have done me a great honor. And I shall reward your trust by serving you faithfully and governing with fairness and honesty." So spoke Huamanpallpa. As he did so, he removed a golden ring from his right hand and placed it upon the like finger of the Captain.

"And this is a testament, honorable Sinchi, of that lasting friendship and confidence."

This produced a further show of acknowledgement among us, for we had witnessed a truly unique display of diplomacy. The meeting thus concluded, Urco declared the coming day one of rest and relaxation, with the townspeople providing refreshment for us all.

On the coming day, various activities occupied our time. Orders came from the Captain that our provisioners, de Cartagena and Tupa, were to fill the *poros* with water before the journey to Atacama. In similar manner, they and their assistants would purchase food for our march that, as we Almagro men remembered, lay over barren and dry ground. La Doña, Pilca Huaca, and Father Lobo visited the place set aside for care of the sick, a small section inside a building's courtyard, and stayed the entire day assisting as best they could. Later, the villagers served food and drink from tables in the center of town. And the *qamchus*, Hidalgo and Paucar, wandered the streets, while large crowds, clapping and laughing, followed them all the while. Meanwhile, Urco and Huaman presided over the serving of refreshments to certain of us at the previous day's meeting site. It offered an atmosphere in which we could meet those who governed the town. Valdivia and Villagran, accompanied by Ancohualla, walked among the Indians and made light conversation. Father remained at Huaman's side and engaged in discussions with him, presumably about their future time together, as Father had a passable knowledge of the language.

A number of Huaman's lieutenants were there and I conversed with one of them, a stout Indian with smiling eyes and a lisping, musical voice. He tended a large guanaco herd, which provided meat for the town's needs. I inquired about the whereabouts of Yupan, our guide from Copayapu to Calama. This man knew him, and said he had business interests now in Angastu and resided there with his family. I asked too about the *caciques* of Angastu, Atacama, Toconao, Peine, and Socaire, who were not in town as they had been years before. The Captain's presence here was of the highest significance, he said, but the travel to Calama takes several days and the *caciques* had learned of our arrival only days before. The Captain would soon meet these men, however, as we would pass through their villages on our travels to Copayapu.

After a while, Urco invited all to walk the streets and enjoy the proceedings and the people. Valdivia, Huaman, and Ancohualla, did so together. The people bowed and clapped when they passed, for the word had spread among them that Huaman would govern the land as he had in recent years, and now do so with the blessing of the bearded lord come from the north. Montesinos and several others of us gave rides to some of the young boys in town, which always prompted yells and shouts of fun and excitement from them. Vicente was the most popular for this, as many of the boys remembered him and his long blond hair from the Almagro visit. As an aside, Sire, de Hoz and his brigands remained in our camp, guarded and denied permission to enjoy any of the day's activities.

Late in the day, several of us gathered at Valdivia's tent, at his invitation, to converse about the day's proceedings. He pronounced himself exceedingly well pleased with all that had transpired on the day, and confident more such occasions lay before us. He looked towards Father de Cabrera and asked him to tell of his meeting with Huaman. Father said Huaman had addressed him as his people's "Priest of the Shining Hair," a title Father found quite pleasing. He went on to say that an important concern of his would be the building of a small church, so he might say mass, baptize those who came to the Faith, and conduct other duties required in his new parish. The *Desert Cacique* replied that he had workers who could build a church, and build it well. Moreover, he made it known that, after discussion with Anta-Accla three years ago about his conversation with Father Molina, he was ready to learn more about the similarities between our religions.[140] Father de Cabrera had found his calling, as he pointed out frequently that evening, and he looked forward to beginning this new part of his life.

Thus passed our day in Calama, an occasion we remembered with pleasure in the years ahead. I remained hopeful that these few days might be a prelude to those years, ones of peace and prosperity in *Nueva Estremadura*.

---

[140] Please consult Volume I: Almagro, Appendix B for the particulars of this meeting.

PART HH-II

OUR PASSAGE TO ATACAMA AND THE DIVERS HAPPENINGS ALONG THE WAY; WE ARE JOINED BY CAPTAINS RODRIGO DE QUIROGA, FRANCISCO DE AGUIRRE, AND THE TWENTY-FIVE MEN WITH THEM

On **June 18, the day of departure to Atacama,** Huaman, Urco, Auqui, and Father de Cabrera, came to bid us a safe journey. The villagers stood at a short distance behind them, to observe our leaving, and wave, clap, and shout their farewells to us and our Indians. The *Desert Cacique*, with his royal headdress again gracing his brow, paid gracious respects to the Captain.

"Most honorable Sinchi, I shall govern these lands for Your King as you would, with honesty and integrity, as I have said. And should you require anything of us while you build new villages in our land, know that I and we are here to serve you." And I may add here, Noble Sire, that Huaman has fulfilled his duties to Your Honor these many years.

The Captain saluted the *Desert Cacique* and, dropping to one knee, bowed his head and whispered silently to himself a short moment. That done, he rose to mount his horse, and we assumed our positions in the order of march. As we proceeded east, I glanced back occasionally and saw the members of our expedition, as they passed the figures behind us, wave to Huaman, Urco, the "Priest of the Shining Hair," and the townspeople, a most gratifying sight to witness. As Valdivia had said, we made friends here, and this would serve us well in the future.

In the afternoon, great dark clouds in the distant east rose into the heavens, with occasional flashes of light and far-off murmurs of thunder, but nothing came of it. Presently, Montesinos rode up for conversation and surprised me when he asked Ayar if he was eager to see his mother and brothers. Disappointed I had forgotten that this faithful companion's family resided only days from us, I offered my apologies for such an oversight and assured him I would gain the Captain's permission for him to leave on the morrow, which I did. Pleased at this, Ayar thanked Vicente and me and said it would be good to see his family again. He arose early the ensuing day, and before he left I asked that he find Apani and seek a meeting with him so we might renew our acquaintance. He assured me he would do so.[141] With that, he rode off, a large smile on his face and with a hearty wave to Montesinos and me.

In two days more, we began to pass the large cacti we had found so extraordinary on our march through here with Almagro.[142] While we gazed at these lofty plants stretching heavenwards for forty or fifty feet, de Ayala and de Almagro both commented on white projections in the distance rising from the desert floor. As we came closer, Vicente and I recognized the formations as snow penitentes caused by the tempest we had seen in the distance days before. We waited for others to arrive; when they did, de Cartagena and Tupa, the provisioners, directed the efforts of Christians and Indians to cut the penitentes at their bases and put them in skin bags for transport. They collected enough to assure us of sufficient

---

[141] See Part V of the Third Letter, Volume I, for the interview with Apani.
[142] Several examples are on display in the images for Part W of the Third Letter on the site.

water during the coming days. While our supply had been adequate until this point, we might have faced a dilemma without the addition from the snow pinnacles.

As we drew closer to the town, Valdivia asked about the strange land shapes off to the south. I did not recall seeing such a wonder, I answered, on our previous visit, possibly because when we left Atacama with Captain Almagro, we took a more northerly route than on this journey. We watched, as others of the expedition had begun to do, while the sun sank lower in the sky. This caused the red sand of the distant ridges to blaze in the late day's sun. Those around us pointed at what they saw and murmured low exclamations of wonder, for this truly offered a marvelous sight.[143] This is merely one example, Your Majesty, of the beauty of the land over which Your Highness now presides.

Late on the day of June 26, we arrived at a location outside the settlement suitable for the night.[144] De Miranda, now assisted by Pedro de Gamboa, and their men had begun to erect our encampment when galloping towards us came Ayar, waving his left arm and gesticulating with welcoming gestures, Captains Francisco de Aguirre and Rodrigo de Quiroga riding at his side. Vicente and I had seen the two men just weeks before. They dismounted when they reached us and we welcomed all three. Valdivia and Villagran joined us and did likewise. There existed a good sum of camaraderie among these men because all four had served in the Italian Wars, though at different times and with different units. This was the bond they shared, and it bound them closely to one another. From this point on, Captain Valdivia's closest advisors and those he consulted with

---

[143] This was no doubt the Valley of the Moon, which sits some eight miles west of San Pedro de Atacama. It has various stone and sand formations, carved by wind and water through the centuries. It possesses an impressive range of color and texture, looking somewhat similar to the surface of the moon, and remains a popular tourist destination. The author and his Chilean friends visited it in 1995.

[144] Today's San Pedro de Atacama lies at 7,900 feet, with a population of around 5,000. It is a tourist magnet, with travelers from around the world. The author visited it several years ago with Chilean friends.

on most issues were Villagran, de Benito, Ancohualla, as well as the two new captains.

At Valdivia's request, de Benito and Ancohualla arrived to discuss activities on the morrow, and the Captain asked Ayar about the town's *cacique*. He replied that a new chief, named Manque,[145] had replaced the previous one, who had passed to the next life, and he wished to meet us. Huaman had told him of the agreement with Almagro, Ayar said, and Manque stood ready to follow the *Desert Cacique's* direction on administrative and religious affairs.

"This, men, is an example of Huaman's leadership. It is further confirmation I have acted correctly in appointing him to the co-governorship. Blessed be Our Lord."

That noted, Valdivia asked the captains about the new men and learned we would meet them on our arrival at Atacama. Altogether, they totaled twenty-five, ten of whom were arquebusiers, or musket men, as they called themselves.[146] They would bring our force to 127 men. We should remain at the town for two days, declared the Captain, so the provisioners might replenish our food stores and our *qamchus* could entertain the villagers. In addition, La Doña, Pilca Huaca, and Father Lobo intended to treat the sick.

Captain Valdivia said too that this should be a short meeting with Manque, one of introduction and brief conversation. After all, Huaman would administer matters and Manque would obey his wishes. With that, he requested that Ayar return to town and prepare for our entry on the upcoming day. At the conclusion of this meeting, I asked Ayar eagerly about the well-being of Apani, the hut builder of Llullaillaco. With a broad smile, he assured me that he remained in good health and wished to see me again.

---

[145] This means "condor" in the native languages of ancient Chile.
[146] De Mérida agrees with the figure given by both de Aguirre and de Quiroga as noted in Medina, Jose Toribio, <u>Collection of Unpublished Documents Concerning the History of Chile, 1888-1902.</u>

On the following day, Valdivia, his four captains, Ancohualla, and Rimac met with Manque and his two advisors in a sunlit plaza with the nearby volcano in full view.¹⁴⁷ All went well, as I learned afterward. Ayar and I visited with Apani, who appeared the same as four years before. This great man, Sire, caused a surprise, for he opened a skin pouch from inside his cloak and took from it a small rock. It proved no ordinary stone, however. It came, Apani said, from the top of the mighty Llullaillaco, at the location of the huts they erected. I voiced my gratitude for such a gift, though I found it difficult to give proper voice to my appreciation. It is still in my possession; I gaze at it frequently and recall the wonderful feat of Apani and his Indian companions.¹⁴⁸

The Captain knew of our meeting, and as I prepared myself to take leave of Apani, he hailed and signaled us to wait. He and Ancohualla strode forth and Anco shook Apani's hand, since he remembered him from years before. He introduced Valdivia, who had special words of praise for him, as translated by Ancohualla. Moreover, he asked Anco to give Apani five llamas, in recognition of his wonderful feat. At this, Apani bowed low in thankful acknowledgement. As we departed, I turned for one last look at him. He still waved towards us, with a large smile on his face.

The new day found soldiers and Indians strolling the streets, the provisioners and their men replenishing our food stores, Doña Inés, Father Lobo, and Pilca Huaca tending the sick in town, and our *qamchus* entertaining laughing crowds. Our Captain asked de Aguirre and de Quiroga to show us nearby items of interest, and they did so. One such was the battlements of a *pukará* called Quitor,¹⁴⁹ of impressive dimensions, although smaller than that of Fortress Arequipa, where we had vanquished the *cacique*, Huanca, and his warriors.

---

¹⁴⁷ This is the volcano Licancabor (19,420 feet), which lies some fifteen miles northeast of the town.
¹⁴⁸ The author has a stone from the top of Llullaillaco, having acquired it on his climb to the summit. See <u>Clawing for the Stars, Chapter 8.</u>
¹⁴⁹ Local natives built this *pukará* more than 700 years ago to serve as protection against marauding Indians.

PHOTO: Please see 4HH-KK.6 for an image of this *pukará*.

Late that day, Valdivia gathered the new men and read them his rules of conduct, and I explained our route from Atacama to Copayapu. A new man, Gerónimo de Alderete,[150] showed intense interest in what I had to say, and asked questions that indicated his previous experiences with de Aguirre and de Quiroga had equipped him well for the journey. The Captain commended this soldier for his astuteness. He came up to me afterwards, said he was from Olmedo,[151] thanked me for answering his questions, and asked if we might meet later and discuss the particulars of our journey to the new land. He seemed a likeable and intelligent man, so I welcomed his company.

When he arrived, Vicente accompanied him, and they were already in deep discussion about something of significance: their military experiences. He had sought Montesinos out purposely, he said, as Vicente had a reputation for battlefield exploits and he wished to converse with him about tactics and strategies. They continued their discussions in the coming weeks and went on to become close friends.

De Alderete paused from military affairs and addressed to me an additional subject of importance to him. He knew we were traveling to the new land to found towns and cultivate the land. But, he said, his talents were those of a soldier rather than a government worker or farmer. This might be said of most of us, I offered in response, except for Valdivia, who with his wife tended their small farm in La Serena for ten years before he came to the New World.[152] I assured him the Captain planned to show us how to plant and sow crops when we found the proper location for our capital city, or before. As to municipal planning, Villagran had knowledge of such things and even now instructed a number of us in the workings of the *cabildo*. I suggested his captains should ask Captain Valdivia's

---

[150] (1518-1556).This man will serve several roles in the coming years. Valdivia mentions him in his Letters III, IV, and V in "Historical Sources" on the site.

[151] This town in Spain is 200 miles north of Mérida.

[152] Both Cunninghame Graham and Weldon Vernon, as well as other historians, agree with de Mérida in this observation.

permission for him to attend with us. They did so later and the Captain approved their request.

A short word, Sire, about this Gerónimo de Alderete, for he made his mark in our new land. He had an askew left eye that looked outward instead of straight ahead. Some, when meeting him for the first time, gazed at that eye instead of his right. He had a means to deal with this, for he laughed, pointed at his right eye, and admonished the other, "Look here, my friend. Look here!" This had the effect of putting the other at ease, prompting an immediate liking of de Alderete. He possessed besides a deep devotion to our Blessed Lady, an attribute noted by the Captain. I will tell more of this man, Exalted One, at the appropriate times, as Valdivia would rely upon him for several important undertakings in the years to come.

At this point, we entertained the return of Ayar, who had taken leave of his family and proclaimed his readiness to depart next day. He thanked Vicente and me for seeking our Captain's permission to leave the expedition for his visit, and asked if we might accompany him to express his appreciation to him. This became unnecessary, however, since Valdivia and Ancohualla approached, with one of Anco's Indians leading five llamas. Ayar bowed low and gave voice to his appreciation for the stay with his family. Valdivia responded that he and Anco wanted to thank him in turn, for the excellent discharge of his duties as the lead guide of the expedition. They wished to do so by bestowing five llamas upon his family as an acknowledgement of his service. Ayar again bowed and replied it remained an honor to serve, and that his mother would appreciate this most generous gift. With that, he took his leave to depart with the llamas for home. Captain Valdivia took the occasion to ask if I might accept an addition to my guide contingent. Ancohualla had asked if one of his men, Paucar, newly appointed as one of his lieutenants, might accompany me and my men, because he had a desire to ride out front. I agreed enthusiastically, since Paucar was a friend of Ayar's and visited regularly with us for discussions and a game of quoits or draughts. A naturally gregarious man when in the role of *qamchu*, he was restrained, composed, and deeply thoughtful when not. A most interesting man, this Paucar, and highly regarded by us.

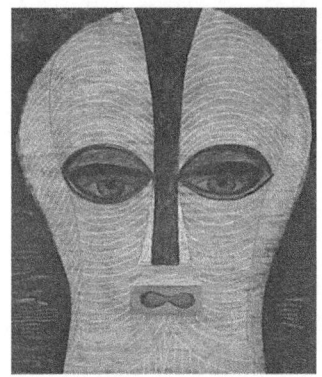

PART JJ

OUR MARCH SOUTH TOWARDS THE DISTANT COPAYAPU; A STRANGE SICKNESS ATTACKS MANY OF US; OUR CAPTAIN NAMES A NEARBY PEAK, "DOÑA INÉS"

On Saturday, June 29, we resumed the steady march south towards the distant Copayapu. My guiding contingent of Ayar, Lope de Ayala, and I, rode out front and led the procession as before, which now included Paucar. The Captain had proposed a different arrangement for our forces on the march, with Captain de Aguirre and a few of his men riding on our left flank and Captain de Quiroga and his men on our right. Valdivia wished our forces more compact, rather than stretched out in a long line of horse soldiers. De Cartagena, Hernando Vallejo, and Bernal Martinez continued to bring up the rear, behind Ancohualla and his people. De Miranda and his men still guarded de Hoz and his two llama dung collectors.

IMAGES: Please see 4HH-KK.7-.28 for scenes upon this journey.

Highness, the small villages we passed through in the coming days I mentioned in my Third Letter to Your Majesty.[153] And, as I recounted then, hundreds of flamingoes on the close by shallow lagunas[154] accompanied us. When we arrived at one of the settlements, the Captain and Ancohualla visited the local *cacique* and introduced themselves. The provisioners purchased needed stores, and our *qamchus* entertained the townspeople.

During this period, Doña Inés shared an event of note one evening about Pilca Huaca. It seems a llama had kicked an Indian as he tried to put a load on its back and tie it down. The sharp strike broke the man's arm. Pilca Huaca was ready to help him, as she had guanaco leg bones to serve as splints for his arm.[155] And where and when did she obtain them, asked our Doña? From the guanaco shoot weeks before! She asked Tupa for them from the four animals the Indians received. Doña Inés characterized Pilca Huaca as exceptionally "resourceful" and able to handle medical affairs with a tranquil composure. "She shall make her mark in the new land, gentlemen, you may be assured of this!" She emphasized this observation by making a small right fist and bringing it down sharply into her left palm. We could tell La Doña had great affection and respect for this woman.

Days after leaving the last village, I observed to Ayar we should soon arrive at the huts north of the great mountain, the small structures that Anta-Aclla Picchu, the High Priest of the High Mountains, had used on visits to that peak and now would use no more. And we did on the succeeding mid-day, for we came to the small stone constructions we had camped by years before, with the view of the great Llullaillaco in the distant south.[156] During the ensuing two days, we marched past the western ramparts of the mountain, and reached eventually the glistening shores of the Laguna of the White Sands,[157] so named by Captain Almagro, and the site of our

---

[153] Proceeding south from Atacama, the villages are Toconao, Socaire, and Peine.
[154] Prominent lagunas are Cejar, Tebenquinche, Chaxa, Bartos Negros, Salada, and several more, all part of the Chilean Flamingo Reserve.
[155] Splints for fractured arms and legs have been used throughout recorded history.
[156] One can just make out the summit, some seventeen miles from this spot.
[157] This is today's Laguna Aguas Calientes, which sits at 12,080 feet.

guanaco hunt on that expedition. The flamingoes on the laguna paid us no mind and went about their business. At the close of our daily meeting with Valdivia and Ancohualla about the itinerary of the ensuing day, the Captain said the ride past the mountain had made him realize what a feat the Indians had accomplished by climbing the mountain and building the huts on its summit. I agreed wholeheartedly.

Valdivia ordered several days of rest here to allow the provisioners and their assistants to fish the Laguna's waters and snare the different birds around its shore. And, since we found ourselves in guanaco country, he commissioned de Aguirre and de Quiroga to muster their musket men and embark on guanaco hunts in the surrounding countryside. Before they returned late the first day, we thought them successful, as we heard frequently the sounds of arquebus discharges close by. Our Doña had other duties and could not participate in the hunt as men with a fever needed her attention.

Close by our encampments lay the skeletons of the animals we had killed and skinned years before. Indians walked amidst the bones, Pilca Huaca and several of her women friends amongst them. I knew what they searched for, splint bones, but wondered what the others, like Paucar, were after. Later, we learned more, for Paucar came and suggested we play a new game. He pulled out a guanaco hoof and said Indians used it in a game they called *chaki*.[158] A player threw it twelve paces in front of him into a circle of sand or mud arranged for the purpose. If it fell on its top side, this meant good luck, and the player won. If it fell on the bottom side, this was bad, and he lost. If it landed on its side, the player lost his next turn. Good players knew how to spin the hoof to give them the best chance to win, and it took practice before a player became good at it. It seemed a useless game to me, this *chaki*. Late that day, the musket men returned, their pack animals weighed down with dead guanaco, thirty-one in all. Captain Valdivia thanked the men and apportioned subsequently twenty carcasses to Ancohualla and his people. Now the task began of skinning, butchering, and preparing the meat for the drying process.

---

[158] *Quechua* for hoof or foot.

During our stay here, Captain Villagran assembled those of us interested in the workings of the *cabildo*, de Alderete, de Quiroga, Bohón, de Miranda, de Monroy, de Gamboa, de Almagro, and me, for further discussions regarding the basic principles of town governance. Father Lobo spent time with Ancohualla, his *caciques*, Paucar, Huayna, and Rimac, and Pilca Huaca, teaching them our language. De Cartagena remained too busy directing the provisioning efforts with Tupa to teach writing skills, but he had been doing that occasionally through the last weeks.

On July 17, the provisioners having completed their tasks and, with the meat, fish, and birds drying in open skin bags, we left Llullaillaco and the white sands of the laguna for the journey south, Paucar and Ayar out front. Our steps south carried us past the western heights of the slightly smoking volcán we remembered from the Almagro journey.[159] It had turned cold during the last weeks, and a light winter snow storm now caused us to pull our warm clothing from Hullaqa tightly around us. Vicente rode up and said Valdivia wished to make camp, as cold and snow hindered our progress. This we did, and as soon as our tents were up and the dung fires in low flame, we were warm and convivial.

It happened here that Paucar said that Ancohualla a few days before had disciplined again the man he had punished south of Putre, for the identical offense and in the same manner, standing him in front of all the natives and telling them of his wrongdoings. This was an uncommon thing for any Inca leader, he said, since a second occurrence usually resulted in death. Paucar declined to name the offense or the man involved, and I cautioned my men not to inquire more about it, since it remained an Indian affair and not ours.

That night I fell asleep easily enough, but I awakened and felt uneasy, about what I knew not. I exited my tent and walked among the silent horses, to see that all were well. The storm had passed, the night was damp and cold, and the *ichu* grass was heavy with icy dewdrops. The tents were invisible, and I saw nothing but the faint figures of our faithful

---

[159] This is the volcán Lastarria (18,691 feet).

animals, breathing deeply, and moving restively as they slept, or still chewing slowly their *ichu*. Far off, beyond the black expanse of the salar, there appeared a dampened light, gradually increasing, akin to the glow of an oncoming inferno; until the wide disk of the moon, blood-red, and greatly enlarged by the desert mist, rose slowly upon the gloom, marked by one or two small clouds. As the light washed across the salar, a fierce and intense howl from a nearby fox[160] seemed to greet it as an unwanted trespasser. All this made for an eerie time and place, for the animals and I remained the only conscious beings around.

In the succeeding days, we continued to follow the route of Almagro towards Copayapu. Most of the peaks seemed familiar and the lagunas and *estanques* too. Montesinos always mentioned when we came close to another water source, since he had vowed to remember them when we traveled with Almagro.[161] One day he let me know we were in the vicinity of the lagunas with a large number of flamingoes, the place at which Diegito had begun the fishing contests among the men. He knew this, he said, because he recognized the peak before us as the mountain that stands above the salar. And indeed, he proved correct, as we came to the laguna there late in the day and stopped for the night.[162] The date was July 26, nine days south from the Laguna of the White Sands.

Although we spent an uneventful night, Sire, events changed, and dramatically so on the coming morning. I sensed something amiss as we prepared to leave, and commented upon it to my men. When Paucar joined us, he said a number of Indians had become feverish and felt too unwell to move. Within moments, runners from the Captain proceeded among us with orders to remain in place, for a sickness plagued some of our men and the Indians too. Presently we knew more, since word came from de Benito that a few Christians and more of the Indians complained

---

[160] On his rides to and from the Andean peaks in the Atacama, the author and his driver encountered occasionally the small Atacama fox.
[161] During this part of the journey, the expedition passed lagunas on the salars of de Azufrera, de Gorbea, de Aguilar, and de Infieles. The altitude varies from 12,000 to 13,000 feet.
[162] This is the Salar de Pedernales.

of headaches, sore throats, and chest and muscle pains. Doña Inés, Father Lobo, Ancohualla, and Pilca Huaca, were identifying all those affected.

Late in the morning, the Captain's aide came to summon Vicente and me to his quarters. When we arrived, others had gathered there. Fifteen of our men and sixty Indians complained of discomfort, Valdivia said. He had put La Doña in charge of the entire matter, for both we Christians and our Indians, and all must take direction from her. Those affected they moved to separate tents, away from the rest of us. Pilca Huaca, Ancohualla, and his *caciques*, did the same with the sick Indians, both the men and the women, with the help of Father Lobo. The duty of the ten of us summoned was to report to Doña Inés and follow her orders as to our actions. We did so, at the place set aside for all the sick.

Doña was quite busy, moving from tent to tent, as were Pilca Huaca and Father Lobo. They saw after the wants of the sick and emphasized the need to rest and sleep, sleep especially. When Doña saw us, she waved us forward. She had planned everything out, she said, and gave us directions as to what she wanted done. Vicente was to gather men, Christian and Indian, to catch fish in the lagunas. Bohón's duty was to entrap *tinamou* and other birds along the shore lines with the help of our men and the Indians. Cisternas would gather the musket men and hunt guanaco. The patients must eat only fresh food, she said emphatically.[163] De Cartagena and Tupa would assist with provisioning needs as necessary. The men left to begin their tasks, with a "Go with God" from La Doña.

She turned next towards me and Diego de Céspedes[164] and asked us to prepare tea for all the sick. Doña had asked Ancohualla for his *caciques* to help with this and they arrived quickly, Rimac and Huayna. She then gave us small pouches of crushed leaves called cilantro and said Father Molina had given them to her for the treatment of headaches. He had

---

[163] This was part of the Middle Ages approach to treating flu virus symptoms, which this sickness seems to be. But, viruses do not thrive at elevation. Since the Salar de Pedernales lies at over 11,000 feet, it is not clear exactly what caused the sickness.

[164] This man's name appears on the list of those who joined in Atacama, but with no birth or death dates.

gotten them from a priest newly arrived in Cusco from Mexico who had used it there to cure heated and aching bodies.[165] We began warming water immediately, the fires kept going by llama dung supplied by de Hoz and his accomplices. La Doña ordered the fires to burn all night, to warm the sick, keep the tea hot, and drive away the evil spirits.

After we had prepared the cilantro tea, what Doña called her "Doña's potion" with a smile and a wink, we carried large pots to the tents for the sick men. She insisted all must consume five cups of her drink during the day and early evening. It surprised me to learn Gerónimo de Alderete was stricken. When we visited his tent, he bid me welcome, but said he felt too poorly to talk. I understood, of course, and wished him good health.

Once we had finished providing the "potion" to our men, we helped Rimac and Huayna. At one tent, humming quietly to herself, Pilca Huaca bid me good-day in well-spoken Spanish, which surprised and delighted me, as she was an engaging woman. She asked for a cup of tea and thanked us for tending the sick Indians. As we walked among the tents, our priests, Father Marmolejo and Father Perez, moved slowly about, saying prayers to drive the Devil and his cohorts from our midst. They did this three times a day. While resting before making an additional delivery of tea, I asked La Doña if she were going to engage in bloodletting. If so, I offered my assistance. She replied she had learned from personal experience that the practice could cause more problems than it solved and she did not intend to use the technique.[166] Valdivia came up and said the guanaco hunters had returned and the butchering was ready to begin. Then Vicente hailed us that he and his men had baskets of fresh fish ready for preparation. Bohón and his men had returned also and now offered us plucked and prepared birds ready for cooking. So events transpired in the ensuing days. And through all this Doña Inés and Pilca Huaca never seemed to rest, rising before the sun and moving among the sick until well after the sun had set. They had their own tent, right amongst the unwell,

---

[165] Cilantro (coriander) was used for a variety of ailments to relieve unpleasant symptoms.

[166] This was a minority assessment among physicians of this time, but certainly of some merit.

so that they might respond quickly to calls for help or assistance. On more than one occasion during these days, I observed our Captain on one knee with his head bowed in prayer.

And now, the most wondrous things came about, Your Majesty, as the sick began feeling well again! Not all of them at the same time, but one by one, until everyone had recovered by the end of the third day. Our Doña informed Valdivia we could resume the march the next day, but allowing one more day to assure all were completely well might be wise. This we did. On the new morning, Father Marmolejo, with his rich baritone, chanted prayers of thanksgiving to Our Lord for his mercy and kindness. He could not say mass, for our wine supply was exhausted. At mid-day of this period of thankfulness and relaxation, Paucar visited and said Ancohualla wished to speak to all who had been sick, Christians and Indians, as well as those who had assisted Doña Inés in caring for them. When all had assembled at the appointed spot, Anco addressed us and said he thought it right to honor Doña Inés for guiding the efforts to heal the sick. At this, a murmur arose amongst us that this seemed most fitting and proper. He continued, and said a way to do this would be to name the mountain before us "Doña Inés" as a tribute to what she had meant to us. There were shouts of acclamation and affirmation that this was certainly a most noteworthy action. After hearing our approval, he said he intended to ask Valdivia that it happen before our departure.

Late in the morning of the fifth day, the Captain called all expedition members together for a special event. When we had assembled, he, with Ancohualla at his side, acknowledged the last days had been difficult for those who had the sickness. Numerous expedition members had contributed to help the sick conquer the illness that had affected them, and they deserved special thanks. And she who had organized those efforts, Doña Inés, merited generous recognition as well, he said. At this, all eyes focused on La Doña, and loud shouts and huzzahs arose from us all.

"As a special honor for her, and to acknowledge the request of all of you, it shall be recorded this day that the mountain at whose foot we stand shall henceforth be known as "Doña Inés."[167] At this, there arose more cries of approval and admiration. Doña Inés bowed in gracious acknowledgement, motioned to Pilca Huaca, and called her by name to come forward. When she did, Doña proclaimed her as the "Protectoress of our Indians," took her left arm in her right, and raised both upwards. More exclamations followed, in particular from our Indians, for her people loved Pilca Huaca dearly. Ancohualla now stepped forward and announced that, as of this day, Pilca Huaca would be his *"Cacica* for Medical Matters" in recognition of her importance to the health of the Indians.

PHOTO: Please see 4HH-KK.22-.24 for images of this peak.

Divine Majesty, Ancohualla's declaration became of marked importance, since the title of *"cacique"* throughout the Indian nations of the New World had been, until now, reserved just for men. So, indeed, this became an event of great significance that would have repercussions in future years, as I shall relate from personal experience. The remainder of the day we devoted to rest, visiting friends, playing games, and enjoying the amusements offered by our *qamchus*, Hidalgo and Paucar. The Captain and La Doña walked amongst us and visited with the men, exchanging pleasantries and encouraging all to rest on this day. Ancohualla and Pilca Huaca did likewise in the Indian encampment. Later, as Vicente, de Alderete, now fully recovered, Juan Bohón, and I sat conversing about the events of the prior days, Paucar and Ayar arrived. Paucar had an item of interest to share with us. Pilca Huaca had proposed to Ancohualla that they name the mountain for La Doña, he said. De Alderete confirmed this at once, saying she had visited the sick Christians with the proposal and all had been in support of it. Now we knew the origin of the naming, and it gave great satisfaction to learn of it.

---

[167] Chilean historians acknowledge that Captain Valdivia named the Volcán Doña Inés, 16,650 feet, for his mistress, although he does not mention doing so in his Letter I. It lies some 25 miles to the east of the mining town of El Salvador and 75-80 miles south from the Laguna of the White Sands (Laguna Aguas Calientes). His failure to mention Doña Inés in any of his letters to the King is due to his illicit affair with her.

As a final comment in fairness, I should add that the despicable de Hoz and his henchmen conducted themselves in a laudable manner during this time, since they kept the fires for the sick burning day and night, which helped contribute to the eventual recovery of all. Valdivia, impressed by their efforts, decided to show clemency and released them from confinement, although he refused them permission to carry a knife or sword. And he permitted de Hoz to ride with a comfortable saddle again. They still had to travel behind and gather llama dung, however. This freeing of those who had tried to kill our leader disappointed Doña Inés and the Captains Villagran and de Benito. Eventually, their assessments of these scoundrels would prove correct.

On July 31, we departed at Terce, with the mountain, Doña Inés, receding slowly in the distance behind us. In one day more, we could see barely its topmost heights, and after that it disappeared from view entirely. The days remained cool and required our wool coats pulled tightly about us. On two separate days, storms passed quickly, dropping light amounts of snow. After eight days, we entered a region that seemed familiar, and in moments I realized the cause of it. I dropped back to visit Montesinos and observed that we were about to reach the spot where Alejandro Velverde[168] met his fate years before. "You are right, my friend. I remember now the close walls on the side of this canyon as the location." That afternoon, after we had groomed our horses, Vicente and I, along with those from the Almagro Expedition who wished to remember this man, found his grave a short distance away, and Father Perez said prayers for his eternal well-being. The serenity of this place struck us as a suitable site for his final resting place.

---

[168] This is the man who probably died from altitude sickness. See Part U of the Third Letter, Volume I.

PART KK

OUR APPROACH TO COPAYAPU

Within two days, Copayapu lay three days ahead. The air became warmer and we could breathe more easily.[169] Late in the day, Valdivia called together the captains and lieutenants, as well as Ancohualla and his *caciques*. He informed us that Ancohualla, Huayna, and Ayar would ride ahead on the morrow and determine the mood of the people. They had been peaceful on the passage through here with Almagro, but the Captain wished to know whether they remained so.

He continued that we would remain a number of weeks in Copayapu to prepare for the last part of our journey. He ordered important activities to happen during our stay, which included the following:

1. Because Indians had attacked Almagro and his men south of Copayapu, at Huasco, and farther south at Papudo, upon leaving Copayapu we must remain ready to encounter hostile

---

[169] Copiapo lies at 1,300 feet in elevation, much lower than the 12,000 to 13,000 feet they have endured for the last several months. Although it is winter, the temperature in the region averages in the 60's and 70's.

Indian forces, if we could not first deal with them peacefully. Therefore, he and the captains planned to direct cavalry battlefield maneuvers several times a week.

2. The musket men, under the direction of Captain de Aguirre, would practice maneuvers without firing their guns. We had to save powder for possible use against hostiles farther south.

3. Since most of the Christians had trained as soldiers rather than farmers, the Captain said he and Ancohualla intended to conduct meetings with all of us so we might learn proper farming techniques, such as soil preparation, planting, watering, harvesting, and the like.

4. The town planners, de Miranda and de Gamboa, were to draw up preliminary proposals for our new capital town and submit them to the Captain for his examination.

5. The training of our Indians in speaking our language, by Father Lobo, and in writing, by de Cartagena, should continue.

6. Captain Villagran's teaching of the workings of the *cabildo* would move forward, and now include Ancohualla and Tupa.

7. Doña Inés, Father Lobo, and Pilca Huaca should be available to the town's medical healers to help with any village health problems.

8. Our priests must make themselves known in the town and seek to spread the word of Christ, our Redeemer.

9. We must have a suitable harbor for the ships soon to come from the City of Kings to our new city in the south. The Captain said he planned to examine the anchorage in the west used by the Almagro Expedition and see if it might provide for our needs.

10. The *qamchus* were to stroll the streets twice a week and spread good cheer and merriment.

11. The provisioners must see after our food stores and other needs before our departure.

Such were the activities our Captain said should occupy us in the weeks spent in Copayapu.

At the hour of None, when one day from Copayapu, Paucar shouted that Ancohualla, Huayna, and Ayar, were approaching, waving their arms in greeting. They were in good spirits when we met and Anco said all seemed well in town. They went past us to greet Valdivia, and within a brief while his aide rode up and said we would stay here for the night. He added that the captains and lieutenants were to gather at the Captain's tent before the evening's repast and hear the news from Ancohualla about the state of affairs in Copayapu.

When we had assembled, Anco told us about the situation in the town.

1. The townspeople appeared quite friendly and ready to welcome us, especially the 200 Peruvian natives from Prince Paullu's entourage who remained there when we passed through here on the Almagro Expedition.

2. Of those Indians from Paullu's force who stayed in Copayapu, two had risen to the position of town *caciques*. Their names were Guasco and Zapana. Ancohualla said he had no memory of these men and could not attest to their good intentions, but they seemed capable, friendly, and thus deserving of our initial trust.

3. The *caciques* said they welcomed medical care since disease plagued several of the townspeople.

At the conclusion of Ancohualla's report, I asked if our Almagro guides, Feliz and Simpa, were in town. He answered that they had left for Tucma two weeks prior leading a caravan with, among other goods, seashell jewelry! Vicente and I nodded knowingly to one another, remembering our Tucma incident of years before.[170]

Majesty, I should here take the time to describe this man, the estimable Ancohualla, so important to the success of my guiding team with Captain Almagro and now the leader of our Indians on the Valdivia Expedition. Our Captain did not mention him in his letters to Your Majesty and I feel it my duty to tell something of him. As I have said previously, he had been a close friend of Prince Paullu for numerous years; he had six summers when the Prince was born[171] and his parents were close to Paullu's father, the Inca Huayna Capac.[172] Thus, Ancohualla enjoyed a certain aspect of royalty, though he conducted himself in a manner that suggested this to be unimportant to him. I offer as attestation to this that he wanted to travel to the new land so he might begin a life of simplicity close to the soil. Further, as the leader of our Indian contingent, there was no task so large that he hesitated to perform it or so insignificant that it was beneath his position to do it. And he always showed himself as prepared as they to endure the hardships of our journey. I think it true that each man finds his distresses less when someone else willingly shares them. And his people enjoyed seeing him openly eating the same food as they or lending a hand with an arduous task. The occasional harshness of the land and weather never caused him anxiety; indeed, he saw these as a natural part of the journey through life, and this attitude he conveyed to others. Because of the man he proved himself to be, Ancohualla won enduring respect and love from his people.

Valdivia had recognized Anco's attributes during our time in Cusco, and he consulted with him every day on our passage about affairs concerning the Indians. He learned some of our language on the Almagro Expedition and furthered this knowledge with the help of Father Lobo. Always a calm and mature man, he nevertheless possessed an ability to see the humor in things. He was slow-spoken, and paused before responding in

---

[170] See, The Adventure Chronicles, the Second Letter, Volume I.
[171] The Prince was born in 1516, so this means Ancohualla was born in 1510. As de Mérida mentioned in the first part of this Letter, Pedro was born in 1505.
[172] Huayna Capac ruled as Inca from 1493-1527.

conversation. But to think this indicated lack of interest or understanding was to misinterpret him completely, since he knew exactly the content and course of the discussion, and this revealed itself in the depth of his responses. A curiosity about our culture created in him an attraction to our Christ and his teachings, which he had pursued with Father Molina years before and continued with Father Lobo, along with others of his people. His natural inquisitiveness also caused him to study civic affairs, and Valdivia had asked him to learn about *cabildo* particulars from Captain Villagran. These pursuits would redound to his importance to his people as well as to the Captain and the governance of our new capital city.

I shall leave this, Sire, for as we returned to our tents at the end of Ancohualla's report, I made a comment to Montesinos about one of our men who disappeared in Copayapu on the Almagro journey. He remembered, he said, and suggested that he and his woman must have left when they heard of our arrival. We both agreed that since Lieutenant Castilla never deemed his desertion an important issue, we should let the incident go unremarked upon to the Captain. But this proved far from the last of this man, as future events will attest.

PART LL

OUR TIME IN COPAYAPU AND WHAT HAPPENED THERE; ANOTHER ENCOUNTER WITH THE LOUT, SANCHO DE HOZ

*Y*our Honor, we entered Copayapu a month ago, on August 19, 1540,[173] more than a month later than planned. Valdivia had stated prior to our arrival our days would be full, and they were. We had no complaints, however, as the activities were a most welcome change from the routine of the last months marching through the high desert and enduring the cold weather. Here in Copayapu, it remained mild and cool, given the season, and very much to our liking. Throughout the weeks of our stay, we followed the Captain's orders assiduously. The cavalry maneuvers were exciting and most instructive, as they gave us the chance to practice battlefield formations and become familiar with the new men we should fight beside in the future. And

---

[173] There is no reason to doubt this date. Historians do not give an exact time for arrival or departure, saying only that it was sometime mid-year and that the expedition stayed for about two months.

Valdivia began the exercises with the words: "Gentlemen, remember. We come in peace, but are always prepared for war."

He led all of our days in the field and directed the practice formations not once or twice, but again and again. Assisting him were Captains de Benito and Villagran, and Lieutenants Montesinos, de Alderete, Bohón, and de Almagro, given their sterling reputations in battle. The configurations remained the usual ones. The most basic, the cavalry charge, we effected by forming a line and attacking forward towards the enemy, in this case, a line of our eleven musket men. The Captain's own word for this charge was "the bolt."[174]

Another was what Valdivia called "the pinch." In this tactic, we formed up in a bolt alignment, and charged forward towards our musket men, arrayed in a stout line of battle and functioning as the make-believe enemy. Behind them was the other part of our attacking force, a line of horse soldiers ready to prevent the musket men from retreating from our charge.[175]

In a different operation, we performed a delicate assault in which one force attacked frontally while the two other contingents assailed the enemy flanks. With the frontal group holding the enemy in place, the flanking forces sought to get behind and encircle the whole lot of them. This presented a difficult method of attack and depended on precise timing and coordination. The Captain liked this formation and called it "the single-hand closure."[176]

A similar combat arrangement was Valdivia's favorite for, though seldom employed, it remained his most satisfying tactic on a field of battle. If

---

[174] The charge is a basic maneuver in which one force advances toward the enemy at high speed in order to engage in close combat.

[175] This is the "hammer and anvil", where the cavalry, the hammer, charges the enemy, the line of musket men, behind whom is positioned the "anvil", in this case another line of horsemen.

[176] This is the envelopment and does, as de Mérida says, require exceptional coordination skills by the commander and instant response to commands by his subordinates.

carried out successfully, he said, the destruction of the enemy would be complete. In this operation, one of our forces advanced towards the center of the hostile formation. An additional unit positioned itself in the enemy's rear, followed by two other cavalry detachments that attacked his flanks. This is quite complex and entirely dependent upon orders obeyed instantly. At a certain point, the Captain gives the command to the front and rear groups to move towards each other. When they come together, this is the signal for the flanking forces to attack, thus creating two surrounded enemy forces. The Captain called this his "double hand closure."[177]

Our ten musket men, besides assisting the cavalry in their maneuvers, conducted their own exercises, led by Captain de Aguirre and his assistant, Cisternas. They did not use gunpowder, at Valdivia's order, as we would need it in future encounters with Indians. The sessions consisted in the proper placement of a high fork, for standing, and a low fork, for sitting or reclining prone on the ground. Absent the use of powder, there was no loading done or lighting of the powder. Yet, the most important aspect of firing the arquebus they practiced over and over. This was the slow squeeze of the trigger. Nothing was more important to the accurate firing of the musket than this basic finger movement, as a quick squeeze sent the bullet off on an unintended course. De Quiroga and the "gunner" worked with five men apiece and called out the words "aim, squeeze, fire" repeatedly to them.[178] And the emphasis was always on the slow "squeeze."

To return to the practice sessions of the horsemen, Majesty, one day the Captain became emotional at the end of a long day in the saddle since he said we were not serious in our preparation and execution. He called out one lieutenant in front of all of us for inattentiveness and extended our practice time until the early evening. He then made the point that similar behavior in the future would result in disciplinary measures or demotion.

---

[177] This complex maneuver has been seldom effected on any battlefield. Known as the "double envelopment" or "pincer' movement, it is carried out as de Mérida describes it. The reader might remember that Captain Almagro used this tactic successfully at the Battle of Laguna Poopo in the First Letter, Volume I.

[178] The author understands this well. During boot camp in the Marines in 1964, our rifle range instructors yelled this at us repeatedly.

There occurred other affairs of importance happening during the days here, for Doña Inés, Pilca Huaca, and Father Lobo, located the medical workers in town and began to assist in caring for those with a sickness similar to the one that had afflicted our people weeks before. The sick resided in a large room under a low ceiling, with openings to admit the warmth of the sun. La Doña suggested they use her "potion," and told the workers of the things she and Pilca Huaca had done to treat our sick. When Doña introduced Pilca Huaca as our Indians' "*Cacica* for Medical Matters," the sick Indians asked that she care for them, along with a young townswoman they respected and loved. Pilca Huaca met this lady, a fine looking woman named Collardis, and learned she was the daughter of the man in charge of treating the sick. He had accompanied the third Inca army to Chile a number of years before and had decided to remain here and tend the sick, injured, and dying. Her older brother followed his father's station in life and served as his assistant. And this woman, Collardis, told La Doña and Pilca Huaca of a favorite elixir they used to treat stomach ailments, made from the leaves, bark, and dark black berries of a tree here in Copayapu. It tasted similar to the pepper spice used to flavor food in Spain.[179] We found this "spice" tree frequently in our new land.

While our activities were associated primarily with work and preparation for the march to our new home, Valdivia recognized that we needed to spend time in other ways. As a result, he declared Wednesday a day of leisure, and the Lord's Day a day of worship and relaxation. We spent these occasions reciting prayers without mass, of course, and engaging in light activities. For example, our *qamchus*, Rodrigo Hidalgo and Paucar, roamed the city streets and delighted our Indians and the villagers with their antics and tricks. Montesinos and other horsemen gave rides to the young boys in town, and the village instrument players walked the streets, playing music for the enjoyment of all. One afternoon, Vicente and I, with de Alderete and Bohón, sought out the cup-and-ball players. When we came upon them, Gerónimo found himself quite competent at the game's

---

[179] This is the *Schinus molle*, or Chilean and American pepper tree. There are several large ones in Copiapo today with a prominent one in the main plaza, Plaza Prat. The author has one in his back yard in California.

complexities, so much so that the Indian players lost interest and declined further matches! Not to be denied his amusement, Gerónimo traded blue beads in the local market to acquire the game pieces and played with soldiers and Indians during the rest of our journey.

One afternoon after our morning horse drills, Vicente, Ayar, and I, spent some time under a large "spice" tree in the center of town discussing matters of little importance and also remembering incidents of humor on our journey to this point. Presently, three young boys approached us and wished to engage in conversation. Ayar served as our translator. These were the same boys who had waved their hats in greeting as we entered the town weeks before and threw flowers at Vicente as a gesture of particular favor for him. They now directed their words to him and said they remembered when he came through their town several years ago. On our return here, all their friends drew wood sticks as to which horse soldier they would watch over and seek to protect and these three had drawn Vicente.

"And what will you protect me from," asked Montesinos, attempting not to smile at their earnestness after his wellbeing. "If you are killed, we will avenge you," replied the one who stood somewhat taller than the others. "And we will tend your grave to see that it is never disturbed," said the shortest among them. "Well," said my friend, "that provides me a great deal of comfort!" "See," said the third boy to his friends, "I told you he would like it." Vicente gave them a serious look and said, "But I do not want you boys to be too disappointed if your plans never come to pass!" He then turned to me. "I hope they do not know something that I do not." We laughed and then gave them rides on our horses. After, we hailed a passing vender of sweet fruits and confections and treated Vicente's new young friends.

I shall leave this and tell of an important issue of concern for the Captain, for he visited the coast to examine the harbor where the *Santiaguillo* and her sister ships had docked on the Almagro visit. Accompanying him were de Gamboa and de Miranda, to aid in assessing the port and a possible site for a town. On their return to Copayapu, Valdivia addressed the officers and declared that, indeed, the region appeared quite suitable for our future port needs, and said he planned upon its construction after we founded our city in the south.[180]

I must relate now, Noble Majesty, a further grave incident involving the malcontent, de Hoz. During the Captain's reconnaissance of the coast, a new band of men rode into town. They came from Cusco, had traveled through Tupiza, and from there, west to Atacama, where they followed our course to Copayapu. It was Gonzalo de los Ríos,[181] along with his twenty mounted men, and accompanied by Juan Jufré,[182] Gaspar de Vergara,[183] and Gaspar de Villarroel.[184] These last three were on poor terms with most of these men, but rode with them for companionship in the search for our expedition. Of especial concern was de los Ríos, as he and a few of his men seemed sympathetic to de Hoz from their days in Cusco, particularly a roguish and hot-tempered ruffian by the name of Alonzo de Chinchilla,[185] a swarthy, brutal looking fellow, with a face as surly and distorted as one of the Devil's Cerberean dogs, and whose outward appearance of crooked teeth and a facial tick reflected his inward repulsiveness.

I became involved in matters when Villagran's aide approached and said La Doña requested my presence at once. I left off sharpening my sword and went to her forthwith. When I arrived, her agitation was apparent. She had heard this de los Ríos, de Chinchilla, and two others hailed by de Hoz and de Chinchilla in seemingly friendly fashion. Doña Inés, armed

---

[180] This is today's port city of Caldera, with a population of around 14,000. Its beaches and restaurants are a popular destination for weekend visitors from Copiapo.
[181] (1515-1575). De los Ríos is on the list of men who joined the Expedition here.
[182] (1516-1578). This man was destined for important government duties in the capital city.
[183] (1507-1576?). De Vergara was a soldier in the Almagro entourage several years prior.
[184] (1510–1590).
[185] This man appears on the list of expedition members but without a birth or death date. Lobera in Ch. XIII, *Crónica del Reino de Chile*, mentions him and much of what de Mérida relates.

with her sword and long stiletto, yelled at the rogues to stand still or she intended to run all of them through. They hesitated to doubt her, for she had the look in her eyes of a demented woman who would take their lives in an instant.

She shouted for me to summon Villagran and the lieutenants, who were on the edge of town practicing cavalry maneuvers, and have them return without delay. I did so, by dispatching Hernando Vallejo to see to it. When I turned back to La Doña, she commanded the miscreants, with language used by a hardened soldier, to get on their knees or they should die without delay. When Captain Villagran rode in, with Vicente, Bohón, de Alderete, and Juan Gómez de Almagro, they knew instantly the state of things. "Take all four prisoners, Captain. They are friends with de Hoz and his accomplices and must surely swing from a tree for their treachery!" This the Captain did without delay, while a close guard watched them until Valdivia's return.[186] When he did, two days later, he was furious and ordered de Hoz, de Chinchilla, de los Ríos, despite his protestation of innocence, and their two friends, confined day and night with less than normal food rations as further punishment. I learned afterwards that when the Captain read his rules to all the new arrivals, he made it a point to promise they would be under close watch for their behavior as a result of these latest incidents. Thus the de Hoz problem remained unresolved for the moment.

I should remark here that Vicente and I, after this commotion had concluded, along with other Almagro Expedition men, saluted an acquaintance from those days, Gaspar de Vergara, an honest, tall, strong man with intense features who would fill important government roles in the new towns in *Nueva Extremadura*. And Juan Jufré was competent in both judicial and medical matters. He asked Doña Inés if he might assist her when needed and she agreed enthusiastically. Those watching after the health needs of Christians and Indians now were four: Doña Inés, Father Lobo, Jufré, and Pilca Huaca.

---

[186] This incident is cited by La Doña, except for the language she used, in Declaración de Inés de Suárez, in Medina, *Documentos inéditos*.

The Adventure Chronicles of *Conquistador* Pedro de Mérida. VOLUME 2, VALDIVIA

Only days after the latest de Hoz affair, Majesty, an event of a significant nature happened among our Indians, and I must tell of it now. It showed how the Inca designated certain crimes as capital ones and the means they used to carry out the punishment for them. It transpired in this manner. One day, Valdivia summoned all the men for an important announcement. There would be an execution of one of the natives, he said, and we must let Ancohualla and his *caciques* carry it out without interference. The Captain explained further that Anco had told him the day before of the transgressions of this man and the means of rendering punishment. It seems the Indian in question stood accused of laziness, a crime in Inca society almost equal to murder, theft, lying, and violence. The punishments for these crimes varied. Hanging, decapitation, stoning, and pushing the guilty man over a cliff were all used, with the means employed determined by the judge of the case. Since idleness deprived the Inca and the workers of the culprit's services, it was a serious crime, first punished with a public rebuke or banishment to serve in a mine or a wet plantation. A second instance of failing to work for the good of all resulted usually in the sentence of death. In the case at hand, the accused had incurred two reprimands from Ancohualla for refusing to work with others, as we had learned from Paucar already. The third occasion happened during our stay in town. Ancohualla, the Captain related, said this man must face execution, since he would continue with this behavior, to the harm of all. He said further that Anco and his *caciques* had decided on death by pushing the man over a steep cliff and they intended to carry it out on this very day. And so they did.[187] Valdivia observed that this action proved Anco the right man to govern the Indians well in our new home.

PHOTO: See 4LL-MM.2-.4 for images of this execution.

With this matter behind us, I must move to other topics, Sire, those activities Captain Valdivia wanted us to engage in during our time here

---

[187] According to Garcilasso de la Vega, the Inca imposed a set of three laws on its citizens:"*Ama Sua. Ama Llulla. Ama Quella*" or "Do not steal. Do not lie. Do not be lazy". De la Vega goes on to say that ".... it was a most infamous and degrading thing among these people to be chastised in public for laziness." See Book II of his <u>Royal Commentaries of the Incas</u>.

in Copayapu, though they be more ordinary in nature in the telling. Through the initial weeks of our stay, Valdivia and his captains, along with Ancohualla and his *caciques,* met on several occasions with the town's *caciques,* Guasco and Zapana. At the end of one such meeting, the Captain called the officers and priests together and told us of the discussions. The *caciques* had asked if some villagers might accompany us on our journey. Valdivia and Ancohualla agreed to this and asked that these people come forward so they might mingle with our Indians and learn their assigned duties. As to an additional issue of our provisions, the *caciques* agreed to provide us with large amounts of fruit and vegetable seeds, like, *papas,* beans, *quinua,* pumpkins, assorted fruits, and salt. On the issue of the governance of Copayapu, that should remain with the two *caciques* for now said Valdivia, and there would be no special arrangement, as with Huaman, the *Desert Cacique.*

One of the Captain's wishes during our stay concerned soldiers learning the ways of the farmer. Valdivia and Ancohualla met with groups of twenty men each and schooled them in the necessary elements of successful farming, such as warmth, sunlight, water, and soil. While this was a most valuable instruction, a few of us learned that perhaps we lacked the necessary skills to succeed in the fields. Soldiering, administering a town government, building town structures, and jobs other than tilling the soil were the things we performed well. Our Captain said he knew this, that some of us would be soldiers, others government workers, and still others builders, but he wished all to know how to farm in case we needed more men, for whatever reason, to plant and cultivate crops in our new homeland.

Another matter important to Captain Valdivia. On the feast day of my beloved St. Francis,[188] as we played games and conversed with friends, the Captain called together all the officers for a discussion. De Gamboa and de Miranda were with him and showed us large diagrams, drawn by de Cartagena, which indicated possible arrangements of our new city's buildings, all laid out conforming to a grid. At the center appeared the Plaza Mayor, and around it lay sites for a Cathedral,

---

[188] The feast day of St. Francis of Assisi is October 4.

the Governor's house, structures for *cabildo* work, corners for open markets of fruits and vegetables, and homes for the officers. Outside this central district, and located at a distance, were large sections for houses for the Christians and our Indians. And near our encampment appeared the buildings for feeding and maintaining our horses and the livestock we brought from Peru. Of course, these drawings showed only the basic things we needed to make the town a pleasant place to live. Valdivia said there would be more plans to examine after we located a site suitable for the city.

Since the day of our departure was upon us, Your Majesty, Valdivia asked me to present the itinerary for our journey from Copayapu to Papudo to our men and Doña Inés, with Ancohualla and his five *caciques* also in attendance, Pilca Huaca included. Below are the contents.

GENTLEMEN AND LADIES:

The Captain has decided our departure date from Copayapu as October 30, ten days from today. The following identifies several of the landmarks and towns we will pass through on the march to our new home. Captain Valdivia has chosen its name as Santiago *del Nueva Extremadura*. May God bless it forever!

The dates of departure and arrival are approximate, since unknown difficulties may present themselves that might alter these estimates.

Departure Landmark or Town	**Arrival Landmark or Town**
Copayapu, October 30, 1540	Huasco, November 12
Huasco, November 14	Cuquimpu, November 24
Cuquimpu, November 25	Limari, November 30
Limari, December 1	Illapel, December 8
Illapel, December 9	Papudo, December 15
Papudo, December 18	Santiago, December 30

Water Availability

With Ayar as our guide, and a number of us having traveled this land already, finding sources of water from Copayapu to Papudo will be straightforward. From Papudo inland to the land where our Captain believes sites exist for our capital city with abundant water, we have information. Captain Almagro sent Lieutenant Alvarado to the interior from Papudo to look for gold deposits during our stay there. In two weeks he returned, but he and his men were unsuccessful in finding any gold mines or even traces of gold.[189] Still, they did find the richest farmland we had encountered so far, on which the natives grew every sort of fruit and vegetable, and in great profusion. We expect this is true today, and this fruitful land therefore might be the location of our new home.

Temperature and Altitude

Most of the journey from Copayapu to Papudo is through low lying land, with cool temperatures because of its nearness to the ocean, and cool also because of the present season of spring.

Roads

We will follow Inca-built roads from Copayapu through the above mentioned towns until we enter Papudo.

Forage for the Animals

Ichu grass is the staple for the llamas and our horses and is available along the entire route. The water sources we encounter have other grasses on their shores that may serve as additional fodder.

---

[189] Historians are uncertain of the extent of Alvarado's search, but most believe that he reached the vicinity of present-day Santiago.

Food Stores

We must purchase large amounts of llama and guanaco *charqui* and stores of dried fish here in Copayapu. We have added extra llamas to provide enough fresh meat when needed. Dried fish, *quinua*, dried and fresh fruits and vegetables, *charqui*, *chuño*, *papas*, and other assorted foodstuffs are available here in town. Huasco has large herds of guanaco that surround it, and there are fresh food stores there and in the other towns we pass through. Our provisioners, Lieutenant de Cartagena and Tupa, will see to our needs.

Seeds and Animals for our New Land

As we found on the Almagro Expedition, the natives of Chile are accomplished farmers and harvest many kinds of fruits and vegetables. And they are efficient at directing water from rivers and lakes to their crop lands by the means of channels and aqueducts. As we now know, the men of the Inca armies who invaded Chile years ago taught this to them, for they were farmers as well as soldiers. Finally, we will find various kinds of seeds in the villages we encounter and will acquire them with our blue beads. Our provisioners will attend to these matters.

Temperament of the Natives

The natives of Huasco confronted us on the Almagro Expedition and prompted our energetic response. We shall know their disposition when we approach the town, as we will send men ahead to determine this. Papudo was the site of a larger battle, one involving war-like natives from a number of miles south of the village. We must expect a similar encounter this time. For these reasons, the Captain has ordered frequent cavalry and musket drills.

Terremotos

We did not encounter a *terremoto* years ago on our march south from Copayapu and our passage back north, until we endured the shaking outside Tacna. We now know they happen often, especially in the coastal regions. So we must stay prepared to experience another one, since most of our route south is near the ocean. As I said before, there is little we can do about such an occurrence except to pray for God's protection.

OUR TOTAL NUMBER OF MEN

You men who rode recently into Copayapu have increased our numbers from 127 to 151. If there are no further additions, and the Captain does not expect any, our current number, along with our Indians, will be those to establish our new home in Santiago.

Such was the content of my report.

I must say, Your Lordship, that those who commented at the conclusion surprised me. Two Indian *caciques*, including Pilca Huaca, asked questions in our language or made comments about an aspect of what I had presented. At one such remark, I glanced at Father Lobo and noticed a smile of great satisfaction upon his face, as it was testimony to how much they had learned from him.

And Father Lobo, as well as Fathers Marmolejo and Perez, had cause to celebrate a momentous event. For on the Lord's Day at the end of our stay, they announced 100 of our Indian men and women had declared their desire to become Christians, including Ancohualla and all his *caciques*, Pilca Huaca, Tupa, Huayna, Paucar, and Rimac. We watched and prayed as the priests baptized the new Christians by pouring water over their foreheads and praying for them. The Captain remained on his knee during this time and clutched his statue of the Virgin Mary. We celebrated with a large meal of meat and fruit afterwards, along with a fermented fruit drink prepared by the townspeople. What a joyous day, Your Majesty. Praise be unto His Name forever.

Two days before our departure, the Captain called the officers together at his tent. Ancohualla was there with his *caciques*, and we learned that thirty men and twenty women from town wanted to be a part of our expedition. This was welcome, Ancohualla said, since he and his *caciques* had talked to them to be certain they understood the hardships and dangers, as well as the pleasures, of beginning a new life. He continued that he felt satisfied all would be valuable members of our new home. And one was the young woman, Collardis, who wished to assist Pilca Huaca with caring for the health of our Indians. At this announcement, both La Doña and Pilca Huaca gripped the hands of Collardis with great joy. On the few occasions that I saw them together in the future, it seemed obvious that these three ladies enjoyed each other's company and had become close friends.

PART MM

OUR DEPARTURE FROM COPAYAPU AND THE JOURNEY SOUTH TO PAPUDO; THE EXECUTION OF JUAN RUÍZ

114

On October 30 1540, Your Lordship, we departed from Copayapu as large crowds bade us farewell. The town *caciques*, Guasco and Zapana, bowed to Valdivia and Ancohualla in a gesture of respectful leave-taking. The families of Indians departing with us, like those of Collardis, pressed close to embrace those embarking upon their journey to find a new life. The town musicians played joyful music with flutes and drums, adding a festive note to our departure as we moved slowly out of town and to the south.

Our order of march was similar to that of the previous months, although now we were on watch for hostile activity by natives, since the first place we would pass was Huasco, the site of the battle several years before. Captain de Aguirre and several of his men rode on our left flank, Captain de Quiroga and his men on our right. Captain de Miranda, with his horse soldiers, de Cartagena, Hernando Vallejo, and Bernal Martinez, still guarded de Hoz and the llama dung collectors and continued to close up our rear. Juan Bohón and five others reinforced them. A posting of the watch occurred each night, commanded by de Miranda. Valdivia reminded those men assigned to this duty that should they fall asleep the punishment would be death by hanging. The journey remained uneventful, marked simply by the unceasing emptiness of the desert land.

On November 10, with Huasco two days farther on, the Captain dispatched Ancohualla, Rimac, and Ayar, protected by de Aguirre and his men, to discover the people's mood. They returned the succeeding day and said all appeared calm and the people were ready to greet us. Anco said the village *caciques* wished us to know that the hostiles who had attacked the Almagro Expedition years before had moved farther south, away from the village and posed no immediate danger. This was important to know, as it meant a possible conflict near the town of Cuquimpu later on our journey. At the evening meeting with the officers and Ancohualla and his *caciques*, Valdivia said we would not stop in Huasco,[190] save to pay respects to the *caciques* and assure them we came in peace. And because of this latest information about the Indians moving south, we would continue to remain on heightened alert.

On Tuesday, November 12, we passed west of the town and came to a stop while the Captain and Ancohualla visited with the village leaders. As we awaited their return, we gazed at the large guanaco herds to the south of town. As we did so, Vicente reminded me of the condors we had seen here with the copper leg bracelets. We laughed about the amusement those great birds had offered us, although they provided a cause of consternation for certain of our companions.[191]

When the captains returned, we continued on until stopping a few miles south. Several of us remember this position well, as events occurred here, Your Honor, of an unexpected nature, so unsettling that most of us refused to believe then and find it difficult to believe now that they actually happened. Things came to pass in this fashion. I tell of them, not from having

---

[190] This is today's Vallenar in the Huasco River Valley, some ninety miles south of Copiapo. Its population in 2002 numbered 48,000 people. There are still large guanaco herds around the town.

[191] See The Adventure Chronicles, Part P of Volume I.

been witness to all matters personally, but hearing of them from Captain Villagran, the man's commanding officer. A soldier by the name of Juan Ruíz, he of a ruddy pink complexion, a stalwart veteran we knew from the Almagro days and a Tacna man, one day began acting strangely and without discipline. There seemed no cause for his actions, at least that anyone could understand, and those who knew him said he had never behaved in this manner before. As an example, one day Ruíz began yelling that he regretted having embarked upon this worthless adventure with Valdivia and that we would all die of hunger and thirst and, if not of those, certainly at the cruel hands of savages. He screamed that he refused to remain on the journey and encouraged others to join him to fight the Captain. Some tried to calm him, although this enraged him even further. Doña Inéz approached him and spoke with a soft, soothing voice in an attempt to settle him. She told him he was a man of honor and must act with more restraint. He could talk with her about his ailments, and she promised to make things better. He looked in her direction with a fierce luster in his eyes, smiled grotesquely, turned away, and then lunged with his sword at those nearby, ran it through the upper thigh of one man, and cut off the ear of another.

The Captains de Benito and Villagran, notified of the affair, appeared on the scene and ordered Ruíz to stand at attention in the presence of officers. This Ruíz took as a challenge, ran toward the unarmed Villagran and might have run him through the chest if de Alderete had not hit him in the face with his morrión. This brought everything to an end, and several soldiers dragged Ruíz, with arms and legs tied by a stout rope and bleeding from the face, to a large rock where two soldiers stood guard over him. Gómez de Benito motioned to Villagran and said they must tell Valdivia what had occurred so he might render judgment and a sentence.

While we awaited what was to happen next, officers and men received orders to gather at a set of trees outside camp in an hour. At the appointed time and place, Valdivia strode forth as two soldiers dragged Ruíz, still tied hand and foot, to the base of a squat tree. He screamed he was a follower of de Hoz and intended to kill Valdivia should he be freed. Amidst Ruíz's loud protestations, the Captain addressed us with stern words that this man presented a danger to all and to the success of our entire enterprise. He had violated two of the Captain's orders, specifically, that any soldier who seeks to foment rebellion against the leaders of the expedition by encouraging desertion or seeks to cause his fellow soldiers harm or injury will suffer death by hanging.

He continued, "Men, Juan Ruíz has injured seriously two of our number and urged others to desert and attack me and my officers. If I fail to punish him, he will attempt further such acts against us. I shall not allow this to happen. Therefore, I sentence you, Juan Ruíz, to death by hanging. May God have mercy upon your eternal soul."

As Father Marmolejo prayed aloud for him and sprinkled blessed water upon his head, two men threw a rope over a tree branch; two others hoisted the condemned man on a horse and fitted the noose of the rope about his neck. As he continued shouting and now cursing, using the name of Our Lord, one of the men, at the signal from our Captain, slapped the horse's haunch. Ruíz dropped heavily, and we heard his neck snap as a result.[192]

PHOTO: Please see 4LL-MM.4,.5 as the possible site of the execution.

Thus ended the Ruíz affair. There were discussions that night about whether de Hoz had been behind the behavior of Ruíz. Indeed, Captain Villagran thought so, according to his aide. Others of us believed it the work of Satan, as did Father Perez and Captain Valdivia, for Ruíz had acted in ways none of us had seen before. With the death of this man, our numbers totaled 150.[193]

We must now return to the march, Majesty, since there is much more to relate. Knowing that the hostile Indians we had encountered in Huasco in

---

[192] Weldon Vernon cites two sources for this unfortunate incident as taking place sometime soon after leaving Copayapu, but does not say where. De Mérida's recounting now clarifies the matter. Ruíz appears on the list of expedition members, but with no birth or death dates. Also, Aurelio Diaz Mesa, in Leyendas y Episodios Chilenos, I,44, mentions the Ruíz affair, but lacks the details offered by de Mérida.

[193] As footnoted previously, this is the number given by Valdivia in his Letter I.

the Almagro days had since moved south, Villagran assigned Vicente and five men to protect me and my guiding group. Besides my steadfast friend, Juan Gómez de Almagro, one of the five horse soldiers was the reputable Sánchez de Morales,[194] a broad-shouldered man of erect bearing and deep-set grey eyes. He was born in a well-met household, the first and only child as his mother died giving him life. His father had not the time or inclination to care for him while he was off to the Italian wars, and so he passed him to his sister, who treated him with the most loving care. He had a dark and heavy brow that became prominent whenever he laughed or frowned. Of noteworthy intelligence, he never used his erudition in an aristocratic or overbearing manner, for he was private and inward-looking, but always ready to laugh and smile with slight hesitation. Possessed of a judicial background, he told me he and Juan Jufré had had frequent conversations about how they might make their legal mark in the new land and had engaged the Captain in several of these discussions.

Our days and nights now were marked by a keen watchfulness for any war-like activity; all remained on alert, our Indians as well. The terrain we traversed in the coming days remained flat, with occasional shallow ravines, and offered little in concealment to those who might wish us harm. But a number of us knew the ground would change. When we were two days from the region where men on the Almagro Expedition had become sick on bees' honey, the ravines became deeper and wooded. As we approached a narrow valley, Vicente sent de Morales back to notify all to be especially watchful, for the country appeared ideal for a surprise attack.

We at the front passed through without incident. A quick glance back seemed to confirm there was no problem for the rest of the expedition either. Suddenly, Vicente yelled for us to halt because there appeared to be disarray in our rear. We could see horsemen galloping in that direction, and a few riding up the eastern slopes. Captain Villagran sent his aide to order us to remain in place until further orders, and we did so. Soon after, we learned what had transpired. Most of the expedition had passed the point of greatest danger, but a number of our Indians and rear guard suffered a barrage of arrows from the heights above. One of them struck

---

[194] (1514-1578). This man is destined for important roles in the coming years.

a Tacna man, Juan Godínez, in the right shoulder.[195] Two of our Indians suffered injuries also. Captains de Miranda, de Aguirre, and their men confronted the savages and killed a large number of them. That evening, Valdivia announced that we would spend an extra day here so as to mend the wounded. We had to remain armed throughout the night and doubled the men on watch.

We saw no more hostiles on our journey to Cuquimpu. Two days from it, Valdivia sent Ancohualla, Paucar, Ayar, Vicente Montesinos and his men, with de Almagro and some horse soldiers along to provide extra protection, to meet the town *caciques*, and determine their intentions. They returned at the hour of None, having ridden back with particular urgency. Ancohualla said the town *caciques* seemed friendly enough. They refused to vouch, however, for the natives outside the town, who were agitated by our appearance among them and wished us ill. These men advised we stop only to restock our provisions and forthwith resume our march south.

When he heard this news, Valdivia summoned his captains in order to determine our response to this latest threat. When they had a plan, they called the lieutenants together. We must bypass the town, said the Captain, to the east, well away from the ocean coast. "Do you know a route around the town, de Mérida?" He asked this while gazing towards me intently. I assured him Ayar knew the land well, as he had traveled up the river that flows through the town with Lieutenant Alvarado looking for gold.[196] This brought an acknowledging head nod from the Captain.

He went on. "We must also avoid this town because it sits at the ocean's edge. Lieutenant Montesinos," he said as he gestured towards Vicente. "I remember you telling me in Cusco of the battle you Almagro men fought on the shores of the lake they call Poopo. The one that sits south

---

[195] (1517-1571). Besides de Mérida telling of this, this man mentions the incident in his *Declaratión de Juan Godínez*, in Medina, <u>Documentos Inéditos</u>, XII.

[196] De Mérida told of this in Part Q of the Second Letter, Volume I. Alvarado marched up the Elqui River to the Puclaro Reservoir in the search for gold, but found none.

of Laguna Titicaca. The Indians had trapped you on the shores in a heavy mist and could have killed you all if the vapors had remained. We must avoid that possibility here, since ocean clouds that may appear as we travel through the area could lead to a similar situation. That is all, men. Go with Santiago and with our Blessed Lady."

Later, Valdivia summoned me, Ayar, and the captains. When all had arrived, he asked me to tell of the course we planned to follow. I had discussed this with Ayar and so was able to do so. My single warning was that there existed two sites where the hills on either side might offer hiding places to natives intent on attacking us in our front or in our rear. After I answered questions, the Captain said he remained uneasy about the hostiles lurking in the vicinity. As a result, he ordered de Benito to take Montesinos, de Alderete, and thirty men and ride ahead of my guiding band as a further protection against an attack. Additionally, he directed de Miranda to bolster his rear guard force with de Almagro, Bohón, and fifteen horse soldiers.

After he excused us, the Captain asked me to remain with him and La Doña. They both gazed over the countryside towards the ocean and its beaches, and saw that trees and plants in all the different colors of green covered the land. While in Cusco, he remembered that Montesinos and I had told him of the uncommon beauty of this region. And it offered an additional attraction, he said. "Ancohualla and I have examined the soil, and we are agreed it should support more than one crop through the growing season, perhaps as many as three. We shall found a town here, Pedro, and call it La Serena.[197] It is of such natural splendor that we must return. We shall be back!" He said this last with much enthusiasm and much emotion.

After prayers on our Lord's Day and while preparing for the day's march, Captain de Benito rode up, bade me good day as was his habit, and said he planned to ride ahead with his men, as ordered by the Captain, and examine the country for possible hostile natives. When we left at the hour of Sext on Monday, November 25, the mist had become a fine drizzle.

---

[197] The Spanish will do just that in several more years.

Nothing happened the first two days. But on the third, a band of hostiles made their presence known. I learned from Montesinos soon thereafter what had occurred. Shortly after leaving us, de Benito and his men came on a large number of Indians defending a narrow pass, brandishing their clubs, maces, and spears with obvious battle intentions. These most likely were warriors who had once lived outside Huasco. De Benito attempted to take the defile with a charge of twenty horse soldiers two abreast, thinking their sword and riding skills should turn the matter to his favor quickly. To the surprise of all, however, the natives fought in a ferocious manner and stubbornly held their position. Fresh Indians who appeared added to their number, and the lot of them managed to fend off our attacks throughout the day.

Later, Captain de Benito devised an assault plan with Montesinos and de Alderete. He also sent a man back to Valdivia to request we remain in camp and await his word. On the ensuing day, they put their one hand closure plan into effect. While de Benito and his men remained at the bottom of the pass, Montesinos and ten horse soldiers moved into position to charge the Indians on their left flank. De Alderete did the same on the right with his ten. At the exchange of signals between these two, they and their men rushed the trapped natives. Besieged from left and right and caught in a vise, some chose to flee south, but found themselves surrounded and annihilated by the lieutenants and their horsemen, who showed no mercy or compassion. Those who tried to escape north, down the gully, met de Benito and his men, who cut them promptly to pieces. No Indians survived this encounter.[198] That late afternoon, we welcomed the men back and heard the story of their adventure, Sire, as I have told it.

Upon our departure on the new day, Montesinos came up to say de Benito had permitted a stop at the site of the drowning of our friend on the Almagro Expedition, Lieutenant Francisco de Valdéz, should they locate it.[199] We had discussed this with the other Almagro men, and Valdivia had agreed to a short stay for prayer and reflection to honor his memory.

---

[198] De Benito in his *Declaración* de Pero de Benito in Medina's <u>Documentos inéditos</u>, *XII*, mentions this skirmish.
[199] De Mérida tells of his death in, <u>The Adventure Chronicles,</u> Part R of Volume I.

Father Marmolejo offered to say prayers over his remains. At mid-day as we planned to stop for refreshment, Paucar said the de Benito men appeared in the distance and seemed to be examining the ground intently. When we rode up, they were looking for the grave, but Montesinos said even though this seemed like the spot, they had not found it yet. Indeed, this appeared to be the location I remembered. The Captain and the rest of the men approached and we searched for the small burial mound of rocks, to no avail. Captain de Benito exclaimed it looked to him as though the river a short distance away must have overflowed recently, since the banks looked disturbed. If so, the water might have swept all before it. This, we Almagro men accepted reluctantly. Father Marmolejo led us in prayer for our departed friend, and there the matter ended. Rest in peace, Francisco de Valdéz. We remember you with fondness and respect.

In the impending days we remained on high alert, now made more necessary by the march to Papudo, the town that saw the fierce Mapuche warriors attack the Almagro Expedition. A day past the small village of Limari,[200] while trodding ground rich with all manner of plants and small trees, de Almagro shouted that the earth was moving and swaying. We felt it as soon as he yelled, a feared *terremoto*. We jumped from our animals to quiet them, but the moving earth stopped within moments. The Captain ordered a halt for the night. With our camp up, the talk the rest of the day was about this frightening event.

A moment that soon would produce an occurrence of historic meaning came about on Tuesday, December 13, Exalted One, and briefly I must tell of it now. It concerned our priest, Father Diego Perez. At prayers he celebrated that morning, he dedicated them to Santa Lucía, as this was her feast day,[201] the patron saint of the blind, and said that he had an exceptional attachment to this saint. No one of us knew the nature of this connection until after the services. During the time for refreshment afterwards, La Doña asked Father as to his special devotion to the saint. With some emotion evident in his voice, he answered that his grandmother had been stricken blind when he was a small boy and

---

[200] This is today's Ovalle.
[201] As it still is today.

his parents, brothers, and sisters, cared for her in their home. And it happened that the entire family prayed always to Santa Lucía, that the old woman might regain her sight. One day, five years after her loss of vision, she fell down and hit her head on the ground. It was not a hard fall and she was unhurt by it. However, the most extraordinary thing happened as a result. She was able to see again. Father said it was a true miracle and that he would always remain close to Lucía. This produced a good deal of discussion amongst us as to the way of Our Lord and His Saints. It had a notable effect upon our Doña, for we could see her with tears in her eyes as she was talking with the Captain.

Three days from Papudo, de Benito and his men escorted Ancohualla and Paucar to meet the town *caciques* and determine the disposition of things. They returned in the afternoon of the next with the news that all seemed calm among the people and the Mapuche Indians remained far to the south. This was welcome news, yet we remained alert to the possible danger of an attack. On December 15, we passed through this town located on the Pacific Ocean shore, with fresh breezes cooling the land, and stayed immediately outside it. Having remained on our schedule, a surprise, Captain Valdivia said we would stay here for several days.

It is now that I shall end this Fourth Letter, Your Exalted Majesty. I pray it finds Your Honor in happiness at knowing more of the wonderful land that profits so greatly from Your beneficent rule.

I Remain, Majesty,   Your Most Humble Servant

Pedro de Mérida (signature)

Don Pedro de Mérida

Signed

November 12 1566

Santiago *del Nueva Extremadura*

THE FIFTH LETTER

Written to the King by Pedro de Mérida from Santiago *del Nueva Extremadura* on May 10, 1567.

PART NN

THE EXIT FROM PAPUDO; THE MARCH TO THE RÍO MAPOCHO; THE GREAT BATTLE OF THE HUELÉN AND THE FOUNDING OF SANTIAGO *DEL NUEVA EXTREMADURA*

Once more, Exalted Majesty, I take pen in hand to relate further adventures in the fabled land of *Nuevo Extremo*, or Chile, with Captain Pedro de Valdivia, in this, my Fifth Letter. In this correspondence, I shall recount events during the years 1540 through 1549 and shall indicate the years in which they took place.

I begin this relation in Papudo on Sunday, the Lord's Day, December 15 of 1540. Upon our arrival and friendly reception there, our Captain called together Captain Gómez de Benito, Ancohualla, Vicente Montesinos, Ayar, and me, to discuss our way to the east. We did not have with us a member of Lieutenant Alvarado's detachment, which Almagro sent from here to examine the land years before. As a result, we needed a guide to show us the route to the region Alvarado found, a place rich for farming and livestock, since that might be the terrain most suitable for settlement and the founding of our Santiago *del Nueva Extremadura*.

Ancohualla proposed to Valdivia that he, his *cacique* Paucar, who rode with me and my guiding group, and Ayar, would search for and locate such a man. They did so in short order, since the next day they put forth the name of a villager who had followed Alvarado and his men on their journey to the southeast. He had remained at a distance behind them, as he was afraid they might think him hostile. In this endeavor, he was obeying a village *cacique*'s order to learn more of Alvarado's intentions, whether warlike or peaceful. This Indian's name was Huenu. A man of twenty years, he was the son of one of the two town *caciques*, both of whom had welcomed Captain Almagro years before and had done so now with us. He remembered us, said Ancohualla, or more particularly, Vicente Montesinos, as my friend had given the young man a ride on his horse when we were here with Almagro. He remembered the ride and Vicente's blond hair. Huenu could not speak our language, but that meant little, since Anco, Paucar, and Ayar, could speak his. All three praised him, and Ancohualla was quite sure that he could be trusted. After consulting with de Benito, Montesinos, and me, Captain Valdivia gave his approval for him to join our guiding team. It was then that Ancohualla mentioned information he had received from Huenu's father, Manque, regarding a *toqui*, their name for a warrior *cacique*, preparing to confront us somewhere to the southeast. His reception would not be a pleasant one, however, for he harbored a deep hatred of all Christians.

I must tell of this *toqui*, Sire, as he would pose a stout force of resistance to us in the years ahead but eventually become our trusted friend. I deem it noteworthy that Anco had known him as a young man in Cusco. This warrior, Michimalongo, by name, possessed a noble heritage, as we learned from Ancohualla.[202] He was the son of an officer in one of

---

[202] For more about this warrior, see de Vivar, Jerónimo, C. XXIV, XXVII, XXX, Crónica y relación copiosa y verdadera de los reinos de Chile (Chronicle and abundant and true relation of the kingdoms of Chile). Also, see Lobera, Pedro Mariño, Chronicle of the Kingdom of Chile, Book First, Ch. X, XIII, XV. Both men arrived from Peru in 1551. See the Bibliography for the website addresses for these two historians.

the Inca armies sent to conquer Chile and a local Mapuche woman; his exceptional intelligence and character brought him to the notice of the Inca governor of the area, who sent the young Michimalongo to Cusco for his education, where he learned the Inca language and the means by which the Inca ruled their land. Ancohualla and Prince Paullu were young boys when Michimalongo took his training in Cusco.[203] Anco's father taught him the particulars of mountain and ravine warfare tactics, since that had been his unique knowledge as a *cacique* in the Inca's armies north of Cusco years before. As such, Ancohualla saw the Indian from the southern lands frequently upon his visits to his father for training. During his time in Cusco, he acquired a *Quechua* accent whilst speaking his native language. Because of this, they called him the Inca *Toqui*. He left the city after four years and returned home when Ancohualla had eight summers. This was the man who awaited our arrival someplace to the east. His circumstances involving Anco posed the possibility for an accord of understanding with him and the avoidance of warfare. Such was our hope. Ancohualla related also that Manque confirmed Michimalongo had not been the warrior *toqui* who led the attack upon us Almagro men during our stay here in Papudo years past. The Inca *Toqui* killed that Indian in a power struggle among the Mapuche[204] and seized the horse he had captured from the Almagro Expedition at the Battle of Papudo.[205] We Almagro men remembered that fight vividly from those days. With this as prelude, Excellency, I shall recount our march to the east on December 18, in the quest for a site to place our capital city and there begin a new stage in our lives.

Huenu had told the Captain and Ancohualla that the land Lieutenant Alvarado reached was on a river named the Mapocho.[206] It lay eleven to twelve days distant at the llama's gait. The order of march was that of the

---

[203] We know from the Fourth Letter that Ancohualla was born in 1510. Thus, he was four to eight years old while Michimalongo was in training in the Sacred City, 1514-1518. See Michimalongo, by Carlos Skeller, in *Pueblos Originarios*.

[204] The Mapuche Indians are indigenous to the Region of Araucania in southern Chile, below Santiago.

[205] The Battle of Papudo is recounted in, The Adventure Chronicles, Part R of Volume I.

[206] The Río Mapocho passes through and divides present day Santiago.

last months, with an emphasis upon readiness to repel any attacks from hostiles. Ten horse soldiers, under the command of Vicente Montesinos, now accompanied me and my guides, Paucar, Ayar, and Huenu. Captain de Benito, Juan Gómez de Almagro, Lope de Ayala, and seven more horse soldiers followed behind us. During this time, Vicente devoted many hours to instructing our new young scout in proper horsemanship, a skill that was to benefit him, and us, a great deal in future years.

On the morning of our second day on the march, Ancohualla, Rimac, and Paucar, rode ahead in an attempt to meet with the warrior *toqui*. Anco had suggested this to Valdivia as a means to convince Michimalongo that we Christians and Indians all came in peace, with the desire to farm, raise livestock, and remain friends with our neighbors. They carried two bags of blue beads as a gift of encouragement to enter into a discussion about our peaceful approach to his territory. They returned in two days with word that the Inca *Toqui*, on horseback and camped with his warriors on the banks of the Mapocho, welcomed Ancohualla, whom he remembered as a young boy in Cusco, and declared that he would not attack him or his people. After all, they were Inca, just as he was. We Spanish Christians, though, were unwelcome and must return north since there would be only bloodshed and death for us here. This response did not deter the Captain, or any of us. As preparation for what lay ahead, he asked those veterans of the Battle of Papudo years before to tell the officers of that fight so they might learn about the warriors we were to face and the tactics and weapons they employed.[207] We did so that evening.

Despite the heightened threat of attack from this Michimalongo, Your Highness, the coming days proved enjoyable as we passed through a land of vibrant beauty on our way southeast. High mountains lay off to the east, while green hills, shady meadows, and well-watered valleys surrounded us. At one point, we entered an impenetrable forest of close set trees with a canopy of thick branches and leaves that imposed a stifling darkness upon the world below. We kept a constant vigil for hostiles amongst the

---

[207] For more on the Mapuche military structure, see Cruz, Eduardo Agustin, "The Mapuche Military Components" in <u>The Grand Araucanian Wars in the Kingdom of Chile, Xlibris, 2010.</u>

silent murkiness, dark like the darkest night. When we emerged into the full light of day once more, the near complete blackness behind us there in the forest was like a shroud drawn about a corpse. And this new light now revealed what seemed another world following our months spent in the northern deserts, since around the few houses of the natives bright purple and orange flowers were in bloom. The colors alone gave the land great wealth. The landscape was gentle, and the deep green grass made us feel welcome in our new home. I knew we could live in contentment here, with wide spaces for crops and livestock and a mellow climate.[208] And provisions for our new town would not be difficult to obtain. Each day we passed through farm land with crops of avocado, *maize*, red and black beans, squash,[209] *papas*, olives, *cherimoyas*,[210] chili peppers, *quinua*, and stores of salt. There was as well an abundance of guanaco and an occasional antlered animal with tasty flesh.[211]

The peacefulness of the land ended on the fifth day, however, and quite suddenly. Traveling east near the river Huenu called Aconca-Hue[212] and south of the village of Llay-Llay,[213] we rounded the flank of a steep hill. Suddenly, one of Montesinos's men galloped towards us shouting that a horde of warriors stood to our front. We remained in place while he rode back to inform de Benito. Presently, the Captains Francisco de Villagran and de Benito rode towards us with thirty horse soldiers, including Gerónimo de Alderete, Juan Bohón, and de Almagro, and rushed past to confront the hostiles. Captain Valdivia came forward and trained his spy glass upon the nearby countryside, searching for Michimalongo, he said. We could hear the natives yelling in the distance for some moments. Then all became quiet. Our men soon drew towards us, and Villagran reported that 200 savages had sought to block our movement forward but

---

[208] The beauty of the land also struck Valdivia. See his Letter I, p. 143, in "Historical Sources" on the site.
[209] *Maize*, beans, and squash were known as the "three sisters" to native Indians throughout the Americas.
[210] The *cherimoya* is a sweet flavored fruit shaped like a pear.
[211] This was the south Andean deer, also known as the Chilean *huemul*.
[212] This is the Mapuche word for "comes from the other side." Its name today is the Río Aconcagua.
[213] This small town's population today is around 21,000.

that now all lay dead or dying. Captain Valdivia asked if they had seen Michimalongo. Villagran said they had not. But he observed that the Inca *Toqui* was most certainly the one who had set this trap for us.

We remained on alert as we continued our journey. On several days hostiles confronted us in bands of forty to fifty warriors, even on the birthday of Our Lord Jesus Christ. Blessed be His Name forever. Since the Indians fought on foot with slings, maces, spears, axes, and arrows, our men quickly dispatched the attackers. These weapons were no match for our horse soldiers and their swords as our men could kill an enemy before he employed fully a short, hand-held weapon. But their arrows, launched from a distance, though they could not pierce our breast chain mail and helmets, still inflicted leg and arm wounds. Our Doña, Father Lobo, and Juan Jufré, remained occupied each day, assisted by Pilca Huaca and Collardis, in cauterizing[214] wounds and applying a cooling cream to them.

On Monday, December 30[215] a half day north from the Río Mapocho, several hills rose to the southeast.[216] The Captain sent two detachments of horse soldiers under Rodrigo de Quiroga and Francisco de Aguirre to search for hostiles on their slopes. In the expected battle with the Mapuche at the Mapocho, our left flank would be exposed to attack from warriors there. The Captains returned in mid-afternoon to report that the hills concealed no Indians. This prompted Valdivia to send forward Montesinos and Juan Bohón, with sixteen men and Huenu, to discover the Indian forces we knew awaited us and report their positions and alignments. I should offer here, Majesty, that Huenu was most eager to continue as our scout, as he knew the country of the Mapuche and enjoyed service to Your Majesty. Also, he did not consider himself to be one of Ancohualla's Inca contingent and was thus eager to fight with us.

---

[214] Cauterization was a common practice during the Middle Ages. The reader may recall that Father Molina used it on several occasions during the Almagro Expedition.

[215] De Mérida corroborates Valdivia's statement in his Letter I, p. 128 that "....I reached this valley of Mapocho towards the end of 1540."

[216] These are Cerros Guanaco, Manquehue, and Peñon,

The men returned before nightfall with the information that several hundred Mapuche were on the southern bank of the Mapocho, a long line of warriors ready to repel our advance across the river. To their east rose a hill that posed a threat to our flank and would require a search for hostiles.[217] Through his spy glass, Bohón had seen an additional three thousand warriors preparing their evening repast below another hill, called by Huenu, Huelén, residing a short distance from the southern bank of the river. That evening, Valdivia assembled the officers, including Ancohualla and his four *caciques*, for discussion and planning before the coming battle. He designated Villagran and de Benito to work with him to form a battle plan, based upon the information from Montesinos and Bohón, that we could employ when he deemed it appropriate to do so. He then addressed us further:

"Gentlemen, the esteemed Ancohualla and his *caciques* are with us, at his request, for he has a proposal he recommended to me that I find compelling and I want all of you to learn of it. I am disappointed in myself that I failed to think of it first." He smiled as he said this and looked to Anco with a head nod of respect and acknowledgement. He continued. "He suggests before giving battle that we allow him and his men to again speak to the Inca *Toqui* and seek a resolution to our circumstances. We come in peace, as we have always said, and Anco thinks he might convince this Michimalongo that we can live with each other amicably. Instead of using blue beads as a sign of friendship, Anco proposes that we make a treaty that promises we Christians shall never attack him or his people. Further, we will share with him seeds of fruits and vegetables that his people need. And we shall provide him pigs, chickens, and goats, when they breed and have offspring. If these offerings are insufficient, the final one will be that of horses, at a number of my reckoning, which will be used only to haul goods and not for warfare."

He then asked us to comment. The strongest words came from the Captains, especially Villagran and de Benito. They argued passionately that horses must not be part of a bargain under any circumstances. Our horses provided the decisive battlefield advantage over the Mapuche

---

[217] This is Cerro San Cristobal.

warriors, as we Almagro men knew from the Battle of Papudo, and that to lose that advantage would doom us. Our Captain listened intently to these comments from his respected Captains, one the veteran of the Italian wars, the other the follower of Hernán Cortés. Valdivia gazed at both men intently, then gripped the hand of each in a tight grasp. "It will be as you say, my stalwart Captains!" I looked across to Montesinos and de Alderete, standing just feet away. Our expressions conveyed our silent relief.

Ii is time to say more, my King, and I deem it a privilege to do so, concerning this distinguished man of mental substance, Francisco de Villagran, since in later years he became the Royal Governor of Chile on three occasions and has served Your Majesty with the highest distinction. He was born in Santervás de Campos[218] to parents of modest means and unmarried. Because of the latter, he took the name of his mother, Ana Velázquez de Villagran. His early education was at an academy for boys, in the nearby city of León, run by an order of priests one day known as the Jesuits.[219] He showed himself to be of a manly spirit and indifferent to most forms of pleasure, except for the kind that honored and successful men earn by their own endeavors. The priests expected their boys from the first to be intensely conscious of what others thought of them, take any criticism deeply to heart as well as to enjoy praise, and any young man who remained indifferent to these sentiments they saw as one who lacked any desire to excel. This kind of ambition his Jesuit education firmly implanted in the young Villagran. On the other hand, he displayed occasionally an inborn deference to those above him, such as one might not expect to discover in those of his standing. But, he saw this as a means of achieving his own ends, a quality that a number of men regard as a necessary part of political calculation.[220]

---

[218] (1511-1563).

[219] St. Ignatius of Loyola, a Spanish soldier who, after being wounded in battle and experiencing a religious conversion, founded the Society of Jesus in 1534. In 1540, Pope Paul III formally approved the new order.

[220] Throughout history, this has been one of the traits of a politician.

His training complete, he joined Your Majesty's service in the Italian wars with Captain Valdivia,[221] and learned the trade of the military man through a number of years and battles. He was left handed, but taught himself to use his right hand and arm to employ his sword. Upon leaving the service, he worked as a minor official in the *Cabildo* of León, a position that he enjoyed and that served him well in his duties as Governor of Chile. The Conquest of the Americas soon caught his interest, and he arrived in Peru in 1538. With friends he made, he planned to free Diego de Almagro, whom the Pizarro brothers had imprisoned in Cusco. Discovered in this attempt, they condemned him to death, but Hernando Pizarro spared him because of his military exploits against Italy. He had to retire from Cusco when Captain Almagro was put to death, but came to the notice of Captain Valdivia in 1540, who recruited him for the expedition to Chile as a captain. He promised Valdivia to enlist men for our southern venture and stay temporarily in Tacna near the coast with them, awaiting word of when to join our expedition and where.

As to his personal characteristics, there was notable dignity in his countenance and bearing, enough to demand one's notice. As an aside, I should add that when he talked he looked to his left a moment or two before returning his gaze to the listener. This was distracting to some, although not to most. Another habit that drew attention was pointing to an object or direction while discoursing. In so doing, he bent his inner fingers to his palm, with the thumb over them, and pointed with the index and little finger fully extended. When in a light mood, he whistled through his teeth, so that those nearby knew of his agreeable temper. He was well-liked by all since he treated those around him with uncommon respect and courtesy.

I shall return now to the peace attempt with Michimalongo, Esteemed One. The following morning Ancohualla, Tupa, Paucar, and Rimac, left on horseback to meet the Inca*Toqui*, with Huayna to remain with us

---

[221] Spain fought Italy on several occasions during the years 1494-1559. In the early years, the Spanish military transformed its procedures, tactics, and weaponry and became a world power. This came at the appropriate time for the conquest of the Americas — Mexico, Central America, Peru, and Chile.

to govern our Indians. Captain Valdivia and the captains wished them success, and Valdivia urged Anco to take the time necessary to obtain a deal since it might involve days of negotiation. If the meetings proved successful, he asked Ancohualla to invite the Inca *Toqui* to join us here for the signing of an official document to record the agreement.

The next day, with Anco and his men still negotiating with Michimalongo, the Captain presented a battle plan for the coming fight, should one occur. The captains to lead our efforts were Villagran, de Benito, Rodrigo de Quiroga, and Francisco de Aguirre, with Lieutenants Vicente Montesinos, Gerónimo de Alderete, Juan Bohón, Juan Gómez de Almagro, Alonso de Monroy, Gaspar de Vergara, and Gaspar de Villarroel assuming important positions on the field. My place was with Montesinos, as I preferred and had requested.

On Wednesday, January 15, 1541, Ancohualla and his *caciques* returned to our camp. We could see at once that their mission had failed, for all of them wore serious, disappointed expressions. Valdivia summoned the officers immediately so that we might learn the particulars of the negotiations. As soon as Anco and his men had dismounted, Doña Inés and Pilca Huaca gave them refreshments. Ancohualla then spoke in this fashion:

"My Captain, Michimalongo was kind to us and treated us well. He listened to your proposal and, though tempted by your terms, I failed to convince him that you have come in peace. His hatred for you Christians runs deep, and that hate prevents him from engaging in any manner with you. He, in turn, gives you an ultimatum that must be carried out by tomorrow, when the sun is at its highest point in the heavens. You must leave this land or you all will die a painful death, for your hearts will be cut from your chests and fed to the condors of the air and the animals of the land!"

There was a stir from amongst the men at these threatening words from the Inca *Toqui*. I looked over at Hernando Vallejo, who had made a fist with his right hand and beat it repeatedly into the palm of his left. The

Captain praised the work of Ancohualla and his *caciques* and stated his reaction thusly: "If Ancohualla and his men, of the same blood as the Inca *Toqui*, have failed to reach an agreement with him upon peace, it seems to me, gentlemen, that it is God's will that this be so and thus unalterable by us." We prepared for battle at the instant and I sent Ayar and Huenu to stay with Ancohualla, since they possessed no military skills, despite Huenu's pleas to remain with us.

On the morning following, after our priests, Juan Lobo, Diego Perez, and Rodrigo Gonzáles Marmolejo, had blessed us all, we arranged ourselves according to the plan designed by Valdivia and Villagran. We all knew our places since we had practiced our positioning while we awaited Anco and his *caciques*. On the far edge of the left wing, Lieutenant de Alderete commanded ten men. This force would search the hill near the Mapocho for warriors in ambush and protect our left flank.[222] These men had left already at daybreak. To de Alderete's right, and still on the left, was Captain Rodrigo de Quiroga, with de Villarroel as his next in command, and thirty men. At the center stood Captain de Aguirre, assisted by Pedro Cisternas, the "gunner," and his ten musket men. On the right wing was Captain de Benito, with Montesinos and me as part of his thirty horse soldiers. Behind this array of our forces, Captain Valdivia placed himself in the middle of the field, with Lieutenants de Monroy and de Vergara as his assistants to carry his orders to any officer on the field. In the rear, the reserve force of fifty horse soldiers, under the command of Captain Villagran, with Bohón and de Almagro as his lieutenants, remained ready to deploy to any part of the battlefield where they might be directed, with Bohón and his twenty-five arrayed to the Captain's left and de Almagro and his men to the right. The remaining men, not deployed, were either recovering from wounds or sickness and were under the care of La Doña and Father Lobo or were guarding de Hoz and the other malcontents.

With the sun still low on the horizon, Valdivia ordered us forward, our banner waving in the breeze with four horsemen guarding the standard bearer, Lope de Ayala. From our position a mile from the Mapocho, we advanced at a walk until we were 500 yards from the river and stopped

---

[222] As footnoted previously, this is Cerro San Cristobal.

at the Captain's orders. We could hear the Mapuche savages chanting, yelling, and calling us women and little girls. De Aguirre and his men proceeded to the river's northern bank, and five musket men took position to the left and five more to the right, the two groups separated by two hundred feet. They used their low forks for aiming and reclined on the ground behind their muskets. The Mapuche on the opposite bank stood in place, yelling, brandishing their weapons, and motioning us to come forward. Little did they know what was about to come their way.

Upon the signal from Valdivia, de Aguirre ordered his men to commence firing, the left most group at an oblique angle to the left of the warrior line, the right set obliquely to the right. The intent was to kill warriors at those places so that the horse soldiers of de Quiroga and de Benito could charge across the river through the openings of dead Mapuche, attack their rear, and strike the Indians behind them clustered about the Huelén. Plumes of smoke rose above the muskets as Indians fell on the opposite shore. They continued shouting, but now with less exuberance. My hands were sweating, as they usually did before battle. I looked over to Vicente. "They have never seen or heard anything like our muskets!" he shouted. After reloading, our men fired again. More hostiles fell and, once they had seen more of their friends dead or dying and hearing again the terrible blasts from the muskets, they all began to turn and flee to the hoped-for safety of the several thousand warriors positioned near the Huelén.

Our time had come. Having received the signal from Valdivia to ride forward, we formed into two columns and moved across the river to the now vacant opposite shore. De Quiroga and his men did the same to our left. Before we reached the bank, Lieutenant Bohón came up behind and shouted the Captain's orders to de Quiroga and de Benito. We formed up in a single line on the river's edge and awaited the Captain's swift arrival. The scene we witnessed to the south was somewhat chaotic among the hostiles, no doubt the result of the encounter with the musket men and their fear of them. The warriors were in no recognizable formations and moved about seemingly without direction. Amidst them, a warrior on horseback, who could only be the Inca *Toqui*, attempted to restore order in their ranks. We remained in place, with our horses snorting, twitching nervously, and straining at the reins, eager to gallop forward. Suddenly, Valdivia shouted, "They want to cut our hearts from our chests and feed them to the birds and the beasts! Give them the bolt, men. Santiago and at them!"

We charged towards the Mapuche, who seemed to have recovered their composure, for they brandished their weapons, screamed their war cries, and called us unspeakable names. We were among them in mere moments, chopping, slashing, stabbing, our Toledo steel slicing their flesh and splashing their blood as we guided our horses through and around them. Horse soldiers had never attacked them before, so there was fear upon their faces as we confronted them at close quarters. Vicente, Juan Almonacid, and I killed savage after savage. Since they could not tell which of us to strike, they hesitated; by the time they had decided upon action, they were writhing on the ground in their death throes.

Then we became aware of a large number of warriors coming at us from behind the Huelén. It must have been two thousand or more. It reminded me of the sudden appearance of countless Indians at the Battle of Papudo years ago with Captain Almagro. Valdivia called out to re-form back near the river. We did so, as he consulted with his captains. We remained at the ready and watched intently the Mapuche and their movements with our stoic, hardened expressions. Soon, Valdivia came up behind and yelled out his new orders. After a few moments, we understood what we were to do and were ready to do it. Just as we were about to charge, the hostiles started to run towards us. Gathered in our battle units behind the captains, we began to ride towards the Mapuche to effect a massive blow to their center, charge through to their rear, and encircle them in a double-hand closure. The savages attacked us at the run, screaming and waving their battle weapons, until they stopped suddenly, to our great surprise, and pointed skyward with hand and arm gesticulations as though they saw something threatening in the sky above. The captains ordered us to halt since the strange events occurring were deeply confusing. I turned and yelled to Almonacid as to what was happening, for we looked upward and saw nothing. He shrugged his shoulders, as though saying, "I don't know."

In the meantime, the Indians began to fall back, still gazing upwards, pointing at what we knew not, then turned about, threw down their arms, and fled hastily to the rear. Montesinos yelled to me that he could see Michimalongo in the distance, the sun's rays lighting up what must be large gold bracelets. As we watched, he rode off to the west. When Valdivia arrived, eager to take advantage of any luck or miracle that presented itself, he ordered us to charge and slaughter the fleeing Mapuche, although to take prisoners as well. Early in the afternoon, after our attack had driven the hostiles to the south and west, the order came to cease hostilities, return to camp with the prisoners, and seek medical help for the few injured among us. Hundreds of dead Mapuche lay across the fields between the Huelén and the Mapocho, their bodies a testament to the fighting superiority of us Christians. May it be forever thus.

Later, when we had returned to our campsite and rested, Captain Valdivia announced that La Doña, Ancohualla, Ayar, and Huenu, had questioned the prisoners to determine what they had seen in the sky. La Doña said the consistent story was that the sky above had opened and a man on a white horse with a long sword in his right hand rode forth and threatened the Indians with annihilation. And just as he seemed ready to descend and massacre them all, they turned and ran for their lives. The Captain then said that the captains and a number of lieutenants were presented to the prisoners and asked if any of our men had been the warrior in the sky. They all responded that the man in the heavens was much superior to any of our men. It was at this point that Valdivia asked Father Marmolejo to join the interrogation and provide his observation. He did so and replied that it had to have been the glorious Apostle *Santo Iago*, come to protect the new city named after him by Valdivia months before! The Captain dropped to his knee, clutched his statue of our Mother Mary, and recited words to himself before rising and thrusting his clenched right fist skyward. These events, Your Highness, made the deepest impression upon us all, and the Captain led us in a heartfelt prayer of gratitude to Blessed *Santo Iago*. On the new day, Valdivia asked Ancohualla and his *caciques* to locate Michimalongo, return the prisoners, and tell him that Valdivia returned his men to him in a gesture of friendship.[223]

And so, the Battle of the Huelén, the first encounter with the Inca *Toqui* and one of more to come, came to a close.[224] Your Majesty may think it strange that Valdivia failed to mention *Santo Iago's* appearance in his first letter to Your Highness. May I explain? I recall the Captain saying that *Santo Iago* had come to protect the town he had decided months before in Copayapu to name in his honor, Santiago *del Nueva Extremadura*.[225] And so this incident was unsurprising to him. As to the fact that only the Mapuche saw the vision, but no one of us Christians, I have no credible response.

We spent time now in attending to the few wounded we had, including Vicente, who had sustained a slight gash from a spear, and preparing large camping areas for us and our Indians. La Doña, Father Lobo, Juan Jufré, Pilca Huaca, the Medical *Cacica*, and Collardis, looked after the injured. Valdivia selected a large area below the Huelén, a spot close to the Mapocho, as the location of our camp. Ancohualla and his people chose a site with rich soil and farmland on the opposite side of the river. This position the Captain had suggested since he wanted our Indians at a distance from our settlement because it might be under attack from the Mapuche in the future and this could put our Indian friends in danger.

Captain Valdivia convened a meeting the next afternoon and said that we would no longer call the hill the Huelén, but Santa Lucía, in honor of the favorite saint of Father Perez. She was not only the patron of the blind but

---

[223] Lobera, in <u>Chronicle of the Kingdom of Chile,</u> Book First, Ch. X and XI, tells of the battle and the appearance of *Santo Iago*. Also see de Vivar, C. XXXVIII, <u>Chronicle and Abundant and True Relations of the Kingdom of Chile</u>. But, since neither was in Chile at the time, de Mérida's description provides more detail than they do.

[224] This battle was the first of many during the Araucanian, or Arauco, Wars, 1541-1883.

[225] See Part LL of the Fourth Letter. Valdivia does not mention the Saint's appearance in his Letter I, so de Mérida's explanation seems to answer the question as to why not.

carried a palm branch besides, the symbol of victory of good over evil. At the base of the Santa Lucía, our men and Indians constructed a structure and put there Valdivia's statue of Our Blessed Mother, which he had carried strapped around the horn of his saddle pommel throughout our journey. Valdivia asked Father Marmolejo to chant prayers there every sunrise, a most noteworthy sign of honor for this highly respected priest.

I should insert here, Sire, that despite our lack of wine these many months we still went to prayers on Our Lord's Day and prayed on our knees and sang the Ave Maria and other hymns, because it was our duty as Christians to do so and a good habit that someday should benefit our souls before the Almighty.

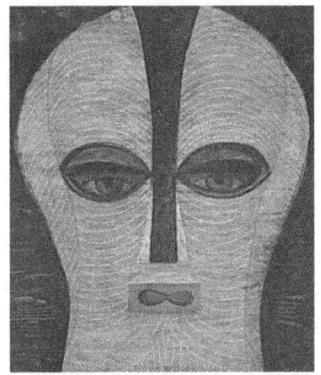

PART OO

CONSTRUCTION OF SANTIAGO *DEL NUEVA EXTREMADURA*; THE FORMATION OF OUR *CABILDO*; ANOTHER ENCOUNTER WITH THE INCA *TOQUI*; THE EVENTS AT MARGA MARGA; LOCATING VALPARAÍSO HARBOR

*N*oble Excellency, the construction of our capital city and the town for our Indian friends began in February of 1541, when Valdivia and Ancohualla conducted the appropriate foundation ceremonies on the twelfth day of that month. This date does not accord with that of February 24, which Valdivia indicated in his Letters I and II to Your Majesty. February 12 is the day recorded by the city *Cabildo* and therefore takes precedence over Captain Valdivia's date.[226] To return to the founding ceremonies, they ended when

---

[226] De Mérida does not offer a reason for the two dates. Thayer Ojeda does. See <u>Historiadores de Chile</u>, I, 67, as cited by Ida Stevenson Weldon. De Mérida is correct, however, that the Santiago *Cabildo* used February 12 as the foundation date.

the Captain placed a large cross in the small structure near Santa Lucía. Our priests blessed it and led us in prayer and song as we all knelt in thanks to our gracious Lord.

Within days, construction work began on Santiago town, guided by the detailed plan of the master builder,[227] or *alarife*, Pedro de Gamboa. The drawing that accompanies this Letter shows the location of the capital city at the foot of the Santa Lucía and to its west. The Río Mapocho is out of sight a half mile to the north.[228] In like manner, *alarife* Captain Pedro de Miranda started a similar town construction effort with our Indians, using his drawing illustrating a layout with streets radiating out from a main square akin to the central plaza in Cusco.

IMAGES: Please see 5NN-PP.8 and .9 for depictions of de Gamboa's grid plan for Santiago *del Nueva Extremadura*.

As to the daily work directed by de Gamboa in building our city, Valdivia was the most determined worker of us all on whatever task, whether it be to carry earth and stone upon his back, or help dig building foundations, carry water, build walls, or make bricks and tiles. We officers and men followed his example, as we knew this was our town and only with our hard effort would we build it. A matter of interest presented itself in a few days. Montesinos, de Alderete, de Almagro, Huenu, and I encountered old stone foundation structures as we cleared the area for the Plaza Mayor. Nearby, a circular set of rocks revealed an underground spring, with water flowing through its depths, no doubt from the nearby Río Mapocho. Gerónimo saw our Captain and *alarife* de Gamboa a short distance off and strode over to tell them of our discovery. They joined us quickly, and de Gamboa examined the sunken stream with his head cocked to the left, as was his habit.[229] Many of our Indian friends were at work with us, and one pointed to the stones and kept saying, "Inca. Inca." Valdivia dispatched Huenu to seek out Ancohualla and have him join us. After a brief examination, he observed that the stonework was that of the Inca

---

[227] Both de Gamboa and de Miranda held this title for many years.
[228] The original design of Santiago is in Appendix C.
[229] This was due to the blindness in his left eye.

army soldiers sent to conquer Chile many years before. He had no idea what had become of those who had inhabited this region in the past.[230]

I shall describe here, Noble Excellency, master builder de Gamboa's grid layout in the drawing so that Your mind's eye may comprehend better the nature of its simplicity and practicality. Parallel streets, nine in number, extended from the base of Santa Lucía and proceeded west at a distance of fourteen blocks. Fifteen other streets intersected these at right angles from north to south. This created fourteen squares measured from east to west, as may be seen. The width of the streets was twelve yards and, as they were cut at right angles, formed squares enclosed by four streets. These squares numbered more than 100, each subdivided into four lots. The Captain assigned officers to reside in selected squares and designated a lot upon which to build their houses. The central square he designated as the Plaza Mayor. On its western side resided the Church and parish house of the priests, and on the northern the government palace and prison. The instructions from the master builders for both our and our Indians' towns were to use clay for the foundations, wood for the walls, and straw for the roofs.[231] This type of construction, though, was to prove disastrous, in light of future events, as I shall relate to Your Honor at the appropriate time.

A brief further word about Pedro de Gamboa, Your Majesty, as his partial blindness was an uncommon physical circumstance. As I stated in my Fourth Letter, he lost his left eye in a battle with Indians outside Cusco. Rather than bemoan this terrible physical loss, instead he prided himself upon it in an unostentatious fashion, in a modest manner and without pretention. Others did not bear the evidence of their brave endeavors, yet the mark of his heroism remained continually upon display. When men saw what he had lost, they regarded it as proof of his valor. If another sought to provide a special favor for him in light of his injury, however,

---

[230] Several Chilean archaeologists testify to these rock foundations as Incaic and wonder that Valdivia did not mention them in his Letter I to the King.

[231] This description by de Mérida is similar to that of Luis Galdames. See his History of Chile, p. 40.

he quickly refused the offer, prompting an even greater respect for him. Such a man was the master builder.

To return to my recounting, in the weeks since beginning construction of our city, Valdivia, in consultation with Villagran, had turned his attention to the city's governance. On March 7, the following *Cabildo* appointments were announced: City mayors: Francisco de Aguirre and Juan Jufré. City council presiding officer: Francisco de Villagran. City council members: Juan Fernández Alderete, Juan Bohón, Martín de Solier, Gaspar de Villarroel, Gerónimo de Alderete. Chief Constable: Juan Gómez de Almagro. Deputy Constable: Gaspar de Vergara. Master builder of Santiago: Pedro de Gamboa. Master builder of our Indian city: Pedro de Miranda. Royal treasurer: Rodrigo de Quiroga. Planning director: Antonio Zapata.[232] City attorney: Antonio de Pastrana. Medical officer: Inés de Suárez. Scribe: Luis de Cartagena. Records keeper: Esteban de Sosa. Representative of the Church: Father Rodrigo Gonzáles Marmolejo.[233] Indian observers: Ancohualla and Tupa. Two of our *Cabildo* appointees were to prove unworthy in their positions, Majesty, as events in the coming months will confirm. As to the functioning of the *Cabildo*, the members found that their duties of building the city, planting, tending, and harvesting crops, as well as the everyday duties of patrolling our settlement, limited the amount of time they had to attend meetings for many months to come.

I must add here, Your Honor, that Ancohualla created a similar ruling structure for our Indians, calling it an *Ayuntamiento*.[234] He was the town mayor and his *caciques* composed the city council and performed other *ayunta* duties as required. Pedro de Miranda served as their *alarife*, as I have indicated before. The Church's representative was Father Lobo. Of course, Pilca Huaca held the important post of medical officer, as she was the *Cacica* for Medical Matters. Some of the *Cabildo* members with special skills, such as our treasurer, planner, and scribe, assisted at the Indian *Ayuntamiento* meetings.

---

[232] (1514-1592).
[233] Ida Weldon corroborates these appointments in <u>Pedro de Valdivia</u>, p. 78.
[234] This is the Indian name for the Spanish *cabildo*.

We celebrated Lady Day, Sire, on her day of Tuesday, March 25. Father Marmolejo in his sermon bestowed great praise upon her and said that she would help us bring the Light, the Light of our Christ, to our Mapuche brothers living in the Dark. The ensuing days and weeks saw four lieutenants chosen every week by Valdivia to lead ten men in different directions from our camp to look for friendly Indians. We wished to convince them of our peaceful intentions and ask that they join us to help build new towns. One of Ancohualla's *caciques*, except Pilca Huaca, rode with each group to serve as translator. Eventually, more than 500 Indians decided to help us.

Here I must tell of yet another encounter, Sire, with the Inca *Toqui*. It came about in this manner. In the middle of May 1541, one of the groups of men mentioned above searching for hospitable natives, the one sent out west, brought in thirty such Indians. Huenu and Ayar happened to engage in conversation with them and came upon remarkable information. Michimalongo and his men had built a large fortress *pukará* near a site called Marga Marga.[235] They seemed to be preparing for war, though the Indians were uncertain of this. They found out as well that near this same Marga Marga there was a gold mine with hundreds of miners working in it. Valdivia learned of this immediately. This matter of gold had been on most of our minds occasionally over the past months. We Almagro men, in moments of idle conversation, wondered aloud where in Chile the gold came from in the gold caravan we encountered north of Tucma.[236] The Captain too had the same question about that shipment. Perhaps this Marga Marga was the place!

Once Valdivia had taken counsel with his captains about what we should do, he informed us of his plans. The first objective was to find the Inca *Toqui* and destroy him and his Mapuche warriors, he said. Our second was to discover the gold mines. And the third would be to look for the port of Valparaíso. Eighty men were to comprise our force, with Captains

---

[235] The area of Marga Marga is some forty-five miles west from Santiago and lies on the southern outskirts of today's city of Quilpué. Nine miles farther west is the port of Valparaíso.
[236] See <u>The Adventure Chronicles</u>, Part I in Volume I.

de Benito, de Quiroga, de Aguirre, and Lieutenants Montesinos, de Alderete, de Vergara, Bohón, and I, as the officers in charge. La Doña would accompany us to care for the sick and wounded, while Huenu was to guide us to where he thought the *pukará* might be. And Ayar, who in the future wanted to lead trade caravans in this new land, joined us as well, to gain knowledge of the land and serve as a translator, if one were needed. The remainder of the men, under the command of Captain Villagran, was to remain in Santiago and protect it from attack. Furthermore, the men there would plant crops and direct Ancohualla and his people in the construction of town buildings while we were away.

The Captain included among our number a man who some thought a possible friend of Sancho de Hoz. This Gonzalo de los Ríos joined us in Copayapu and seemed, from the way he had hailed him, to be a compatriot of de Hoz, but had maintained his innocence ever since then. He took his grievance to Father Marmolejo, who found merit in what he had to say. Father accompanied him to a meeting with Valdivia and La Doña, and they convinced them that de los Ríos bore no evil intentions towards our leader and, in fact, had acted in the Captain's favor on occasion since then. And Doña Inéz said that she might have been mistaken in thinking that he was one of those calling to de Hoz when they entered Copayapu. De los Ríos thanked her and begged Valdivia for a new chance to prove his worth. He had heard about the recent report of gold mines to the west, and said that he had worked as a boy in the silver mines of the Pyrenees with his father until embarking for the New World. He made the argument that he could be of worth in various aspects of our mining endeavors. Upon hearing the testimony of those involved, Captain Valdivia pardoned de los Ríos forthwith and included him in our contingent of reserves.

On June 9, we left Santiago, expecting to arrive at the *pukará* in two or three days. Ayar, Huenu, Montesinos, recovered now from his slight wound, and I rode out front at a brief distance from the rest of the force. Valdivia told us to use caution, since we did not want to alert the Mapuche to our approach. So our orders were for the four of us to seek concealment should we sight warriors or their fortress. Late on the Wednesday of

June 11, we became sensitive to sights and sounds since we were close to the warriors and their *pukará*. Vicente said he could "feel" them nearby. When we came to a slight rise of the ground, both Huenu and Ayar stopped abruptly in front of us, dismounted quickly, and pointed west to a hillside with a large, strange looking collection of branches, trees, and stones. Its lower slopes presented a good deal of open ground, while dense shrubs and trees obscured the upper part. Vicente commented that this was no Fortress Arequipa, only a collection of earth, rocks, intertwining tree trunks and branches.[237] Still, it was formidable in appearance notwithstanding.

We dismounted as they both came to us and motioned us back down the incline. When we were lower and out of sight, Vicente rode back and consulted with Valdivia. They joined us and we walked high enough for Valdivia to use his spy glass. He stared intently at the distant collection of rocks and trees and declared it was a fortress that surely must be Michimalongo's. Studying carefully the surrounding terrain, he noticed a point where the open ground met that of dense foliage at a trough that stretched a half mile from north to south. He noted also that there were no trenches perpendicular to it to protect its flanks. Were the Mapuche still building this *pukará*? The Captain thought so, for the warriors he could see were not in war-like dress or mood. Instead, they appeared to be performing construction tasks. "It seems to me that this is in our favor, gentlemen. We will take them by surprise, despite tonight's near full moon. And furthermore, our center forces will have the rising sun at their backs and the Mapuche will have its light straight in their faces." Upon returning to camp, Valdivia summoned all the men and explained what we had seen. Then, he arranged another meeting with the captains and lieutenants to discuss the battle plan.

IMAGES: Please see 5NN-PP.13 for a Google image of the possible site of this fort.

---

[237] Eduardo Cruz says that Mapuche forts were intended for temporary use and were typically constructed of the materials here used by Michimalongo. See p. 163, <u>The Grand Araucanian Wars</u>. Montesinos refers to the Battle of Fortress Arequipa in Parts X-Z in Volume I, the Third Letter.

The stratagem devised I shall describe briefly, as I know such details interest Your Highness. First, the deployment of men. On the left wing was Captain Rodrigo de Quiroga, with de Alderete as his next in command and twenty horse soldiers. At the center stood Captain de Aguirre, commanding a force of seventeen with Bohón as his second in command, with the musket men to remain in reserve until daylight. On the right wing, Captain de Benito was in place with Montesinos and me as part of his twenty horsemen. Captain Valdivia stationed himself in the middle of the field behind de Aguirre, with de Vergara as his assistant to carry his orders to any officer on the field and to command the reserve force of ten horse soldiers and five musket men. La Doña remained with the reserves.

Second, the plan of attack. Events were to commence before first light, as the moon would grant us the vision we needed. De Quiroga was to position his men perpendicular to the left side of the ditch and *pukará*, about a half mile south of its center. De Aguirre was to locate his force in a line frontal to the long trough, while de Benito was to array his men perpendicular to the northern right side of the ditch and fortress, distant by a half mile from the center. We were to remain silent as we advanced and our actions must be slow and deliberate so our movements made no noise. Once in position, and upon hearing the second of two musket shots, all three groups were to charge. The flanking forces would get behind the farthest extension of each end of the trench, while de Aguirre would attack forward and engage the center. At some point, the north and south extensions of the trench would be under our control, and the flanking elements could move behind the center of the Mapuche line and link with de Aguirre to complete the encirclement. This plan presented a difficult method of attack and depended upon precise timing and coordination. As You are aware, Majesty, the Captain was partial to this formation and called it "the single-hand closure."[238] Yet, as we all know, things often go awry in battle and tactics must change as a result. But we were prepared

---

[238] This is the envelopment and does, as de Mérida says, require exceptional coordination skills by the commander and instant responses to commands by his subordinates.

for any exigency, for the Spanish cavalryman is the best and most efficient of any horse soldier in history.

We left our camp fires unlit that evening to avoid giving away our positions to the Mapuche, and arose when the moon first shed its light above the dark horizon. Vicente and I shared llama *charqui* and red berries[239] we had picked near camp. Soon thereafter, Valdivia ordered us to mount and proceed at the quiet towards the assault positions. "Go with God, my men," was his hushed admonition. Captain de Benito, with his order to, "Follow me!" given with marked determination in his voice, led us in columns of two bunched closely together so we might find the way. We proceeded northwestwards slowly and silently to a point of his choosing north of the trench and *pukará*. When he raised his hand and arm to halt, the moon was higher in the heavens and first light appeared on the eastern horizon. We gazed towards the ditch and *pukará* in silence as gradually the light granted further definition. De Benito gestured to us to gather round him and, in a hushed voice, commented that we had succeeded in getting to this spot undetected, for there were no Mapuche in the trench or outside it. "This *pukará* is their Tenochtitlán, and we will take it from Michimalongo as we did that one from Montezuma!" He said this with considerable emotion in remembering those times. He then ordered us to form files facing south, with Montesinos on the right, me on the left, and de Benito behind us ready to help when and where necessary. Vicente's task was to lead his ten men to the right of the trough's end and try to maneuver in behind it. My orders were to proceed with my men to the front of the ditch. Then, both our lines were to turn towards one another and crush the Mapuche between us.

In a short time, we were in position and silently awaited the two musket shots, our horses snorting nervously, shaking their heads, and moving restlessly forward and back. Times like these are difficult for me also and my mouth goes dry in response. Just as the sun had created enough light to see clearly, a musket shot rang out from the east. After that, another. This was the moment. When de Benito shouted, "Santiago,

---

[239] These would have been the Chilean strawberry, still cultivated in this area today.

and at them, my men!" we set off at a full gallop towards the trench and *pukará*. We could see movement now, with Mapuche running from their fortress towards the trough in a piecemeal and uncoordinated fashion. Obviously they were confused and surprised. When we arrived at our end of the trench, only a few warriors had reached it. De Benito yelled, changed my orders, and directed me to lead my men to the ground above it and support Montesinos in confronting the Indians trying to attain it. It became quickly a bloody affair since most of the hostiles had left their weapons in the ditch the day before and this forced them to hurl rocks and swing tree branches. This end of the trench was almost ours when de Benito shouted to Montesinos to shift towards the center, for de Aguirre and his men were fighting Mapuche who had made it to the middle of the trough and were putting up a spirited fight. At this instant, something demanded my attention. Off to one side I saw Vicente's man, Rodrigo Sánchez,[240] clinging to his saddle with a spear in his side. His horse galloped from the scene and stopped a short distance from us, where he fell lifeless to the earth.

152 My concentration returned to the ditch as we were beginning to turn the battle in the center to our favor. Abruptly, shouts rang out from the south, from de Quiroga's troops. The Inca *Toqui* had surrendered and was in the custody of Captain de Quiroga! Then we heard a singing noise above us, like that of a flute our *qamchus* used to entertain us. After that, another. Surprisingly, the warriors near us, those still alive, sat down where they were and stayed motionless. De Benito yelled to hold our positions and watch the hostiles for any sign of movement. They remained silent and inactive, however, and presented no threat. We learned later that this singing arrow was Michimalongo's signal that all fighting should cease.

Valdivia arrived with his men and proceeded to the south side of the trough and *pukará*. Once there, he waved to de Aguirre and de Benito to join him and de Quiroga, and we saw them talking with Michimalongo. Vicente observed that the *Toqui* was taller than any of his countrymen

---

[240] This man's name appears on the expedition list of Errazuriz, but nothing else is known of him. Lobera mentions him in C. XIII, but not the details of his death.

and stood as straight as the barrel of a musket. Near the hour of None, de Benito rejoined us and said that we were to return to our encampment, with the Inca *Toqui* and his *caciques* as our prisoners. There, Valdivia and the captains would continue the negotiations. We left the trough and *pukará*, the Mapuche still silent and unmoving. We killed three hundred and fifty warriors in our surprise attack, in this, the Battle of Marga Marga. Our causalities were one man killed and twenty wounded, most of them struck by stones or tree branches. La Doña saw to their needs in a special part of camp reserved for them.

Late the following day, June 13, Valdivia gathered all of us to reveal the state of affairs. Michimalongo had offered to show us the location of the gold mines and to give them to us, along with four large sacks of gold, in exchange for his release and the free passage of his warriors from this place. This the Captain had agreed to. Additionally, the *Toqui* offered 1,200 young men, with their *yanaconas*,[241] and 500 women to work the mines. As it happened, these women and their children had been in another part of the *pukará* during our attack. Captain Valdivia refused the tender of the women, as he believed it a grave sin to treat them in such a manner, and said they must accompany the Inca *Toqui* instead. Still, he accepted the offer of the men.[242]

In two days more, things had become more stable as Michimalongo and his people had departed the scene, and Valdivia had the bags of gold he needed to purchase tools and goods from Peru to build and grow our capital town. Two men, Pedro de Herrera,[243] a man who held himself excessively erect while riding as well as while standing, and Diego Delgado,[244] a facially creased man with unusually yellow skin, both familiar with mining operations in Peru, Captain Valdivia put in

---

[241] In the Inca system, these men were a level above the common Indian. In this case, these are the mine's supervisors

[242] De Vivar, C. XXXI and XXXII, tells most of the Marga Marga story, but lacks the intimate details provided by de Mérida. So too with Lobera and his recounting of it in C. XIII.

[243] (1510-1589). He was one of de Aguirre's men who joined Valdivia in Copayapu.

[244] Lobera tells of this man in C. XIII but we know little else of him since de Mérida does not mention him again.

charge of the mining natives. And Gonzalo de los Ríos, the man pardoned by the Captain, was given fifteen men and appointed as protector of the mine and miners from hostile attack.[245] On another matter, Your Honor, de Herrera learned later that the Marga Marga Station mines were the source of gold tributes to the Inca in Cusco in years past. This confirmed what most of us had thought to be the case.

The time was now propitious to accomplish Valdivia's third goal, to identify the port area of Valparaíso, as the first two, the defeat of the Inca Toqui and the finding of the gold mines, were now complete. To these, the Captain added a fourth –- the building of a small brig to sail to Peru to purchase supplies. Since our entire force was not necessary for this, the Captain directed the men to return to Santiago and guard it from possible attack. To accompany him west, he chose Villagran, de Benito, Vicente, me, twelve men from the overall force who knew something of ship building, Huenu, Ayar, and our Doña. She came with us since the wounded men had recovered or were able to make the journey back to our town and there enter the care of Juan Jufré and Father Lobo.

Concerning the port for the new city, Valdivia declared that in a visit with Francisco Pizarro in the City of Kings before our departure to this new land, he had met Captain Juan de Saavedra,[246] who had ventured south of Papudo in a failed attempt to locate the Almagro Expedition years ago. Instead he had found a harbor site that might prove ideal to serve our needs. Captain Saavedra provided a description of the region and its latitude coordinate, with which the Captain could use an astrolabe to locate the port.[247] Saavedra had named this harbor Valparaíso, in honor of his native village in Spain.

When camp was broken at mid-morning of June 16 and the rest of the force was on their journey back to Santiago, Vicente, Ayar, Huenu, and I, led our small band to the west. Huenu seemed to know exactly our

---

[245] See Lobera, Ch. XIII.
[246] This is the Captain of the *Santiaguillo* who met the Almagro Expedition in Cuquimpu several years before. See Part S of the Second Letter, Volume I.
[247] Apollonius of Perga invented an early astrolabe around 220 BC.

destination before attaining it, which seemed amusing. After a short while, Valdivia ordered a halt for refreshment, as there were berries nearby. While we enjoyed their sweetness, Valdivia pulled the astrolabe, or "ring,"[248] as he referred to it, from his saddle bag, clutched the disk, and began to explain its operation. Made of brass and seven inches in diameter, its rim was graduated in degrees of arc, with several flat plates made for specific latitudes, all engraved with circles denoting azimuth and altitude. I looked over to Vicente, who seemed engrossed completely in the description. I found myself incapable of understanding the explanation concerning the "ring," however, and looked occasionally towards the lush landscape all about us. The Captain having finished his lecture, we resumed our journey.

PHOTOS: Please see 5NN-PP.14 for a photo of an astrolabe.

When we drew closer to the ocean in mid-afternoon, Valdivia ordered a halt and adjusted his instrument to mark the latitude setting given him by Captain Saavedra, at 32°54′S. Meanwhile, we examined the landscape of the soon-to-be port station of Valparaíso. A spit of land to our left rose almost 400 feet high and formed the southern boundary of the harbor area with numerous sites for the docking of ships and placement of warehouses. The shoreline continued in a gentle curve to the north, producing additional land ideal for the storage of goods and locations for buildings and homes for those to work and live here. There were also level areas that would serve as salt harvesting sites. This place offered great beauty and a pleasant atmosphere within which we Christians could survive and prosper, and we all commented to this effect.

PAINTING: Please see P5.1 for the scene of the men looking upon Valparaíso harbor.

PHOTOS/IMAGES: See 5NN-PP.15 -.18 for depictions of the town and harbor of Valparaíso.

Captain Valdivia found a spot to build a ship, a wide forest with large stands of tall trees. As I have said, this boat one day was to sail to Peru,

---

[248] Mariners termed it a "ring" because of its circular construction.

Sire, the men to use the Marga Marga gold to purchase the goods we needed, after we had apportioned for Your Majesty the Royal Fifth.[249] The pleasant days here, marked by Valdivia directing the ship building efforts and La Doña preparing our meals, ended at the close of the month. For one late afternoon at the conclusion of work, we heard the sound of galloping horses and loud shouts. We all left our tents to welcome Juan Almonacid, Francisco de Galdames, and Manuel Anaya. Yet, this was not a visit to engage in pleasantries, since they brought word from Captain de Monroy that de Hoz and his sympathizers were surprised in a plot to kill the Captain. As a result, it was imperative that Valdivia return forthwith to take charge of matters. He said he intended to do so, and we were all to leave with him except Huenu and the twelve brig builders. I offered my services to remain with these men, but Valdivia said this would be a short matter to attend to and that we should be gone but one or two days. Anaya, a tall, upright man, having hailed the men upon arrival and obviously friends with them, petitioned the Captain with the same request, to remain here until our return. This Valdivia granted.

---

[249] The Royal Fifth was a 20% levy for the Monarch on all precious metals and other commodities acquired by his subjects.

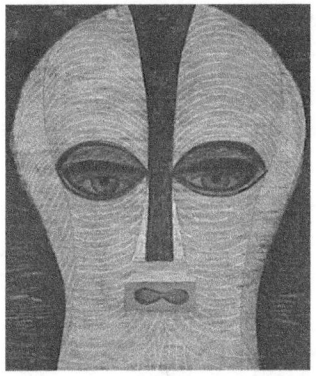

PART PP

CONFRONTING THE CONSPIRATORS AGAINST CAPTAIN VALDIVIA; HIS ACCEPTANCE OF THE GOVERNORSHIP; A GOLD DISTRIBUTION; THE DESTRUCTION OF OUR CAPITAL CITY AND THE BEHEADINGS OF SEVEN *CACIQUES*

Two days later in early July, we arrived in Santiago at mid-day, and the Captain consulted straight away with de Monroy on the matter of a mutiny and the threat to kill him. De Benito and Villagran were part of these discussions, but the rest of us traveled around town to renew friendships and admire what was taking shape as a recognizable capital city, with foundations for residences and a rising cathedral, fruit and vegetable shopping places, La Doña's medical treatment building, a main plaza with roads leading from it to the four compass directions, all things important to the beginning of any town and all according to de Gamboa's meticulous plan.

In the late afternoon, his meeting concerning the de Hoz affair at a close, Valdivia summoned all the officers to the Plaza Mayor to tell us the fate of de Hoz and his compatriots. There was no crime or plot by him, the Captain said, without elaboration. The evidence presented was unconvincing; and so the matter was at an end. I looked aside at La Doña. One could tell by her pursed lips and body movements that this was not what she desired to hear. Yet, she remained silent. Another accused, however, Alonzo de Chinchilla, was of a different lot, he said, and ordered the villain guarded by our Constable, Juan Gómez de Almagro, and put on reduced rations until further notice.

I must say something more, Your Honor, about this good-for-nothing, de Chinchilla. He was like others of the time, of the times past, and certainly those times yet to come, who exhibit a mindless disregard for principled human affairs and seek only worldly enrichment and political power. This scoundrel had begun life honorably enough, as he was born the second son in a family of admirable circumstances. His father was a member of the León *Cabildo*, and his mother tended to women of the lower caste in need of shelter and food. Yet, despite this responsible environment that might have directed him to a life inclined towards the good of society, he embarked upon a discordant path of shameful behavior, for reasons that remain unclear. As I mentioned in my Fourth Letter to Your Majesty,[250] his swarthy and brutal outward appearance reflected his inner repugnance. During the months after he joined our expedition in Copayapu, several of the lieutenants learned that when given an order he did not agree with or did not want to carry out, he would mutter oaths and ribald words toward the officer, out of his hearing, and use hand and arm gestures of mockery behind his back. Thus, we knew that he harbored the possibility of joining others, like de Hoz, who wished to overthrow the Captain and take control of our government. Enough for now of this repulsive man, Sire, since I have gone on too long about him.

Valdivia decided to remain in town two days before returning to the coast, since he wished to inspect the building projects, for one thing. Furthermore, he wanted to see how the fruit and vegetable plantings

---

[250] See <u>The Adventure Chronicles</u>, Part LL of Volume II: Valdivia.

were faring, and to visit with Ancohualla to assess the progress he and his *caciques* had made in building their town for his Indians. Some of us accompanied Valdivia and La Doña on this call upon our friends. A large village had begun to take shape, arranged around a main plaza that resembled the one in Cusco,[251] and designed by Captain de Miranda working with Ancohualla and his *caciques*. Small residences for them were located on the south side of the plaza, a partially constructed chapel, built by Father Lobo, stood on the northern. On the plaza's west, there were large structures to store the fruits and vegetables from the cultivated fields that stretched far into the distance. Two blocks away, Pilca Huaca and Collardis treated the sick in a three room structure, and we found them directing workers in the placement of beds and tables. Matters were going well, said Pilca Huaca, and she expected to add more rooms in the future. She was truly a dedicated lady who had found her proper calling. The radiance of her countenance, which was the case always, made me take notice, as I had previously. But all was far from well, Majesty, as the Captain registered concern that the crops were too meager and soon might prove unable to sustain us. The seeds we had brought from Peru were insufficient, and we needed more. Indeed, within months this situation became much worse, as I shall relate at the proper time.

A matter of great importance occurred now, and to tell of it even at the distance of these many years causes in me feelings of satisfaction and gratitude towards Valdivia, sentiments shared by all. It occurred thus. Once we had returned from the visit with our Indian friends, the Captain's aides passed the word that all were to gather at the Plaza Mayor to hear important news. Within a brief time all had assembled there, including Ancohualla and his *caciques*. Presently, Valdivia and La Doña strode forward from a side street, accompanied by the captains. I turned to Vicente and Gerónimo standing beside me. They met my shrug of "What is this?" with similar expressions of perplexity. We then heard the reason for our gathering.

"Christians and our Indian friends," the Captain intoned. "The time has come to provide rewards for the hardships we have suffered and those

---

[251] This refers to today's Plaza de Armas in Cusco.

that are still to come." He beckoned to Villagran, who stepped forward followed by four men carrying a long pallet, two men at each end, with two large skin bags sitting atop it. Vicente nudged my elbow. "It's the gold from Marga Marga, my friend!" And so it was, for Valdivia continued to explain that a portion of the gold ransom from Michimalongo was for us, including Anco and his *caciques*. For several moments there was no perceptible sound in the entire Plaza. Then, shouts and exclamations of surprise and joy exploded from us all. A few men dropped to their knees and bowed their heads in thanksgiving. Others embraced those nearest them, some with tears on their cheeks. Vicente, with a wide smile, patted me on the back and shook de Alderete's hand with a firm grip. I looked over to our Indians and saw a wide smile on the face of Pilca Huaca. This was a fitting remuneration for our efforts and sufferings to arrive at this land, Your Majesty, and, what is more, this was but the first distribution of gold to us from the Marga Marga Station, as there were more in the years to come. Each allocation was determined after the reckoning of Your Majesty's portion, and all such transactions we recorded faithfully in *Cabildo* records.

We must leave this event that brought so much pleasure to us, for as we returned from placing our bags of gold under guard day and night, there were shouts from the main plaza that men in great distress were approaching and needed medical attention. We watched intently as they came into sight from behind low shrubs and clumps of bushes and soon recognized de los Ríos and three of his men who had been guarding the Marga Marga Station, de Herrera, Anaya, Huenu, and five of the men left to work on our ship at the Valparaíso Station. All were exhausted and leaned forward in their saddles; one man even slumped to the left side of his pommel, fell to the ground, crawled a short distance and, with a look of complete unhappiness, sat down upon the grass. Gerónimo and Vicente went to his aid as the rest of us helped the other men from their animals. De los Ríos suffered a great deal, as his cheeks were emaciated and sunken in the hollows of his jaw. Anaya was affected too as his lips were dried-up and drawn back from his teeth like a dead man's. Huenu was tired but in good condition, and I hugged him in welcome.

The Adventure Chronicles of *Conquistador* Pedro de Mérida. VOLUME 2, VALDIVIA

La Doña motioned to some men to bring bags of water and her medical supplies. They then moved the wounded into the shade as Pilca Huaca and Collardis arrived to provide assistance. Most of the inhabitants of our town were at the scene and heard de los Ríos and Anaya explain the disaster that had befallen them. The Indian miners had revolted, killed the *yanaconas* and several Christians, and gone on to the coast, where they slaughtered more of our men and burned the small boat. Only these men had survived the terrible events. Captain Valdivia knew we faced formidable problems and he responded by designating forty of us, including Villagran and de Benito, and a number of lieutenants, to ride with him to the coast. We set out late in the day and avoided the Marga Marga Station on the way as de Benito thought a trap might lie there. When we attained the shore in two days we discovered the truth, for the brig lay in blackened ruins. But our men's bodies were nowhere to be found. During our brief stay, Valdivia became suspicious that the Inca *Toqui* had had a hand in all this and decided we must return to Santiago forthwith, since it might be in danger of attack.

We arrived back in our capital town to discover that de Hoz and his followers had been found out yet again, this time with decisive evidence uncovered by the attentiveness of de Almagro that they intended to murder Valdivia. Their plan was to kill him, take over the government, seize the bags of gold, capture the brig on the coast, and sail back to Peru. At de Almagro's insistence, de Monroy had detained the guilty men and required them to sign confessions of their guilt. This they did and their declarations given to Valdivia, who convened a court proceeding composed of the captains and our two judicial authorities, Francisco de Aguirre and Juan Jufré. When the meeting concluded, the Captain retired and spent much of the night deciding upon the fate of these men. On the new day, all gathered in the main plaza to hear the decisions. Five of the conspirators were to die, by hanging or decapitation.[252] As for Sancho de Hoz? His sentence was imprisonment. The subsequent morning saw the executions carried out. The dastardly Chinchilla, as the greatest offender,

---

[252] The five were: Alonso de Chinchilla, Martín de Solier, Sebastián Vázquez, Bartolomé Márquez, and Antonio de Pastrana. See Ida Weldon, <u>Pedro de Valdivia</u>, p. 90.

they led to a tall tree on the flank of Santa Lucía and soon his lifeless body swung heavily from one of its branches. The others were beheaded or hanged. As to Sancho de Hoz, I beg Your Majesty's pardon. I cannot explain his sentence and shall let history render its own explanation.[253]

Two of the executed five men, Exalted Excellency, were members of our city's governing *Cabildo*, a truth most would find difficult to believe. Antonio de Pastrana was the city attorney and Martín de Solier a council member. Both planned to stay in Santiago and rule Chile as co-Governors. This treason prompts the observation, Your Majesty, that excess in all things is harmful, since it proved deadly for these men. It swept them into discernible folly and intrigue as they sought great power and refused to regard what is honorable behavior as glorious but considered what is glorious as good and honest.

To assume the duties of these two blackguards, the Captain chose my friend de Morales as the replacement attorney, a noteworthy choice. To my surprise, he selected me as the new council representative, a post I knew I could fulfill because of the training from Captain Villagran on our journey here, although one I thought beyond my station. When Villagran, the senior member of the council, visited to congratulate me upon my appointment, I gave voice to my reservations. He disabused me quickly of my hesitancies with many words of praise and a resounding declaration of my competencies. For this kindness, I was most grateful. As for my friends, they celebrated my appointment with words and actions most gracious and appealing.

That evening, I talked about the day's events with other lieutenants on the town plaza. Most of the discussion was upon the perfidious actions of these malcontents and the just rewards they received. There was unanimous agreement that de Hoz was guilty, and no one could understand how the blackguard still survived. On another matter, Montesinos said something that had escaped the rest of us. Our numbers, the numbers of men we needed to fight the Mapuche, build our town, and plant our crops, were

---

[253] Several historians believe that Valdivia still thought the King favored de Hoz and thus would react adversely to his execution.

decreasing. We had lost the eleven at the mine, seven on the coast, and the five villains dealt with on this day. "That's twenty-three," he observed. "Twenty-five if you count Juan Ruíz and Rodrigo Sánchez," added I. Right then, de Monroy and de Miranda passed nearby and de Alderete hailed them in greeting. They joined us, and Gerónimo and Vicente took the opportunity to register concern about our decreasing numbers. Both men commented that it was a matter of worry to them and to the Captain as well. The loss of the brig was an event of great importance, and Valdivia was planning on another effort to build a ship to bring men from Peru. But there were so many things happening at present that it might be some time before decisions were made. De Monroy commented further, though, that he thought there could be a plan shortly, since he had a proposal to present to Valdivia. Thus the matter rested for the present.

It was on July 20 that the *Cabildo* of our town persuaded the Captain finally to accept the governorship of our new land. He had refused our previous request, for reasons unclear, yet accepted it on this occasion because the *Cabildo* told him that it would benefit Your Majesty.[254] He was now, in formal fashion, the ruler of our town and this land. Praise be unto His Name. As a further guarantee that Governor Valdivia and we were not subservient to the rule of Peru, we learned by word conveyed overland by Inca *chasquis* in late July that Francisco Pizarro had been assassinated and thus was no longer in charge of our affairs. The Governor and the *Cabildo* could govern now on their own, until we heard otherwise.[255] A few of the Almagro men observed that Pizarro had received a just payment for the theft of the gold from the gold caravan that was rightfully ours. Every man's death lessens mankind, though this man's lessened it but a trifle.

And now, Sacred Majesty, it is an honor to relate another incident that concerns our Doña, the worthy Inés de Suárez. I shall tell how she demonstrated great courage and manly attributes when we needed

---

[254] Valdivia says in Letter I (p. 130 on the site) that he accepted when the *Cabildo* convinced him "… through showing me the advantage to Your Majesty, …"

[255] Diego de Almagro II, Diegito, and his followers, assassinated Francisco Pizarro on 26 June 1541.

both desperately. Matters transpired in this fashion. In late August 1541, Governor Valdivia invited seven *caciques* from nearby to join us and arrange the transfer of food from the surrounding country to both Christians and our Indians. This was to help relieve the shortage of food from our meager crops. Matters turned unpleasant, however, as various of these Indians seemed more interested in delaying the movement of goods in order to cause us harm. Also inviting alarm was the way they strode about town and examined the buildings and the layout of the streets. Captain Villagran commented that two of these men had been among the prisoners captured at Marga Marga that we had released. Others noticed their behavior and that several wore clothing colored and cut like the Inca *Toqui's*. The Governor reacted to this apparent hostility and their possible planning for the same by taking the seven as hostages. He sent word to Michimalongo that he would release them if the Inca *Toqui* agreed to provide the food arranged for delivery and meet with Valdivia to discuss again living in peace with us.

In early September, while awaiting an answer from Michimalongo, the Governor received an urgent communication from Captain de Benito. Governor Valdivia had sent the old warrior south with de Almagro and ten horse soldiers with orders to break up any gatherings of Indians that might threaten our capital city. They were now in great peril, though, and needed immediate assistance since nearly 500 warriors on the northern bank of the Río Cachapoal surrounded them and they needed immediate assistance.[256] It was unclear from the message if the Inca *Toqui* was involved, although that is what Valdivia suspected. He left that evening with Captains Villagran, de Aguirre, de Miranda, de Quiroga, and a number of lieutenants, leaving Captain de Monroy in charge of the remaining fifty men, with de Alderete, Bohón, Gaspar de Villarroel, and me as his assistants.

Two days later on September 12, Huenu and Ayar returned from a *huemul* hunt with word that Mapuche warriors were massing in the forests to the south. In response, de Monroy sent me, with Francisco Rubio[257] and

---

[256] The Río Cachapoal is some 55 miles south from Santiago
[257] (1513-1565).

Sánchez de Morales, to ride around the town's perimeter to assess the extent of the danger. Within a short time, we were able to determine that several thousand warriors were a brief distance to the south, as Huenu and Ayar had reported. They were forming quickly and might attack at any time. Furthermore, we saw Michimalongo among them! He was not threatening Captain de Benito as we had thought, but had engaged in a ruse to lure most of our force to the south and away from the city. In addition, he was violating the understanding reached with Governor Valdivia at Marga Marga Station. We hastened back to town and notified de Monroy without delay of what we had seen. He was in the company of our Doña Inés who, upon hearing my estimate that 5,000 Mapuche were preparing to attack us, strapped her double-edged sword belt quickly about her waist and tugged at it to make sure it was in position. As she shoved her long stiletto inside the belt, there was a look of forbidding determination upon her face. Glancing at me, she said determinedly, "We will teach this Michimalongo some Christian manners, Pedro!"

In the meantime, de Monroy summoned the lieutenants and placed them in defensive positions on the southern border. He ordered that two horsemen must be close to one another so as to provide the best protection against charging warriors, who would be unsure which man to attack first. In addition, he kept five horse soldiers in reserve, with me in command. We guarded our flanks, and the Captain could send us forward at his discretion to bolster our line where needed. The shortage of men prompted de Monroy to release Sancho de Hoz, thus freeing the two men guarding him. He unshackled de Hoz, allowed him the use of his sword, told him to prove his worth by fighting bravely, and assigned him to me and my reserve force. The Captain knew we would need every man to do his duty, and this scoundrel needed to do so more than most.

Fortunately, we had five musket men with Cisternas in command and de Monroy placed them in front of the horse soldiers. They were to fire first at charging warriors and then retire behind the line of horses to reload. I was to ride behind the line and await developments. As to the seven *caciques* detained by the Governor, they were tied hand and foot and arranged against the side of a storage building to await the fight's conclusion. Early in the afternoon, we heard war cries in the distance as the Mapuche ran towards us, yelling their war chants and brandishing their weapons. At the most propitious moment, Cisternas had his men fire their muskets, with lethal effect. The hostiles paused, stunned by the sound and the dead among them, and then resumed their attack. They reached our horsemen and the killing began in earnest as our swords slashed arms and necks. After one charge of Mapuche had had enough, they retreated, those who still lived. Later, another wave rushed forward, enduring our musket balls and deadly swords. Then, we heard the seven *caciques* behind us yelling encouragement to their comrades. They left off when Doña Inéz rode over and smashed her sword's guard into the face of each one with the loud shout of an oath used only by men.

During one charge, Mapuche bowmen were able to escape our notice and launch arrows with tips afire at town buildings and structures. The foundations of bricks withstood the fires, but the walls of wooden planks and roofs of straw burned readily and swiftly. My men and I tried to quell the flames as soon as the Mapuche retreated to form for another attack, but, in the end, our efforts came to naught. This firing of our town prompted de Monroy to use different tactics. He ordered me to ride out when the new rush of Mapuche came into contact with our line, maneuver to the rear of the hostiles, and then attack them from behind wherever our men needed help. This we did, with de Hoz yelling support to those near him. We rode past the rightmost extension of the Mapuche line and came in behind them. Recognizing that de Villarroel on the leftmost part of the Christian front was in difficulty, I pointed my sword in that direction and yelled, the sign to the men to charge that area of the line. I had no sooner done so than de Hoz galloped off in the lead with two other men. They engaged the Mapuche there, de Hoz fighting like a madman, lunging right and left with his sword. As a result of their attack, the Mapuche in that part of their line retreated, and, as they did so, the rest of the Indians followed. We had time to rest before the following onslaught, and I led my reserves back to join de Monroy, who had words of praise for us all, especially for de Hoz. During this lull in the fighting, the Captain regrouped us, as the Mapuche prepared for the next attack, and gave a rousing speech of encouragement. Then,

La Doña strode forward in a resolute manner. De Monroy asked her if it might be propitious to release the *caciques* as a peace gesture. "Not while I still breathe, sir!" She said this with such intensity that we knew she was now in charge. When he asked what should be done, she answered, "We must kill all seven!"

She left hurriedly. Within a short time, she returned, astride her white horse and dressed in a horse soldier's coat of heavy leather and breast mail, but without the morrión. When de Monroy asked her how the *caciques* would be killed, she shouted, "Sir, in this manner!" And brandishing her sword, she rode over to where the *caciques* sat tied up, dismounted, grabbed each one by his head of hair, and promptly cut off his head. De Alderete, on horse beside me, let out a low whistle of amazement at what we were seeing and smiled in appreciation. "Pedro," said he, "she is our Joan of Arc!" La Doña then put the seven heads in a bag of llama hide as we watched, and galloped through our lines with her long hair streaming in the wind. Once she was between our battle position and that of the Mapuche poised for the next charge, she let out a loud shout in their direction, rode slowly between both lines, and dropped a *cacique* head to the ground every fifty feet, all the while yelling and shaking her head from side to side so that her hair fluttered in the breeze.

IMAGES: See 5NN-PP.20 and .21 for renderings of these beheadings.

She returned and called us all together, for the Mapuche had not moved since seeing the heads of their chiefs thrown to the ground in front of them. She exhorted all of us with words of extravagant praise about our great deeds in battle and told us to demonstrate that prowess, as victory was close at hand. A great shout arose from us all, for our courageous Doña was no longer simply a woman looking to our medical needs but now, on this occasion, a lady serving as one of our bravest captains. We Christians now found a new resolve to kill all the Mapuche that came our way and reformed directly into our battle positions. When we stared south to the Mapuche lines, though, there was little activity. A number of Indians braved the danger and ran forward to retrieve the heads, ordered to do so by the warrior on horseback, Michimalongo himself. La Doña told us to stand firm, that this battle was at an end. And indeed it was, for the Inca *Toqui* retreated from the field, his Mapuche warriors running behind, a fitting end to the battle for our town.

A hostile captured two days later, Majesty, had been one of the Mapuche on the field that day. He claimed that we Christians all would have died if it had not been for the warrior woman with the long, flowing hair riding a white horse. And Father Marmolejo, who had saved our chapel from destruction during the battle, later said that the fight resembled the Day of Judgment for the Christians and that we were saved by a miracle. Such is my everlasting memory of the great feat performed by Doña Inés de Suárez on that day of the Battle for Santiago Town.[258]

As to the aftermath, the town suffered the loss to fire of most of its buildings and their contents, including our stored clothing and other goods. Yet, we knew we could rebuild our city. We lost two Christians, with several injured, and six horses, two killed and four captured; we knew we would see those four with Mapuche on their backs in the future. De Hoz had fought bravely, as had all the Christians, and de Villarroel and I mentioned to de Monroy that perhaps a word to the Governor about his performance might be in order upon his return from the south. He agreed, as did the lieutenants. The Mapuche lost at least 1,000 warriors on this occasion, and it took three days to burn their bodies. Not all was lost, however, since Ancohualla and our Indians had twenty pigs,[259] fifty cocks and hens, eight goats, thirty guanaco, and numerous baskets of wheat, *maize*, beans, squash, *charqui*, and hot peppers that survived, since the Inca *Toqui* had not attacked our Indians, as he had promised, a most fortunate occurrence.

---

[258] Incredible as this story is, it is told by several historians. Lobera, in <u>Chronicle of the Kingdom of Chile,</u> C. XV, tells of Doña Inéz and the beheadings, and also the destruction of Santiago, but de Mérida brings it all "alive" for us. Valdivia refers to the attack and destruction of the town but says not a word about the deaths of the seven *caciques* (Valdivia's Letter I, p. 131), perhaps knowing that the King would not approve of his relationship with Doña Inés.

[259] The Expedition started with two pigs and they have multiplied, as have the other animals.

This battle required much from each of us. I noticed among several men afterwards that they lacked energy and were reluctant to do anything more than sit and rest, some staring blankly without focus, neither responding to others in words or physical action. I had seen this in prior years, notably after the Battle of Papudo and the Battle for Fortress Arequipa. For most, this behavior lasted for hours. It left off at different times for different men.[260] We veterans knew to let those so affected take their respite, if we were able to do so.

The destruction of our town prompted differing sentiments. On an afternoon while talking with friends on the wide Plaza Mayor, de Morales gave voice to his point of view. "There will never be peace in this land. We will be in constant conflict with these Mapuche until well past our going."[261] Other men agreed, but de Alderete had a different view of things. "Yes, that may be true, Sánchez. As for me, I have understood that things would be unsettled here in our new land ever since Pedro here told us of the Battle of Papudo fought by the Almagro men. So, I acknowledge what you say, but I know that our Spanish cavalry can defeat any force deployed against it. And, being a resourceful people, we will rebuild our city and found more. Someday, rest assured, we shall live in a modicum of peace with these people. Our precious Savior will see to that." Such were the thoughts expressed by some of us as to the nature of things, Your Highness.

---

[260] De Mérida has remarked upon battle fatigue after previous battles.
[261] De Morales was correct in his assessment. The Arauco Wars with the Mapuche continued until the mid-nineteenth century.

PART QQ

OUR CROPS FAIL OUR NEEDS; THE MAPUCHE CONTINUE THEIR RAIDS; DE MONROY, DE MIRANDA, AND FOUR OTHERS LEAVE FOR PERU; A SURPRISE SHIP ARRIVAL; THE RETURN OF DE MONROY AND DE MIRANDA

Our most immediate concerns now became planting food crops, protecting ourselves from Mapuche harassment raids, and rebuilding our town. The low amount of seeds proved a continuing problem. To defend ourselves against the constant threat of attack from the Mapuche, the Governor divided us into groups, one to watch the town, and several others to ride miles into the countryside each day, on what he called "seek and subdue" missions, to raid gatherings of Indians who might pose a threat. On these rides, we sought as well to trade our beads with friendly natives for fruit, vegetables, wheat, *maize*, seeds, anything we might take back for us and our Indians. Those who remained in town were responsible for protecting our settlement from attack, planting and harvesting our small crops, and rebuilding the city.

Exalted Majesty, the two men we lost in the fight for our town brought our losses to twenty-seven, and we now numbered 123 Christians. Few of us felt comfortable or safe with so few men, above all de Alderete and Montesinos, as cited previously. One evening, they met with all the lieutenants to discuss the situation, proposed that they would speak for us as a group, and make it known to Captains de Monroy and de Miranda that they should approach the Governor with a request to send word to Peru that more men were needed here. Before they were able to arrange this meeting, however, the Governor announced that de Monroy and de Miranda had volunteered to strike out for Peru to find more men. Four others were to accompany them: Juan Pacheco, Juan Ronquilla, Martín de Castro, and Alonso Salguerro.[262] This cheered us immensely, Your Grace, for reasons understood.

Before the men's departure, we learned from the Governor the particulars of what he wished accomplished and how de Monroy and de Miranda were to effect his orders. This he failed to mention in his Letter I to Your Majesty, so I record it here. The highest priority was the identification of men in Peru eager to begin a new life with us. Another was to satisfy the need for fruit and vegetable seeds, young pigs, chickens, goats, and especially wine so our priests might say mass once more.[263] And we needed priests, in particular one to assist Father de Cabrera in Calama. Last, they were to find a ship and captain and pay him to sail to our port. To help the men carry out their orders, the Governor gave them two bags of gold from the Marga Marga Station. As to the need for priests, Governor Valdivia and Father Marmolejo signed a letter with their requests for delivery to Bishop Vicente Valverde.[264] And, for our friend the *Desert Cacique* in Calama, the Governor gave de Monroy a large gold ring with the Lord's cross carved upon its face as a sign of our friendship.

---

[262] Valdivia, in his Letter I (p. 132), Lobera in his Ch. XX, and Ida Weldon Vernon, p. 96, agree with de Mérida as to the number of men on this mission to Peru.

[263] European vines were brought to Chile around 1554 and were first cultivated by Captain Francisco de Aguirre.

[264] The bishop had attended the ceremony marking their departure from Cusco more than a year earlier.

On a warm morning in early December of 1541, after prayers and the singing of hymns led by Father Marmolejo with assistance from the other priests and enjoyed by us Christians and our Indian Christian friends, the men rode off to the west for Peru by the route we had come. De Villarroel and I watched them until they were barely visible in the distance. There was not one of us who could foresee that we were not to welcome them back for a full two years, and merely two of them at that. I shall tell of their exploits and trials upon their return, Sire.

Our lives were difficult following the departure of de Monroy, what with the meager plantings and raids by the Mapuche. Yet we continued with our tasks, such as the reconstruction of our town, since these activities gave us hope. Its destruction had taught us the danger of straw roofs and wooden walls. Governor Valdivia directed the rebuilding efforts, with needed assistance from Ancohualla and our Indians. We used adobe bricks this time in the structures and paid heed to the need for fortifications. The Governor explained the walls we built around town in his Letter I, Exalted One, and their thickness and height would provide shelter during Mapuche attacks.

It was now that a matter of great importance presented itself, one that was to have lasting effects in the years to come. For it happened that Ancohualla had spoken to the Governor on occasion, that it would be fitting for various of his Indian women to marry those of our men who were interested. Governor Valdivia approved of this and explained matters to the officers and *caciques* on a sun-lit afternoon. It was time to settle and people this new land, to marry, raise families, farm the land, start businesses, create thriving towns and cities, and participate in their governance, our Governor said. We all accepted this. And, with the coming arrival of children, our town of Santiago would have the feel of our homes back in Spain. De Gamboa, de Villarroel, de Cartagena, Jufré, and de Morales, were a few of those who stepped forward to legalize their love for their chosen Indian women. Our Indians took wives as well on this occasion, the most notable marriage that of Paucar and Collardis. This did not surprise me as Pilca Huaca had spoken of their affection for one another a number of months before. Our priests performed the ceremonies for every couple over the period of a week and there was a joyful celebration after each one.

The happiness caused by these marriages and by the celebration of the birth of our Blessed Lord did not lessen the direness of our situation, since the shortage of food caused continued distress. We fed ourselves with roots, oat seeds, and other herbs this land grows without sowing and in profusion. Governor Valdivia led the survival efforts, and we all dug, ploughed, and sowed, while remaining armed and our horses saddled. We planted the little amounts of *maize*, bean, squash, and wheat seeds we had, and benefited from the three crops this fertile land supported. As soon as the seed was sown, we kept guard over the fields and the town in likewise fashion. Cisternas and his musket men embarked occasionally on forays to shoot guanaco and *huemul*, but were often unsuccessful. And during this period, we patrolled outside and around the town at the Governor's direction on seek and subdue raids to rid the land of Mapuche war bands. We were merciless in these encounters, since we were fighting for our lives and those of our countrymen and Indians. Any warriors raising weapons against us were disarmed and had their hands or an arm chopped off. Not one of us hesitated to inflict these injuries, and we did so with alacrity. A number of men went further, like de Morales and Antonio Carrillo,[265] by cutting the back of the leg behind the knee[266] or the back of the foot at the ankle,[267] both of which meant the man could never walk again without assistance. Such was the state of affairs while we awaited the return of de Monroy and his men.

I shall move my relation forward, Honored One, to September of 1543, when an event of astonishing significance transpired. On a cool afternoon as we were engaged in construction and planting activities, a shout arose from the lookout on the heights of Santa Lucía that a number of Indians were coming towards us from the west. Gerónimo joined Vicente and me as we walked towards the town's western border in company with some

---

[265] This man appears on the list of those who founded Santiago, but with no more information than that.
[266] This is the hamstring tendon.
[267] And this is the Achilles tendon.

friends. Of the three natives, the man in the lead called for Governor Valdivia, as he had important events to relate. The Governor and La Doña came forward forthwith and we heard the extraordinary report that a ship had been sighted sailing along the coast, although it seemed hesitant to land. Was it de Monroy and the men? Shouts of joy arose from the crowd, composed of most of our 118 souls, practically skeletons of our former selves, as we dared to hope that deliverance presently might be at hand. Valdivia immediately shouted to Lope de Ayala and Alonso del Campo to mount up, hasten to the coast, and signal the ship with fire and smoke, as its captain had found the right location. We all cheered as the men rode off. On the ensuing morning, the Governor also commissioned de Benito and de Quiroga to ride with thirty men and pack horses to protect the ship and its contents from attack and to transport its goods inland to us.

There was a good amount of excitement amongst us. Who was on board? What was the ship's cargo? All that we had hoped for? We received our answers days later when the lookout heralded the advance from the west of many men and horses laden with goods. We all ceased our activities and joined the Governor, Doña Inés, Ancohualla, and his *caciques* to welcome the visitors. As they drew closer, Valdivia shouted out a greeting to a gentleman of distinguished appearance, who dismounted and came forward hurriedly to embrace him. This was Lucas Martínez Vegaso, a man of means and a friend of Valdivia's who, we later found out, had stocked the ship with goods asked for by de Monroy and had paid for it all from his own monies. He introduced the ship's Pilot-Captain, Diego García Villalón,[268] who bowed to Governor Valdivia and declared that his ship, the *Santiaguillo*, no stranger to those of us from the Almagro days, was loaded with cargo and that it should be an honor for him to help unload the shipment meant for the Christians of Santiago town. With much joyful shouting from us, Lucas Martínez went on to proclaim that the Captains de Monroy and de Miranda would arrive soon with seventy men to bolster our meager force.[269] At this, the Governor raised

---

[268] Valdivia mentions Lucas Martínez and Captain Villalón in his Letter I, p. 136. See "Historical Sources" on the site.

[269] The Declaration of Diego García Villalón supports this, in Medina, <u>Documentos inéditos</u>, XII, 166.

his arms for quiet and requested Father Marmolejo to lead us in prayers of thankfulness and gratitude to our Lord Jesus Christ for His mercy. As he did, we knelt with relief as Father prayed.

IMAGE: 5QQ-SS.1 is a rendering of the *Santiaguillo*.

It was then time to store the ship's cargo in town using wheeled carts to move all the goods. Lucas Martínez proclaimed the cargo's contents as large bags of fruit and vegetable seeds; more pigs, chickens, and goats; large bags of salt; flagons of wine for our priests; shirts, pants, and shoes to replace our tattered clothing; iron for our horseshoes; and wood working tools and instruments. This rekindled hope amongst us and we felt ready once more to settle in this land.

A surprise awaited us, however, for after the cargo contents had been distributed and stored, Lucas Martínez said that there was another item he had purchased for Governor Valdivia, a gift that would provide a worthwhile benefit for us all. Without saying more, he beckoned the Governor to come closer and subsequently pulled from a carton a time clock of metal and glass! There were remarks of wonder and amazement amongst us at this. We had seen clocks at home in Spain and in Cusco, but had purposely not carried one with us because of the rough passage over tortured land to attain our home. Now, to have such an instrument made us feel as though we were living in the present, like many men of our day, and not in the past.[270] Governor Valdivia said that it would occupy a place of honor in the town hall where the *Cabildo* met. To mark the arrival of the new time piece, Noble Prince, in future I shall reference time as portrayed by the clock instead of the canonical hours, as Governor Valdivia does in two of his letters to Your Highness.[271]

IMAGES: Please see 5QQ-SS.2 for what this clock probably looked like.

---

[270] Please consult Appendix D for more about the clocks of the 16th century.
[271] Valdivia uses clock time references in his Letters I and III.

On the new morning, our priests said mass for Christians and Indians for the first time in many months, and we much rejoiced at this as Our Lord was amongst us yet again. Later, with the wealth of seeds brought by Lucas Martínez, Christians and Indians began planting with a renewed hope that our sufferings might be at an end. And so it came about, as on a warm day in early December, 1543, musket shots rang out to the west. Our musket men were busy planting and building, so it was not they making such noise. In an instant, all knew who was coming — Captain de Monroy! His name rang out in loud shouts as he and Captain de Miranda rode towards us at the head of a long column of horse soldiers, seventy in all, as Lucas Martínez had said, with twenty of them musket men. As they rode around the Plaza Mayor and waved, we shouted, sang, and gripped tightly the hands of all our friends, since we had all endured much misery these last two years and we knew that now it was over. Riding behind the two Captains was a man we understood as the gentleman de Monroy had enlisted to finance the seventy men, their horses, their arms, their clothing, and their food for the journey from Arequipa, by name, Cristóbal de Escobar Villarroel (unrelated to Gaspar). He dismounted and introduced himself to Valdivia as a man most interested in the Governor's foray into this new land and a merchant eager to finance business undertakings. Further, the men he had recruited possessed needed talents, since some were wheelwrights, ironsmiths, structure builders, master masons, and carpenters, and they were to have much to do in the building of our town. In addition, two of them had medical skills and were welcomed warmly by Doña Inés. The Governor expressed his heart-felt thanks to Cristóbal de Escobar and then suggested that he needed further medical attention, at which he submitted readily to the ministrations of our Doña. This was necessary, Majesty, since the cold had frozen the nose of de Escobar on the journey and he had lost part of it as a result.[272]

Upon welcoming de Escobar and the new men, Valdivia moved to embrace warmly Captains de Monroy and de Miranda. Over the ensuing days, they told us of their exploits, Sire, and I must take the opportunity to

---

[272] Weldon Vernon corroborates this in her <u>Pedro de Valdivia</u>, p. 98.

add to the Governor's brief account of their journey²⁷³ north to Peru, what they encountered along the way, and what happened when they reached that northern land. All went well until they entered Copayapu. Guasco and Zapana, the *caciques* friendly to us when we passed through the town in August of 1540, had been killed and replaced by the *cacique* Andequín, a man hostile to us Christians. He had four of our men executed, imprisoned de Monroy and de Miranda, and seized the gold so important to their plans. While detained, they were visited secretly by one of our own, the soldier in Lieutenant Castilla's command who had deserted when we were there on the Almagro Expedition.²⁷⁴ As he has since passed from this life, I may reveal his name as Francisco de Gásco.²⁷⁵ He had a wife in town and numerous children. De Gásco explained that Andequín trusted him and so allowed him to visit the prisoners, which our men used to their advantage. Because of their good behavior, the *cacique* allowed our men time to themselves occasionally. Having acquired sharp knives by stealth and deception, they stabbed and killed Andequín and forced de Gásco to show them the course north, which he agreed to do.

Having escaped harm, they proceeded farther north, paid their respects to Huamanpallpa in Calama, and presented him with Valdivia's large gold ring, which Huaman kissed and put upon his index finger. They visited with Father de Cabrera as well, received his blessings, and assured him they would convey his need for another priest to the Bishop of Cusco for action. Eventually they entered the sacred city in September of 1542 and, despite finding themselves with no money, quickly convinced important men with influence and wealth to help them provide for our needs in Santiago town. A man of such caliber was Vaca de Castro,²⁷⁶ then in

---

²⁷³ See p. 136 in Valdivia's Letter I in "Historical Sources" on the site.
²⁷⁴ De Mérida tells of this incident in Part U of the Third Letter, Volume I.
²⁷⁵ Lobera, in his Ch. XXII, corroborates de Mérida in revealing this man's name.
²⁷⁶ In 1540 Vaca de Castro was sent by Emperor Charles V to restore order between the factions of Gonzalo Pizarro and Diego Almagro the Younger (Diegito) after the assassination of Diego de Almagro the Elder. De Castro had a reputation as a man of integrity, sagacity, and courage. His official title was "special investigator." He took over the government after the death of Francisco Pizarro.

political control of Peru, who allowed de Monroy to recruit men for the journey to Chile. He promised also to send a shipload of goods as soon as he had restored order to Peru. Other important men were Lucas Martínez and Cristóbal de Escobar Villarroel, both already mentioned,[277] and the results of de Monroy's recruitment of them I have related above, Excellency. As a further note, it transpired in future years that these two men became the leading merchants in our capital town and rather wealthy as a result. Lastly, the Captains met with Bishop Juan Solano, Bishop Valverde having suffered death at the hands of renegade savages, and received his oath that he would seek to identify a priest to help Father de Cabrera in Calama. Such was the sum of the captains' work in Peru.

Noble Sire, I must take the opportunity here to tell of this Alonzo de Monroy, an extraordinary man. He had spent his youthful years in Salamanca, the town of his birth. Born in 1506 to parents of considerable means, he attended the University of Salamanca,[278] where he took studies in law, although he found this learning tedious and unfulfilling. Briefly attracted to the religious life, he studied under Dominican tutelage until, excited by the discoveries in the New World, he sought to make his name here. He abandoned his religious studies and embarked for Peru in 1537, arriving in Cusco at the close of that year. When friendship with Valdivia presented itself, the Governor saw to Alonso's instruction in all the necessaries of making war. He and I met in 1539 when introduced to one another by Valdivia and found we had much in common. Before we departed from Cusco, he accompanied Captain Villagran to Arequipa to find men interested in joining us in our new land and was with those who met us at Putre, having ridden from Tacna. This is where we renewed our friendship. Alonso was a man of few words, until presented with a topic of great interest to him. Such matters as the destiny of man, as an example, prompted eager observations from him. Likewise, the life

---

[277] See Valdivia's Letter I, p. 134-136, on the site.

[278] Founded in 1134, The University of Salamanca received the Royal charter of foundation from King Alfonso IX in 1218. It is the oldest university in Spain and the third oldest university in the world. The title of "University" was granted by King Alfonso X in 1254 and recognized by Pope Alexander IV in 1255.

style and fighting abilities of our Indian adversaries elicited thoughtful comments, ones of interest to many. To our misfortune, his was a life too short, as I shall relate, yet one full of purpose and accomplishment notwithstanding.

To return to my relation, the months between de Monroy's departure until his return were ones of such pressing events, like repelling Mapuche attacks and trying to keep ourselves nourished, that we engaged rarely in municipal matters. However, with our prospects improving, Governor Valdivia convened the *Cabildo* a week following de Monroy's return, and he and Captain Villagran presided over the formation of laws and regulations to govern the economic, legal, and social interests of our citizens. We passed legislation concerning such issues as citizen safety; proper land usage; taxation of land, goods, and services; protection of our town and its citizens; proper conduct in public; amounts the priests could charge for their services; the hours of work for those building our city; experience requirements for city construction workers; fruit and vegetable seed prices; establishment of zones of commerce and housing; and other such matters. This involved four days of work before we adjourned.

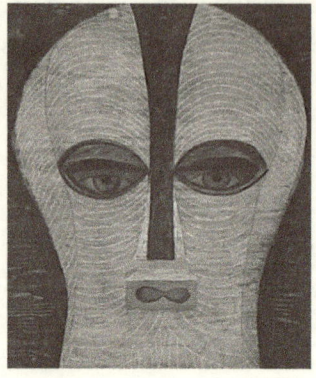

PART RR

DISTRIBUTION OF OUR LAND; MOVES AGAINST THE MAPUCHE TO THE SOUTH; RE-DIRECTION OF THE FIGHTING NORTH; MICHIMALONGO AND THE BATTLE OF LIMARI IN THE NORTH

*I*n late January of 1544, Your Grace, Governor Valdivia decided to allocate land to many of those who had embarked originally from Peru with him, had joined us along the way to the site of Santiago town, or had just arrived with de Monroy. He, with the assistance of the *Cabildo* council, had identified sixty land areas of various sizes for apportionment among the Christian captains, lieutenants, and a select few of the soldiers, as well as Ancohualla and his four *caciques* and *cacica*,[279] and likewise Father Marmolejo.[280] These

---

[279] Valdivia mentions this division of land, but not the particulars, in his Letter III to the King, p. 163 in "Historical Sources" on the site.

[280] Valdivia and Marmolejo engaged in this land grant despite Rome's ban on such land transfers to the clergy.

distributions were transferrable from one owner to another at an agreed upon price, and used for the growing of crops, or for the grazing of cattle, pigs, goats, and the breeding of chickens. The *Cabildo* administered all land matters. For those owners engaged in either agriculture or animal cultivation, our Indians were available as hired labor. Ancohualla saw to this by assigning his *caciques*, Tupa, Huayna, Paucar, and Rimac, to portion out the workers to the land owners at wages paid in gold. And as to the distributed land sizes, 120 acres were awarded to the captains and to Ancohualla; eighty acres were given to each lieutenant, each *cacique*, and to Pilca Huaca, the *cacica*; and thirty acres were bestowed upon those horse soldiers chosen by Valdivia as deserving such an award. The allocation of land to us, Your Excellency, drew us even closer to our new home, as the gold distribution had done previously.[281]

I must leave this matter of the land allocation and relate that with the arrival of de Monroy and the new men, the Mapuche had ceased their attacks upon us. After the new arrivals had recovered from their long, tiring passage from Peru, however, Valdivia thought the time propitious to search for the Mapuche to the south, as we had heard that they were massing for an eventual strike upon us. We left town on Tuesday, February 8, with a force that numbered 110 horse soldiers; the rest of the men, under the command of Captain Villagran and a number of captains and lieutenants, remained in town to protect it from possible attack. After we crossed the Río Cachapoal, the land we journeyed through was new to us, with black shapes, dim light, and a greenish gloom pervading vast territories. While traveling through this darkness to seek and subdue Mapuche forts and armed bands of hostiles, we felt ourselves residing within a colossal wilderness, so dark as to be almost black. Montesinos referred to this landscape as "the dark," a name we all took up quickly, for it described these murky places perfectly. And the spaces all seemed the same — a proliferation of heavy, burdened forests with close bound trees whose branches embraced one another and created a shadowy roof over all beneath. When we entered such sinister enclaves, many

---

[281] Land grants occurred in different forms throughout the New World and were called *repartimientos, encomiendas,* or *estancias*. Valdivia's approach draws upon aspects of all three of these for its structure and implementation.

of us, including the Governor, crossed himself, asking silently for His mercy. Large leafy fronds, several feet wide and several long, repeatedly obscured our view and made it difficult to see beyond them. But we knew what was beyond them, more leafy fronds, huge tree boughs that bent to the ground, and great tufts of grass that rose two feet off the jungle floor. All this vegetation posed the darkest and blackest curtain that concealed from view anything or anyone that might do us harm. In the death-like stillness, we heard only the tramp of our horses. Fighting in this terrain would prove much different and more difficult than we had encountered heretofore. The closeness of the forest prevented us from arranging ourselves in formations across a wide battlefield, as we were more accustomed to do. Since we could not see around us more than ten yards, we had to close our positions and travel in column so that we could keep the other men in sight. This made us more vulnerable to attacks as a unit, and we disliked this type of warfare as a result.[282] Some of us learned to adjust quickly in these jungle-like places. We had to, for understanding meant life. If one did not comprehend the hellish black and all it encompassed, it could cause a thought as to whether this was a bad place, a wrong place, perhaps even a last place and whether a terrible mistake had been made. Still, we adapted to it as best we could, as our efficient killing of the Mapuche attests. As for me and my guiding team's adjustment, I wanted us always to watch intently left, front, and right for movement or for the outline of a body or weapon. We had to listen as well, to listen beyond the *caa-caa*'s and other sounds and songs of the myriad birds of the forest. I insisted upon our silence and devised finger, hand, and arm movements to communicate. We used also sharp whistling sounds that mimicked those of the forest birds to attract one another's attention. Such were the means we employed to adapt to our jungled surroundings.

Late on a cool afternoon six miles south from the Cachapoal, we set camp near a swift flowing stream. As the sun rose on the new morning, a white, silent fog enclosed completely our lonely jungle outpost nestled amongst the forest bushes and branches, warm, wet, and more blinding than the

---

[282] This land is much like that encountered by our forces in Vietnam in the '60's and '70's.

darkness of the night. It did not move, yet remained there, its pallor close and suffocating, confining all in its suffocating embrace. The mist seemed to rise from the decayed trees and gloomy brush and bushes, a pestilential and mystic vapor, dark, dull, sluggish, that made us faintly discernible to one another. We exited our tents when the white pall began to lift and as the guards began to change. I went to stoke the fire for the morning's repast and met my friend Lieutenant Gaspar de Vergara, who exited his tent next to ours to do the same. As we wished each other good day, he suddenly twisted to his left, looked at me with an expression of disbelief, and fell to the ground at my feet. He uttered not a sound as he did so. I knew forthwith the cause of it all, since he gripped the point of an arrow in his hands that had come through his side at the hip. He looked up at me with a questioning gaze. There were shouts throughout the campsite to arm, as others nearby had seen Gaspar go down. Yet there were no warrior screams from the shadowy, silent jungle around us, simply a deathly quiet. Men were armed and mounted in an instant, and Valdivia directed deployments of the men to protect camp and charge into the wilderness to find the cause of this one arrow. I felt warm liquid on my feet and saw it was Gaspar's blood. I knelt down to hold him, now assisted by Antonio Zapata, to ease his pain. He kept looking upwards at me with glistening eyes, fixated upon my face as if they would never leave it. Juan de Oliva, a de Escobar man from Peru and one of the two of their number competent in medical matters, ran over to take charge and I broke away from Gaspar's unremitting stare.

IMAGES: 5QQ-SS.3-.5 show pictures of landscape called "the dark."

Within an hour, loud shouts welcomed our men back from searching for those responsible. They had found ten Mapuche, tied them by the feet, and dragged them back to the outskirts of our campground. Each one was a mass of bloody tissue, their faces unrecognizable from being dragged over rocks and fallen tree branches. De Quiroga ordered them arranged against nearby tree trunks to serve as grotesque reminders to Mapuche passing by what they would incur should they run afoul of us. The danger of further attack abated, I returned to discover Gaspar alive, with the arrow pulled free from his side and in a great deal of pain.

Days later, de Vergara now able to ride, we crossed the Río Maule[283] and entered another forested jungle of "the dark," one virtually impenetrable, as Huenu, Ayar, and I rode forward at a short distance in front of the main group while a light rain fell. Little distance separated us from our protective force, Vicente and his five men, as the visibility was such that the green hell forced us to stay close. We looked side to side and ahead continually, seeking the best direction, the best path. Huenu was expert at this, since his instincts at these times never wavered. I found myself distracted time and again, however, as I kept looking for Mapuche. Not their full shapes, since they were skilled at concealment, but for things that presented a dislodgement of order in the low jungle growth, anything that was at variance with the implacable dark forest undergrowth, such as eyes, Sire, yes, eyes. I knew they were there, though I could not see the rest of their human form.

When I glanced at the back of Huenu seeking to follow his lead, he slumped forward suddenly while still clinging with both arms to the neck of his horse. What was that for? Then, I heard a sound we had heard before, a vibration that an arrow or spear makes as it passes close by. But these were stones that were flying about us. We were under attack! All this while the woods, the trees, the branches, the leaves, were silent, excepting the hissing of the stones. One passed near my right ear; another hit the shoulder of my patient horse and caused her to rear on her hind legs; still another bounced off an overhead tree branch and hit my morrión. I rode to Huenu, who had righted himself, although he held his right shoulder in pain. He yelled that he was all right, so I turned to see about Montesinos. Vicente and his men were trying as best they could to withstand the onslaught. I turned to the right and saw amongst the leaves at the same height as my own, a face staring at me, vicious and steady. After that, I noticed in the knotted murkiness, naked breasts, arms, legs, and glaring eyes. The green darkness was full, Excellency, of human parts in motion this way and that. And now shouts from behind startled me and Huenu, as de Benito and thirty men rode past shouting and yelling that the Mapuche were ours, their swords drawn and slashing left and right as they plunged into the wretched forest shadows. I bade Huenu

---

[283] The Río Maule is some 145 miles south from Santiago.

to remain in place and rode to join my compatriots. When I caught up to them, the Mapuche were already prime targets; they ran before us exposing themselves to our relentless slashing and jabbing. We came to a large clearing with scant vegetation in its midst and, for some unknown reason, the hostiles ran into it, failing to stay within the protection of the sheltering murkiness. When Captain de Quiroga and fifteen horse soldiers came to assist us, together we slew every one of them as they cried out and begged for mercy. It never came, as we were merciless in meting out the sentence of death to them all. And so the skirmish ended, with some hundred dead Mapuche littering the clearing's expanse.[284] After another week in this threatening land without an encounter, Valdivia declared that the Mapuche in the south, now driven well below the Río Maule, were non-threatening at the present and that we should turn our course north on the morrow for the journey back to Santiago town. Despite this assurance from the Governor, we maintained double guards and still slept fully clothed at night with our arms within easy reach.

Upon our return in mid-March of 1544, we saw the outlines of our town's new buildings when we were still miles away. We were welcomed warmly by our friends, treated to fruit and vegetable dishes from our new crops, and entertained by our *qamchus* and flute players. The next day, Captain Villagran had both pleasing and unsettling news for Valdivia and the officers. The daily seek and subdue patrols had come upon a gold mine, called La Campana, near a village north of the Marga Marga gold Station. This area, known as Quillota,[285] possessed as well rich farming land. As a balance to this welcome information, natives friendly to us in the northwest had reported to our men that Michimalongo was leading a large mass of warriors in building forts along the coast to the north and inland and making war-like movements as he had years before. And more to our interest, these natives said that there was word of yet another gold mine that Michimalongo was working with a large force of Indians at an area named Andacollo, between the towns of Limari and Cuquimpu.

---

[284] Valdivia refers to the skirmishes but absent the real-life details we have from de Mérida. See Letter I, p. 137, in "Historical Sources."
[285] Quillota is seventy-five miles north northeast from Valparaíso.

With the southern Mapuche under control for the present, the Governor, following extensive consultations with his captains, decided that we should strike out in full force to the northwest to counter this latest Mapuche threat. But first, in recognition of the weeks long campaign against the hostiles to the south, he declared the ensuing days as ones of relaxation and recuperation, time much appreciated by us. While in town, Sire, an important matter to those awarded land distributions presented itself, for Valdivia and Ancohualla met with us to tell how to maintain the land, whether used for agriculture cultivation or the care of animals. As stated previously, Anco had designated his *caciques* to see to our needs and assigned several hundred of our Indians for this work, each of whom would be paid in gold. Paucar was my *cacique*-in-charge, as he was to various of my friends, like Jufré, de Morales, de Alderete, Bohón, and, to my pleased surprise, Pilca Huaca, whose land was near mine. We met with Paucar and learned the particulars of how matters would work. It all seemed reasonable and gave us the assurance that things would benefit our Indian workers as well as the land holders. Afterwards, I paid my respects to Pilca Huaca. She invited me to visit with her and Collardis at their medical facility; when I did, I enjoyed the visit immensely. Later, this caused me to reflect that I should call upon her more often in the future, since her conversation and presence always lifted my spirits.

On Thursday, March 30 our force, composed of seventy horse soldiers and our guides, Huenu and Ayar, rode out of Santiago in a light mist traveling west. In two days we came upon the peak of La Campana and the hospitable *yanaconas* in charge of mining operations on the mountain's slopes. Subsequent to much discussion among the Governor, de Benito, de Quiroga, and de Monroy, they decided that Captain de Benito would take twenty men, including Montesinos, Bohón, and the guides, and conduct a patrol in force to determine the strength and activities of Michimalongo. His orders were to return for assistance if the enemy proved formidable. Next morning the men left, while the rest of us remained behind. De Quiroga and de Monroy, with twenty men, were to study the extent of the La Campana mining operations and assess how we might enlist the aid of the *yanaconas* to work for us. The rest of us accompanied Valdivia to the village of Quillota, five miles to the west, a region of rich farmland watered by the river we knew, the Aconca-Hue.[286]

I should say here, Sire, that this matter of locating more mines lifted our moods, and especially that of Governor Valdivia. He observed frequently that if there were a mine at Andacollo, as the natives said, then it, La Campana, and Marga Marga would provide enough gold to buy construction materials for Santiago, Valparaíso, and other towns we would found, as well as seeds, animals, clothes, and the goods necessary for our communities to thrive and prosper. He was excited about these possibilities the gold would finance and referred to our future as destined by God to build a Chilean nation composed of us Christians and more Indians that our priests would convert to our Holy Faith. Thus, the "Light," as he referred to our Lord, would watch over and guide us the rest of our lives. Such was his vision, Your Honor, and so it was to be.

In three days, we received a visit from de Quiroga and de Monroy. They reported that all was well at the mine and negotiations with the *yanaconas* had yielded an agreement about wages for the mine workers and their hours of work. Upon the return to Santiago, we would have to identify men to oversee the mining operations, take charge of transportation of the ore to our city, and designate a force to protect us against possible attacks from hostiles. The Captains had no sooner left to return to the mine than shouts arose in the west. It was de Benito and his men, and we knew quickly enough that they had been in a serious fight, since two men had their arms bandaged and were in obvious discomfort. Governor Valdivia and we rushed to help them dismount and see to their needs for water, food, and comfort, and I welcomed my friends, Vicente and Gerónimo. Presently, the old veteran de Benito reported to the Governor that they had encountered hundreds of hostiles a day's ride north from Illapel. In the skirmish with them, which lasted over two hours, they were forced

---

[286] As noted above, this is the Río Aconcagua. When the HMS Beagle arrived at Valparaíso in July 1834, Charles Darwin visited the area near Quillota and wrote of its rich farmland, which remains lush to the present day. Today, it is composed of 80,000 inhabitants, many of whom work in Valparaíso.

to retreat in haste when a thousand more Indians led by the Inca *Toqui* himself entered the fray.

Upon hearing this news, Valdivia declared that an attack on Michimalongo must wait, since we should return first to Santiago to obtain further medical care for the wounded and replenish our food, powder, and other supplies before engaging the Inca *Toqui*. He wished additionally to increase our effectiveness by including musket men for the encounter, a decision that was to prove decisive. We left the coming day for our town and, after seeing to our provisioning, we departed in mid-April with 105 men, including fifteen musket men and Pedro Cisternas, the "gunner." Captain Villagran remained in charge of the town during our absence. We came to La Campana in two days and turned north at Quillota, passing Papudo to the west. Two days farther on, we entered Illapel and learned from the town *caciques* that they thought Michimalongo was one day away to the north. Governor Valdivia sent Montesinos, de Alderete, and the guides on a scouting mission to locate our old enemy. They returned the next afternoon to report that the Inca *Toqui* and several thousand Mapuche were proceeding slowly northward near to three miles from us. Valdivia sent them forward again to keep close watch upon their movements. They returned the subsequent afternoon to say that Michimalongo had ended his march, no doubt advised of our approach by his sympathizers and spies, where it appeared he wished to stand and fight, since his men were arrayed along the western side of the Río Limari and preparing to give battle. The Governor then asked Vicente and Gerónimo to take him and de Benito to a position of concealment where they could use the spy glass to view the river scene before returning to discuss a plan of attack with us.

When they returned, Valdivia summoned the officers to tell what he had seen. We were to experience something new on the battlefield, he said, a weapon he had encountered in the Italian Wars, yet not here in the Americas: the long pike.[287] With his spy glass, he and de Benito had been able to estimate their length at fifteen feet. In answer to a question from

---

[287] The pike was used effectively in Europe in the Middle Ages until around 1700. The Mapuche and Michimalongo had created a new weapon for themselves.

an inexperienced young officer from the newly arrived Peru contingent about their use, the Governor responded, "To skewer your horse from chest to tail and unhorse you!" This brought knowing murmurs and nods from many of the men, accompanied by the realization that this required a change in tactics, since a charging horse soldier is no match for a skilled pike man. If we failed to charge the enemy, asked the same man, how might we prevail? The Governor said he would soon make that clear and continued with his observations. The enemy, numbering near 2,000, occupied the western bank of a narrow river, he said, and extended about a mile in length. They appeared armed as we had encountered them in previous battles, with slings, darts, javelins, and bows and arrows, but this time they possessed the more dangerous weapon, the sharp pointed long pike. Several hundred of the men were so equipped, and it appeared that they would occupy the center of the line. He went on to observe that, if this were so, the farther extensions of their line should be composed of fewer men than usual. Furthermore, since they were facing east, they would have the sun in their eyes when we attacked early in the morning.

IMAGES: 5QQ-SS.7-.12 are images of this area's landscape.

Then Valdivia answered the young soldier's question by presenting his battle plan and explained it thusly. The sure counter to pike men, as learned in the Italian Wars and earlier, he observed, was the long bow in past days, and in our day the musket. Hence, we would position our fifteen muskets, under the command of Cisternas and his assistant, Lázaro Pérez de Santiago, across the river from the pike men and proceed to kill as many of them as we might. If they stood close to each other in rows, a single shot could kill two or three of them at a time. During the musket fire, the cavalry would remain in place arrayed in this manner: Captain de Monroy, with de Alderete as his second, would hold the left side of our line with twenty men. Captain de Benito, with Montesinos and me, was to anchor the center with thirty-five. Captain de Quiroga, with Gaspar de Villarroel as second, would secure the north end with twenty horsemen. Valdivia remained in the rear, along with Captain de Aguirre in command of the fifteen reserves, with Bohón as his second.

Yet, not all our formations were to attack forward at the conclusion of the muskets firing at the warrior pike men. Rather, we would employ a surprise by having de Benito and his men join de Quiroga and his, at the Governor's signal, and jointly they were to attack the northern side of the Mapuche line in a surprise move, where there were fewer men, and seek to enclose them in a half-pocket. At the same instant, de Monroy was to engage the southern part of the line and attempt to do the same. De Aguirre, meanwhile, would move his men into the center vacated by de Benito and charge forward, at Valdivia's order, towards the decimated pike men and through them to join the other captains. These maneuvers should create eventually two pockets of surrounded Mapuche that we could slash and cut until their surrender or decimation. The Governor's presentation ended with a last comment. "Gentlemen, do not think less of the men we are about to face because of the weaknesses I have cited that we will exploit. They are tough, hardened warriors and will fight to the death. Gather with your captains and men and plan for the coming fray. We will leave at first light. And remember. Attack first! Hit first. When in doubt, attack!"

That night we doubled the guard, slept fully clothed with swords and long-knives at hand, and arose in the dark of first light. The sun still lay below the mountains in the east as we came upon the battleground in the gathering light. The Mapuche were already in position and aligned exactly as our Governor had thought they would be. Vicente looked at me and yelled, "They will be ours, my friend!" The musket men moved to a position directly in front of the pike men on the opposite shore line and deployed according to the shouted commands of the "gunner." Up and down the Mapuche line the warriors continued yelling that we were little girls, chanting their warrior songs, and shaking their weapons. The 400 pike men were arranged four rows deep, their pikes angled upwards and forward. I could but thank our Lord that the muskets were to engage them first. Soon, more shouts arose from the horde, since who should appear behind the pike men but Michimalongo himself, astride his horse and arrayed in a shirt and pants of varied colors. He waved to his men and, in a display of horsemanship and a rebuke to us, rode the extent of the line to the north, turned, galloped all the way past the center and to the end of the line in the south. He then turned to take his place in the center rear with his *caciques*. All the while he gestured towards us with hand and arm in a threatening manner, beckoning us to come forward, and this excited his troops to a frenzy. They jumped up and down, brandished their weapons in the air, and sang words that referred to us as lazy dogs and women cowards. I captured the eye of de Villarroel to the right and gave him a nod, just as I heard de Benito behind me exclaim a blasphemy in derision.

All of us knew the time for action was upon us. When finally the sun lifted above the peaks behind us and caught the hostiles full in the face, Valdivia signaled to Cisternas. Within minutes, the muskets began their booming. The first rounds tore through the pike men, and many fell twisting and writhing as the huge bullets ripped their flesh. The next round produced the same devastation. And the next. I looked upon the scene and felt an admiration for the warriors we faced. They remained where they were and stood their ground, unflinching. Cisternas continued to yell his firing command until, in truth, Sire, there were few pike men left standing, perhaps 150, and they appeared confused and dazed from what they had endured. Valdivia signaled Cisternas to withdraw the muskets and rode forward into our midst, yelled his "Santiago, and at them!" and we kicked our horses into the charge. De Benito led us to the right to join de Quiroga and his men, and as one we dashed through the shallow stream and plunged into the warriors at the line's north end. Stones from their slings and darts from their bows filled the air, and one dart stuck in my lower right leg. I had no time to pull it out, as I was too busy swinging and thrusting with my sword. Presently, as if by command, the hostiles seemed to lose spirit, for they began to back away slowly and then run to the rear, where Michimalongo and his *caciques* were nowhere in sight. De Benito shouted for us to let them go and ride towards the center, behind the pike men. As we did so, de Monroy and his horsemen rode towards us, the Mapuche at the southern end having retreated from the field as well. With Bohón now in their front, we had the pike men surrounded. Some put the points of their pikes to their chests and fell forward on them. The rest threw their weapons to the ground, except two of them. These men displayed their bravery and courage by pointing to their chests and motioning us to run them through with our swords. At this, Valdivia shouted for us to cease the killing. He called the captains to join him and invited Ayar forward as well. We watched the Indians intently for any sign of hostility, yet they remained quiet and subdued. Their meeting concluded, the captains rejoined us and Valdivia ordered the fighting and killing to cease. This gesture might create goodwill towards us in the future, he said. At least, that was the Governor's hope. Ayar shouted to the hostiles that they had been granted their freedom through the goodness of the Lord we worshipped and by the kindness of Governor Valdivia and could leave once they had buried their dead. So ended the Battle of Río Limari, an encounter that we all found difficult to believe had ended so quickly.[288] There was a cost, of course. Eleven of us sustained injuries, none of them life threatening, thanks be to our Lord. We lost two horses, with two wounded, one by a mace blow to the head.

---

[288] De Quiroga mentions this battle but does not provide the particulars that de Mérida has. See *Información* de Rodrigo de Quiroga, in Medina, *Documentos Inéditos*. Also, see Weldon Vernon, p.105.

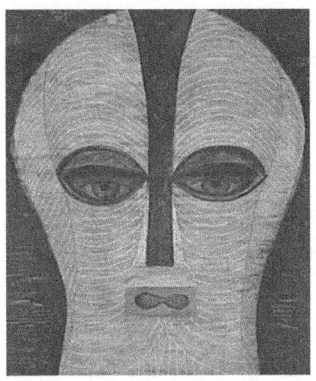

PART SS

A VISIT TO THE SITE OF VILLANUEVA DE LA SERENA; MY MARRIAGE TO PILCA HUACA, THE INCA PRINCESS AND *CACIQUA*; THE LA SERENA FOUNDING; THE VOYAGE OF EXPLORATION TO THE SOUTH AS RECORDED BY PASTENE IN HIS JOURNAL; MICHIMALONGO BECOMES A FRIEND

*A*fter we had returned to our previous night's camp and brushed down our horses, I allowed Pero Estéban, one of the men from Peru with medical skills, to treat my leg with a salve to stop the bleeding but only when he had looked after the other injured men. Later, after our evening's repast, Valdivia invited the officers to join him to discuss the events of the day. Talk turned to the brevity of the fighting, as we were unused to such behavior from the Mapuche. De Alderete offered that our enemy was not well trained or well led. "Following the *Toqui's* ride between our lines, did anyone see him again? What happened to him?" None of us could recall seeing him either. De Benito felt they expected too much from their pike men. "When the muskets killed so many of them, they lost heart. And they were an undetermined foe. They yelled and sang before our charge, but when it came time to fight, they were not there." Montesinos thought the sun in their eyes played a part. "Just as I charged into their line, the first hostile I encountered acted as though he had trouble seeing me. He was dead before he did see me. Moreover, there were no reserves to call upon, and that was poor leadership, as Gerónimo said." Governor Valdivia gave his view of things. "It occurs to me, gentlemen, that all you have said is true. It could be too that our other skirmishes with the *Toqui*, every one of which we have prevailed, have taken a toll and may have weakened his desire to give battle. Time will determine if this be so."

Still, there is more to the story, Excellency. As the Indians gathered their dead and prepared to burn the bodies, Vicente noticed that many of them had grooves in their foreheads, like the mining *yanaconas* at the Marga Marga and La Campana Stations who carried gold from the mines. They used bags with straps that they draped across their heads while the filled bag rested on their backs. "They must work at the Andacollo mine, my friend. Perhaps they can take us there and explain the workings of it." He left at once to inform the Governor of his observation. He proved correct, since the men with the indentations did work at the mine and were quite ready to lead us there in appreciation for the Governor granting them their freedom. Our entire troop, along with twenty-five Indians, left the day following for the mine and also to hunt Michimalongo. We failed to locate the Inca *Toqui* but we did find the mine. It sat upon a raised plateau and gold was not the single thing of value in its depths. Copper existed in abundance,[289] although more men mined the gold because of its value. Valdivia designated Captains de Quiroga and de Monroy to stay here and determine how we might employ the natives in our service, as they had done at La Campana. Forty horsemen remained with them while Valdivia

---

[289] Today's Andacollo gold/copper mine is located some twenty-two miles southeast from Coquimbo/La Serena. The handsome town of Andacollo, with 22,000 citizens, lies upon its outskirts.

led the rest of us to Cuquimpu, the region where he had vowed to me that we would someday build a town.[290]

On the ride to the town, we remained on watch for Michimalongo and his Mapuche, yet neither he nor they made an appearance. That afternoon we entered the settlement, and the day after we traveled six miles to the north until Governor Valdivia led us to the east for another two miles. After we halted, he declared this as the site of our second town, and remarked approvingly upon Cuquimpu's nearby compact harbor, stating that it and our new village would offer rest and shelter to ships sailing between the City of Kings and Valparaíso. It would provide respite as well to those riding overland by horse. "And soon we will use the harbor to transport gold and copper from Andacollo to our city." Juan Bohón, as we had learned the night before, was to be its Governor, a most admirable choice, as he was an honorable man. Upon arriving in Santiago, he and Valdivia were to identify the men to return here and begin construction of the town and harbor using plans drawn by the *alarife*, Pedro de Miranda. Valdivia declared the name of the new settlement as Villanueva de La Serena, the town of his birth in Spain and a most fitting choice.

This done, we began the trek back to Andacollo to join the men there. That evening Valdivia gathered us together for a notable occasion. He recounted the exploits of Pedro Cisternas in directing the fire of the muskets upon the Mapuche pike men. "This broke their spirit and gave us the victory," he declared. Subsequently, he announced the "gunner's" promotion to Lieutenant, Junior Grade, a reward richly deserved. This done, we departed in the early hours of the morning and arrived back in Santiago town in late May, with no sighting of the Inca *Toqui* during the journey. Had the Governor been correct in his observation that perhaps he had no more stomach for battle?

I shall take a brief opportunity here, August Majesty, to relate that upon our return I visited with Pilca Huaca to discuss a subject of great importance. The next day, I met with Ancohualla and asked him for her hand in marriage. This did not take him by surprise, since he knew of our affection for one

---

[290] See Part MM of the Fourth Letter.

another. "This will please her parents immensely, Pedro. I promised them I would find a suitable husband for her, and you are that man." On the coming morning, after Ancohualla presented Pilca Huaca to me, Father Lobo, joined by Father Marmolejo, performed the marriage ceremony at the chapel in our Indian village. Vicente Montesinos, my loyal and trustworthy friend, was beside me the entire time. And Doña Inés assisted Pilca Huaca affectionately throughout the ceremony. Hundreds of Christians and Indians attended, for Pilca Huaca was much loved and respected by all. As was our custom in this new land, she chose her Christian married name as "Doña Maria de Mérida y *Caciqua* de Cuzco," in honor of our Blessed Virgin.[291] Governor Valdivia, at the cheerful proceedings afterwards, presented us with a gold cross one foot tall fashioned out of gold from Marga Marga Station, a most valuable gift and one we still possess and have always cherished. Ancohualla gave Pilca Huaca five Indians to serve as assistants at her medical facility, a present most valuable, as our Indian population was growing quickly with the addition of new babies now a frequent occurrence. I should add here, Your Honor, that my wife used her marriage name of Doña Maria de Mérida y *Caciqua* de Cuzco on formal occasions. She preferred, otherwise, to be addressed by her birth name, Pilca Huaca.

I must go to other affairs of interest, as I hesitate to distract Your Lordship since this relation is about the Valdivia years in Chile and not about me. One such topic was Captain Juan Bohón's preparations for his leaving to found La Serena. A matter of concern to him was his land, which stood between my distribution and Pilca Huaca's. He asked that we manage it with the Indians in the same fashion as we did with our lots. I assured him we should do so and would send him the proceeds from fruit, vegetable, and animal sales, after deducting the expenses. He found this quite satisfactory and gripped my hand tightly. At the next meeting of the *Cabildo*, I asked that this agreement be entered into the city records.

In early June of 1544, Captain Bohón and his men departed to found La Serena, with Captain de Benito and twenty men providing their protection

---

[291] It was the custom of the Spanish to name Indian women taken as brides with Christian names. Bernal Díaz tells of this in his, <u>The Discovery and Conquest of Mexico</u>, p. 155.

during the first year before returning to our city.²⁹² I should tell something of this man, Noble One, as Juan Bohón was a gentleman of a singular constitution. The oldest of nine children born to poor farmer peasants outside Madrid, he resolved at a young age to rise above the low station bequeathed him at birth. With the blessing of his parents, he left the family's home and farm and sought a new life in the city of Madrid. By great good fortune an elderly couple, the man a member of the Madrid *Cabildo*, having lost their son in the Italian Wars took him in and saw to his education in the arts, town governance, and soldiering. He possessed these talents in abundance, and projected an outward appearance of competence and trustworthiness, both traits well deserved. The New World beckoned eventually, and he traveled here to make his name and succeeded in doing so most admirably. He had a number of interesting traits. One was a continual worry about whether he would have enough food for himself. This came no doubt from his early years when food was scarce and the children received but a small portion at their meals. This prepared him for the years in Santiago, when the crops and harvests were meager. But even while food was plentiful in the later years, his was a constant uneasiness. There were occasions I noticed him receiving his meal serving and placing part of it in his guanaco skin bag, supposedly apprehensive that our supply might run out. He was notable as well for the tenor of his voice. It was a deep, low, powerful tone that we all recognized instantly as that of Bohón's. If he were within voice range, even if out of sight, his every utterance identified him directly. This was especially true during singing at mass and the recitation of daily prayers. Such is my memory of this unforgettable man.

I shall move forward, Sire. Notable events occurred frequently during these times, for in just two months word came from Valparaíso that a ship had arrived there and rested at anchor in the harbor roads.²⁹³ The

---

²⁹² There was some early confusion about the exact date of the founding of La Serena. So modern historians now give the middle of 1544 as the date, in line with de Mérida's dating of it.

²⁹³ A "roads" is a roadstead, or a body of water sheltered from rip currents, spring tides, or ocean swell where ships can lie reasonably safely at anchor. In maritime law it is described as a "known general station for ships, notoriously used as such, and distinguished by the name," such as "the Valparaíso harbor roads."

Governor gathered several officers and men and rode forth to greet the unexpected arrival. When he returned, in his company was a man who was to make his mark upon us all and our town in the years to come, by name, Pilot-Captain Juan Bautísta de Pastene.[294] In addition, Vicente and I were old friends of his and welcomed him warmly since we had not seen him for some twelve years. He had transported us and others from Panamá to join Captains Pizarro and Almagro in Peru in 1532, as I shall relate to Your Highness in future letters.[295] Only months prior, the Viceroy of Peru, the admirable Vaca de Castro, named him the Senior Pilot of the Pacific Ocean and Captain of the ship, the *San Pedro*. In light of the order from Your Royal Highness to explore the coast of southern Chile and declare it part of Your Kingdom, de Castro named Pastene to do so. This was the primary reason for his appearance in Valparaíso harbor. But he carried as well seeds, animals, food provisions, wine, guns, gun powder, and construction materials and tools. These had been loaded onto the ship by Juan Calderon de la Barca, a servant of the Viceroy's, who had honored de Castro's promise to de Monroy months prior that he would send supplies to our town.

The Governor, upon meeting with Captain Pastene and learning of his bona-fides, recognized straight away his steadfast and honest character and named him his "Lieutenant-General of the South Seas," calling him a man of much faith, honor, and truth,[296] as Vicente and I knew him to be. Within days, the Governor and his captains conceived a grand exploration plan, and he explained it to us. Captain Pastene in the *San Pedro* and Captain Villalón in the *Santiaguillo* were to explore the sea coast to the south and declare the land down to the 40th S parallel in the name of Your Excellency. De Alderete was to accompany the ships as he had experience at sea. He served also as the Governor's representative to declare the lands in the south those of the Spanish empire. As land

---

[294] (1507-1580). This Captain held several Santiago *Cabildo* posts during future years, one as mayor in 1564.
[295] See The Adventure Chronicles, Volume III: Pizarro, for de Mérida's early days in the conquest of the Incas.
[296] De Mérida here uses the Captain's words of description. See p. 138 of his Letter I on the site.

support, Captain Villagran, with Captain de Aguirre, and accompanied by several lieutenants including Montesinos and forty horse soldiers, was to clear out hostiles along the coast in the region of "the dark" down to the Río Maule where it enters the ocean and meet the *Santiaguillo* there. The *San Pedro* was then to sail farther south, take formal possession of the territory and bestow names upon prominent land and sea features. Both land and sea contingents moved south on Monday, September 4 in the year of Our Lord 1544.

I did not accompany the land or sea forces on their journeys. Captain Villagran had ordered me and numerous *cabildo* members to remain in town and work on the considerable amount of council matters that needed attention. Mine was not all work, however, since Pilca Huaca and I oversaw the completion of our modest home at the northern end of Calle Rodrigo de Quiroga and close to the Río Mapocho, where boats carried people across to the Indian side of the river.[297] A handful of our friends had dwellings near us.

Let us return to the exploits of the two contingents, Exalted Highness, and especially the discoveries made by those men on the southern voyage since they became important in later years.[298] When both groups had returned to us by early October, they each told of their adventures. First, I shall treat the sea voyage events and rely upon Captain Pastene's journal to present the details of what occurred on selected days of his travels, as he generously made it available to me. As an aside, Excellency, he provided also his journals for his early voyages to Peru, as I will relate in future letters to Your Majesty.

IMAGES: 5QQ-SS.15-.34 are images of interest on the voyage south and the return. Also, please consult Appendix F for an understanding of the nautical terms used in Pastene's journal.

---

[297] One may locate the home's location by consulting Appendix C. As one can see, the captains received home sites around the Plaza Mayor. The lieutenants were located farther down the streets.

[298] The reader may consult Valdivia's Letter I to the King for his brief comments about Pastene's journey south: pp. 138-139. However, he says nothing equal to what de Mérida and Pastene tell us. Also of interest is Weldon Vernon, pp. 108-111.

September 4, Monday, 1544, Lat 33°01'S. At first light and upon my signal to Captain Villalón in the *Santiaguillo*, we both weighed anchor and, with *San Pedro* in the van, left the Valparaíso roads sailing due W on parallel 33°01'S with the prevailing moderate westerlies and Peru Current. Knowing of Lieutenant Gerónimo de Alderete's prior sailing days, we discussed the finer points of the astrolabe, or ring, as he called it, and compass and he became quite adept at their usage within days. Also, Gerónimo commanded fifteen soldiers, including five musket men. At a distance of five marine miles from land, I ordered the helmsman to tack S by W and, after one mile, to tack again due S, with strong winds and current upon the bow.[299] As is my daily custom, at the end of the afternoon watch we gathered mid-ships. I read the Vespers prayer, we sang the *Salve Regina*, and at the whistle the new watch stood forward.

September 6, Wednesday, Lat. 35°19'S. At two of the afternoon watch, my ship's first mate[300] called out that the sea water was brown in color, an indication of nearness to the Río Maule's ocean entry. Then, at the end of the afternoon watch, the lookout in the foremast nest shouted that the Río's entry point was off the port side bow. We signaled the *Santiaguillo*, reefed the mainsail, and hove to at 35°19'S and lay to. It should be noted that the distance from the Valparaíso roads to this latitude is approximately 160 miles; we made some seventy miles each day tacking before light westerlies and the strong

---

[299] A ship's distance and speed were measured by throwing a piece of wood from its bow. The pilot then used a half-hour sandglass to time the piece's movement past two marks on the ship's side. This provided a rough guide to the speed and thus the distance traveled.

[300] A sailing ship mate was the superintending officer next in command to the captain.

current. With shouts of farewell and Godspeed to Captain Villalón, we hoisted sail to continue our way S.

September 10, Sunday, Lat. 38°22′S. At the end of the forenoon watch, a call from the seaman in the mizzenmast nest alerted me of an isle to the forward beam standing at a distance of 235 miles S from the Maule. I saw it with my spyglass bearing S by SE near four miles distant. We sailed around it to assess its aspect and dropped anchor when the seaman called out, "By the mark, nine!" at full fathom nine[301] two miles offshore to the ENE at 38°22′S, according to de Alderete's readings of the astrolabe and compass. A mountain chain 500 feet in height bores five miles N to S covered by a rich verdure of trees and shrubs. In certain areas, the land is clear of trees for the planting of crops. The natives appeared friendly, as a crowd of them waved and pointed at us, seemingly in merriment. I took de Alderete and ten men and rowed the longboat to shore, at which the natives began to sing in Mapuche, words that we could not understand. However, they proved welcoming and, in exchange for our blue beads, we acquired baskets of beans, *maize*, squash, and dried fish to supplement our food stores. After bartering, I took the cross from around my neck and, with de Alderete and our men as witness, declared this island as Isla de San Nicolas de Tolentino in the name of His Majesty.[302] We then departed amidst more singing and waving by the islanders.

---

[301] One fathom is equal to six feet. Mariners have taken water soundings since Greek times using a lead weight attached to a thin marked rope. On the Mississippi in Mark Twain's day, they used "twain" for the word "two". Thus, a depth of two feet was called out as, "By the mark, twain."

[302] The island retained this name until early in the 17th century when it was renamed Isla Mocha. Today it is a recreational resort for tourists.

September 12, Tuesday, Lat. 39°15′S. Our progress to the S was slowed early on the morning watch as unfavorable westerlies blowing lustily at 39°15′S caused me to tack frequently 80 degrees to port and starboard as we beat before the wind, the ship rolling scuppers under in the ocean's swell. At one of the afternoon watch, we were in a full gale that blew with such violence that the *San Pedro* was almost driven forecastle under with the booms tearing at the blocks, the rudder shifting from port to starboard, the whole ship rasping and moaning, until I ordered to reef the mainsail, which eased the situation considerably. We remained lying to until the next morning, when we bore away under shortened sail. But during the afternoon watch, the sea ran so high that it was unsafe to stand on. I then brought her into the wind and remained lying to through the night. The next day the winds abated and we again bore away S.

September 14, Thursday, Lat. 39°30′S. At the first dog watch, the winds increased, making the waves frightful as they ran counter to one another and crossed our course so that we could not make headway or get from between them. The wind and sea increased further and, recognizing the danger great, I scudded with the wind wherever it would take us as there was nothing left to be done.

September 15, Friday, Lat. 39°38′S. Early the forenoon watch, the winds shifted to the S and we scudded before the wind with the sea very agitated. During the last dog watch after the setting of the sun, the sky cleared to the W, telling me the wind would come from that direction. Soon after the first dog watch stood to, a heretofore distant dark bank of haze turned threatening and I ordered the top-gallant lowered and the top mast studding sails hauled and clewed up. We stood awaiting the first explosions, which hit with such force of high winds and heavy rain that the *San Pedro* lay almost over her beam ends, the spars and rigging snapped and cracked, and the fore and main masts bent like weak sticks. I had waited too long, but now yelled to clew up the fore and main top-gallant sails as the decks stood at an angle of forty degrees with the ship heaving the tortured seas, the entire bow in overwhelming foam and spray. I then ordered to let go all sail halyards fore and aft. The violent wind, rain, and sleet that flew horizontally across the sea made it hard for the hands aloft since the wet and cold slowed their efforts. After what seemed like a lifetime to haul in all sails, I hove and lay to to ride out the still roaring tempest. At the middle watch, the winds and sea began to abate and we thanked our blessed Lord when a clear and calm sunrise bathed the sea.

September 17, Sunday, Lat. 40°34′S. After seven days to sail the 154 miles from Isla de San Nicolas de Tolentino, we reached 40°34′S, the southern parallel Governor Valdivia and our King wished us to reach and declare for the Crown. A mile offshore and at a place of Gerónimo's choosing, we hove to and he pronounced the formal words marking the establishment of this territory for His Sacred Majesty.

September 19, Tuesday, Lat. 39°50′S. Late the morning watch, we weighed anchor and, staying close inboard to the coast, sailed N running with light westerlies and a strong current in a calm sea. That late afternoon watch, after a pleasant voyage of fifty miles, a wonderfully wide bay appeared in my glass some four miles wide at parallel 39°50′S, the entry point of a río which extended out of sight to the E. We hove and lay to within the broad bay that I named San Pedro since our Governor is named Pedro and the ship that found it is called *San Pedro*. The

Río that empties into it I called the Valdivia. De Alderete remarked that he thought all of this appropriate and rather amusing. Our soundings revealed that the Río mouth had twelve fathoms and is wide enough to beat in without danger of shoals. At ten miles upriver, I ordered anchor dropped midst a land I had never seen the likeness of, with trees along the shores, beautiful and green, and many birds that sang very sweetly, some even from the masts' trucks. Gerónimo and I then disembarked with ten men including three muskets and marched inland two miles amidst the vibrant green growth of grass and trees. Here, we learned from the natives that a town named Anil[303] lay inland farther on, although we had no time to visit it.[304] They told also of two gold mines nearby, one to the E of Anil and another to the N. This caused a stir amongst us. More mines![305]

September 20, Wednesday, Lat. 39°12'S. Early the morning watch, we weighed anchor and set sail N for the entry point of the Río Bio-Bio and a nearby island I had seen in the distance upon our voyage S. Calm seas and light westerlies marked our passage.

September 21, Thursday, Lat. 38°59'S. Sailing a favorable current at fourteen miles in ten hours[306] setting N by NE, we encountered at nine of the forenoon watch a very heavy rain, during which time we nearly filled all our empty water casks.

---

[303] This was a thriving town at this time, according to archaeologists. They style it as "a kind of little Venice," as it had large areas of wetlands and canals. Valdivia later founded the town named after him with this village as part of it.

[304] This would soon be the location for the town of Valdivia.

[305] Several years later, the Christians were to populate this mine to the east and name it Madre Dios. The one to the north was in today's town of Carahue.

[306] As mentioned above, mariners used a one-half hour sandglass to track the time.

September 23, Saturday, Lat. 38°22'S. We came upon the island of my interest at 38°22'S, 206 miles N from Río Valdivia. As we sailed around it, several natives waved from shore in seemingly friendly fashion. The island bores seven miles N to S with a high point of 120 feet; the majority of it is flat and cultivatable. We dropped anchor when the seaman called out, "By the deep, eight!" at full fathom eight two miles from shore at heading ENE and put ashore to the welcome of only fifty natives, as it was sparsely populated. Curiously, there were more sea lions on the southern shores, several hundred, than there were islanders. We traded our blue beads for enough sea lion meat to last a week.[307] I performed the founding ceremony, with Gerónimo's assistance, and named it Isla Santa Maria in honor of our Blessed Virgin.[308]

September 24, Sunday, Lat. 36°49'S. During the forenoon watch, we sailed twenty-two miles ENE in mild breezes to a bearing one mile N from the entry point of the Río Bio-Bio at 36°49'S. That afternoon, we rowed ashore and were met by a crowd of natives who escorted us inland to their village of Penco. There we met their *cacique*, of venerable age, Leochengo, who proved quite friendly.[309] After accepting his invitation to a repast of baked fish and *papas*, we said our farewells upon finishing, accompanied by my promise to Leochengo that I would return one day for the purpose of trading with his people. Once more at the shore and before entering the longboat, de Alderete

---

[307] The South American sea lion populates the Ecuadorian, Peruvian, and Chilean coasts.

[308] Historians do not know the exact date of the founding, but agree that it was sometime in September 1544. Today, a large sea lion colony resides on its shores.

[309] This area later became the port city of Concepción.

performed his founding ceremony for this land in the name of our Sovereign Majesty.

September 26, Tuesday, Lat. 35°19'S. At the mid-forenoon watch, the lookout shouted from the mizzenmast nest that the *Santiaguillo* lay dead ahead six miles distant at the Río Maule's entry point. With waves and shouts to Villalón and his men upon our arrival, we hove to athwart ships to his vessel and dropped anchor midst calm seas. That evening at the repast with the Captain and his men, I learned that Captain Villagran and his troops had arrived quite safely and without conflict, although deep in Mapuche territory, and had departed the previous day for Santiago.

September 27, Wednesday, Lat. 34°03'S. After the morning watch yielded to the forenoon at the whistle, we weighed anchor for the return passage to Valparaíso, bearing away to the W by N before tacking due N midst favorable winds. Our progress was marked by occasional high gusts, but being mostly from the south gave us a fair wind, before which we scudded under full topsails and foresail right regally. Though we weathered a very heavy sea, we incurred no damage, the *San Pedro* demonstrating herself a splendid sailing vessel.

September 28, Thursday, Lat. 33°25'S. Late the middle watch, my first mate awoke me from a light slumber with the sad report that seaman Francisco de Saucedo, a man of character and an able sailor, had passed during the night of an unknown cause. Our medical man surmised that it might have been that his heart suddenly ceased to beat. At the changing of the forenoon and afternoon watches, we gathered on deck to recite the Lord's Prayer, followed by my reading the Twenty-third Psalm. At its conclusion, six seamen bore de Saucedo's body, wrapped in a weighted cloth bag, to portside mid-ships and let it fall into the sea at the whistle from my first mate. May he dwell in Your house forever, O Lord.

September 29, Friday, Lat. 33°01'S.[310] At mid-day, our voyage of 164 miles at an end, we dropped anchor at the Valparaíso roads. We knelt upon both knees, as I led the men in the *Gloria in excelsis Deo*. Thanks be to our Blessed Lord for our safe return.

Captain Pastene having ended his diary voyage recounting, we heard from Captain Villagran about the land journey down to the Maule. It was quite strange, he said, because they failed to encounter fierce Mapuche warriors eager for battle. Rather, at the settlements they came to, the friendly natives were eager to trade with the Christians "in the north." Another matter of note, he said, was that despite the heavily forested areas that we knew so well, there were many wide clearings filled with grasses taller than a man, obviously fertile land for crop growing and animal domestication. Although unknown to us at the time, high grasslands similar to these offered complete concealment to Mapuche warriors intent upon our destruction, as I shall relate at the proper time, Your Highness.

Governor Valdivia was excited to hear of the men's exploits on sea and land and the news of the rich farm land, the good harbors, the seeming friendliness of the natives in the midst of Mapuche territory, and the prospects for more gold mines. "It seems to me, gentlemen, that the captains have found our King hundreds of miles of new territory to add to His Kingdom. As time allows, we will found new towns and settle them with Christians and friendly Indians. May God bless our efforts to bring His light to the dark."[311] He inquired further of Captain Villagran about the unexpected hospitable nature of the Mapuche. Had they changed their attitude towards us Christians? Perhaps our bloody encounters with

---

[310] This and the previous days of the week correspond to those listed in the historical calendar available on-line.

[311] Pastene describes some of the particulars of his voyage in Medina, <u>Documentos inéditos</u>, VIII.

them had taken away their fighting spirit? He reminded us of what he had said following the Battle of Limari, that our killing of so many pike men in that encounter had weakened their desire for further battle. Captain Villagran had no answers to the questions, nor did any of us.

But we had an answer forthwith. In late October, a southern border guard rode into town to report that a band of unarmed natives was approaching from the south, led by an Indian on horseback. Our chamber sentry brought the word to Valdivia, who was speaking to the full *Cabildo* about land grant matters and new tax boundaries in and outside town. He adjourned the meeting forthwith and we all followed him to the Plaza Mayor to observe the matters to unfold. As we watched, the gathering of Indians stopped in the distance and a single native of regal bearing walked forward towards us. Once within hailing distance, he bowed gracefully and spoke in the Mapuche language. Valdivia beckoned Ancohualla forward to interpret. After moments of discussion with the man, Anco stated to our Governor that Michimalongo and his *caciques* were here to discuss a peace proposal and wished to draw near. The Governor assented with a wide smile and Anco sent the man on his way. Soon Michimalongo, the famed Inca *Toqui* rode up with his men, nodded to Valdivia and gestured to him as his friend. He then stated that he wished to talk about surrender and the terms of a truce. Upon hearing this, I looked around to my friends nearby, particularly to Gerónimo, with an expression of surprise and astonishment. The Governor had been correct that the *Toqui* had had enough of battle! Michimalongo went on to say that he preferred to conduct the meeting on the coming day, since he planned to bring with him gifts and offerings that would secure our new found peace. In conclusion, he requested that Ancohualla return with him to his encampment so that they might renew their friendship and discuss the next day's proceedings. Ancohualla assured the Governor that this was a peaceful offer and asked his permission to visit, which Valdivia granted promptly.

On the ensuing day, the *Cabildo* chambers were prepared in lavish fashion for the peace proceedings. Doña Inéz, Pilca Huaca, and our Indian *caciques* sat on one side of the room. At the hour of ten, the crier announced the approach of the Inca *Toqui* and Ancohualla, while some

200 other Indians waited outside the chambers. The *Toqui* and Anco were ushered into the *Cabildo* office, and Michimalongo was shown a large, comfortable chair in front of the Governor. This he declined, saying he preferred to stand as a sign of respect.

I shall take but a brief time to describe this Mapuche chief, the notable Michimalongo, Your Honor, so that You may obtain a sense of the man. Tall for an Indian, he stood taller than most of us Christians and even more so over his Mapuche followers. Possessed of piercing black eyes, he stared forward, seemingly unfazed and unafraid of walking into the midst of his former foes. Plain clothing draped his body, allowing his strong, symmetrical form to impress all those who saw him, and his long, braided black hair and a singularly resonant voice captured the notice of all. Such was the presentation of this great warrior, who seemed completely at ease in our midst.

He began the proceedings by bowing to Valdivia and proclaiming, with Ancohualla as translator, that he had become convinced that we Christians could not be driven from the land. Therefore, it was appropriate for him and his people to recognize the truth of this and forge a treaty of peace with us so that we might live together amicably. He had persuaded his followers, who we were to learn numbered some 10,000 Mapuche, that their lives must be ones of peace rather than warfare in which so many of them had been killed. "Tata,"[312] he said, as such was the name by which he referred to the Governor, "I know you to be courageous and brave in war and I trust that you will be gentle and affable in peace." He continued on to say that he and his people promised to be loyal and subject to us Christians and to serve with all obedience. "And, Tata, I have seen a vision of *Santo Iago*, he who we saw at the battle here, and he ordered me to become a Christian and lead my people to Christ and that I would find lasting salvation should I do so."

Governor Valdivia rose from his chair, addressed Michimalongo as his "brother," and welcomed him "to the peace he had come in search of

---

[312] The derivation of this name for Valdivia is unclear. De Mérida does not tell us nor do any of the historians.

because it is well understood that you, Michimalongo, as a prudent man and leader, have the best interests of your people at heart. I want to tell you why we have come to your lands. You already understand that we are Christians, and this is our name, because we worship and adore Jesus Christ, the Son of God, who became man and died on the cross for our sins. He Himself is God, as is the Father and the Holy Spirit, and all three are the true God and Lord of heaven, and earth, and sea, and of all that has been created, because He it is who created all, and everything is governed by His will and sovereign disposition. And to teach you of this Eternal One and to lead you out of the darkness, as told to you by the holy *Santo Iago*, we have our priests who will see to the instruction of your people in the knowledge of His will and bring you to the Light." He gestured towards our priests standing at the side of the room as he said these last words.

Valdivia stepped forward, grasped the hands of the Inca *Toqui*, and continued. "As to the terms of our alliance, *Toqui* Michimalongo, first you and your people will become Christians. Second, you must agree to work in our fields, to plant and raise our livestock, with generous compensation supplied by us and arranged by Ancohualla and his *caciques*. Third, we need you to work in our gold mines, again with fair treatment and generous remuneration from us. What say you to these particulars, Michimalongo?"[313] The Inca *Toqui* raised both his hands, put them upon the shoulders of the Governor, and declared his acceptance of all that he had said. Valdivia then withdrew the knife at his waist and put his left hand forward, exposing the palm. Michimalongo did the same. Valdivia then made a slight cut to his left thumb, enough to draw blood, and did the same to Michimalongo's outstretched thumb. The two next pressed them together and grasped each other's full hand, in a gesture of lasting friendship. There were murmurs from among some, but others of us knew this as the Mapuche expression of friendship. I learned it from conversing

---

[313] De Mérida has summarized the speeches of both men. Lobera, in his Ch. XVIII, provides fuller versions. Weldon Vernon mentions the treaty meeting on p. 111, but without details. Valdivia says not a word about this truce and never mentions the *Toqui's* name in his Letters, which causes a mystery as to why not.

with our Indian friends on the long journey to this land. "And now, Tata, to close our agreement, we shall bestow upon you many gifts and presents. Come, and you shall see."

We all followed outside to the Plaza Mayor, where his retinue of Mapuche awaited, and gazed in awe at the many large rectangular boxes with long beams that the Indians had supported on their shoulders and carried here. Michimalongo led Valdivia, now joined by La Doña, whom the *Toqui* addressed as "the warrior woman with long flowing dark hair who rides a white horse," to the boxes, and took from them pieces of gold jewelry of exquisite form and shape. Cups and plates of pure gold he brought forth also, every piece shining in the day's bright sun. Then he gestured us forward to two containers with a broad smile upon his face as he commanded their tops removed. Within were many bars of pure gold that glittered and shone and caused Pilca Huaca at my side to gasp at their brightness. Exclamations from the crowd attested to the surprise and wonder of it all.

"This gold, Tata, is this year's tribute to the Lord High Inca in Cusco. But our loyalty is to you and your King, so accept it as a measure of our allegiance." Governor Valdivia reached out to the *Toqui* and grasped his hand firmly in gratitude. "There is another matter, Tata, that will bind us to one another, since we have many women who will make good wives for you Christians and your Indians from Peru. Many children will come from these marriages and that will be good." This was the occasion for a surprise, for he put his hand upon the shoulder of Ancohualla, looked to the crowd of Mapuche witnessing the occasion, and beckoned with his hand to someone there. A woman of dark and handsome beauty strode forward and held her hands out to Anco, who took them with a quiet tenderness. "This woman, Tata, is the oldest of my five daughters, Millaray.[314] I have awarded her to my friend of many years as he will make her a good husband and she will bear him many sons. In this manner we will bring our nations together." As the word of this spread among the crowd, there were loud exclamations of congratulations and much clapping as well. Doña Inés, Pilca Huaca, and Collardis, went to

---

[314] Millaray is a Mapuche girl's name and means "golden one."

Millaray and welcomed her with embraces and words of congratulations. Many of us crowded around Ancohualla, the first being Valdivia, and then his *caciques*, to wish him good fortune, for all of us admired and respected him.

Late that afternoon, a banquet was set out to celebrate the new treaty. The *Toqui* hailed our fermented strawberry beverage as "refreshing."[315] Particularly of satisfaction to the chief and his *caciques* were the dishes of pork, which they had not tasted heretofore, prepared in several different ways that pleased them. At the after dinner refreshment inside the *Cabildo* chambers, we were witness to a memorable encounter between our Doña and the *Toqui*. Anco translated as Doña Inés gave him medals of gold, combs, scissors, beads, and a silver mirror. The last fascinated him, and he looked at himself in wonder many times the rest of the evening. Presently, he asked for quiet, as he wished to present Doña Inés with a gift of great value and symbolism to him and his people. He produced from his tunic a gold box and withdrew something he said was a sacred feather from a bird that lives amongst the highest mountains, those that send flame and smoke into the sky. His soldiers had found it in an enemy hut burned down in a raid upon them. It possessed magical powers, he declared, as it would not burn. He asked that a brazier be lit so he might demonstrate its uniqueness. Then, he placed the feather in the flames, where it retained its shape and texture and failed to burn. There were many gasps of amazement from the on-lookers, since we were witness to magic or deception, which one was unclear. La Doña accepted her gift with a smile and a gracious bow. This feather, Your Majesty, lies at present under glass in the foyer of our *Cabildo* building.[316] Later, the *qamchus*, Hidalgo and Paucar, appeared and engaged in their comic antics. The Mapuche had never seen such behavior, we could tell. But they became involved quickly in

---

[315] At the time of Valdivia's appearance in Chile, the strawberry was widely grown in small garden plots. Under Christian rule, larger plantings were grown. In the following years, Chileans carried the fruit with them up the western coast to Peru and Ecuador.

[316] For more about the feather incident, see Lobera and Weldon Vernon cited previously.

the merriment, in particular the *Toqui*. For the while, he put aside the serious countenance of a man of importance and permitted himself to engage in hearty laughter and clapping. Such was the beginning of our friendship with Michimalongo. However, as we were to learn, he was but one Mapuche *toqui*, and many of the other chiefs to the south remained hostile to us.

Sire, it is time to leave these historic events and take up the matter of the gold tribute the Inca *Toqui* bestowed upon the Governor. Valdivia summoned Diego Delgado, one of our men managing the Marga Marga Station mining operation, and asked him to assay the weight of the gold tribute. His judgment was that the total weighed 200 pounds and its texture was extremely fine.[317] He suggested that the source of this treasure should be determined, since it would be a mine of great value to us. When told that soon he would have a thousand more Indians for mining work, Delgado promised that he could run both Marga Marga and La Campana Stations around the clock, thus increasing the amount of gold withdrawn for us and the Royal Fifth for Your Highness.

In the ensuing weeks and months, the Inca *Toqui* and his people took up residence on land near Ancohualla and our Indians and began to sow and harvest the crops. They tended as well the growing herds of thousands of pigs, guanaco, chickens, and *huemul*.[318] Others went to work the mines in the Marga Marga, La Campana, and Andacollo Stations. And all started instruction in the basics of our Christian Faith. Father Marmolejo, at the request of the Governor, assigned our priests accordingly. Father Lobo began educating Michimalongo and his Mapuche. Father Perez traveled to Quillota to teach the miners in La Campana and Marga Marga. With the increased work of instruction, Father Marmolejo realized that we needed additional priests if we were to bring more natives to our Faith. A similar situation existed with the care of our sick, both among our Indians and us Christians, since there were not enough medical workers. Michimalongo

---

[317] At the price of gold in 12/17, this amount would be worth $3,159,777.
[318] Valdivia says that at this time they had as many as eight to ten thousand pigs and thousands of chickens. See p. 142 of his Letter I, in "Historical Sources," on the site.

gave Pilca Huaca and Collardis three of his men of medicine, which helped a good deal. Doña Inés had added three new medical workers, Juan de Oliva, Pero Estéban, and Juan Francísco de Ríberos, all from the de Monroy Peru group, but she required more.

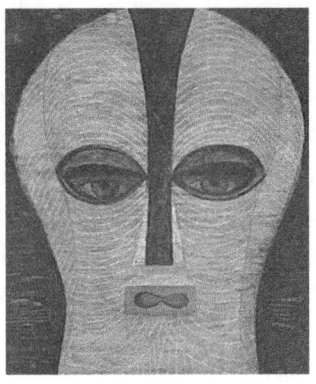

PART TT

DE MONROY SENT A SECOND TIME TO THE CITY OF KINGS TO HIRE MEN; THE KILLING FIELDS OF QUILACURA; WE REACH THE BIO-BIO AT PENCO AND RETURN TO SANTIAGO TOWN; PASTENE RETURNS, WITHOUT DE MONROY; GOVERNOR VALDIVIA LEAVES FOR PERU TO FIGHT GONZALO PIZARRO; DE HOZ FINALLY MEETS HIS DESERVED FATE

*T*he increase in the number of workers provided by Michimalongo in our mines, Honored Prince, supplied more gold to hire additional men from Peru to join us so that we might bring the southern lands, down to the Bay of Valdivia identified by Pastene on his journey, under the rule of Your Majesty. And not only to declare these lands for Spain, but to identify an area south of the Maule for town sites to serve as bases from which to carry forward future operations of settlement. In particular, the Governor was interested in the area known as Penco, a location Pastene and de

Alderete had visited on their voyage and praised as ideal for a new town. Accordingly, in September of 1545, Valdivia ordered the faithful de Monroy and the worthy Captain Pastene to depart for the City of Kings to bestow numerous gold pieces of great value upon Vaca de Castro and to search for more men and priests. Cristóbal de Escobar Villarroel, Lucas Martinez Vegaso, and Juan Calderon de la Barca, our thriving merchants, he designated to accompany Monroy and bargain for the goods, men, and materials we needed. To pay for these necessaries, Governor Valdivia gave the men two large boxes filled with gold bars worth an exceptional sum.[319]

Despite the need for more men from Peru, Valdivia decided to march south without them, since we needed to found towns and recruit more Indians to work in our fields and mines and convert them to our Faith. Accordingly, the next months saw determined activity to prepare for this expedition. La Doña Inés, who proved herself a superb planner and organizer for these kinds of activities, led these efforts.[320] The Governor chose sixty horse soldiers, including ten musket men under the command of Lázaro Pérez de Santiago, an intense man of serious countenance, rarely known to laugh but occasionally to smile, for this foray. A number of us thought the force should be doubled, and Vicente and Gerónimo said as much to Captains de Benito, now returned from his duty in La Serena, and de Quiroga, arguing that we should wait upon more soldiers from Peru before setting off to the south and that they should make this known to Valdivia. Despite their request, there was no change to the plan and, upon bidding farewell to our loved ones, we departed in mid-February of 1546 in the usual formations. This time, though, we were joined by 150 of our Indians, supplied by Michimalongo and Ancohualla, to carry our baggage and equipment, a duty for which they were duly rewarded.

We met welcoming natives as far south as the Maule, since our previous incursions had evidently convinced hostiles in the area to move farther

---

[319] Valdivia refers to the gold sent in his Letter III, p. 160 on the site. He continues with the coming expedition to the south on pp. 161 and 162, but he lacks the vivid details supplied by de Mérida.

[320] Weldon Vernon supports de Mérida in his observation of La Doña. See p. 114 of Pedro de Valdivia.

south below that river. We had returned now to the land of the oppressive "dark," and we knew it would be with us for the rest of the journey, with its fetid vapors, its perpetual nocturnal black even at mid-day, its silence that screamed at us from all sides, its green vibrancy that pressed so close we thought it a second skin. We were prepared, however, as we had fought in this land many months before and were accustomed to its dangers as well as its advantages and knew that the terrain would shape the Mapuche's maneuvers and dispositions as well as our own.

As to the friendly behavior of the Indians we encountered, matters changed in early March upon nearing the Río Nuble, sixty miles south from the Maule,[321] when on a warm afternoon Huenu and Ayar, riding ahead in their usual position, signaled that something needed my attention. As the countryside was open, without overhanging branches and thick vegetation, I saw within a few gallops the cause of their concern, for 300 warriors appeared a short distance away at the edge of a forest. They were not arrayed in battle lines, but clearly were upset and obviously agitated. I signaled Vicente to join me. Once he had assessed the situation, he left to inform Valdivia, who rode up presently with de Benito and de Quiroga in his company. The Governor forthwith sent Huenu and Ayar to converse with the chiefs to ascertain their concerns, and found upon their return that these natives demanded our withdrawal or they should kill us to a man. Valdivia, with a stern visage, summoned de Santiago and his musket men forward. They and the rest of our troop arrived quickly; the Indians meanwhile did nothing but yell and shake their weapons. The Governor ordered de Santiago to arrange the muskets in a line and commence firing when ready. In minutes, they were in position and, with still no advance from the hostiles, began firing upon de Santiago's command. Within a short time, many dead lay upon the ground. Valdivia then ordered de Benito and de Quiroga to attack and drive the others off. Those still alive took flight into the thick forest upon the charge, although our men did not follow. As a warning to other hostiles planning to cause us harm, we dragged twenty bodies of the fifty dead strapped to bundles of branches and sticks and dumped them into the river so that unfriendly natives downstream might see them.

---

[321] The Río Nuble lies seventy-five miles, not sixty, south from the Maule.

Having suffered no injuries to men or horses, we continued on. In two hours, we crossed another river[322] and came to a place to camp amongst a grim nest of trees and bushes that surrounded a wide expanse of tall grass. We were once again in "the dark" and, as Gerónimo said, "I could sleep without closing my eyes." As I mentioned before, Majesty, the nature of what Vicente Montesinos called "the dark" begins with a layer of thick low grass and dense deep bush. Then low trees, with branches bent heavy with shroud-like green leaves, loom above the lower grass and bush. Above these, tall trees with heavy hanging branches and moist leaves darken the scene below. These three layers create a gloomy, leaden, ominous darkness that resembles surely the farthest most regions of Dante's Hell. Huenu and Ayar were uniquely competent at finding the way through this gloom, since they maintained a sense of direction, though blinded by the dark, which they rarely lost.

IMAGES: Please see 5TT-UU.2-.5 for images of the rivers mentioned.

The Governor dispatched horse soldiers to scout the forest for hostiles and sent Ayar and Huenu out to look for natives who might provide information about Indians in the vicinity. In the meantime, we positioned our campsite on the northern periphery of a wide expanse of six foot high jungle grass turned light brown from the hot summer of late March. While we made camp, Ayar and Huenu returned and told me they must talk to the Governor without delay. I accompanied them to his tent, where he was speaking with Montesinos and de Alderete. After his welcome to us, my scouts told the incredible news of coming upon two squash and bean farmers in their fields who, upon receiving two bags of blue beads, revealed that 6,000 warriors[323] planned to arrive from the south late at night, at this place called Quilacura, led by a *toqui* named Malloquete, a chief with large, rounded golden rings in his ears, and seek to surprise

---

[322] This is the Río Chillán, six miles south from the Nuble.
[323] Valdivia states in Letter III on p. 161 that the Quilacura number was 7-8,000. Lobera in his Ch. XVII says there were 80,000! Later historians think both to be hyperbole. The author believes de Mérida's is closer to the correct number. Also, see Weldon Vernon, p. 115. None of these sources, however, provides any detail as to what happened on the field, as does de Mérida, except that it occurred at night.

us under the dark cover of night before sunrise on the morrow. Upon hearing this valuable piece of intelligence, de Alderete and Montesinos requested permission to study the surrounding landscape and devise a plan of attack that they would present in an hour. Governor Valdivia granted the request enthusiastically and the two retired, talking excitedly as they did so.

I should take a moment, Exalted Prince, to describe the dimensions and characteristics of the coming field of battle, since they require an explanation. The forest and jungle were in the form of the letter "n," with the closed, curved portion in the north and the open area to the south. The distance from the forest curve to the open section was about a mile and a half; the length from east to west at its widest point within the enclosure was a half mile. The tall grass began somewhere to the south outside the opening and stretched northward through the inside of the "n," with its entire length separated from the forest at its sides by about fifty feet. As I said above, Majesty, this grass was some six feet high and offered perfect concealment. Our encampment lay at the topmost portion of the curve and down its flanks nearly 200 yards on the northeast and northwest sides of the arc. With these dimensions as stated, we anticipated that the Mapuche would enter the "n" through the southern opening and crawl towards our camp to attack us upon the orders of this Malloquete.

Vicente and Gerónimo returned in less than an hour, both with expressions of confidence, and Valdivia summoned the captains and lieutenants to listen to their plan of engagement. I should say, Excellency, it was one of genius, as we all expected from these two ardent students and practitioners of tactical warfare maneuvers. The proposal they presented was the following: Surprise, terrain, and vegetation must all be used to our advantage, they said. Two units of fifteen horsemen each should be deployed in the forest, one on the eastern side, the other on the western. Captain de Quiroga was to head the eastern contingent with de Alderete as second; de Benito, with Montesinos as second, would captain the western group. Governor Valdivia, with Your servant as second in command, was to anchor the center at the top of the "n" with ten men while Gaspar de Villarroel led the reserve contingent behind us with ten horse soldiers. Lázaro Pérez commanded the ten musket men, arrayed in two teams of five placed at the top sides of the curve, one facing southeast, the other southwest, and both ready to fire upon the Mapuche should they charge us from the high grass before we launched our strike. Upon the signal of the second of two musket shots, the men at the top of the curve and those along the east and west sides of the tall grass were to toss lit tree branches into the grass. Since the hostiles would no doubt break for the southern opening to seek escape, de Quiroga and de Benito should be ready to move towards that quarter and kill them as they fled. Such was the nature of their presentation.

Once the lieutenants answered questions involving the coordination of movements and positioning of units, the Governor signaled his approval by his raised clenched fist and congratulated both men with effusive praise for their splendid plan, as such it was. The problem at present for Valdivia was when to initiate the assault. This was a decision for him and him alone to make. The farmers had said the Mapuche might strike just before dawn. We had to launch our attack before that to cause maximum surprise and inflict the most casualties. Yet how should we know when the majority of the warriors were in the high grass and thus most vulnerable? We had the answer at the end of the second watch,[324] for the Governor summoned the officers to announce that we were to deploy, take our positions, and await the second musket blast to begin throwing burning branches into the grass. Our movements had to be silent, and conducted with the utmost stealth so that we remained undiscovered by the hostiles. In our favor was the weather, as high clouds hindered star light from revealing our movements and positions. The clouds also prevented the formation of fog, which would have endangered us all.

IMAGES: See 5TT-UU.8-.10 for images of the Quilacura battle site.

To continue, Exalted Majesty, I shall summarize in brief what transpired. Since I was in charge of the center force, I sat on horse beside the Governor. He remained calm throughout and trusted the sentries to our front to respond immediately when they saw hostiles emerge from the grass. I

---

[324] This would have been at midnight.

looked out into the brooding night, watching for the enemy's movement, listening for it, by savages intent upon our complete destruction. I knew they were there, sliding on their bellies towards us, closer, ever closer. My hands were sweating and my mouth was dry in anticipation. Valdivia waited, wishing to make sure our men were in position and the majority of Mapuche were in the grass. Presently, upon the shout from one of our sentries, he said to me, "It is time, Pedro!" and called to de Santiago standing two yards in front of us to commence firing the two shots. I signaled my men to light the tree branches but to keep them hidden as best they could. The second shot sounded, and I charged off with my men to throw our burning branches into the grassland to our front. Within minutes, I saw the flickering of light in the distance on the western and eastern sides of the huge pasture. All was beginning as planned. We waited, and watched. In minutes, as the flames began to rise to our front and in the distance, the yells of frightened men were heard distinctly, shrieks such as only the tortured make. As the fire increased in intensity, we were able to see indistinct outlines of men rushing away from us, jumping, writhing right and left, screaming, shouting, yelling, crying. The scene before us seemed one straight from the depths of Hell, yet witnessed by us the living. The carnage had begun. I ordered my men down the western side near the burning grass to join de Benito and Vicente so we might assist them if needed. The fire now had engulfed the entire high grass enclosure, with brightened flames rising more than a hundred feet into the heavens that created a light so intense in the night darkness that we had to shade our eyes from the glare. The heat it gave off was so severe that we rode farther to the side near the forest to obtain relief. Suddenly, eight screaming Mapuche burst from the grass to our left seeking to flee the blazing field. The hair of one was alight, and he ran in twisted fashion this way and that trying to put it out. Another found himself smothered completely in flames from head to foot. After vain attempts to slap the fire from his body, his movements slowed until he stopped, stood there momentarily, and then fell forward to the earth, his body consumed entirely by the implacable flames. There was more screaming thirty feet away as eleven more broke through the burning brush with fire upon their bodies. They were brave but fought in a disorderly fashion with their clubs and spears and could not survive our sword slashes. Cries of the burned and dying like we had never heard before continued from inside the vast, flaming inferno and filled the night air as we rode slowly south. Soon, we joined forces with de Benito and Montesinos and arrayed ourselves at the southern end of the enclosed space, with de Quiroga and de Alderete across from us at a distance of 300 yards. The fires continued to flare and cast eerie shadows upon the forest trees and their undergrowth as warriors ran through the border of the high grass periphery and dashed between the kill space created by our two forces as they sought safety south of the flaming grass fields. We all charged into the fleeing Mapuche, currently too frightened and dazed from their confrontation with the hot, terrible flames to offer any resistance, and the slaughter continued.

At length we left off our killing, Your Honor, as there were no more of the enemy to slay; they had escaped, died by our swords, or burned to death in the raging fires. Later, the smoke clouded morning revealed all the high grass as black ash and cinders that covered the entire enclosure, over which hundreds of dead bodies lay like a blanket, all blackened by the fires and no more than charred stumps of burned flesh still smoking in the cool, silent air. Truly, this had been a complete Hell for the Mapuche in a very small place. The Governor ordered two men to count the number of dead. After we heard that near to 3,500 hostiles had met their fate in the death fires of Quilacura, there was no rejoicing on our part, simply relief that we had been spared an agonizing death within that fiery conflagration. We failed to locate the body of the *toqui*, Malloquete. He either escaped or was burned beyond recognition. We rested well into the afternoon. As after previous fights, some men only stared, at nothing in particular. We knew to let them have their peace. One of our new men recently joined from Peru, young and youthful looking, had come to make his fortune in our fabled land of Chile. But he did not understand that any new land can be cruel and tempestuous and may require being taken by force of arms. He sat slumped against a tree's trunk with one of those faces sometimes seen after a battle, all the youth sucked from the eyes, the color drained from the face, cold white lips, the blank stare, seeing nothing. And I must confess that this battle caused me to retreat into myself, oblivious to that around me, the men, the terrain, the happenings. I witnessed all with a vacant gaze, perceiving naught, not the men, the land, the goings on.

Quilacura now for many was not a name; it was an emotion. I responded only when Vicente came to me and offered his hand that I might rise.

At one point, Valdivia directed our Indians to make sleds of wood, put thirty dead bodies upon them, take them to the river, and dump them there as a warning to hostiles downriver. Although we lost two of our horses, as a matter of good fortune we sustained no injuries to ourselves, thanks be to the mercy of our most beneficent holy Savior and Lord.[325] That evening, Governor Valdivia paid tribute to Vicente Montesinos and Gerónimo de Alderete for their superb battle plan. Afterwards, we all joined in congratulating them, and Captain de Quiroga said that he and the officers would host a party for them upon our return to Santiago. And so, the affair of the death fires of the killing fields of Quilacura came to a close, Your Highness. And our two lieutenants, the designers of the operation, were soon to have their abilities rewarded appropriately and handsomely for this and past achievements.

The day following the battle, we left behind us the charred and blackened fields of Quilacura and continued our journey, now to the west and the ocean coast where the Governor wished to find a site for future settlement. In two days we came to where the Chillán and the Bio-Bio empty their waters into the sea and stayed near the small village of Penco.[326] The *cacique*, Leochengo, a man of many years and the chief de Alderete had met two years prior with Pastene, came forth alone to meet us. He greeted Gerónimo with a bow and kind words of salutation. Valdivia and the two captains bid him good day as Ayar translated. This man spoke haltingly, for part of his tongue was missing, perhaps lost in battle in his youth. What he had to say was valuable to us, since he spoke quite directly of what was happening south of the Bio-Bio amongst the Mapuche there. Since he wished to remain friends with us Christians, he warned of the imminent joining up of the Mapuche warriors to the south with those north of the river in order to push us back above the Río Cachapoal. The

---

[325] Rodrigo de Quiroga says this battle occurred in the early morning hours but says nothing more about it. See *Información de Rodrigo de Quiroga* in Medina, *Documentos inéditos*, XVI.
[326] Penco, with 46,000 citizens, lies five miles north of today's city of Concepción.

leader of this uprising of warriors was none other than *toqui* Malloquete, who could perhaps call upon as many as 30,000 Mapuche. This chief had survived the recent forest battle, said Leochengo, and was even more intent on driving us from the land. His attack could happen within the coming months. De Alderete commented upon hearing this that the encounter with the hostiles at Quilacura no doubt was a precursor to this rebellion.[327]

IMAGES: Please see images 5TT-UU.11-.16 for the Penco area.

Late that day, Valdivia announced that we were to leave for Santiago town on the morrow, since the present threat of attack was too worrisome and because our numbers were too few. This district of Penco would serve as an excellent site for a new town, he said, and we would return when more men joined us from Peru. The next day we began the journey back by following the coast rather than the route through the center of Arauco territory. I recall the following days with distinct emotion, as I was uncomfortable much of the time and was so ill that rarely could I walk without feeling I must fall over at any minute. When I rose from sitting upon the ground, the land around me grew indistinct, trees from the dark forest swung from side to side, and the ground before me rose and fell like an ocean swell. To mount and dismount my horse required assistance from Ayar or Huenu, and Vicente took charge of my guide duties at the direction of the Governor. In our new land, where a man's life depended upon his alertness to danger and his ability to use his sword and long knife to preserve his life and the lives of his friends, my condition caused distress and worry. For medical care, I had Juan Francisco de Ríberos, a man from Peru with de Escobar Villarroel, who possessed a most attentive manner towards me during my affliction. The occasional sleeping upon damp ground and the frequent soaking from rain showers worsened my suffering. So too my attempt to control what I consumed. For days I ate little, and felt the better for it. Yet, when I began to resume gradually a less rigid diet, the detested symptoms of the "bloody flux"[328]

---

[327] This gathering rebellion is referred to vaguely by Galdames in <u>A History of Chile</u>, p. 42.

[328] This is the Middle Ages term for diarrhea or dysentery.

returned once more, although without its previous strength. When finally it finished having its way with me, I had lost enough weight that my friends commented upon it.

Within a week, we entered Valparaíso Station and turned east for Santiago, which we entered at the end of March. Our families and friends welcomed us with great joy, especially my Pilca Huaca, not only because we were safe, but also because Villagran and de Aguirre had learned from friendly natives in the south that our town was in danger from Mapuche attack, perhaps by warriors with the *toqui* Malloquete. This confirmed the warning given us by Leochengo. We strengthened our defenses quickly around the town as a necessary means of security. As further protection, the Governor ordered my friend de Villarroel, with twenty men, to take up a position north of the Río Maule to watch for and warn us of any war-like movements of *toqui* Malloquete.

Our immediate activities returned to sowing, planting, harvesting, gold mining, town construction, and the like. And during this time important events occurred, Your Excellency, since by September of 1546 a year had gone by with no word from de Monroy and Captain Pastene on their venture to Peru. Governor Valdivia was not only worried about the men and supplies, but desirous of clarification about his position as Governor of our land. Although the Santiago *Cabildo* had bestowed this honor upon him, there had been no word from Your Majesty approving it. Accordingly, in September of 1547, Valdivia commissioned Juan Jufré, our co-Mayor with Francisco de Aguirre, to sail to Peru with seven men and attempt to locate de Monroy and Pastene. The Governor provided Jufré with a considerable number of gold bars to pay for men and purchase the supplies we needed. We had no intimation upon their departure that another year would pass before we heard from them again.[329]

We continued at our city tasks as we awaited word from the north, but matters soon became unruly. In September of this same year, the Governor and Captain de Quiroga departed for the mines of La Campana Station to assess the operation there for its efficiency. With the Governor absent,

---

[329] See Valdivia's Letter III, p. 163, in "Historical Sources" on the site.

the hopeless lout and ne'er-do-well, Sancho de Hoz, and his compatriot in evil, Juan Romero, attempted once more to rouse various of our men to overthrow Valdivia and seize control of the Governorship. He tempted Captain Villagran, in charge during Valdivia's absence, with a promise of great riches should he assist in the plot. The Captain asked for time to consider the proposal and consulted directly with our Doña about how to confront this latest threat. Her advice he heeded quickly and sent a messenger to La Campana Station to summon Governor Valdivia. Upon his return and upon learning from Villagran the nature of the plot, he forthwith ordered de Hoz and Romero jailed and shackled in chains while he pondered their fate.[330]

Days after this incident, Juan Bohón rode into our city from La Serena with news that Captain Pastene, gone these two long years, had arrived in La Serena in the *Santiaguillo*, but the ship was in such poor condition that repairs were required before coming on to Valparaíso Station. He bore a letter from Pastene counseling the Governor to beware of de Hoz, as he had come upon information of a proposed scheme to unseat him. While Valdivia weighed this new information that corroborated that of Villagran and La Doña, de Hoz confronted Bohón and begged him to intercede on his behalf with the Governor and save his life. My friend was sympathetic to this request and pleaded with Valdivia, at a certain point even doing so on bended knee, to forgive de Hoz and give him yet another chance. Despite the rogue's history of having attempted already to take our Governor's life, Valdivia pardoned de Hoz, but banished him to a remote valley to the southwest of our town. Remarkably, this completely worthless ruffian had found yet another way to escape his deserved fate. Later, I heard from an anonymous source that Doña Inés was furious that de Hoz was not hanged for his assassination scheme. I must admit, Your Highness, many of us were astonished yet again at the Governor's leniency towards a man of his ilk.

We must leave this briefly, for it was at Juan Bohón's return to and brief stay in Santiago that Pilca Huaca and I invited him to a repast of

---

[330] Doña Inés corroborates de Mérida's story. See *Declaración de Inés de Suárez* in <u>Documentos Ineditos</u>, XXII, 625-628.

pork, *maize*, and warm wheat bread one fine evening. In conversation afterwards, he said that he wished to sell his land, which lay beside ours and asked about our interest in it, as he owned many acres near the new town of La Serena and that property was his sole concern. Following a brief discussion, we agreed on the purchase price and on the coming day, I put that amount in gold in his possession. In the future months and years, we used some of our expanded property for the growing of the large strawberries that are a favorite in our city. The rest we devoted to the breeding and caring of our livestock of pigs and chickens, all maintained by our Indians, whom we paid handsomely for their faithful service.

I shall return now to my relation, Sire. When Captain Pastene finally arrived in early December of 1547 after two years away, he had much to convey to the Governor about the events in Peru, events that were to cause Valdivia soon to take drastic action. I shall summarize briefly the story Pastene told, as the Governor mentioned it in much more detail in his letter to Your Majesty of 15 October 1550.[331] He and de Monroy entered the City of Kings in late October of 1545 and learned of the civil war in Peru between Gonzalo Pizarro, the brother of the assassinated Francisco, and the new Viceroy, Blasco Nuñez Vela, who had replaced Vaca de Castro. On the day they, along with Cristóbal de Escobar Villarroel, Lucas Martinez Vegaso, and Juan Calderon de la Barca, had left the ship to identify merchants to supply the goods they desired, de Monroy complained of pain in his chest. A doctor suggested rest because of fatigue, but that proved a worthless remedy, for my friend died within two days. Once Captain Pastene had arranged a funeral mass and seen to his proper burial, the men resumed their attempts to obtain supplies and men, yet agents with animosity towards Valdivia prevented them from doing so for many months. It was then that the Captain encountered and joined with Jufré and his men. While they all languished in the City, word arrived from Cusco that Nuñez Vela had been killed in a battle with Pizarro. Within a week, Sire, Your representatives appointed Father Pedro de la Gasca, arrived recently from Spain, as the new Viceroy. With the former individuals with enmity towards Valdivia who had prevented

---

[331] This is Letter III. A fuller rendering of what de Mérida recounts is told by Valdivia in the Letter, pp. 167-169, on the site.

the purchasing of goods now weakened by this new appointment, Pastene loaded the ship and found thirty men eager to travel on board to seek adventure and wealth in our new land. In addition, forty mounted men said they planned to ride to our new city with Jufré and join us here in several months, which they did in January of 1548. Pastene's return voyage was a tumultuous affair as ruffians from Los Reyes attempted to capture the *Santiaguillo* and seize our goods and supplies. Fortunately, the Captain outmaneuvered the pursuing vessels and at last reached the safety of La Serena and the protection of the harbor and our men there. Presently, he entered the Valparaíso roads with his ship loaded with goods and supplies, thirty new soldiers, and our three merchant men. But, unfortunately, he brought no new priests. Such, Majesty, was the sum of his journey.[332]

Governor Valdivia, upon hearing the Captain's story, was determined to take the strong action I referred to above, Your Honor, as he decided to embark for Peru to help la Gasca against the rebellion of Gonzalo Pizarro, a man he had come to detest before leaving Cusco. He summoned the *Cabildo* to special session and identified ten men to accompany him, the most noteworthy among them Gerónimo de Alderete and Vicente Montesinos, my great and good friends. As further testament to their past and future worth to him, he promoted both to the rank of captain, so as to assist him in the anticipated battles against Pizarro. I was with them after they heard the news. De Alderete, in a moment of reflection common to him, commented, "I thought coming here I could put my sword away, settle down, raise crops and livestock, find a woman, and live the rest of my days in peace. I suppose that will have to wait." Also, Valdivia designated Captain Villagran as Lieutenant Governor in his absence, a post quite familiar to him. The *Cabildo's* approvals of these appointments were unanimous.

I am compelled to pause briefly here, Honorable One, for I must say more about my friend, Gerónimo de Alderete. I mentioned earlier his askew left eye and his amusing manner of calming others who saw it for

---

[332] Lobera in his Ch. XXV briefly mentions the journey of Pastene and de Monroy to Peru, de Monroy's death, and Pastene's return to Santiago.

the first time. He was born in Olmedo in 1518 to religiously observant parents, the youngest of five children. Suffering from a mysterious ailment at the age of seven that crippled both his legs, he used wooden sticks to carry on with his life. His parents prayed fervently every day to St. Giles for a miracle to save their boy. Indeed, their prayers were answered, for after eight months of affliction his legs began to regain their strength and movement. "This cross I bore in my youth," he once said, "made me a stronger person. I realized that I could confront and overcome all obstacles I might encounter in my later life with prayer and perseverance."[333] He acquired an early interest in the sea and, at the age of twelve years, embarked upon a Spanish ship trading in foods and goods throughout the Mediterranean Sea. In the course of his two years seeking adventure, he learned all the parts of a sailing ship and how each contributes to the functioning of a vessel. When the attraction of the New World called him, he paid his fare on board ship by serving without recompense as the third deck hand, a position that received the more difficult jobs.[334] This knowledge of sailing vessels made him a valuable assistant to Captain Pastene on the voyage of discovery to the south that I mentioned previously. Further, all who knew him regarded with great respect his ability to learn of things, even the most difficult of things, by touching the object of interest, feeling it with his fingers, moving its parts, and within a short time understanding its workings. An example of this was his comprehension of the astrolabe, which he acquired by simply touching and moving the mater and the tympan.[335] He possessed a keen eye too, for he watched others as they performed certain activities and, by imitating them, succeeded in doing whatever it was better than they. This talent carried over to personal affairs, where he studied intently the behavior of others and how that behavior affected those around them. Because of his abilities, others consulted him often if they found themselves confronted by something beyond their understanding. A

---

[333] It is not clear what caused this affliction. St. Giles (650-710) is the patron saint of cripples.
[334] A third deck hand's job involved aiding the deck officer in (un)mooring, anchoring, and performing odd jobs on board a vessel.
[335] The mater is a disk deep enough to hold a flat plate; the tympan is made for a specific latitude.

leisure pursuit of his was the study of warfare. As I related previously, he and Montesinos used to amuse themselves by drawing up battle plans to address situations of their contrivance and discussing the ideal means to vanquish the enemy. Such activity led to their design of the battle plan for Quilacura, as I have related. From all of this, one may see why Governor Valdivia chose Gerónimo for this important assignment of accompanying him to Peru and why he valued him to the degree that he did.

I shall return now to events that followed Governor Valdivia's departure on Monday, December 15 of 1547 to Peru. He had been gone no more than a week when the indefatigably evil Sancho de Hoz, assisted by the blackguard Juan Romero, launched a new attempt to overthrow the Governor and take control of the government. Juan Gómez de Almagro, our city's Chief Constable, learned of the plot when informed by Father Lobo and Alonso de Córdoba,[336] one of de Escobar's men, that they had learned of a letter that de Hoz and Romero were circulating in town seeking others to join their conspiracy. Juan Gómez took their petition to our Acting Governor, Captain Villagran. Having read the letter, Villagran initiated instant action by directing de Almagro and his constables to seize de Hoz and Romero. Within an hour, we learned that Juan Gómez had found Romero and had him in custody at Francisco de Aquirre's house. In one hour more, Villagran received further word from de Almagro that he had detained de Hoz and that both he and Romero were ready for questioning.[337] Upon his arrival at de Aguirre's house, the Governor demanded to know if de Hoz had authored the letter. After the brigand protested and declared that he was a gentleman and deserved treatment as such, Villagran had had enough. He called for our scribe, Luis de Cartagena, and dictated to him the order that Sancho de Hoz's head be cut off for treason. Governor Villagran signed it and

---

[336] (1505-1589). De Córdoba was to hold several Santiago council positions during the coming years.

[337] De Córdoba refers to the capture of these two in the *Declaración* de Alonso de Córdoba, in Medina, <u>Documentos Inéditos</u>, XXII, 172. Also see Marmolejo, Alonso de Góngora, <u>History of All Things that have occurred in the Kingdom of Chile and of those who have ruled (1536-1575)</u>. See the Bibliography for the website address of this work.

put him in de Alderete's custody. As for Romero, Villagran declared that he should hang until he rendered up his soul and signed the order forthwith. Father Marmolejo gave both men the last rites of Holy Mother Church and, the following morning on the south bank of the Cañada de San Francisco[338] near the southern side of Santa Lucia and with the entire *Cabildo* as witness, Juan Gómez handed the executioner, one of his constables, his sharpened sword. At de Almagro's shouted command, the sword strike severed the head at its base even while Sancho de Hoz pleaded for his life, the words echoing for seconds after his head lay in the dust. Afterwards, it swung from a high branch of the lone tree at the side of the Cañada. The next day, it was Romero's turn, again with the *Cabildo* as witness. From another branch of the same tree, a rope with a noose twisted from side to side in a slight breeze. A constable escorted Romero, with a blind over his eyes and sitting upon his horse, to the end of the rope and placed the noose about his neck. At de Almagro's command, his officer slapped the horse's haunch and it galloped off, leaving Romero at the end of the rope, his neck snapped and his body swinging slowly in the light wind. Later, the Governor called the *Cabildo* to formal session and ordered all of us to sign a document attesting to the deaths of both men. Such was the end of these two malcontents, de Hoz the perpetrator of a number of assassination attempts upon the Governor and Romero his witless accomplice in this, de Hoz's last attempt to take control of our government. Notably absent from the execution proceedings was our Inés de Suárez. Medical matters had prevented her from witnessing them, as an outbreak of sickness amongst our Indians had required her to render assistance to Pilca Huaca and Collardis. But, as she told me later, the sick were more important to her than these evil rogues and that she knelt upon her knees and thanked our Lord when she heard the news of their deserved departure to Hell.

PAINTING: Please see P5.2 for the de Hoz reaction to his sentence.

---

[338] This is today's major thoroughfare of Bernardo O'Higgins.

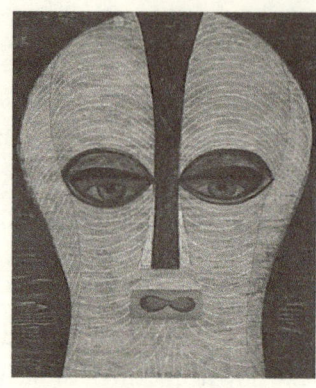

PART UU

SANTIAGO DEFENSES STRENGTHENED; VICEROY LA GASCA APPROVES VALDIVIA AS GOVERNOR OF THE PROVINCE OF CHILE; THE VICEROY'S LEGAL CASE AGAINST OUR GOVERNOR; HE REACHES VALPARAÍSO STATION AND HEARS OF THE DESTRUCTION OF LA SERENA; THE SEPARATION FROM INÉS DE SUÁREZ; HER MARRIAGE TO RODRIGO DE QUIROGA

With our Governor and two of our best officers away on the venture to Peru, Lieutenant Governor Villagran decided to place an emphasis until their return upon a rigorous defensive system around our city, since we still worried about *toqui* Malloquete leading an uprising from the south. Even with Lieutenant de Villarroel and his men stationed on the Maule to provide an early warning of trouble, we needed more protection. Accordingly, having consulted with the captains, Villagran decided upon the following. We would establish four "advanced warning-watching posts," as he referred to them, manned by eight men apiece, commanded by a lieutenant and situated at the four compass corners eight miles from the outer limits of our growing city. The men at each post would be replaced every five days by a new contingent. Their primary duty was to watch and listen for Mapuche encroachment and notify our city command of the danger. Each day, all warning-watching camps were to send two horse soldiers to the two posts closest to them, while those camps did the same. Upon the soldiers meeting, they were to return to their home encampment. In these movements of our men, we sought to encircle the city with a means to warn us of possible or imminent threat of attack. Meanwhile, the men left in camp were to seek out nearby natives and attempt to gain their friendship. As to the sustenance of the camps, we supplied them with food and needed goods from town by weekly llama caravans driven by Michimalongo's people. And, in an unexpected demonstration of his friendship with us Christians, Michimalongo pledged to train a force of 2,000 of his and Ancohualla's Indians to serve as our battle allies, protect our city, and help us colonize the southern lands, an action much appreciated. No doubt his willingness to help proceeded from a deep animus towards *toqui* Malloquete, who had rebuked Michimalongo's leadership in the past.

To coordinate these activities and all matters military, Governor Villagran created a new *Cabildo* position called the Captain General of Military Affairs, a post subject to the orders of the Governor. And the man he appointed was Captain Pedro Gómez de Benito, our highly respected battlefield commander, whose experience went back to the conquest of Mexico days with Hernán Cortés. His wide-ranging responsibility was to coordinate the ring of protection encampments around the city, manage the seek and subdue missions in the nearby countryside, train and deploy our forces throughout our growing land, assure that the soldiers were well housed and fed, see to our weaponry, and care for the horses. In sum, all matters concerning the maintenance of our forces were subject to his authority. The creation of this command position proved fortuitous in the coming years. As we founded new towns and our land of Chile began to grow, the military grew in size and for that reason needed organization and control.

To return to Governor Valdivia and the ten men with him who had left for Peru to confront the Pizarro uprising, they had been gone several months when the prestigious men of our community became worried about their fate. Eventually, Lieutenant Governor Villagran presented a proposal to the city *Cabildo* that we authorize Pedro de Villagran, his cousin,[339] to sail to Peru to determine their whereabouts and learn if Viceroy la Gasca[340] had confirmed Valdivia, in Your name, Sire, as Governor of Chile. This journey we on the *Cabildo* approved. Others wished to accompany Villagran, however. A number of new men believed that Valdivia had failed to govern fairly, especially in the awarding of land grants, and consequently should not be designated the Governor by the Viceroy. There were other complaints as well, all of which Lieutenant Governor Villagran treated in fair-minded fashion. He allowed all of them to go, and they arrived in Peru in late October, 1548.

I shall return to what effect these different groups had upon the thinking and actions of la Gasca concerning Valdivia, but now, Your Honor, asking Your Grace's patience, I shall provide a summary of the events that transpired in Peru involving Valdivia and our men and their return to us.[341] Viceroy la Gasca has provided Your Excellency with his account,[342] so my telling, learned from Montesinos and de Alderete upon their return, will be brief and to the point. Valdivia and the men arrived in mid-January of 1548 at the port of Callao. La Gasca welcomed them in Cusco and put Valdivia in charge of the Viceroy's armies, a fortuitous decision on his part. A meager band of rebels led by Gonzalo Pizarro was defeated by Valdivia's force on April 9 of 1548 in the Battle

---

[339] (1513-1577). It is not clear why de Mérida has not introduced this man prior to this. History tells us he was likely a Tacna man. He served in several Chile political posts in the coming years.

[340] Pedro de la Gasca, 1485-1567, a Spanish priest and diplomat, was appointed by the King as the second Viceroy of Peru. Along with his religious bona-fides, he was a ruthless disciplinarian.

[341] One may read Valdivia's account of his Peru venture in his Letter III, pp. 175-189, in "Historical Sources." Also, see Weldon Vernon, Ch. VII.

[342] See La Gasca's letter to the Council of the Indies, March 9, 1548, in Medina, <u>Documentos ineditos.</u> Also, Marmolejo, Ch. IX.

of Jaquijahuana.[343] Refusing to pardon the mutineers, Father la Gasca had the lot of them beheaded. And within the hearing of Vicente and Gerónimo at the conclusion of the battle, he addressed Valdivia thusly: "Ah! Sir Governor! What a lot His Majesty owes you!"[344] Two weeks later, on April 23, he formally installed Valdivia as the Governor and Captain-General of, as it was now designated, the "Province" of Chile, from the Copayapu Valley at 26 degrees south latitude to 41 degrees south latitude at San Pedro Bay, the farthest point to the south reached by Pastene and de Alderete on their 1544 voyage.[345]

IMAGES: Please view 5TT-UU.18-.21 for images of the battle and its aftermath as well as the Fortress of Sacsayhuaman.

The goal the Governor had pursued for years at last come to pass, his primary purpose now was to hasten back to Santiago with as many men and supplies as possible. He identified over 200 men who wished to begin new lives in the Province of Chile, eighty of them with horses. He put these under the command of Montesinos for the return ride. He and de Alderete finished loading three ships with goods and 120 new men and were prepared to leave in mid-October when, in a surprise to the Governor, an officer by the name of Lorenzo de Aldana,[346] who had once been part of Pizarro's men but renounced him for la Gasca, insisted to the Viceroy that Governor Valdivia had left the City of Kings with stolen goods and should be called back to provide restitution. The Viceroy sent his aide to locate the Governor and found him in Callao as he was about to sail. Of course, he honored the request of la Gasca, who told him that he had begun an investigation into the charges and that this would delay Valdivia's departure for several weeks. It was at this point that those from our city arrived, those I mentioned above, Your Honor. La Gasca agreed to hear all that they had to say, thus further preventing the Governor and

---

[343] In *Quechua*, this is Sacsayhuaman, the Inca fortress above Cusco. The author has visited it three times through the years.
[344] Valdivia mentions this exclamation in his Letter III, p. 182.
[345] For a detailed recounting of the Pizarro uprising, see Prescott, William H., History of the Conquest of Peru, Book V, Ch. III. It resides on the site in "Historical Sources."
[346] (1508-1571).

his men from leaving. Finally, in late November of 1548, a trial was held and the verdict and decree rendered, which I shall present shortly. The Governor returned to his ships and saw to their re-provisioning and the stocking of goods. With those tasks completed in mid-January of 1549, he sent Captain Montesinos and the eighty men on their ride to Santiago while he and de Alderete embarked for Valparaíso Station with the new men and supplies.

At the end of February on their journey back to us, Vicente and his men were aghast as they approached La Serena Station. He told me later that he knew something was amiss whilst still a mile from the town, as things did not seem "right" to him. His fears were confirmed quickly, for they beheld the horror of the destruction of La Serena. All the buildings had been burned to the ground and the bodies of our men, including that of my friend, Juan Bohón, were scattered all about, some with their limbs missing, some beheaded, and a number of them swinging from trees. It was a sight, Montesinos told me, that caused him to become physically sick. He and his men buried the bodies and rode to us to tell of the tragedy. This caused much sorrow among us and our priests said masses asking our Blessed Lord to look mercifully upon the souls of our friends. Lieutenant Governor Villagran appointed Constable Juan Gómez de Almagro as his replacement and left town with Captains de Benito, de Aguirre, and sixty men, including thirty musket men, to ride to the destroyed town, knowing all was lost yet determined to kill every savage they might find to mete out punishment and send the message that any future such incursions would invite annihilation.[347]

Meanwhile, Montesinos, in a presentation to the *Cabildo*, made it understood that la Gasca had confirmed Valdivia as the Governor, and this produced loud shouts and applause. Valdivia, he said, would share the other details of the Viceroy's decree, upon his return. But one particular soon became known, for there were among Vicente's troops various men who were unwell physically and needed attention by La Doña and her

---

[347] Valdivia mentions the destruction of La Serena in his Letter III, pp. 188,189; by Lobera, in Ch. XXVII and XXVIII; by Marmolejo, Ch. VII; and by Weldon Vernon, p. 154.

medical workers. It seems that she overheard talk among them and their visitors about the decision of the Viceroy that she and the Governor must cease their relationship, and that she must either leave Chile or marry one of the men in Santiago. With her usual decisiveness and with no doubt that Governor Valdivia must obey the Viceroy's order, Doña Inés resolved not to wait for the Governor's return and have to live through difficult months of unpleasantness before separation. For that reason, she chose to end their friendship and remain in Santiago to marry another. She had her medical mission to oversee, and it had become the primary purpose in her life. She possessed also ample property from the land grants to provide for her well-being. She consulted with Father Marmolejo about these matters. He agreed with her decision to leave the Governor, stay in Chile, marry another, and suggested as well that she erect a chapel and pray every day before its altar for both hers and Governor Valdivia's souls. Within weeks, on Monday, May 2, Father Marmolejo performed the wedding ceremony, which brought Inés de Suárez and her chosen husband and close friend of Valdivia, Rodrigo de Quiroga, to blessed union[348] before a select group of the friends of both, with my Pilca Huaca and Collardis her mistresses in waiting.

To return to my accounting, Noble One, summer storms delayed Governor Valdivia's voyage back to us, and the vessels entered Valparaíso harbor in the middle of April. There he heard the terrible news of the destruction of La Serena. When he had received details of this disaster and learned that Villagran had ridden to the scene to exact deadly revenge, he decided to remain at Valparaíso Station with our stores and men until his return. When he arrived, the two embraced one another warmly and Villagran told of the bloody penance he had levied upon 150 savages for their killing of our men. The next day, they all left Valparaíso, reached our city on June 12 of 1549, and received a warm and excited welcoming.

Two days later, Governor Valdivia summoned the *Cabildo* to special session and closed it to all except Council members. Then he read the

---

[348] Weldon Vernon supports most of what de Mérida says. See Pedro de Valdivia, pp. 158-159.

entire decree of Viceroy la Gasca with its fifty-seven rulings. Below are the most noteworthy of those findings, Your Honor, in summarized fashion.

1. The Viceroy confirmed Valdivia as the Governor of our Province of Chile.

2. Within six months upon arrival in Santiago, he was to cease his relationship with Inés de Suárez and either marry her to someone else or send her from the Province. In addition, he was to ask his wife, Marina Ortiz de Gaete González, to join him here in our Province.[349]

3. The Governor must repay the loans he obtained from some of us that he used to pay for the journey to Peru.

4. He must allow those who wished to leave the Province to do so.

5. Future awards of land grants must have enough Indians assigned to them so that they were not overworked.[350]

As I said, these were the most significant of the Viceroy's judgments. I shall refrain from commenting upon them, Your Eminence, since that is a matter to keep historians employed. At the reading's conclusion, the Governor stated that he intended to follow the Viceroy's directions in all matters and he charged the *Cabildo* to assure that he did so. Upon the conclusion of this dramatic and historic proceeding, Lieutenant Governor Villagran thanked the Governor for his honesty and forthrightness. To mark the occasion of Valdivia's appointment, Villagran proposed that the coming days be given over to celebratory functions. This the Governor asked not to be carried forth. He wished to dedicate himself only to the implementation of the verdict's findings, he said, and planned to begin without delay in doing so. One of his priorities was to march south to found towns so that he could bestow land grants, pacify the natives, and

---

[349] We will learn more of Marina Ortiz, 1509-1592, later in the Sixth Letter,
[350] See La Gasca's letter to the Council of the Indies, November 26, which details all the charges against Valdivia in Weldon Vernon, p. 185.

employ them in our mines and fields. Our numbers, now increased by more than 300, would help provide the men to start such an operation. But first, he said, we must re-establish our destroyed La Serena. Accordingly, on June 30 he declared Captain Francisco de Aguirre as its Lieutenant Governor; the estimable de Aguirre left our city with thirty men and on 26 August of 1549 founded San Bartolomé de La Serena in the name of Our Precious Lord and Savior, Jesus Christ.

I shall end this Letter, Your Excellency, with words about this gentleman, Francisco de Aguirre, as his appointment to this post compels me to say more about this most notable and accomplished man. He was born in 1507 to parents of the upper middle class, who provided him with an education in the arts and military affairs. He joined the army and participated in the Battle of Pavia and the assault on Rome in 1527. While in the Eternal City, he protected a convent of nuns and, as a reward for this service, the Pope allowed him to marry his cousin, Maria de Torres y Meneses, while the King appointed him Mayor of Talavera de la Reina.[351] He traveled to Peru in 1536; when he heard that Valdivia was on his way to conquer Chile in 1540, he joined with Rodrigo de Quiroga and, together with their troops totaling twenty-five, met us at Calama, Majesty, as I have related in my Fourth Letter.

As a result of his years of military and political accomplishments, one might have expected him to possess a nature somewhat aloof and distant. But this was not the case, as his friendly countenance and easy affability, notable in the way he greeted people and chatted with them, and his unusually deferential manner for a man of his stature, earned him a great deal of respect and loyalty from his men. His appearance was gentlemanly and dignified, with his shaped beard, wide forehead, and broad shoulders adding emphasis to his overall presentation. His temper flared upon occasion, yet he was quick to control it. Since he was best when life did not present surprises or events he was unprepared to confront, a number felt

---

[351] Medina, Jose Toribio, Collection of Unpublished Documents Concerning the History of Chile, 1888-1902. Talavera de la Reina is a city in the western part of the province of Toledo, which in turn is part of the larger community of Castile–La Mancha, Spain.

that he might be a poor choice to re-found La Serena. But future events proved these worries unsubstantiated, as he served in an outstanding manner in the rebuilding of that town and its subsequent governance. As to a personal peculiarity, he was interested in the proper maintenance and shaping of his hair and meticulously guided those who cut it with elaborate and exacting instructions as to where and what to cut, how close to the scalp, and the shaping of the overall at the conclusion. He and our Governor were close, as I have disclosed previously, and they enjoyed immensely each other's company.

This brings to a close, Honored One, my Fifth Letter to Your Majesty. The Sixth follows forthwith.

I Remain, Majesty,   Your Most Humble Servant

Pedro de Mérida

Don Pedro de Mérida

Signed

May 10 1567

Santiago *del Nueva Extremadura*

THE SIXTH LETTER

Written to the King by Pedro de Mérida from Santiago *del Nueva Extremadura* on September 12, 1568.

PART VV

SKIRMISH AT THE RÌO NIVEQUETEN; BATTLE OF THE ANDALIÉN; THE BATTLE OF FORTRESS PENCO; VALDIVIA ORDERS THE HANDS AND NOSES OF THE CAPTIVES CUT OFF

Once again, Blessed Majesty, I take pen in hand to relate further adventures in the fabled land of *Nuevo Extremo*, or Chile, with Captain Pedro de Valdivia, in this my Sixth Letter, wherein I shall recount events during the years 1549 to 1554.

I begin my relation in Santiago where the Governor now turned his attention to bringing our Province to peaceful productivity. Accordingly, in early July of 1549, he sent Captain Francisco de Villagran, with several of our men and Indians, to Peru with eight crates of gold bars to hire more men and purchase supplies, goods, and horses. Also, he carried reports from our Governor to deliver to Viceroy de La Gasca concerning his actions in fulfilling the findings of the Viceroy's decree.[352] In addition,

---

[352] See Valdivia's Letter III, p. 189 in "Historical Sources" and Lobera, Ch. XXIX.

the Governor entrusted a letter to Villagran addressed to his wife in Villanueva de La Serena, the aforementioned Marina Ortiz, asking her to join him so that they might resume their lives together.[353] I shall tell more of this honorable lady, Your Eminence, when appropriate.

With such matters attended to, we now prepared to depart for the southern lands in order to build a fort at Penco and one day found a town there. The land force was to be a seek and subdue offensive operation to find the *toqui* Malloquete and his followers, pacify them, locate mines, found our new town, and cultivate the land. Additionally, spies sent by the Inca *Toqui* to determine the disposition of the Mapuche months before had returned with the news that another Mapuche *toqui*, Ainavillo by name, had joined his forces with Malloquete's and that both intended to drive us from our land.

Commander of Military Affairs Gómez de Benito designated 200 men on foot and mounted, with twenty musket men commanded by Lázaro Pérez de Santiago, as the land fighting force. Our captains were Montesinos, de Alderete, Pedro de Villagran, and Juan Jufré. The lieutenants were Sanchez de Morales, Antonio Carrillo, Luis de Cartagena, Hernando Vallejo, Francisco de Riberos,[354] Juan Godínez,[355] Gregorio de Castañeda,[356] and Your humble servant. One hundred of our Indians chosen by Ancohualla, well recompensed by us, carried our equipment and food. Michimalongo and 300 of his warriors accompanied our land force, a most welcome addition, to protect our flanks and rear.[357] As for sea operations, Governor Valdivia directed Captains Pastene and Villalón to command the naval forces that were to meet us at Penco with reinforcements and supplies, as well as goods for the fort we would build there, and medicines for any wounded we might have. De Benito assigned

---

[353] The reader may recall that Valdivia and Marina Ortiz were married for ten years and living in La Serena, Spain, tilling the land on their small farm before he departed for Peru.

[354] (1512-1580)

[355] Godínez was a Tacna man mentioned in the Fourth Letter.

[356] (1517-1567)

[357] Lobera, in Ch. XXXIII, mentions Michimalongo providing warriors for the move south, but does not indicate the number of them.

forty men to the captains for this effort. They were to wait until two weeks after our departure, then sail to Penco and remain there until our signal to come ashore.

But on our day of departure in September, an event of painful consequence occurred. It happened in this manner. I was about to depart with my guides, Huenu and Ayar, when behind me I heard the neigh of a horse and a loud noise like that of an object striking the ground. When I turned, I saw the Governor lying on his side with his right arm twisted under his body and screaming in pain. His aide, de Cartagena, immediately dismounted and ran to his side to provide comfort. Captain Jufré and de Ríberos, our medical man for this journey, were quickly with him to ease his pain and assess his injuries. As it turned out, he had broken all the toes of his right foot and dislocated his right thumb.[358] These injuries were so painful and debilitating that there was no question whether we might embark upon our mission to the south. It would have to wait.

With our commander unable to ride or walk, his rest and recuperation were of paramount importance. In the meanwhile, he asked de Benito to use the time to engage in the tactical training of all the men in the particulars of fighting the Mapuche in the close, dark forests — the dark, as Vicente referred to it. We veterans welcomed this training, since forty of the men were newly from Peru and had no experience fighting in such surroundings. Accordingly, an area fifteen miles to the south, which resembled the terrain we were to encounter on our expedition, became our training ground five days a week. The captains re-created the encounters we had had with the hostiles in the south on previous journeys there and the tactics we had used and, while remembered by us veterans, were completely new to our Peru men. We practiced also "the bolt," "the single-hand closure," and the "double hand closure" maneuvers, since some of our encounters with Mapuche might be in open spaces and permit such formations.

In these days awaiting our Governor's recovery, a disturbing incident occurred that one day would prove prophetic. For one Saturday evening,

---

[358] See Valdivia's Letter III, p. 190, in "Historical Sources" on the site.

a pleasing respite day from our training maneuvers, I invited Vicente and Gerónimo to dinner. After enjoying our repast, Pilca Huaca excused herself so she might direct our helpers in the after dinner tasks.[359] As the three of us amused one another by recalling the humorous incidents that had occurred on our journey to Chile from Peru, Vicente became uncharacteristically quiet. After a few minutes, I asked of my friend if he might be uncomfortable and whether we could assist him in any manner. He replied in an even and controlled tone that he thought Governor Valdivia's accident was an omen of future catastrophe, a prophecy of darker events to come. "I confessed to Father Marmolejo this morning," he said, "as I do not expect to return from this venture to the south. I have never felt this way before and so I believe these portents to be true. I feel I have an appointment with destiny, that which has always faced mankind. And mine will be presently upon me." This unsettled me, Your Grace, since I had never before heard him voice such sentiments. Gerónimo was at a loss for words. But I felt compelled to make answer. "I believe, Vicente, that we either live and die by accident or we live and die by plan. Some say that we shall never know and that we are like small bugs that children kill upon a summer afternoon. But I believe, to the contrary, that even the sparrow does not fly without a gentle push from the hand of God. And so, Vicente, my dear friend, whatever happens to you, our Governor, Gerónimo, or me will be caused by our Lord and Savior, Jesus Christ, so let us remain at peace with His plans for us." Gerónimo, with a serious and reflective expression, nodded in agreement. Yet, my friend was not at ease. "We shall await the verdict of our Lord," he said. And so this disquieting matter ended.

Your Excellency, the Governor summoned at last the strength to begin our journey, and we left our town on Saturday, January 7 of 1550, with our Constable, Juan Gómez de Almagro, in charge during our absence. Valdivia could not ride his horse, however, and so our Indians carried him in a chair formed of llama hides.[360] My guiding band of Huenu and Ayar, accompanied by Lieutenant Antonio Carrillo with four men for

---

[359] Such servant duty must have been highly prized by the Indians in those days.

[360] De Mérida's account of the next several months corroborates a good deal of what Valdivia wrote to the King in his Letter III found on the site.

our protection, took the lead. Behind us at a distance, the lead force of 150 mounted and unmounted soldiers followed, joined by Michimalongo and his 300 warriors. The Governor rode with this force, with Captains de Alderete and Pedro de Villagran commanding the mounted men, and Juan Jufré in charge of the unmounted. Our Indians carrying our equipment and food came next. Fifty men under Captain Montesinos brought up the rear. At the Río Maule on January 17, we met my long-time friend Lieutenant de Villarroel and his twenty men at the Río Maule who had served as our early warning contingent for an attack by Malloquete during the Governor's journey to Peru two years prior. We celebrated that night with large amounts of fish, vegetable dishes, and generous portions of fermented fruit juice, all prepared by our Indians.

Honored Sire, in a past letter, You thanked me for telling of the men seeking to bring this land to Christ, and I find this the proper time to discourse upon the well-regarded Gaspar de Villarroel. Born in 1510 in Villarreal[361] to kindly, deeply religious parents of modest means, his father was a tailor and his mother a seamstress. He and his older brother grew of age learning the basics of both occupations, while the youngest brother became a cloistered monk of the Cistercian Order. The exploits of Hernando Cortés in Mexico gained Gaspar's interest at a young age; those of Francisco Pizarro in Peru convinced him that his destiny resided in the new world. Bidding farewell to his parents, he set sail for that fabled land, arrived following our departure from Cusco with Valdivia in 1540, and joined the ne'er-do-well, Sancho de Hoz, and his vagabond followers as they were on their way to meet us at Copayapu. I told of our encounter with these brigands in my Fourth Letter to Your Grace.[362] Although Gaspar and his companions did not share the scoundrels' desire to overthrow our Captain, various men still regarded Gaspar with suspicion as to his leanings, until his constant and relentless devotion to duty to the Captain erased all ill feeling. As to other matters, he possessed certain attributes that set him apart from others. For example, he wished to be first in all he undertook: he had in him intensity and determination

---

[361] Founded in 1274, Villarreal (Royal Village) today is famous for its ceramic tile industry and has a well-regarded soccer team.
[362] See Part LL of the Fourth Letter.

that allowed him to surmount all barriers with alacrity. And, he was so ready and eager to obey authority that he did whatever was demanded of him. This proceeded from a strong sense of principle, not of fear, and he was far more sensitive to rebuke than to any kind of hardship. As to other characteristics, he was small of stature, and that lent the impression of an insignificant presence. But his cheerfulness and high spirits at occasions of crisis and his ability to raise a smile or laugh at such moments made him an agreeable companion. In his dealings with others, he acted with more principle towards those who wished him ill than those who wished him well. By this I mean that he never acted against the former without just cause, but occasionally associated himself with injustices committed by the latter. In like manner, he was generous in giving credit to those opposed to him, if they were in the right, yet often unable to condemn his friends if they were in the wrong. In brief, he felt he had done nothing dishonorable if it were to help a friend. And if any adversary encountered misfortune, he was the first to tender his sympathy and an offer to help if the other desired it. On a more personal note, he was one of the first among us to take an Indian woman to wife,[363] one Curi Illpay by name,[364] a woman known for her devotion to our Christ and her good deeds amongst those less fortunate in our midst. All in all, Excellency, Gaspar de Villarroel was a man respected and admired, and I hold it an honor that we were close friends.

In seven days more, we crossed the Río Itata north of Penco and moved east. The Governor was able to ride now, with assistance from de Cartagena to mount and dismount. In days, we passed the still blackened fields of Quilacura, the memory of the battle still fresh to those of us who had fought there, and turned south. One day beyond that battlefield, we entered a thick forest as dark clouds settled over the three canopied cover above, only faintly seen by us in the dark below. Heavy and cruel winds that bent tree branches downward, exposing the pale undersides of their leaves, suddenly blew furiously upon us. Wind blow after blow

---

[363] See Part QQ of the Fifth Letter.
[364] Curi Illpay was the wife of the Lord High Inca Huayna Yupanqui, who ruled from 1493 to 1527, and so her name was popular for the naming of new-born girls.

followed upon one another, thrashing the branches above us violently up and down, to this side and that, creating a chaotic scene that we tried to maneuver through. The thunder was continual and deafening. I called to Huenu and Ayar, to my front and hardly visible, to halt and shouted to Carrillo to go back and ask the Governor for orders regarding advancing farther. In a quarter of an hour he returned and yelled that Valdivia had ordered us to halt and set up camp. The wind and rain were now so violent that even my horse seemed to shudder amidst the uncomfortable conditions. Our site at first was a confused affair, with tents raised hastily and our goods and supplies placed in scattered piles by our Indian bearers. Lieutenant Vallejo, the watch officer, with assistance from Lieutenant de Castañeda, set our double ring of watch posts around our lonely outpost. The rain continued to pour down in almost overwhelming amounts, as the thundering went on as though it meant to continue forever. Our Indians, who seemed undisturbed by the watery conditions, deposited our food rations of pork *charqui* and vegetables at our tents. Until now, we had endured a number of storms, but this one was of real import. Though the officers of the watch set our sentinels and monitored them hourly, we slept on nights such as these fully armed and ready to give battle in this hostile land of the hostile Mapuche. This was their land and they had lived here since long ago in the past and were at home here. But a number of us had fought battles and skirmishes in the darkened confines of their deep forests and felt we knew how to fight in their home too. Yes, this was the world of the Mapuche, but we were mounted horse soldiers, the most deadly fighting force our new land had ever seen. I say this, Honored Sire, not as boastfulness but as a statement of proven fact. Of course, we would suffer wounded and dead, yet in the end we would prevail, and in triumphant fashion.

IMAGES: See 6VV-ZZ.1-.3 for images of the scenes below.

The rain all through the night was over, although it was damp, gray, and wind-blown at daybreak. Low, dark, oppressive clouds drifted across the dull sky, as the high treetops roared with a deep droning and the foliage underneath, the tree branches, shrubs, and grass, rustled in the fretful breezes. It was a melancholy morning. We remained vigilant, with

Captain de Alderete and twenty men now riding in front of my guiding group each day to seek out the enemy. On February 5, we approached the Río called Nivequeten,[365] two musket shots wide and as deep as our stirrups; the dark brown current ran slowly amidst the shadows on both shores. Surprisingly, we had not been attacked by Mapuche, something unexpected. This soon changed, however, for when we met the Bio-Bio just to the east of its junction with the Nivequeten, Huenu called to me that de Alderete and his men were fighting hundreds of Mapuche to our front. I shouted back to Carrillo, who rode up quickly. We joined Huenu and Ayar and saw that our horse soldiers were in a skirmish across the Bio-Bio. He left to inform our Governor and I yelled to his four men to follow me. We galloped forward, in seconds broke through the high brush, and beheld de Alderete and his men arrayed on the southern shore a musket shot away, slashing and stabbing at hundreds of Mapuche.[366] The río was shallow in this part, near to our horses' knees, and we crossed easily to enter the fray at the left or eastern side of the line. Gerónimo saw us and rode over yelling to follow him. We pivoted round the fighting and galloped south through the low brush so as to, I now understood, maneuver to their rear. Upon covering 150 yards, we found ourselves behind the savages, now to our north. With no warriors in their rear as reserves, we were in a perfect position to annihilate them all. Gerónimo waited a few minutes, until the center of the Mapuche resistance began to waver. At his, "Let's at them, men!" we charged forward into the gap offered by the weakened hostiles and began our slashing and stabbing, wreaking great havoc with our steel as we did so. At one point de Alderete shouted to Lieutenant Vallejo, his second in command, to have twelve men form up north to south and push forward to the west. Gerónimo, with the five of us and his other eight, did the same and sought to surround the savages at our end and drive them east. Within fifteen minutes, the Mapuche will collapsed and Indians ran to the south and west to escape our deadly swords and long knives. Hundreds lay dead or dying in the brush and grass before de Alderete ordered a halt to the killing. Governor Valdivia and several captains and men had arrived by now on the northern

---

[365] This river has since been renamed and is today's Río Laja.
[366] Valdivia puts the number at 2,000 in his Letter III. See "Historical Sources" on the site.

banks. The Governor raised his right fist to signal a job well done and rode across to assess the carnage. He congratulated us for our deeds and said that we should celebrate this night on guanaco, since Michimalongo had found hundreds grazing nearby. We returned to the northern side of the río and positioned a camp with double guards around it. So ended the skirmish at the Río Nivequeten.

The day following, we crossed the Nivequeten above its juncture with the Bio-Bio and made camp on its northern shore. We remained here nine days, with daily forays by patrols to seek out the Mapuche hoards we knew must be nearby. Our Governor ordered all to stand guard throughout the nights, half of us on the first watch and the rest on the second. By great good fortune, the plans of Malloquete and Ainavillo were surprised and made known to us, Sacred Majesty, through the wisdom and foresight of Michimalongo. He convinced the Governor to dispatch his *cacique*, Quepuanté, and ten of his warriors to seek out the location of the Mapuche to the west. When they returned in three days, they had four hostages with them, men they had captured thirty miles to the northwest. They were remarkably fine men, fairly complected, six feet tall, with slim waists and broad shoulders. It happened that these four were warrior *caciques*, who possessed especially valuable information about the numbers of Mapuche awaiting us, their positioning, location, and the battle intentions of the *toquis*. We officers watched the proceedings as the Inca *Toqui* conducted their questioning. The first two spat out replies that they did not know anything of the matters in question. Michimalongo looked at Valdivia, who motioned with his right hand at his throat. The *Toqui* gestured to four of his warriors, who dragged the two forty feet distant, forced them to their knees, and then cut them at their necks until their heads dropped to the ground. They uttered not a word during their ordeal. The third answered also that he did not know, and added, "Do likewise to me. I am a man and can die!" Our Governor made the same sign to the *Toqui*, and this man proved as brave as the previous two. Not one of them had betrayed the united cause of the Mapuche nation! I glanced over to Montesinos and de Alderete. At my pursed lips indicating admiration for their behavior, both conveyed their agreement with positive nods. The conduct of the fourth *cacique* was exceptionally different, however. He saved his life by betraying the location of a large force of 20,000 warriors,[367] who were camped west of a place called Andalién thirty miles to the northwest. They had planned to move north towards Santiago in two weeks. We knew they would abandon that plan at once, however, and direct their forces at us. The questioning concluded, our Governor ordered Michimalongo to keep this Indian prisoner for the present. With this valuable information, we felt confident of coming success. That evening in conversation at our evening repast, de Villarroel observed that Valdivia's decision to behead the three *caciques* seemed out of character. Carrillo suggested that our Governor had become angry and moreover had not been himself since his forced separation from Doña Inés, and that his behavior might be an indication of his changed temperament. Vallejo offered his agreement with Antonio's observation and added that we might see more of this in the future. "Nonetheless," he said, "we are arrayed against an implacable enemy who gives no quarter and would do even worse to us in a similar situation. I say Valdivia behaved correctly."

254 To continue, on Wednesday, February 15, we made our way west following the Bio-Bio at a slow, determined pace, with de Alderete and his men in front. We were highly vigilant, since we knew the Mapuche somewhere near the coast would have cancelled any plans to attack Santiago town, and focus instead all their efforts upon killing every last one of us and dismembering our bodies. We rode on close to the Bio-Bio for two days until we came to a sharp bend with a small settlement on shore, a place where Michimalongo said that Andalién was a brief distance to the north. The *Toqui* mentioned that the men here were miners working at a nearby gold mine, by name, Quilacoya.[368] At our arrival, he greeted the village

---

[367] De Mérida agrees with Valdivia as to the number of hostiles. See his Letter III, p. 192 on the site. If we may believe this figure and others in previous battles as true and not hyperbole as to the number of enemy the Christians faced, to think 220 mounted and unmounted men could take on 20,000 of an enemy as fierce as the Mapuche attests to the *conquistador* "killing machine," for such it was.

[368] Today, there is the small town of Hualqui, of 20,000 citizens, at this crook of the Bio-Bio. The Quilacoya mine's rich deposits were exhausted after only several years.

caciques, whom he knew, and introduced them to our Governor. After brief discussions led by the Inca *Toqui*, they agreed to our management of their operations, provided that the mining *yanaconas* received generous compensation. At Valdivia's direction, de Cartagena wrote a contract of agreement that the Governor signed and the head *cacique* marked with the imprint of his thumb.

This concluded, Valdivia dispatched Michimalongo and his *cacique*, Cayancura, a warrior with a stern and noble bearing, north on horseback to determine the location of Ainavillo and Malloquete. As another battle loomed, Your Honor, I should tell of the arrangement of our officers and men. Captain Montesinos commanded fifty men, with seconds of Lieutenants Carrillo and me; Captain de Villagran's company included fifty men and seconds of Hernando Vallejo and de Villarroel; Captain de Alderete commanded fifty, with seconds of Francisco de Riberos and de Morales; Captain Jufré's unit included thirty unmounted soldiers, with Juan Godínez and Gregorio de Castañeda as seconds. Also under his command was Lázaro Pérez de Santiago with twenty musket men.

Upon the coming morning, Your Highness, we journeyed north nine miles until we reached a small laguna. The Río Andalién flowed east to west a quarter of a mile to the north of this laguna.[369] Michimalongo and Cayancura awaited us and said that the Mapuche were located close to Penco on the coast, nearly eight miles distant, and showed no signs of movement yet towards us. With this intelligence, our Governor conferred with his captains and decided to place our encampment 100 yards to the east and not directly between the laguna and río, this at the recommendation of Vicente and Gerónimo, our expert tacticians. Their reasoning was that, assuming the Mapuche attacked from the west, they would bunch up on the constricted ground of only 300 yards between the laguna and río and thus present a handsome target for annihilation. As to this small body of water, it measured 530 yards from west to east and 510 yards north to south. It was not filled completely with water, though, as a peninsula 320 yards long and 150 yards wide stretched down

---

[369] It's name today is Laguna Pineda.

its center from the north shore towards the south. Such was the nature of the terrain.

IMAGES: See 6VV-ZZ.4-.6 for pictures of the Andalién terrain.

As soon as the tents were up, the Governor met with the officers and Michimalongo and gave us our orders. The Inca *Toqui* and his men were to guard our Indians and the rear of the site. We Christians were broken into two groups, half for the first watch from sundown to midnight and half for the second from then until daybreak. Both were composed of mounted and unmounted men with ten musket men assigned to each. The watches were further set into two groups, with half the men serving as the outer perimeter sentinels and the other half the inner. Thus, two layers of protection encircled our campsite. In addition, I should add that our captains designated de Cartagena for the first watch and de Morales for the second of ten horse soldiers deployed at the southern end of the laguna's inner peninsula. This group would provide a flanking charge directed at the Mapuche that we expected to mass between the laguna and the río. A further employment consisted of ten horse soldiers positioned thirty yards in front of our outer perimeter in the area between the laguna and the río. They were our forward listening post. These men were to listen, while our horses' sense of smell would cause them to snort and whinny when they detected something unfamiliar or uncommon nearby, such as the presence of 20,000 Mapuche![370]

That afternoon, Vicente spoke to all his men before we took the second watch. He thought it highly probable, he said, that the Mapuche planned to attack at night. "I think they have come to believe that our horse soldiers will be less effective in the dark. So be attentive and listen intently for strange sounds. And our horses just may smell them before you hear anything since there is a steady breeze blowing from the west." Lieutenant Carrillo volunteered to command the ten men in front of our outer perimeter. "I can hear those Mapuche already, Sir." We laughed at this show of bravado. A brief word here, Sire, concerning my friend, Lieutenant Antonio Carrillo. He had a high, narrow forehead, keen eyes,

---

[370] A horse's smell acuity is stronger than a human's but less than a dog's.

a small, sharp nose, and long, thin lips. Premature wrinkles in his cheeks suggested recovery from illness. Yet he was well and healthy. A practical and plain spoken man, unpretentious in his bearing, he possessed great self-confidence and courage accompanied by a bent to the humorous.

Our first night passed in unremarkable fashion. There were times during nights like these in the jungle when all sounds stopped at once. They did not just fade away slowly but were gone in an instant as though some signal had been given to all life: bats, birds, and insects, to cease their natural soundings. This left me to wonder what I did not hear now. Might it be the Mapuche stealing across the jungle floor seeking to slash our throats even before we knew them amongst us? Of course, this is why we posted sentries. Still, the thought that the secretive, stealthy, silent Mapuche might steal their way past our guards had a dampening effect on my ability to sleep midst the dead silence of the night and it kept me awake that I might confront the fiends before they had their way with me. I could endure this for a long time, either until the shrieking of the jungle had begun again or something familiar pulled me out of it, a horse neighing, the rain falling.

The morning of February 19, we of the second watch slept while horse soldiers of the first watch the previous night patrolled two miles out on our perimeter. Late that night, we replaced our men of the first watch. Carrillo left to move in front of our outer perimeter and I clasped his hand warmly as he went with a "Go with God!" as exclamation. "This might be the night, Pedro, and I'm ready for it!" I moved behind my men, watching, listening, exactly as they. Vicente rode over slowly and we gazed out together through the gloomy night. The half moon provided a certain visibility, although faint notwithstanding.

After two hours of quiet, there was shouting to our front! It was Carrillo. "They are here! They are here!" The moment was upon us. Vicente ordered us forward, and within fifty yards we recognized our men slashing and thrusting at half visible images yelling, shouting that we were old women, waving lances, and swinging heavy-headed mace clubs. To join the fray, we tried to insert ourselves into the mass of our men and the heathens but it proved impossible. The pallid moonlight revealed an impenetrable multitude of warriors so close to one another they had difficulty using their weapons. To the best I could see, which was none too well, this mass of savages covered completely the ground between the laguna and the río, just as Vicente and Gerónimo had predicted. All our mounted men had joined us by now, and the scene was one of disarray and chaos. The darkness and the hordes of screaming Mapuche created an impression of an overwhelmed land. The closely packed crowd of the enemy continued to prevent us from getting into their midst, thus thwarting our attempts at their slaughter. And we found out later that de Morales was having no success with his flanking attack from the laguna peninsula. After approximately an hour, I heard the loud report of muskets firing behind us. A scream went up from one of my men to the right. I looked that way and saw that Martin de Ibarrola[371] had fallen from his horse. Our musket men had shot one of our own! I broke off my engagement and wheeled about to find Vicente. He was behind me vaguely visible. As I rode up, he yelled that he had seen what happened and had sent his aide back to ask the Captain to cease firing until daylight. Why he initiated such action in the first place I never determined.[372] Even after three hours, the fighting raged on. Truly, none of us had ever encountered such determined resistance to our superior arms and tactics.[373] On occasion, we were able to move in amongst them, yet their sheer numbers and the density of their throng prevented our effectiveness.

In another hour, the Governor behind us cried out to yield position to our unmounted comrades, as they might be able to break the Mapuche wall. In minutes, Captain Jufré, Juan Godínez, Gregorio de Castañeda, and their foot soldiers, brandishing their swords and short knives, lent their sturdy presence to our efforts as we horse soldiers backed away to give

---

[371] (?-1550). De Ibarrola is on the Errazuriz list of the 150 men who accompanied Valdivia to Chile. See Appendix A.

[372] Valdivia tells of this incident in his Letter III, pp. 192-193, in "Historical Sources" on the site.

[373] In his Letter, Valdivia says, "I give my word that in the thirty years I have been serving Your Majesty, I have never seen such stubborn men for fighting as were these Indians."

them the space they needed. Godínez and de Castañeda were particularly effective.[374] They led their men into faint openings in the Mapuche line and began killing in earnest. In half an hour the huge mass began to splinter in the northern part as our soldiers worked their will upon the luckless hostiles. Villagran and his horse soldiers now entered the fight on that side. De Alderete and his men began to exploit similar openings in the south of the line and de Morales and his men from the peninsula linked up with them. The center of the line also began to show weakness, so we reinserted ourselves into the fray, creating a space for us to work our will. With the sun now above the horizon behind us, the Mapuche had the full force of light in their eyes and the rout was on. The killing lasted for a brief time until orders to cease came from Valdivia, since the Mapuche were now in full flight to the west. Michimalongo, upon orders from the Governor, began the pursuit of the fleeing hostiles with his *caciques*, Quepuanté and Cayancura, and 300 warriors, and killed more. The end result of the Battle of the Andalién was more than 3,000 Mapuche dead, one dead Christian, sixty injured horses, and sixty wounded Christians.[375]

As I have said, Excellency, we had not encountered such resoluteness in our enemy before this battle. They were a hard foe and, as a result, earned our respect. Fortunately, though we had many injured Christians and horses, the wounds were not serious. Most were the result of blows from the large-headed mace the Mapuche wielded and many were to our knees and lower legs. The resulting bruises and pain lingered a number of days and de Riberos tended to our injuries in tireless fashion, as good medical men do. A few men had the vacant stare that had become common to some. This lasted several hours and we knew to leave them alone but to watch them closely for untoward behavior. De Riberos was expert at this. We stayed here two days to recover from our injuries. We then set off on February 23 on the slow ride west to the site that years before our Governor had determined as the location of our next settlement in our new land, at the place called Penco, where we arrived that afternoon. This proved a most favorable location, since to the northeast two miles distant the Río Andalién flowed

---

[374] Marmolejo in his Ch. X makes brief mention of these two men.
[375] Lobera mentions the Inca *Toqui* in his Second Part, Ch. XXXI and the resulting losses on both sides in the battle.

with fresh, clean water before its entry into the ocean. Four miles to the south, the Bio-Bio ran into the sea, an area that provided excellent fishing, with sardines, bream, tunny-fish, cod, lamprey, sole, and a host of other species.[376] Two miles to the west, a spacious harbor, bounded on north and south by headlands that protected it from ocean swells, provided us with what our Governor called, "the best harbor in the Indies."[377]

Valdivia wasted no time in directing the building of a fort to offer protection and to limit the number of men to stand guard duty through the night. Accordingly, the work details had specific duties. One unit erected a fence or barricade ten feet high of tree trunks driven into the earth and set against one another. Another group dug a trench three feet deep and three wide in front of the walls with the dirt and rocks placed behind it. The fences and trenches described a rectangular configuration that stretched almost one quarter mile in length. A different band of workers constructed four gates of sturdy tree trunks permitting entry and exit points. It was hard work, and to relieve the strain on our bodies we chanted lusty songs de Alderete recalled from his sailing days, and this provided entertainment that took our minds away from the physical exertion. Michimalongo and his men supplied us with ample food for our daily needs, as they fished in the harbor and in the nearby Bio-Bio and Andalién for many different kinds of fish. Furthermore, our Indians gathered fruits and vegetables very plentiful in this bounteous land and prepared them as we preferred. At night, they served fermented juice that brought smiles to all. We completed the walls of our fort, Fortress Penco, in eight days on Friday, March 3 of 1550. Afterwards, we saw to our living arrangements inside and other such important matters.

IMAGE: See 6VV-ZZ.7-.9 for an artist's depiction of a typical fortress layout of the time and the terrain around Fort Penco.

However, to remain in a closed, defensive position, Sire, seemed like surrender to a few of the men, and they were outspoken about it. "We

---

[376] Valdivia told the King that this place offered "the best fishing in the world."

[377] The Captain's words exactly. See Valdivia's Letter III, p. 193, in "Historical Sources."

were born to kill, not to sit on our hands and do nothing."[378] So said Sergeant Antonio Zapata, a thick-set, dark-faced, stern-looking man whose ferocity and fiery temperament on the battlefield had earned him the titles of "the remorseless one" and "the Mapuche slayer." Our Governor heard of this restive mood and addressed it forthwith at an assembly of us all. "My Christian soldiers and brothers, you know of my exhortation to you of attack, attack, when in doubt, attack." There were murmurs of acknowledgement at this. "And this is your true nature, for you are the deadliest soldiers the world has yet seen, and I am proud of you to a man. And with your preference to attack, I know the feelings of a number of you that remaining inside the walls of this fortress runs counter to your basic warrior instinct. Well, it does mine as well. But this will last only a short while, as I am on the watch for the first indication by these Indian hordes of a weakness in their formation or position that we may use to our advantage. And, trust me when I say this, I shall find that weakness and exploit it to the fullest. And when I do, once more I shall encourage you to attack, attack, when in doubt, attack!" At this, all voiced our loud approval and smiled in satisfaction. He had more. "And my men, my stalwart men, be assured that when we drive these savages to their version of hell, each of you will be recompensed with an allotment of gold from Quilacoya upon our victory. Such is my promise to you. So let it be written. So let it be done!" This raised loud huzzahs from all of us with much back and shoulder slapping as well.

On March 9 of 1550, Michimalongo's scouts patrolling the hills to the east reported large masses of Mapuche moving through the forest there. And an important piece of intelligence we forced from a captured heathen that Malloquete had been wounded at Andalién and was near death. Now Ainavillo and a young, inexperienced *toqui* by the name of Colo-Colo, whom Michimalongo did not know, led the enemy hordes.[379] In preparation for the coming battle, we reinforced the fortress walls and

---

[378] This phrase and ones similar have colored men's emotions throughout the centuries. "Born to kill." appeared on several Marine and Army helmets in Vietnam.

[379] Lobera mentions this *toqui* in his Second Part,Ch. XXXIII. He will gain further experience in future battles with the Christians.

strengthened its gates. In mid-afternoon of March 12, we saw thousands of Mapuche at the base of the distant eastern ridges begin a slow walk towards us, with much waving of their large spiked clubs, short swords, and long pikes. Later, Valdivia said he estimated their number at over 40,000 Indians on the plain that day.[380] As they came closer, Michimalongo remarked to our Governor that with the absence of Malloquete, Ainavillo might have trouble commanding their vast numbers. "That should work to our favor, Governor," said Montesinos. Valdivia pursed his lips and nodded in assent. But how? We were to find out quickly. When the mass of warriors was almost two miles away, they began to split into four separate throngs, now yelling insults at us that we heard clearly, ones we recognized from previous encounters, about us being old women and animals akin to snakes. It became apparent that the formations intended to assault our gates, behind which five musket men commanded by de Santiago had taken position ready to fire. At the distance of a quarter mile from our gateways, all four formations stopped and began to chant songs and phrases intended to increase their courage and stamina. Many wore cloaks we had not seen before, various coverings of llama hides, others of guanaco skins, and a few even of seal skins from the sea. Also unseen before were the colorful hats or plumes of animal skin and feathers they wore upon their heads, not all, but some.

Ainavillo and his formation took their position in front of our eastern gate, and de Alderete commented that the other three had no leaders, except the young Colo-Colo, and appeared uncoordinated and unsure as to how to cross our ditch, although they shot arrows at us. "That is their weakness I promised to exploit," shouted Valdivia. "If we attack and break the *toqui's* formation, the others seeing their leader flee the field will do the same!" It now being mid-afternoon, it was the time to strike. He thus ordered de Alderete and his men to prepare to attack. Villagran was to move to the south, at Valdivia's orders. Captain Montesinos and our men would charge the enemy before the northern and western gates. Captain Jufré and the unmounted men would remain in reserve until

---

[380] Valdivia says 40,000, with many more behind streaming over the eastern ridges "like water over a falls." De Vivar gives 60,000 as the number. Lobera says 150,000! Today's historians say the amount was probably around 6,000.

needed. When all were in position and at the ready, I looked to Zapata, "the Mapuche slayer." He was about to get his wish. The Governor yelled that Ainavillo was moving forward and to open the gate. He motioned excitedly to de Alderete and his men with his upraised right arm and bellowed, "Attack, my men. Attack!" Out they charged through the eastern gate, the musket men at its opening ready to fire. Our scouts at the top of the walls cried out that the other three groups remained in place and seemed content only to shoot arrows. At the approach of de Alderete, the Mapuche clustered close together, as they had at Andalién, and prevented our men from getting in amongst them. The Governor quickly ordered Jufré and his unmounted corps to enter the fray. At the same instant, he directed de Villagran to charge to the south and take on the enemy there, and shouted to us under Montesinos to assail the formations in the west and north. Michimalongo's men opened the western gate, and we galloped out to confront the enemy before us. It was evident from the first that their leader, the youthful Colo-Colo, lacked battle experience for his men were disordered. They resisted our charge in manly fashion at first although there was no strength to it. We got in amongst them and began slashing our way through at our will. At one point Vicente called a withdrawal so we might assess matters. We looked to the north and saw the Mapuche there running to the east, away from us. And the Indians to the west now began to flee too. What we soon understood was that Ainavillo and his force had been routed completely by de Alderete and this had caused the rest of the hordes to retreat too, just as the Governor had surmised. It was now merely a matter of chasing the fleeing scores and killing as many as we could and we set off to do just that. Occasionally, the brave ones stood to confront and fight us. We respected such warriors, yet that did not deter us from doing our duty. I came upon four Mapuche who had stopped to confront us. As I charged them, they broke and ran, making easy targets for my sword slashes.

The sun was nearing the western horizon when word reached us to cease the slaughter and return to the fort. Weary from the killing, we welcomed the safety and protection of our fortress walls. The occasion was now Michimalongo's. He, his *caciques* on horseback, and his warriors, Valdivia dispatched to the east to find and kill as many Mapuche as they could. We rested, and ate a refreshing meal. Michimalongo and his men returned near midnight, having extinguished several hundred hostiles they trapped near where the Río Andalién enters the sea. The next day, we determined that near 2,000 Mapuche had met their final fate, although Ainavillo and Colo-Colo escaped.[381] As to our Christian forces, there were no injuries to us or our horses, a further testament to our prowess and, yes, good fortune. Such was the Battle of Fortress Penco, Your Honor, a fight we won because of a lack of Mapuche leadership, the cowardice of many of the warriors, and because of our leadership and battle efficiency.

We took 200 prisoners and, as Your Highness knows, since the Governor mentions it in his Letter III to Your Grace, he ordered the hands and noses of them all cut off for refusing to accept us in peace.[382] Michimalongo's warriors did this. A number of the savages cried out for mercy, while most endured this torture with a manly silence many of us respected. And, I should note that there were differing reactions as to the appropriateness of this punishment among the men, not unlike the sentiments after the execution of the three captured *caciques* before the fight at the Andalién. Some felt it justifiable, some not. And Carrillo, as he had said after that incident, observed that the Governor's behavior had changed after the separation from Doña Inés and this cruel act proved that. Godínez offered a new observation. "It is clear to me that none of us may risk capture because of our treatment of them. They will torture and keep us alive as long as they can while doing so. I will not let that happen to me as I shall die upon my sword first." This gave us pause, for no doubt he would be proven correct.

---

[381] Valdivia says the count was 1,500 to 2,000. Again, Lobera seems to exaggerate the numbers. He writes that 4,000 were killed in this battle.

[382] Valdivia gives his reason for doing this in his Letter III, p. 195, in "Historical Sources." The reader may decide if this is a suitable justification. The Spanish continued to use this type of mutilation for many years to come in the Arauco Wars.

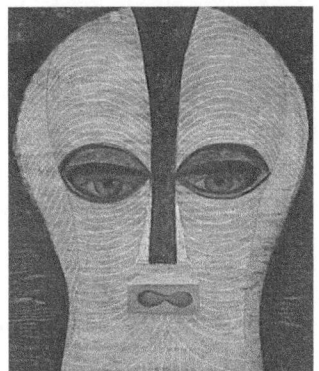

PART WW

THE FOUNDING OF CONCEPCIÓN DE MARÍA PURÍSIMA DEL NUEVO EXTREMO; MY BRIEF RETURN TO SANTIAGO; MEETING MY NEWBORN SON, VICENTE; VALDIVIA'S MAPUCHE 'PAGE,' LAUTARO; THE FOUNDING OF LA IMPERIAL

On March 21 there was great excitement when a shout arose from numerous men that sailing into our harbor were Captain Pastene in the *San Pedro* and Captain Villalón in the *Santiaguillo*. We welcomed them warmly and thankfully as they brought generous amounts of *maize*, squash, *papas*, beans, seeds, pigs, and chickens, as well as building materials needed for the construction of our new town. Also aboard was Father Marmolejo, summoned by the Governor to bless our settlement, now accompanied by a new priest, Bartolomé del Pozo.[383] They blessed us all in a brief ceremony of prayer and thanksgiving and we now looked forward to daily mass again as they had bags of wine with them. They had been sent for so they might

---

[383] Weldon Vernon mentions this priest on p. 178 of her <u>Pedro de Valdivia</u>.

begin to Christianize the Indians in these southern lands. Twenty new men also joined us, skilled in carpentry and foundation construction. Captain Pedro de Miranda commanded them, another long-time friend, and assisted by Lieutenant Marcos Veas,[384] a man destined to play an unwitting part in a coming tragedy. Aboard too was a Captain Alonzo de Aguilera,[385] newly arrived from Peru and an old acquaintance of the Governor's, a man with a stooped bearing, round eyes that glistened, and a wan smile permanently upon his lips. But to return to Father Marmolejo, Sire. He conveyed a request from our acting Governor, Gómez de Almagro, that *Cabildo* members here return to our capital town to help with the accumulation of city affair activities since our departure. We *Cabildo* associates, de Morales, Jufré, de Cartagena, de Villarroel, and I, were eager to return, as we wished to see our wives again, if only for a brief time. Furthermore, de Miranda told me that Pilca Huaca was well and should give birth to our first child in six months. But our Governor said he could not honor de Almagro's appeal for some time since the highest priorities were to build our new town, make friends with the Indians here, arrange for them to supply us with food, start the formation of the town *Cabildo*, and supervise the mining at Quilacoya. Our return home thus would have to wait.

Briefly, Your Grace, I shall tell of our activities over the next months. We Santiago *Cabildo* members began to train those chosen by our Governor as the new *Cabildo's* initial representatives here, men who possessed the required skills and had indicated their wish to reside here permanently. The Governor chose de Alderete as the city council's presiding officer. And we discovered that Valdivia planned to name this settlement, Concepción de María Purísima del Nuevo Extremo, when he felt the time right and appropriate. As to mining affairs, a new lieutenant recently arrived from Peru by the name of Carlos Santos,[386] embarked for Quilacoya with ten men with mining skills to strike an agreement with the natives there for deliveries of gold. Michimalongo, Cayancura, and some of their warriors

---

[384] (1515-1597).

[385] (1514-1609).

[386] The historical record is silent about this man.

accompanied our men. The mining operation enjoyed such success that we began receiving pure gold dust a month later.

As for the Indians near our growing town, to determine the mood of the natives of two close islands and to acquire more food, our fleet captains visited them. One, thirty miles south, Captain Pastene had discovered six years prior, in 1544, and named it Isla Santa Maria, as I recounted in my Fifth Letter. The other, founded by the Captain as well, he named Isla de San Nicolas de Tolentino.[387] The natives on these islands proved exceptionally friendly and provided us with many fruits and vegetables, as well as sea lion meat, in exchange for our blue beads on this and our visits to come. As to the natives on land near us, the Governor dispatched Captain de Alderete with his men to the south to establish friendships with the Indians along the coast and was no less successful, for they were eager to trade with us and many offered to help build our new settlement. When Gerónimo and his men returned in a week, 150 natives from the village called Arauco accompanied them.[388] They brought bags of seeds, full baskets of fruits and *maize*, barley, *papas*, squash, and beans, and worked tirelessly in the coming months with construction activities and the planting of crops. I should observe here, Your Excellency, that Governor Valdivia during dinner with the officers one evening, in a candid statement not unknown to him, commented that the friendliness of the Indians here was due to cutting off the hands and noses of the 200 warriors following the Battle of Fort Penco. History may judge if this be true.

As to the town's building work, the master builder and *alarife*, de Miranda, after surveying the land, presented his detailed street and building layout to the Governor and officers. At its center was Fort Penco, with the streets radiating out to the four compass points. Proceeding on to the area near the Fort, nearby was the Plaza Mayor, with locations marked for a cathedral, a building to house the *Cabildo*, and other necessary edifices

---

[387] The first island retains its name today, but the second has been renamed Isla Mocha.

[388] Present-day Arauco resides thirty-five miles south from Concepción and has a population of 36,000.

every city needs. Two miles distant to the west stood our harbor, so the diagram showed that region with storage and dock sections for incoming and outgoing vessels. To the east, the chart indicated the Rio Andalién as the outer limit, and the Bio-Bio as the limiting boundary to the south. In the north, the ocean two miles distant was our town's border.

By mid-June, Your Highness, we had received a number of gold deliveries from the Quilacoya mine, all duly recorded in the township's *Cabildo* records. One afternoon, de Cartagena and two other soldiers rode throughout our growing settlement to announce that all were to gather at the Plaza Mayor to hear an important announcement. Many suspected the nature of this meeting and they proved correct, as Valdivia announced that the day of payment had arrived as recompense for the difficult days prior to the Battle of Fort Penco. Our Captains bestowed upon each of us a small skin bag of gold dust, and Valdivia added a firm hand grip in acknowledgement of our efforts that day. He also gave bags to Michimalongo and his *caciques* and, in a gesture applauded by us all who were present at the Battle of Quilacura, bags to Huenu and Ayar for their surprising the intent of the Mapuche to attack at night in the high grass. I assisted the new *Cabildo* members in recording these distributions.

By October, the Governor felt it proper to christen our village, as the Indians around us were friendly and working with us in construction, in our fields, and at the mine. Accordingly, on Thursday, October 5 of 1550, we held the ceremony and Concepción de María Purísima del Nuevo Extremo was entered officially into the *Cabildo* records as the name of our new town. The Governor and Father Marmolejo placed a large wooden cross, with a cross of gold in its center, at the northern edge of the Plaza Mayor, across from the adobe foundation of the new church. After that, Father celebrated a High Mass to commemorate this momentous occasion and to pray that Our Lord might watch over us in His mercy.

This done, the Governor decided he could honor Gómez de Almagro's request for help with Santiago *Cabildo* matters, and so on October 15 we aforementioned members boarded the *Santiaguillo* with Captain Villalón, departed the harbor roads, and stood our way north for Valparaíso harbor. With us, Your Honor, was Captain Alonzo de Aguilera, the gentleman named above, carrying the Governor's letter to Your Grace. Valdivia respected and valued this man, as You read in the letter.[389] In three days, we entered the growing and busy Valparaíso harbor, dropped anchor at the roads, and said our farewells to those on board. They were going on to the City of Kings, where de Aguilera was to obtain passage on a ship bound for Spain and Villalón would seek new men with gold given him by the Governor. Upon paying for spare horses, the five of us set off with a good deal of excitement, as we had not been home since January. We followed the now well-worn dirt road; and, when we crested the hills to the west of our city, its profile of buildings came into view, a beautiful sight to witness. Not long after that, when we were a few miles from its limits, Jufré shouted that the town bells were ringing, and so they were. When we drew closer, the crowds of people on the Plaza Mayor were waving and calling to us. What a moment. When we rode up, Gómez de Almagro and Gómez de Benito were flanked by our smiling and clapping wives. And my Pilca Huaca was holding our first born! Upon dismounting, I learned our son, Vicente de Mérida de Santiago, had been born a month prior on September 23 and, thanks be to Our Lord, was in excellent health and disposition. Pilca Huaca had awaited my return before baptizing Vicente; and so, on the appointed day, October 24 of 1550, Father Lobo christened our son while I held him. If only Montesinos had been here to do it for me! We and our friends welcomed our Vicente to Holy Mother Church with a joyful celebration that afternoon.

Since we had to return to Concepción by the end of January 1551, we devoted ourselves to the *Cabildo* work needed by Juan Gómez, a considerable amount that kept us busy every day. But we found time to spend with our families and to meet with our friends. One day, Pilca Huaca and Collardis showed me their expanded medical facility, now comprising two levels and sixty rooms for medical attention and recovery. I met with Paucar too, who explained how he was following our directions regarding the use of our land. He and his people were doing an exemplary

---

[389] Valdivia's words of praise for Aguilera are in his Letter III, p. 205, in "Historical Sources" on the site.

job in cultivating our strawberry plants and selling the fruit in the markets in Santiago. In addition, he managed the raising, care, and sale of our many pigs. As to our other activities, we shared occasions with our friends and dined often with Paucar and Collardis, Ancohualla and Millaray, and Juan Gómez and his new wife, Illaray. And we had special moments with Doña Inés de Suárez de Quiroga and her new husband, Rodrigo. Pilca Huaca and I found them truly happy in their marriage, and we thanked the Lord that this was so.

I am honored to provide here, Your Majesty, a concise accounting of this gentleman, Rodrigo de Quiroga. Born in Santiago de Compostela in 1512 of religiously minded parents, he grew of age close to the city's cathedral where the bones of *Santo Iago* reside.[390] His parents served the cathedral's bishop by helping clean the church and keeping it presentable for the many worshippers who arrived every day to pray to our cherished saint. As I have said previously, he was a veteran of the Italian Wars. In a certain engagement outside Florence, he was struck on the right side of his helmet, a glancing blow by a metal bolt that unhorsed him. He might have died right there, except that one of his aides helped him quickly to re-mount and leave the field to seek help. As it happened, he lost his hearing in that right ear and from then on had to incline his head to the left in order to hear better. He was a man who preferred his privacy, yet quick and ready, as the occasion demanded, to engage with others. Having a natural cordiality, warmth of disposition, and good humor, he could be high-spirited, although always in control of himself. Being human, he had moments of self-satisfaction, even of pettiness. Yet these rare incidents he balanced with basic common sense, instinctive goodness of intent, and an appealing nature. As to his military abilities, he was partial to and adept at the maneuver the Governor called "the pinch," in which our men form in a bolt alignment and charge forward towards the enemy, with the other part of the force positioned behind them to prevent their retreat.[391] In

---

[390] The city houses the shrine of Saint James the Great, now the city's cathedral, a destination on the Way of St. James, a leading Catholic pilgrimage route originated in the 9th century. It is still popular today.

[391] As mentioned previously, this is the "hammer and anvil" formation used since warfare began.

sum, he was a man of exceptional merit whose company we enjoyed and appreciated. Doña Inés had made an admirable choice for her husband.

I might comment here, Excellency, on the changes that have occurred in our town through the previous years. This is the tenth year since the original 150 of us arrived in this land and founded Santiago del Nueva Estremadura in 1541. All of us were experienced in warfare and tribulations, especially those from the Almagro and early Valdivia days. Among us there existed an air, a sense, that one might rely upon the man beside him in battle, as the other had seen many fights and probably had been wounded at least once. This sense of camaraderie came from our shared occasions together of great danger and great discomfort, not only upon the battlefield but away from it, like the initial days in Santiago with the burning down of the town and our near starvation during the many months afterwards. Having endured these with one another, we treated fairly and honestly our brethren in financial and social matters, since we were a large family of brothers with a shared upbringing. Yet the hundreds of new men who had arrived since those early days had little in common with us. Many had not yet fought the Mapuche here and lacked basic skills in tactics. These were taught, of course, and in rigorous fashion by our Captain General of Military Affairs, Gómez de Benito. But when these men joined our forces in battle, their first exposure to combat sometimes caused us concern. Besides this, their sole motivation in our land was the acquisition of wealth, in gold, in land, and even if this meant creating ill will with another. I shall leave off, Your Majesty, with this prolix digression.

IMAGES: 6VV-ZZ.10-.16 depict scenes and images in the above text.

I shall now return to my account. Although the days in our town with our families and friends were too few, on Wednesday, January 15 of 1551, we rode to Valparaiso to meet Captain Villalón and take passage to Concepción on the *Santiaguillo*. I did so with a heavy heart at having to leave my Pilca Huaca and Vicente, but duty to our land remained foremost. On the day after our arrival and following a full moon, we boarded ship and, the anchor weighed, we left the roads and stood due west for twenty miles. Encountering favorable winds, we tacked south and enjoyed their blusterings leeward. Our three day voyage was without incident, but our arrival at the harbor roads provided great excitement, for I saw Vicente Montesinos standing on the quay and waving when he saw me. I thrust both fists upwards, our agreed upon signal that Pilca Huaca had given birth to a boy. As I had told him upon departure, should our child be a boy, we would name him Vicente. Upon dropping anchor and taking the landing boat to shore, we embraced one another in friendship. His first words to me were ones of inquiry concerning Vicente's eye and hair color, his weight, his disposition, all those things important to him to know about his namesake. I could tell our son would have a devoted admirer the rest of his life.

In the coming weeks we prepared for another move south to found more settlements while I devoted attention besides to assisting and instructing the new *Cabildo* members. I think it fitting to relate now, Noble Sire, an incident that later would have momentous consequences. It happened in this fashion. During my months away in Santiago, Captain de Alderete made visits to Arauco to replenish our food stores. Upon his return from one such outing, he brought a young Mapuche with him who had approached Gerónimo and requested employment in our service, as he knew of Michimalongo's turn to our side and wished to do likewise in imitation of the Inca *Toqui*. De Alderete introduced him to the Governor, who, having conversed with him as regards his intentions and qualifications thought him of future value in bettering relations with the Mapuche and agreed to accept him as his aide, or "page," as he called him. His name? Lautaro, although our Governor called him Alonzo.[392] He was a young man of erect stature, well-formed muscles, and a skin color darker than most Mapuche. The direct gaze of his dark eyes upon those with whom he conversed caused some to think that he did so in a menacing manner. But his actions belied this, for they were ones of neither sympathy nor animosity, but merely indifference. Among his

---

[392] Lautaro means "daring and enterprising" in the Mapuche language. Marmolejo in his Ch. XIV mentions that Valdivia named him Alonso, or possibly Felipe, but never concludes which name was used. Neither Lobera nor Vivar mention Lautaro by name until an important battle soon to occur.

daily tasks was to care for the Governor's horse and accompany him into battle and military exercises. This is how he learned not to fear horses and even became a good rider himself. Throughout this period he had a certain level of friendship with one of Valdivia's new lieutenants from Peru, the aforementioned Marcos Veas. This man taught Lautaro, at the Governor's order, how to use different kinds of weapons and instructed him in our cavalry formations. This was important tutoring, because as Valdivia's page he was responsible to serve as his assistant in battles, as I said, although not bearing arms against our enemies.

Huenu did not like or trust him. He said he heard him remark once to one of Michimalongo's warriors that he had witnessed the depredations to which Valdivia subjected the 200 defeated Mapuche after Penco, mutilating them and releasing them later as examples to deter future rebellions. This affected him deeply, Huenu said. In light of what transpired later, it is certain that as a result of those violent acts towards his people, a deep animosity existed in this youth towards the Governor and us Christians. As we were to find out, he had maneuvered himself into the page position in order to learn our battle tactics in the hope of using them against us in the future. In the meantime, he awaited the arrival of the opportunity to escape and return to his people.[393]

So much for all that, Sire. Now I shall tell of the journey south. It began on Monday, February 12 of 1551[394] with 120 mounted and 50 unmounted men, including Father del Pozo. Michimalongo, Quepuanté, Cayancura, and 150 warriors, accompanied us, while 150 stayed to protect our men and work in the fields with our Arauco Indians. Captain de Miranda remained in town commanding fifty soldiers to protect it and continue the building activities. On the second day out from Arauco, we entered a dense canopy of forested jungle, with its clean smells of damp earth and trees of pine with the cries of *caa caa* from small birds with brownish feathers. Close together in our usual fashion, Huenu and Ayar were now only twenty

---

[393] See Alegría, Fernando, <u>Lautaro</u>, pp. 8-10 for s description of Lautaro similar to de Mérida's. Also see Mackenna, Vicuna, <u>Lautaro Y Sus Tres Compañas</u>, pp. 4-8.

[394] See, once more, Valdivia's Letter IV.

yards before me, yet the tortured darkness and oppressive green hell restricted sight of them. Lieutenant Carrillo and five men followed behind to provide protection. We advanced slowly and deliberately through the dark, looking all about us, listening all about us, feeling the presence of this close, gloomy land. Suddenly, lightning flashed through the covering above, followed by deep, resonating thunder claps. I called to Huenu and Ayar to halt, thinking that the Governor might not wish us to continue. Carrillo shouted that he would go back and discern Valdivia's intention. As we waited, the rumbling continued to disturb the land. The booming now was directly above and, for everlasting minutes, brightened bolts of white-hot light crackled across the darkened land and through the canopy above, so bright it were as though the heavens had quickened their usual course of turning and unleashed the full light of day. Down they came, heaven hurtled beams filled with fire that exploded nearby. We looked at the brooding spaces all around, spellbound by the light that played before us. When stiletto-like stabs hit a short distance to the north, a noise like splintering wood detonated above us. The flashes brought to life each leaf and each shrub, leaving each luminous in the jungle night. Presently, the lightning passed and heavy drops of water sounded upon my morrión and bathed all around in a heavy falling of water from the thickened covering above. The wet poured upon our overhead jungle covering and descended upon us like a raging stream falling over a steep escarpment so heavy and dense that I could scarcely determine Huenu and Ayar just feet from me.

Carrillo rode up and yelled that the Governor wished to make camp, as the storms were too violent to continue. We rode back and participated in a most unruly affair, as might be imagined. Yet, the soldiers that we were, we set in place our encampment in excellent fashion. The captains sent word from Valdivia that we must stay alert, since this was Mapuche land and they knew how to exist in these conditions as well as how to kill in these conditions. The Officer of the Guard set sentries around our lonely outpost at a distance of 100 yards, with a secondary defensive line fifty yards inside that. And thus we endured as the heavens continued to spew downward through the night vast amounts of water that created a shallow lake that flooded our tents. Once, the torrent was such that the sound itself drowned out all thought. It was a dreary night.

After a number of days, we crossed a río Michimalongo called the Cautín.[395] The Governor wished to find a suitable place near it for another settlement, so we followed its gently flowing crystal waters through rich fertile lands until we arrived at a site twelve miles from the coast where the río called Damas joins it. The day following, on March 16, Governor Valdivia led the founding ceremony for La Imperial,[396] so named, Excellency, in Your honor.[397] After the blessing by Father del Pozo, we began building a fortress of such stoutness that in two weeks its sturdiness calmed our uneasiness about possible attacks from the Mapuche. As it happened, the natives were quite friendly here and traded in an eager fashion, pleasing us all. And Father found the Indians receptive to the word of Christ. After Valdivia had tended to such matters as how to parcel out the land for future land grants, we departed for the return to Concepción on April 7, but left forty men, including Father del Pozo, under the command of Captain Pedro de Villagran with orders to further good relations with our Mapuche neighbors. Our return proved uneventful. We entered Concepción in late April of 1551 and resumed our previous duties there whilst awaiting our next venture south.

In June, Captains Pastene and Villalón entered our harbor carrying the usual supplies as well as 100 more men from Peru. And, in a surprise arrival, a Captain Diego Maldonado[398] rode in two days later with eight men and a letter from Francisco de Villagran, whom our Governor had dispatched to Peru two years prior to hire more men to help us found towns and pacify the land. De Villagran was riding to us with 200 men. The arrival of new men with Maldonado and the promise of more to come impassioned the Governor to embark upon another journey to the south. Before our departure, Valdivia appointed Maldonado, whom Villagran had praised highly in his letter, to drill the new men in battle tactics, assisted by Lieutenant de Villarroel with his knowledge of forest battle

---

[395] The Cautín is 150 miles south from Concepción.
[396] The original site of La Imperial was destroyed several times through the years by the Mapuche and was relocated twelve miles east and named New Imperial. The original town site has been re-founded as Carahue.
[397] See Lobera, Second Part, Ch. XXXIV.
[398] (1504-1570). Valdivia mentions this Captain in his Letter IV, pp. 210,211.

practices. This arranged, in early October we departed for La Imperial. The officers and men were those of the previous journey to that location as well as Michimalongo and his warriors.

On this journey we did not encounter large numbers of Mapuche ready to give battle. Still, a number of us sensed matters seemed possibly threatening. Vicente gave voice to this one evening when he remarked upon the sullen expressions of farmers we had passed on the day's march. As to my team and me, we had seen a small village on our route that I thought looked menacing, for some reason. I chose to lead around it to the east and avoid it entirely. Despite these incidents, after nine days on the march we arrived at La Imperial and that evening shared beverages with our friends. During our brief stay, the Governor professed himself quite satisfied with Pedro de Villagran and the work he and his men had done to strengthen the fort, plant crops, and make friends with the surrounding Indians. And Father del Pozo related that it excited him so many natives were receptive to his message of God's word. Things seemed well here, although an incident involving Lautaro occurred that caused various among us to have concerns. It seems Vallejo had seen him in a nearby field one afternoon at the end of the day, practicing slashing and spearing movements with a sword while mounted. He quickly left off when he was seen and departed, although Vallejo said it seemed to him that Valdivia's page exhibited too much enthusiasm in war tactics than should be the case. I shall leave this incident there for now.

I mentioned that the natives here were amenable to God's word, Your Grace, and that compels me to comment upon Father Bartolomé del Pozo, who had become a favorite amongst us all. He possessed an outgoing manner, and engaged those near him in comradely fashion as though he were one of us, regardless of rank or position, for he believed every man equal to him. One could engage him in any topic for discussion, whether to seek advice upon a personal matter or only to pass the time in light-hearted fashion. As to this last, one evening at our leisure hour, Montesinos queried him about his uncanny ability to toss a quoit shoe so accurately that few of us could best him at this popular game. "It's all in the wrist, my boys," he said. "It's all in the wrist!" This brought smiles and laughs and typified his lighter moments with us. His inveterate good humor, I believe, possibly came from his closeness to our Savior and the deep happiness this provided him. Of course, when discharging his religious duties, he proved most restrained since this required a serious composure. At leisure times, however, he was a pleasure to be near as I have said. As to other characteristics, when among us and the Indians he frequently bestowed Christ's blessing by placing his right hand upon one's forehead, saying a few short words of blessing, and then making the sign of the cross. This touching of others, as Father Cabrera used to do, created a bond that remained long afterwards. In addition, he was an exceptional horseman, in fact, more adept than many of our newly arrived horse soldiers. Physically, his presentation was similar to that of the esteemed Father Suarez of the Almagro Expedition days, with wide shoulders, thick arms, and excellent physical coordination that communicated to others that, should he be threatened in battle by a Mapuche, he could care for himself quite adequately. A prime admirer of Father was the Governor. They had formed a strong bond of friendship from the first moment of their meeting. I believe what attracted Governor Valdivia was the juxtaposition of a man of God caring for our spiritual needs, while doing so with a light and engaging manner and at the same time projecting an air of physical distinction. Such is my memory of this holy man, Your Eminence, and it is how I shall remember him since his tragic leave taking from our midst, an event I must relate eventually.

PART XX

THE CLASH IN THE MARIQUINA VALLEY; THE FOUNDING OF VALDIVIA TOWN; A TERRIBLE SHAKING OF THE EARTH FOLLOWED BY FLOODING WATERS FROM THE SEA; VILLAGRAN RETURNS FROM PERU WITH 200 MEN; THE FOUNDING OF VILLARRICA AND ARAUCO

We left La Imperial on Thursday, February 1 in November of 1551 with the intention, as the Governor told us, of founding a town on the shores of the Río Valdivia, so christened by de Alderete in 1544 on his journey south with Captain Pastene.[399] Upon our arrival at a handsome valley named Mariquina[400] according to Huenu, we settled in for a brief rest near a slow moving río the Governor named the Cruces. The next morning, he dispatched de Alderete and his fifty men to follow the Cruces south to

---

[399] See Part SS of the Fifth Letter.
[400] Mariquina, with 20,000 citizens, lies on the Río Cruces 20 miles north from the city of Valdivia.

the río he had named the Valdivia and identify a proper location near it for the establishment of the new settlement. One afternoon, ten men from La Imperial rode in with word that Francisco de Villagran had finally returned from Peru, arriving in Santiago with 200 men and 500 horses and mares, most welcome news.[401] At this, the Governor sent Lieutenant Carrillo and a number of men back to La Imperial to accompany them here to Mariquina. We were surprised days later when the guards shouted that several riders were drawing near from the north. It couldn't be Captain Villagran, since we expected his 200 men with him. But indeed, it was Carrillo leading Captain Villagran with only fifteen horse soldiers from Peru. Obviously, something had happened involving the rest of the men since they remained in Santiago, yet we never learned the reason for their absence.[402] Our Governor and his old friend embraced with a great show of happiness after two years apart, and we all celebrated that evening with a special repast of boiled pork, *papas*, and squash, cooked by our Indians, with beverages created by Michimalongo's men. The day after, the Governor dispatched Jufré back to Santiago with eight men to lead the remaining soldiers from Peru to La Imperial and asked Villagran to journey there and await the arrival of his men. He could spend the weeks in La Imperial assisting his cousin, Pedro, with settlement duties.

IMAGES: 6VV-ZZ.20-.28 are images to accompany the following text.

Eager to establish the new settlement, one we knew would bear the name of our leader, on December 15, a day marked by bright sunlight and a pleasing coolness, Valdivia ordered us forward. As we wended our way south with the Río Cruces to the east, suddenly the fog settled so thick we could not see ten paces to our front or anywhere surrounding us. Bushes appeared as high trees and rocks and gullies as cliffs and inclines. All about us, on any side, Mapuche might be only ten paces away. Yet we kept advancing, Huenu and Ayar expertly pushing forward in the constant

---

[401] Lobera, in his Second Part, Ch. XXXVIII, corroborates this.
[402] Lobera remarks on this number of men, but does not give the reason for the missing 185. He spends more time telling of the happy reunion of the two close friends.

murky darkness of the fog over tortured and unknown ground. And then, the gloom and shadows began to lift and we were able to distinguish the forest's true nature.

Later that day, Ayar whistled back to me with his distinctive bird-like call that danger lay ahead. I rode forward slowly amongst the pressing foliage until I saw him crouched and pointing ahead to something not yet visible to me. Then he pressed his forefinger to his lips for me to stay quiet on my approach. I dismounted, crept to his position, and saw in a wide field before us at least 1,000 Mapuche. Their number was not the worry. It was their weapons, since some stood holding long-stemmed pikes, with sharp spike ends at their tips that glistened in the noon-day sun. The savages held them forward, arrayed in an obvious manner to obstruct our advance. We had not seen pikes since the Battle of Limari, and this alarmed us. The 300 or so pike men stood in two lines facing forward. The remaining savages were massed at either end of the lines, enfiladed. The disposition of these Mapuche assumed that we would attack forward towards the pike men and, thus engaged, the flanking forces at either end would move to encircle us. I sent Huenu to Carrillo with word that Mapuche were in battle position to our front, ready to oppose our progress, and instructed him to notify the Governor. After several moments Montesinos rode up, beheld the scene before us, and in short order said he had a plan and that it should be effected in the quarter hour, unless these Indians decided to attack. If they did, we were to retire to the main group immediately. In the meanwhile, the warriors kept their order and remained where they were. Soon, we heard the rush of men behind us, and five musket men with Pérez de Santiago positioned themselves in a line in front of us. Then, Juan Godínez and Gregorio de Castañeda, in charge in Jufré's absence, and their unmounted men appeared in a long line behind us. Still no movement from the Mapuche. Were they leaderless? Inexperienced? Our horse soldiers, whom we could not see, had moved into position on either of our flanks, commanded by Valdivia in de Alderete's absence. At de Santiago's shouted command, our muskets began firing into the pike men. As at Limari, they had not seen or heard of muskets, did not comprehend the danger they faced, and so they stood there, unmoving. I could not believe what we witnessed. When six volleys from our men had brought down scores of the Mapuche, Godínez and de Castañeda ordered their men forward directly at the pike men. At that instant, we saw our men on the left and right gallop towards the Indian flanking forces. Carrillo and I remained where we were, it feeling strange that we were not involved, and witnessed the wholesale carnage of the Mapuche forces. The Governor called a halt to the slaughter an hour after it began, with 450 warriors dead or writhing in their death throes on the field.[403] Michimalongo and his men followed the Mapuche survivors as they fled to the west and killed another seventy. We suffered not one casualty to man or horse in this fight, thanks be to our Blessed Savior, and Father del Pozo afterwards said prayers of thanksgiving for His blessed mercy.

The Governor permitted half an hour's rest before ordering us to pack and mount, for we needed to leave this place with so many dead bodies rotting in the sun. Accordingly, we left that afternoon and had been on the march a brief time when it began to rain so hard the Governor sent word to halt and make camp. The rain continued through the night, and at daylight the Río Cruces had risen so high that we had to move to nearby higher ground. Still it rained, without a pause through the day and into the night, not ending until the following afternoon. We were high enough that we were safe from the flooding; the surrounding ground below us, however, was like a large lake. Valdivia said that we should remain here a few days and celebrate the birth of our Lord and Savior Jesus Christ before moving forward. On the eve of His blessed birth, Captain de Alderete and his men rode in with the news that he had located an ideal site for our new town. We had much to be thankful for, Your Honor, on the next day, the day of His birth.

It continued to rain over the coming days. At last, on Tuesday, January 8 of 1552, with a clear sky above, we rode forward, my team now joined by my friend, de Alderete, who would show us the ground he had identified as the location of a fortress to guard the new settlement. Among the

---

[403] Lobera refers to this encounter in his Second Part, Ch. XXXVII and says it was a slaughter but is brief with details, certainly not to the extent we learn from de Mérida.

pleasantries exchanged between us and his congratulations to me about my new son, he said that he would be off to Spain in several months to carry news and reports to Your Majesty from the Governor, an exciting trip he eagerly wished to undertake. I shall tell more of this later. In three days, Gerónimo led us up upon the rising land until to the south we saw the Cruces joined by the Río Valdivia. We continued going higher until we reached a wide area that looked down upon the juncture of the rivers a hundred feet below. We enjoyed the stirring sight whilst awaiting the arrival of our men. When the Governor rode up, his expression and exclamations were ones of awe and satisfaction at the beauty of the land.

After setting camp, the Governor and captains formed us into construction teams and work began. The fort's foundation took shape within four days of hard laboring, with the officers and the Governor participating in the strenuous activities. On day five, Valdivia stood upon a slight hillock directing the efforts of fifteen men in hoisting the last of the logs comprising the western end of the fortress walls when, without warning, the earth beneath us began to move right and left and back and forth, motions that caused me and others to fall to the ground. A *terremoto*! The Governor fell from the knoll upon which he stood and rolled down its slight incline. The logs inserted vertically in the western wall swung forward and backward and fell with roars as they struck the earth, crushing a number of the Indians helping us. A few of our horses, although tethered, broke their pickets and galloped away in fright as the violent shaking continued for minutes before subsiding. I lay there upon the ground with Vicente in astonishment that the falling logs had not struck us, a testament to the mercy of our Lord, Jesus Christ.

Valdivia yelled out as to casualties, but there were none, except our unfortunate Indian helpers. We ceased our activities to savor our delivery from a harsh fate as Father del Pozo led us in prayers of thanksgiving. Then, an incident of singular concern unfolded, for a half-hour past the violent trembling, de Morales shouted that the water at the river juncture was rising as water flowing in from the sea began flooding the flat land below.[404] It did not rise to our height, yet it served as a warning to future

---

[404] This is the *tsunami* of today.

citizens here of the devastation caused by *terremotos* and the flooding they cause.[405] The day after we began to rebuild and, in nine days more, Fortress Valdivia stood in redoubtable fashion above the green landscape below. Truly, this site was auspicious for our new settlement. Accordingly, on February 9 of 1552 the Governor, assisted by the captains, carried out the founding ceremony of Santa Maria la Blanca de Valdivia, with blessings bestowed upon her by Father del Pozo. May she reign in peace and prosperity for time without end.[406] We stayed a number of months here, Your Honor, constructing our fort, trading with the Indians for seeds and food and seeking their friendship, while Father del Pozo proselytized amongst them. Ninety men wished to make this township their home,[407] and they were awarded land grants as a result.

A surprise was at hand, Sire, as a week later our sentries heard the loud shouting of many men, and soon Captain Villagran and Jufré appeared, with Lieutenant Carrillo leading the soldiers Villagran had recruited in Peru.[408] This provided a most appreciated addition to our forces, and the Governor took advantage of the increased numbers forthwith. Eager to establish more settlements, he acted upon information Michimalongo had passed to him recently that a large lake stood three days ride to the northeast, with gold and silver mines on its western shores. Additionally, the Inca *Toqui* made available his *cacique*, Cayancura, and ten men with mining experience, to accompany our forces to the lake and mines. With this notable offer the Governor, on February 15, sent de Alderete and his men, accompanied by *cacique* Cayancura and his, to assess matters and found a town, if warranted, and inspect the productivity of the mines. A further comment concerning Cayancura, Excellency. It happened that

---

[405] Earthquakes have struck Valdivia several times through the centuries. Lobera does not tell of this quake but he does record a Valdivia quake in 1575 in his Third Part, Ch. I. The city was almost completely destroyed in 1960 by another violent *terremoto*.

[406] Valdivia refers to the founding in his Letter V, p. 215. So does Marmolejo in his Ch. XII. But neither mentions the earthquake.

[407] This does not match Valdivia's number of one hundred. See his Letter V, p. 215, in "Historical Sources."

[408] The historians, Jerónimo de Vivar, Mariño de Lobera, and Góngora de Marmolejo, were part of this contingent.

he had two brothers who worked at our Marga Marga Station and thus had knowledge of mining affairs, a knowledge that would prove its worth.

At the same time as de Alderete's foray to the northeast, the Governor, with ever an eye for the southern lands since he one day wished to reach the Straights of Magellan, as he had told Your Majesty,[409] chose 100 men and, accompanied by Captain Villagran and several lieutenants, set off to the south on a fine morning with a favorable sun. Montesinos and those of us in his command were to stay in Valdivia to protect it and to continue with construction activities and our friendly dealings with the Indians.

I should tell of the results of these two efforts. The Governor and Villagran identified a number of sites for new settlements, bettered their understanding as to the requirements of a future journey to the Straights, and returned to us on April 12. De Alderete and his seventy men had a more exciting adventure to relate, as one day out from Valdivia his scouts discovered 500 Mapuche engaged in war-like preparations. Their proximity to our new settlement and fort suggested that they might launch an assault at any time. Gerónimo, therefore, designed a masterful plan of attack and presented it to his lieutenants, Riberos and de Morales. Once they had explained things to their men, two columns of thirty horse soldiers each formed up, Riberos heading the left most and de Morales the right, with de Alderete and ten men behind in reserve. The columns approached the Mapuche camp from the southeast where heavy forest provided concealment. At Gerónimo's shouted command, both files charged forward from their dark sanctuary and into the midst of the stunned savages as they were finishing their morning repast. Both columns galloped through the center of the encampment, slashing and stabbing to right and left as they rode through its width of 300 yards. When the Christians were at the far perimeter, Riberos turned his men to the left to encircle the divided warriors, while de Morales and his men did likewise to the right. Within a quarter hour, two groups of more than 200 Mapuche were surrounded in two pockets that, as more were

---

[409] Valdivia mentioned to the King on several occasions his intent to do so and declare them for him and for Spain. See his Letter V, p. 216, 217, in "Historical Sources."

slashed and killed, each gradually closed in upon itself. De Alderete and his men then added their swords to the massacre and, at one point, a warrior with distinctive headgear of colored llama skin pulled his tunic apart to expose his bare chest to one of our horsemen, de Santos by name, who thrust his sword straight into its center. In another quarter hour, Gerónimo ordered a halt to the carnage. The thirty Mapuche still alive were shown mercy and given to Cayancura and his men for guarding. Such was the first, and perfect, execution of the double envelopment of an enemy force in Mapuche country. As a further comment, it happened that Cayancura learned from the captured Mapuche that the savage with the demonstrative headdress was none other than the *toqui*, Ainavillo, last seen by us fleeing with Colo-Colo from the fight at Fort Penco. This, observed Gerónimo, should warn us that Colo-Colo and others were fomenting unrest throughout Mapuche land, an observation that later events confirmed.

Following a day of rest two miles from the battlefield, Gerónimo and his men continued forward to the western border of the lake, brooded over by a volcán to the east,[410] and entered a village of mining natives. These proved friendly and, at a meeting with de Alderete and Cayancura, the villagers professed themselves most willing to join with them to increase the output of gold and silver, should they receive fair reward for their work. This agreed upon, de Alderete asked for those among his men wishing to stay and participate in the mining efforts. A man called Jesus de Maria,[411] with mining experience, and thirty others stepped forward, and the Captain approved their taking residence here. Cayancura said that he and his men wished to stay also and that Michimalongo had approved his request for doing so. As a final matter, Gerónimo awarded land grants to his men and Cayancura as compensation for their future work to expand the mines' output.[412] This matter of foremost importance concluded, de Alderete identified a flat space between the river flowing west from the lake[413] and its western shores as the site of our new village. Accordingly,

---

[410] This is Volcán Villarrica, elevation of 9,300 feet.
[411] The historical record is silent about this man.
[412] These mines remained active until 1598.
[413] This is the Río Tolten.

on Tuesday, February 19 of 1552, the Captain performed the foundation ceremony, naming it Santa María Magdalena de Villarrica. May it remain always prosperous and faithful to our Blessed Lord.

After remaining two months to supervise construction activities and identify locations for Villarrica's cathedral, its *Cabildo* building, sections for homes for the men, and other such sites, the Captain and his remaining soldiers returned to us at Valdivia three days before our Governor and Captain Villagran rode in from the southern lands. While we tended to the construction needs of the town, Valdivia asked one day to know those who wished to stay and develop the settlement, grow crops, and see to the transportation of gold and silver from Villarrica to Santiago. Ninety-five men said they would do so and these the Governor awarded generous land grants for cultivation and civic development.[414] With Captain Villagran remaining here to oversee the construction of the fort and the betterment of relations with the natives, we set off for Concepción in mid-April of 1552 on a day of light rain.

286 An incident occurred on the journey, Excellency, that caused some to think that we were being spied upon from within our ranks and it deserves the telling of it. It happened on an afternoon once we set camp. While most of us were brushing down our horses, Lautaro did likewise for his mount and the Governor's. At one point, he moved to where Pérez de Santiago, the leader of our musket men, was combing his animal and, wishing him good afternoon, began a conversation at first upon the weather, the day's journey, and so forth. This gave way, however, to queries concerning the maneuvers of our musket men. At what moment in a battle was their deployment ordered and why, was one such question. How long did musket reloading take, was another. In what kind of terrain were muskets ineffective and thus not brought to bear in the fight? De Santiago answered these inquiries, thinking that knowing musketry was part of the page's training approved by the Governor. When Pérez mentioned this encounter to Jufré, the Captain voiced his unease to Valdivia about Lautaro knowing such things about our muskets and tactics. The reply he received was, "Lautaro is our friend and one day will

---

[414] Valdivia says the number was 100.

be, like Michimalongo, a true ally of us Christians." Some of us learned of this response from de Santiago, who swore us to secrecy. We promised as much. Nonetheless, in light of what would befall Valdivia and others, I believe it my duty to report this to Your Kingship. For here among us was this wanton savage who now possessed intimate knowledge of our muskets along with our cavalry tactics as taught him by Veas.

I must move on from this, for two days from Concepción, at the Indian village of Arauco, the Governor wished to locate another settlement. Accordingly, he summoned de Miranda from Concepción to supervise the construction work. He broke us into construction and work groups and, assisted by the natives we had been trading with since the founding of Concepción, we all began the work that was becoming all too common. In several days, at the end of April in 1552,[415] the Governor, his captains, and Father del Pozo carried out the ceremonies to establish San Felipe de Arauco. While here, we learned of important activities by the Mapuche. Michimalongo told the Governor that spies he had sent out when we left Valdivia town had returned with disturbing information. For they learned that Colo-Colo and a new warrior *toqui*, by name, Caupolicán,[416] were moving through the villages in Mapuche country attempting to stir the warriors to rebellion against us Christians. And, these *toquis* were on horseback, something we feared since we had lost a number of animals. They had either been captured from us or had wandered off from loose tethers. Until now, these *toquis* had convinced thousands of young warriors to take battle training with them. When their efforts would result in attacks upon our towns remained unclear, nevertheless this served as a forewarning to us of conflicts to come.

---

[415] The initial location of the town was seven miles inland on the south bank of the Río Carampangue. The Spanish moved it to its present site on the coast in 1590.

[416] This *toqui* will play an important part in events soon to unfold.

PART YY

THE RETURN TO SANTIAGO TOWN; WE ADOPT OUR DAUGHTER, INÉS; MICHIMALONGO RETIRES; LAUTARO ESCAPES AND IS REPLACED BY AGUSTINILLO

With de Miranda in charge of construction and Vicente Montesinos and his men providing men for building work and protection from the rising threat of Mapuche attack, the rest of us departed for Concepción. Upon our arrival, we resumed our tasks there; for many this was construction work and for others that of assisting the new *Cabildo* members. The major interest now of Valdivia was to prepare de Alderete to visit Your Excellency. One purpose of the journey would be to inform Your Grace of all that our Governor had done and planned to do to bring our new land and people to our Christ's loving embrace and to Your Honor's growing domain. Another was to escort the honorable Marina Ortiz de Gaete González, our Governor's wife, to this land that they might resume their lives with each other, as Viceroy de la Gasca had ordered.[417] Accordingly, the Governor, Gerónimo, and those of us to assist our Santiago *Cabildo*, departed on the *San Pedro* with Captain Pastene for Valparaíso. At the harbor roads, we dropped anchor at the seaman's call of "By the mark five!" at full fathom five and feasted on board ship that evening in farewell to Gerónimo and with earnest hopefulness for his success in his meeting with Your Grace. The following day, upon taking our leave of both captains, the *San Pedro* cleared the harbor roads and stood towards the northwest, her canvases billowing in the southerly breezes, bound for the City of Kings to find a ship sailing for Spain. I could not know that this was the last I would see of my friend, Gerónimo de Alderete, Sire. Your Grace knows what befell him.[418] The rest of us left for a ride of two days, and upon our nearing Santiago town we heard musket shots in the distance announcing our arrival. When we rode into the Plaza Mayor, there at the front of the crowd stood my Pilca Huaca holding Vicente as she raised his arm to wave. This being Friday, September 26 of 1552, our young son had turned two years old three days before; we celebrated that evening this important day.[419] I now began in earnest upon my *Cabildo* duties, as they were considerable. And added to these activities were those to honor a request from our venerated veteran, Gómez de Benito, our Captain General of Military Affairs. He asked that I spend whatever time I had available to help train new soldiers from Peru in the maneuvers and tactics we used in the forests and jungles of the southern lands. I did so, and readily, since this effort would bear results in our battles with the savages of Mapuche land.

Another development of great importance occurred during our stay here, Excellency. The Governor announced that Juan Gómez de Almagro would replace de Alderete until his return. This proved a most exemplary appointment, and it reminds me that I should say more here, Exalted Prince, regarding my admirable friend and worthy

---

[417] See Part UU of the Fifth Letter.
[418] On his return to Chile, de Alderete contracted yellow fever in Panama and passed away in 1556.
[419] Weldon Vernon says they entered Santiago sometime in the spring of 1552. See p. 172 of, <u>Pedro de Valdivia</u>.

companion, Juan Gómez, a man of great distinction and honor whom I knew from the days in Cusco. He was of notable lineage, the nephew of Diego de Almagro, as Your Honor knows already. To some, he seemed unapproachable and difficult to understand and know. They interpreted his perceived lack of friendliness as the mark of a deep-seated arrogance towards others because of his ancestry. Yet this was to misunderstand the man completely. For his initial reticence at camaraderie came from a natural shyness in dealing with others and a need to take the other man's measure as to his intentions towards him before offering his companionship. If, after awhile, he determined that no harm or ill will towards him was intended, he responded in ways most congenial. If he suspected otherwise, however, he turned tight-lipped and closed-mouthed towards the other. From the first moment of our meeting one another, he understood that my respect for his father and uncle and the high esteem in which I held them made me almost like a brother. We remained close companions, therefore, through the years. As to his personal traits, with his friends he was quick to laugh, when the occasion permitted, and swift to see the humor in things. A heavy-molded man, he had a broad, appealing face that exuded self-confidence. He also possessed a degree of stubborn fidelity to principle, an insensibility to danger, and a kind of instinct or sagacity whilst others seemed at a loss. Furthermore, others could receive confidently a service or gift from Juan Gómez and understand that he gave it freely, without the expectation of reciprocity. And he was swift to commend those he found truthful and prompt to excoriate those he found untruthful. These and other attributes served him and our people well in our new land, as he would hold numerous important *Cabildo* posts in the coming years, the most enduring that of township Constable. As to his private life, he married one of our Indian women from Peru, Illaray[420] by name, as I have said, a lady of great sagacity and warm humor who posed a counterpoint to the sometimes serious nature of Juan Gómez. She enjoyed playing the game of draughts, and the four of us met occasionally on Sundays following High Mass to play and take food together. Such are my memories of this most worthy man.

---

[420] This is the *Quechua* word for "rainbow."

It behooves me now, Sire, to relate a matter of personal importance to me. I will be brief. In mid-November the lady helping to care for Vicente, Miski by name,[421] visited me at my *Cabildo* office and said that Pilca Huaca desired my presence "quickly." When we arrived at her medical station, Miski led me to a room down a short hall to where Pilca Huaca sat holding a baby girl just born. As Vicente slept nearby, she said that a sheriff making his daily rounds found her by the roadside wrapped in a warm blanket of llama wool and brought her to the station for care. Who had abandoned her, no one knew. "She has no home, Pedro. May we claim her as our own?" She said this with such loving emotion that I knew that we would add a daughter to our family. When several days of searching for the parents or anyone who might know of the child's circumstances came to naught, we petitioned the *Cabildo* council for permission to take the child as our daughter. My colleagues granted this and our records keeper, Esteban de Sosa, recorded her birth name as Inés de Mérida de Santiago de Chile, with a date of birth of the 12th of November of 1552. Our Doña Inés held her namesake as Father Lobo poured holy water over her forehead at her christening.

Another event of import transpired during these days, for on a morning in early December an Indian on horseback advanced towards us from the south, was stopped by our guards, and escorted by one of them to the office of our Constable, Juan Gómez. As it happened, the man was a *cacique* of Michimalongo's who had come to tell us that the Inca *Toqui* would arrive shortly and wished to meet the Governor and Ancohualla, in private. Before relating what transpired, I should say that Michimalongo had suffered numerous wounds through the years, most recently at the Battle of Fortress Penco, when he and his warriors pursued and slew the retreating Mapuche. In that affair, he took a blow to the head that occasionally affected his balance and sight. Thus, he had decided to return here and resume his peaceful activities before the wars in the south intensified, such as working at Ancohualla's direction in the assignment of his people to the mines; planting, tending, and harvesting our crops; and assisting in the construction of our township. Such are the circumstances that prompted this meeting with our Governor and Ancohualla.

---

[421] Her name means "honey" or "sweet" in *Quechua*.

In mid-afternoon, the sheriff's deputy who controlled entry to the *Cabildo* chamber announced the approach of the three. It was clear to all when they entered that Michimalongo was in bodily difficulty as he used a hand pole for balance. The Governor, after a brief statement about Michimalongo's physical situation, went on to recount the early opposition of the Inca *Toqui* to us Christians and his transformation from our ardent foe to our ardent friend, by laying down his arms, embracing our Christ, directing his people to manage our properties, and supporting us in battles with the Mapuche to the south. The Governor, following our applause in acknowledgement of the *Toqui's* importance to us, asked the *Cabildo's* approval to award one/fiftieth of all future gold deposits from Marga Marga as recompense for his outstanding service. Of course, we did so, with loud acclamations. Such is the substance of this occurrence, Majesty, an event that marked the close of this era of the Inca *Toqui's* life, and the beginning of a new one for him.[422]

I must now leave these matters and return to those at hand, Your Grace. Several days later, 120 men under a Captain Martín de Avendaño[423] entered our town after their ride from Peru. The Captain was of an unusual sort, since in two weeks he and thirty of his men professed themselves eager to return to Peru. Never knowing the cause of this change in thinking, the Governor sent them on their way.[424] None of us ever determined the cause of their displeasure. Also during this period, the Governor presented to the *Cabildo* his plans to explore more of the southern lands of this continent. He intended, he said, to send orders to Captain Villagran, presently commanding the construction work in Valdivia and Villarrica, to take 100 men and strike out to the east to locate the Atlantic Ocean and establish a settlement there[425] at an appropriate location. This would enlarge the land under Your rule, Excellency, and identify more souls to come to Our Christ. Upon the *Cabildo's* unanimous approval, four horsemen set off next day for Valparaíso and the sea passage to Valdivia town.

---

[422] We only know of Michimalongo's retirement from de Mérida. The last mention of him was by Lobera, Second Part, Ch. XXXIII, at the Battle of Penco.

[423] See Weldon Vernon, p. 173.

[424] Marmolejo, Ch XIV, corroborates de Mérida's recounting of this incident.

[425] See Valdivia's Letter V, p. 216, in "Historical Sources," on the site.

The Adventure Chronicles of *Conquistador* Pedro de Mérida. VOLUME 2, VALDIVIA

IMAGES: 6VV-ZZ.29-.44 depict the characters and scenes of the tumultuous times to unfold.

Moving forward to May of 1553, the Governor decided to return to Concepción and resume the establishment of villages and the betterment of relations with the Mapuche. Accordingly, he and his men, including Huenu as a guide, as Valdivia was quite pleased with him and his performance, left early in the month for the journey south, while at his orders Juan Gómez and the rest of us were to follow two weeks later. As we were not with them when the following event happened, I tell of it after learning the particulars after entering Concepción weeks later. On their second day out of Santiago town, Excellency, something transpired, of which no one could have foreseen the consequences, and they still affect us to this day. It happened thusly. Lautaro, riding to the right of our Captain and two horse lengths behind, as was his custom, rode up to him and made a request. He pointed to a cluster of bushes and plants 300 yards to the west with orange colored, rounded flowers. These small bulbs when pressed, he told Valdivia, gave off a thick liquid that the Mapuche used to heal open wounds and to calm stomach pain.[426] He asked permission to gather these bulbs and take them to Michimalongo and Juan de Oliva, our medical man on this journey. The Governor granted his request and signaled to those nearby to let his page pass. The scoundrel got to the bushes and began picking the bulbs and placing them in his bag. In the meanwhile, our men continued forward, of course. When Lieutenant de Villarroel, in charge of the rear guard and his men came upon him, Lautaro waved and held up his bag. Not knowing the real state of affairs, our men continued forward with no suspicion of treason on their minds. When the men stopped in mid-afternoon to set camp, the Governor and his officers were in consternation as to the whereabouts of Lautaro. Valdivia made known the page's request and that he had granted his permission. Others said they had seen him amongst the bushes but did not suspect anything untoward. Valdivia sent Vallejo and five men in search of the aide, although they returned in two hours without having found him. When we of de Almagro's troop arrived later

---

[426] This herb, matico, has been used by the Mapuche for these ailments for hundreds of years.

in Concepción at the end of the month and learned that he had escaped, Huenu commented that he had been correct in his first assessment that he would desert at some point at a time of his choosing. He observed further that the information gathered months before by Michimalongo's spies that Mapuche *toquis* were stirring unrest in the countryside no doubt suggested to him that the moment had arrived to abscond. Whatever the cause, that was the last any of us saw of the reprobate until that fateful day soon upon us.[427]

Returning my narrative back now to Santiago, the time had arrived for our departure to Concepción. The morning of our leaving, I embraced Vicente, Inés, and Pilca Huaca, with a fervor of reluctance at my going. My son looked at me, in that innocent manner of children, and keeping his eyes fixed upon mine, he placed his favorite plaything made for his amusement, a little bird made of llama skin, into my hand. At first, his gesture puzzled me, until Pilca Huaca explained. "He wants you to have it, as it is a charm to work its magic so that you may return to us." I pondered this moment long after we left.

On our journey to the south, we crossed a shallow stream flowing into the Río Itata, advanced through a muddy field where the ground had been liquefied by the recent days of rain, past grass and bushes touched with green here and there, and entered a woodland of darkened gloom the likes of which we knew so well. In this heavy, forested enclave, the trees and shrubs with their motionless branches and leaves warned us of the Mapuche presence lurking perhaps in their murky depths. The times we entered one of these forlorn forests of latent iniquity, my every sense was at its utmost expectation of an attack from our front or our flanks. And this fear brought forth anger in me. I did not want to appear fearful or afraid. And my countenance and attitude at these instances turned to that of a dark and menacing glare with an intention to kill any and all hostiles I should encounter. Such is how conflict and battle alter our beings into instruments of death and destruction.

---

[427] The major historians of the time do not mention details of Lautaro's escape, only that at some point he became one of the Mapuche's foremost leaders, as we shall soon see.

After we entered our busy city of Concepción on Friday, May 29 of 1553, I met with Montesinos to tell him of our new daughter and especially of the health and playful nature of young Vicente. He brightened at the news and commented that he felt part of our family, as indeed he was. The conversation turned to Lautaro's escape, which turned out fortuitous, since Michimalongo suggested a replacement that proved superior in all respects. His name, Agustinillo.[428] He had served as *cacique* Quepuanté's *yanacona*, who looked after his well-being, saw to his every need, and to his personal protection as well. Upon his introduction to our Governor, Valdivia questioned him on a number of topics of importance. Satisfied with the answers, he appointed him as his personal aide. To say more of him, he exhibited a friendly and benign countenance, unlike the often sullen and withdrawn expression of Lautaro. He was a man of conversation as well, able and willing to engage in discussion with the Governor on topics of interest to both. And he was devoted to Valdivia, showing his respect with a slight bow of his straight and erect frame when entering or leaving his company. Also of note, he was as uninterested in learning our battle tactics as Lautaro had been interested in learning them. He eagerly and quickly became skilled at riding the horse given him by Valdivia, and his riding abilities even surpassed those of a number of our men. Interested in the teachings of our Christ, he followed Michimalongo's example of several years earlier and was baptized into the Church by Father del Pozo. As to his appearance, the guanaco skin band he wore around his head that captured his long strands of dark hair created almost an impression of royalty about him. The Governor was pleased with his new attendant, and many of us heard him say so on a number of occasions. He called him Agusto, perhaps as a testament to his noble bearing and manner. Such is my memory of this man.

To return to my relation, Your Grace, it happened that a priest joined us in Concepción newly arrived from Spain. Father Martín de Robleda, of the order of my beloved Saint Francis, was the first Franciscan to enter our new land and a pleasing addition to the priests here in Christianizing

---

[428] Marmolejo mentions Valdivia's new aide in his Ch. XIV.

our Indians.[429] Father and I talked regularly of St. Francis and his good works amongst the poor. He possessed medical skills too, a notable talent always in demand, and declared himself eager to learn more of this new Province of Chile. Hearing this, I suggested that he make his desire known to the Governor, as we were presently to depart on another fort founding expedition.

---

[429] See Lobera, Third Part, Ch. XLII. Also, the "Franciscans in Chile" website says that Father Robleda founded a Franciscan church in Concepción in early 1554.

PART ZZ

THE GOVERNOR'S UNPOPULAR DECISION TO ESTABLISH MORE FORTS; THE FOUNDING OF FORTS TUCAPEL, PURÉN, AND LOS CONFINES; DE MÉRIDA SUFFERS A CRIPPLING WOUND; EVENTS PRESAGING A TRAGEDY; THE FATED BATTLE OF TUCAPEL

On August 20, an incident of importance transpired, as Captain Francisco de Villagran and his men returned from their journey to the Atlantic Ocean and had a remarkable story to tell the Governor, the captains, and lieutenants. Although they had crossed the mountains, more than a few incidents forced their return, one being the inability to cross two very wide rivers.[430] On their march back, the Captain located the site for a future settlement south of Valdivia but needed more men to begin the construction work.[431] They left that area, passed through Valdivia, and continued north towards La Imperial

---

[430] It is not clear which rivers these are.
[431] The place he located would soon be founded as the city of Osorno.

when his scouts learned from local Indians that some Christians had been attacked at a site called Pucureo.[432] When Villagran entered upon the scene, he learned that Mapuche warriors had killed a Captain Alonso de Moya, but his ten horse soldiers had fended off the enemy. They stayed there for the night and 300 Mapuche attacked them the subsequent morning. They fought bravely and two hours later had managed to kill 125 hostiles and capture three of their *caciques*. To make examples of these men, the Captain ordered their noses and hands cut off to serve notice that such attacks in future should meet the same response. That the land was in turmoil was obvious when they entered La Imperial. The Captain's cousin, Pedro de Villagran, welcomed them with the disturbing news that bands of Mapuche were massing at locations throughout the region in the north, led by the *toquis* Caupolicán and Colo-Colo, and now joined by the infamous Lautaro. This did not surprise any of us listening to his story, as we knew that this traitor wished us Christians harm and death. He left ten men with Pedro before leaving for our town.[433] As de Villarroel commented after the Captain's presentation, this was the information given us by Michimalongo a year before when we were at Arauco, that the Mapuche were seeking followers to drive us from their land. Gaspar commented further that these hostiles would reveal themselves at some point and that the Governor must recognize this possibility and prepare for it.

In the days following this sobering report, many expected the immediate actions taken by the Governor would be to strengthen the defenses of our current townships of Concepción, Arauco, La Imperial, Valdivia, and Villarrica, as de Villarroel had observed. Yet he did not do so, to the surprise of many. "This is not right. We are jeopardizing the safety of our people and that of our Indian friends if we disregard these threats." So said Lieutenant Vallejo one evening at relaxation. De Villarroel and de Morales agreed, among others. To increase these worries, our Governor directed Captain Villagran to take forty men and march south to found a town at the site south of Valdivia mentioned above, Excellency. Many

---

[432] No such place exists today. This might have been Pitrufquén, a small commune of 20,000 people.

[433] See the *Proceso de Villagran* in Medina, <u>Documentos Ineditos</u>, XXI, XXII.

thought we could not afford the loss of these men in these threatening times.

It occurred during these worrisome days that my great and good friend, Vicente Montesinos, sent his aide to ask if we might dine in private. I agreed, of course, and that evening over our fermented beverages we reminisced about the times we had spent together through the years and turned emotional reliving those occasions, some of great joy, some of great danger, and some of great sadness. At a certain point, his manner and expression recalled to me his misgivings months earlier concerning his premonition about the battles with the Mapuche, and I now saw in his eyes the feeling that its fulfillment was upon him. "We have sought great adventure together, Pedro, since the Almagro days, and you have been my closest and dearest companion, always." I replied in the same fashion. He continued. "I must tell you that our Governor is going to embark us all upon expeditions to found new settlements rather than to improve our defenses. You should know in private that I disagree with this, especially the departure of Captain Villagran, and have told him as much, with a certain heatedness. But he is driven by forces that many of us cannot understand, and I fear that the coming campaigns will see my undoing. There are only two realities, Pedro, life and death. And I feel that I am soon to leave the first and enter the second." Before I could comment, he withdrew from his blouse an envelope and held it out to me. "Here," he said with a hint of emotion. "I want you to have this. Should something happen to me in the coming months, you may open it. If not, keep it still, for my reckoning is close at hand notwithstanding. I can feel it." We embraced one another warmly, in the manner known only to those who have faced death together. When we parted, I harbored a deep trepidation as to what might come his and our way.

Events now proceeded quickly and in an uncoordinated manner, Your Excellency, so much so that the correct dates and exact details of several events still remain in question.[434] The frenzy to establish townships by Valdivia began with his departure on Wednesday, October 14, from Concepción with two contingents composed of one hundred men each.

---

[434] And they are still to this day.

One group included Captain Montesinos, Captain Martín de Ariza,[435] a new man recently arrived from Peru, Lieutenants de Morales and de Riberos, Huenu as guide, and Father del Pozo. This force totaled forty-five men. Captain de Almagro headed the other troop whose numbers consisted of Lieutenants Carrillo, de Villarroel, Alonso Coronas, Your humble servant (Vicente Montesinos had asked that I not be part of his command), five musket men, Father Robleda, and Ayar, for a total of fifty-five. The plan the Governor explained before our departure had us marching south to the Río Tucapel, a region we had passed on our expeditions to and from the south, there establish a fortress, and leave men to start construction. From there, Valdivia would continue due east and build a fort at a place of his choosing. In the meantime, Juan Gómez was to journey southeast to a location on the Río Purén, a section we had gone through on numerous occasions, and start construction of a fort there. This was not all, however. For then de Almagro was to journey south to La Imperial and direct Pedro de Villagran to lead a force to the southeast to find a salt mine, which Michimalongo some years ago had indicated was in the vicinity. I must interject here, Your Honor, that when we heard this I looked to de Villarroel, who wore an expression of incomprehension that such an activity should have any merit in the face of the danger we faced. Salt was important, yet so were our lives, he remarked privately. Many others expressed perplexity at this in the succeeding days.

I shall tell now what transpired. We reached the Río Tucapel on October 18[436] and went through the founding ceremony with the blessing administered by Father del Pozo. After four days of fort construction activities, Captain Ariza, with fifteen men,[437] was left in charge, and Valdivia, Montesinos, and the rest of the men departed on October 22 for another founding to the east. As Vicente and I said our farewells, we could not know this was the last time we were to see one another. On Saturday, October 24 of 1553, they founded Los Confines where the Ríos

---

[435] (1518-1587).
[436] There is no exact founding day for Fort Tucapel, but de Mérida's fits admirably.
[437] Marmolejo, Ch. XIV, confirms this number of men.

Malleco and Huequén converge[438] and, upon leaving men for construction work, returned to Concepción.

Meanwhile, we marched south, and Ayar and I had little difficulty finding the general vicinity our Governor had indicated as proper for a fort's placement. Juan Gómez surveyed possible locations and decided upon land to the west from where the Río Purén divides into two separate channels. The site he chose proved admirable, as one river branch flowed east to west one half mile to the north and the other one half mile to the south. The surrounding country was flat and open, providing little cover for attacking warriors. Still, there were heavy forests above the northern branch of the río that required extra scrutiny by our patrols. We set the watches, and next day on October 25 Captain de Almagro founded the fort of Purén, with Father Robleda performing the Christian ceremonies.[439] That evening, Juan Gómez gave us our orders. Lieutenant Coronas would remain here with fifteen men, including the five muskets,[440] since the guns provided sturdy protection in case of a Mapuche attack. In the meanwhile, we were to advance south with the remaining men and meet with Pedro de Villagran. The new day dawned cool with a light drizzle, and we set off after bidding our men a hearty farewell. That afternoon, we entered a forest that prompted our deepest attention because of the constant Mapuche threat, before we exited the gloom and entered a vast zone of low grasses and shrubs. Now without the arching tree branches over us, the darkened clouds above heralded the coming of a violent tempest. It moved towards us, swiftly upon a swift wind, and its watery torrents broke over us with an inundation of downward cascading water that formed watery pools and within half an hour large, lake-like collections. Carrillo brought word from the Captain to cease our march and make camp, which we attempted with the greatest difficulty upon rising ground with vacant

---

[438] This is the correct founding date and location, according to the historical record. The fort was later destroyed by the Mapuche and re-founded as Angol in 1560.

[439] The record is silent as to the exact day in October, but de Mérida's date appears to fit.

[440] See Lobera, Third Part, Ch. XLII, as he tells also of this incident.

land all around us. When double sentries were set, we endured a fitful sleep.

At noon on Friday, October 30, we came to the Río Imperial and followed it west towards the outline of La Imperial's fort and low buildings. A sentry hailed our approach, and upon passing through fields of beans, squash, and *maize*, we entered the Plaza Mayor to a cheerful reception from Captain Pedro de Villagran and his men. After partaking of a meal of roasted fish and boiled *papas* with hot peppers, discussion began as to the orders Juan Gómez bore from the Governor. "Yes," Villagran responded. "We have a salt mine here to the east, for we barter with the natives to acquire it, as you see it here at table. If the Governor wants us to take charge, I am happy to determine what resources we need to assume its ownership." In response to a question, he said that Mapuche activity here was not apparent now; their attention seemed focused upon our forces in the north up to Concepción. "Yet, we remain on the alert day and night, for their interest in the north could quickly change to us here in the south."

On the coming day, Villagran and ten men set off on their journey.[441] We were to await their return, assist with construction activities, and work with the natives to maintain the rich crops all around the village. Father Robleda visited the Indians nearby and made known the blessings of our Christ. At his daily masses, local Indians began to attend, until by the day of our going there were more natives than the 140 Christians in attendance. One evening during conversation amongst us he said, "My brothers, this is my calling and I could not be happier!" Such is the working of our Lord.

At the close of November, Villagran returned with the news that they had found the mine. Nevertheless, they needed at least ten more men to organize the Indians and set in place procedures for salt shipments north to the new settlements and asked Juan Gómez to convey his request to the Governor. This determined, our Captain decided to linger here

---

[441] See, *Información de servicios de Pedro de Villagran*, in Medina, <u>Documentos ineditos</u>, Ch. XIII.

a few days more and enjoy the peacefulness while we could. But this respite ended abruptly when, on December 13, one of our men from Fort Purén rode in with disturbing news. Coronas had found signs that the Mapuche were preparing assaults throughout the region and requested our immediate return. Without delay, we set off traveling with urgency, remaining constantly on alert for savages, and reached our fort in three days. The men there expected an attack at any moment and were armed and at the high ready. According to Coronas, he had learned from the local natives that the three *toquis* and their forces were preparing for large, coordinated attacks on our new forts. He had notified the Governor of this, now in Concepción, but had heard nothing in reply.

On Friday, December 18 of 1553, a shout arose from the sentries on the northern walls that horsemen were approaching. In minutes, Captain Ariza and thirteen of his men rode in to tell of the attack upon Fort Tucapel by Colo-Colo and hundreds of hostiles. They had fought in determined fashion, said Ariza, until the point when two of his men were killed and he realized that they were hopelessly outnumbered. He then decided to break away and flee here to safety.[442] We were the next to experience the weight of the wretched hordes, for early the morning following, our perimeter sentries on their ride around the fort, rode in yelling for us to arm since hundreds of Mapuche were massing in the forest on the northern side of the Río Purén. Juan Gómez shouted out our deployment positions, and we were no sooner at the ready than flaming arrows began striking our outer walls and landing inside the fort. None of these caused much damage or alarm, as we extinguished them quickly. After a half hour of this the Mapuche, led by Colo-Colo, as identified by Ariza, advanced from the forest in menacing fashion towards us. Juan Gómez shouted to Pedro Niño, one of Coronas' men, to align the musket men to the front of our wall and begin firing at the instant. When they did so and Mapuche began to fall, they turned to retreat, recognizing that the flat, open land from the Río Purén to our walls made them prime targets for annihilation. At this withdrawal, Captain de Almagro ordered de Villarroel and me to advance with eight horse soldiers apiece

---

[442] Marmolejo, in Ch. XIV, attests to this attack upon Tucapel and the withdrawal south by Ariza.

and attack the hostiles at their flanks, with Captain Ariza to charge at the center with ten men. In the haste to mount and move off, I failed to strap my legging fully about my right boot. This offered vital protection, but I could not make it right as we moved off so quickly. When we were in line formation in front of the walls, Ariza yelled his "charge" command and we bolted forward. We were upon them swiftly and began their slaughter easily, for they seemed to lack resolve, perhaps stunned by the damage wreaked by our muskets.

And then, it happened. I knew the instant I felt the arrow point enter my right boot at the ankle that, though not a death strike, it was a blow that would alter my life. If only I had cinched the legging correctly, I could have avoided this! I pulled the reins to the left to move from our line and ride back to the fort, for I knew that with my right foot unable to guide my horse I could not direct my men in the fight. I yelled to Sergeant Zapata, the relentless warrior, to take charge as I did so. Blood streamed from the wound and oozed out from the boot. The physical pain was excruciating, although bearable. My all too real fear was whether I might ever walk again. "My merciful Lord," I asked, "will I be a cripple the rest of my life?" I cantered back to the fort as yells and screams from the butchered savages behind me swept across the open fields. Father Robleda ran to meet me as I entered through the open gate, and he and Juan Gómez eased me to ground at his medical station. His spiritual abilities now gave way to his medical skills. He pulled the boot off slowly, wiped the blood away, and applied orange paste to the wound to slow the bleeding.[443] With Ayar's help, he cut the rear end of the arrow and pulled the remainder of the shaft from my ankle. After applying more paste, Father bound it with thin llama skin to stop the bleeding and provide stability so that I might stand without falling.

As for the battle, Sire, our men drove the Mapuche back across the Río Purén, and having seen to the threat for now, Ariza ordered a return to our camp. We watched intently for movement in the trees, yet saw none. To determine Colo-Colo's location and intent, the Captain sent Carrillo out with ten men on a scouting mission. When they returned in late

---

[443] This is from the matico bulb, mentioned above.

afternoon, Carrillo said the enemy was camped deep in the forest two miles to the north. Ariza and Coronas thought that the Mapuche were here to block us from going north, for what reason they did not know. As matters were to transpire, their observation was correct, since they were preventing us from riding north to Tucapel.

In mid-day December 22, two horsemen galloped in from the west. Their mounts frothed heavily upon their arrival and our men washed them down to cool them. They bore a message from our Governor that he meant to attack at Tucapel with forty men[444] and ordered Juan Gómez to meet him there for reinforcement on December 25. The Captain decided to leave the day following and designated Ariza and his thirteen men, all to a one eager to return to Tucapel, to accompany him. As an aside, Your Majesty, these fourteen men, who fled from Tucapel only weeks before and were now returning to wreak havoc upon the Mapuche heathens, Juan Gómez called the "Famous Fourteen" as testament to their courage and dedication.[445] The Captain learned from the two messengers that they had come from the northwest and had followed the shores of a ten mile long lake. This route let them pass to the west of the Mapuche to our front and so this is the track de Almagro followed.

Early on Wednesday, December 23, the men rode off to the west for the twenty mile ride, our earnest shouts of "God be with you" accompanying them. That afternoon, as they were traversing the northeast shore of the lake,[446] the forces of Colo-Colo attacked them. The ensuing fight was a daunting affair for the Famous Fourteen, since they had the lake at their backs. This prevented encirclement by the enemy, but the Mapuche kept them in this position until nightfall. It was a restless night for our men and all remained awake throughout. On December 25, the holy day of our Blessed Lord's birth, they saw Mapuche in the bushes and nearby

---

[444] This is the number given by Marmolejo in his Ch. XV. Lobera says there were sixty-three in his Ch. XLII.

[445] See *Información de servicios de Juan Gómez de Almagro*, in Medina, <u>Documentos inéditos</u>, Ch. XIV, for confirmation of de Mérida's statement. De Almagro was one of the Fourteen.

[446] This is today's Laguna Lanalhue.

forest, yet they failed to attack. This kept our men in position, as the number of hostiles was difficult to determine, and thus they missed the meeting date with our Governor. At the sun's rise on December 26, the Captain decided to force his way to Tucapel no matter the opposition, but, surprisingly, there was none.

Juan Gómez and his men entered the Tucapel fort area from the southwest in the afternoon and beheld a stark and unsettling scene. Parts of bodies lay here and there, most obviously roasted over fires and with chunks missing from their appendages as though they had been eaten. Our men could not believe what they saw and sat there on horseback without saying a word. Then, to the east, loud shouting alerted them to the Mapuche, who appeared from the forest holding the severed heads of many of our comrades. They dropped these and charged towards the Captain and his men. Hundreds followed, seeking to overwhelm our men, who broke away in a frenzied gallop. After riding three miles to the west of Tucapel and after turning south to return to us, hundreds of Indians ambushed them and killed six of the Famous. The Captain and the eight remaining rode off into the night, thinking that the darkness would be in their favor. It provided safety, until they entered a shallow valley to the west of our fort in the hours before dawn.[447] Mapuche commanded by Colo-Colo surprised our men again, and they fought desperately for their lives. They killed the horse of Juan Gómez and wounded him seriously. Realizing the nature of things, he pleaded for his men to leave him and flee to our fort. They refused. An injured man, my friend Gregorio de Castañeda,[448] rode to us to sound the alarm, while Ariza and the other men mounted the Captain on the horse of the dead Alonso Cortes. In the meanwhile, de Castañeda yelled to the sentries as he approached and they aroused de Villarroel, in charge in de Almagro's absence. He hastily identified ten men, and they rode off to the west to save Juan Gómez and his companions.

---

[447] This area today is the site of the town of Contulmo, six miles west from Purén.
[448] (1517-1567). This man served later as the Mayor of La Imperial in 1564 and 1565. As mentioned previously, he died in a sea storm on the return to Chile from Peru in 1567.

As the sun rose slowly in the east, the sentries announced their return. De Villarroel shouted that the wounded Captain needed Father Robleda. They rode through the open gate and our men rushed to provide assistance. Captain Ariza helped Juan Gómez off his horse, as he had injuries to his face and both legs. Father tended him as best he could while we gave water and food to the men. In half an hour, the western sentry yelled that hundreds of Mapuche were advancing towards us from the west. The Captain, still sound of mind despite his injuries shouted for all to make ready, since we had to leave without delay for La Imperial. "Men, this is the wrong ground to die upon! And remember this. We are not retreating. This is an armed advance to the south by you, my Chosen Few!" With his words ringing in our ears, we gathered what we could and set off. After two miles, Carrillo exclaimed that the fort was in flames behind us, and so it was, with the blazes lighting the morning sky.[449]

The subsequent three days proved difficult. Father tended to Juan Gómez at our frequent stops for rest and to me and de Gregorio as well. We were in considerable pain and unable to mount and dismount our horses without help from Ayar. On the march, Captain Ariza and de Villarroel set guards on our flanks and to our front and rear, for the danger from Mapuche resided all around us. We entered La Imperial on Friday, January 1 of 1554 to the welcome of Pedro de Villagran and his men, who saw to it that our every need was seen to. The Captain and his men were astounded to hear de Almagro's story, as they had heard nothing of the tragedy. And the natives here and down to Valdivia and Villarrica were peaceful and friendly, as best he knew. He related also that his cousin, Francisco, had recently passed through on his ride south to found the aforementioned township south of Valdivia, as ordered by the Governor some weeks before.

Thus it seemed that the Mapuche *toquis* were concentrating their forces to destroy the northern towns and forts while leaving the far south alone for the time being. During our stay, it became evident that Captain de

---

[449] Marmolejo attests to some of these events in his Ch. XIV and XV. Also, see *Información de servicios de* Juan Gómez de Almagro, in Medina, <u>Documentos inéditos</u>, Ch. XIV,

Almagro, de Castañeda, and I needed more specialized medical care and that we and our men had to return to Concepción and maybe Santiago. Specifically as to injuries, a thrown mace had struck Juan Gómez in his morrión, causing bleeding cuts to his head and face. The fall from his horse was upon jagged rocks that cut through his pants and opened a bloody gash in his right thigh. As to Gregorio, a wretched Mapuche had thrust a long knife into his lower right leg just as his downward sword swing separated the despicable flesh eating hostile's head from his shoulders.

Of course, we still had heard nothing further concerning events to the north, although we assumed that the land there must be in great turmoil, with rampant bloodshed and warfare. Thus, the Captain decided the safe way to return must be to march south to Valdivia, notify Captain Villagran of the Tucapel tragedy, and seek passage back on a visiting supply ship. Our Chosen Few of forty-eight men departed January 3 on the eighty mile ride to Valdivia, bidding farewell to Pedro Villagran and the men of La Imperial. Throughout the journey, we talked constantly about what matters were like in Concepción. Without any news, a few imagined that the heathens had perhaps attacked and burned it. One evening, Zapata wondered aloud if Santiago were in danger. Arauco? Valparaíso? And other like questions were asked repeatedly. Who had accompanied the Governor? How many men and who were they? Of course, Vicente remained on my mind at these times, and I wished earnestly for his safety and well-being. However, his repeated comments to me about feelings of his impending doom caused me to ask, "Could Tucapel be the realization of those premonitions?" And why did he ask that I not ride with him when we left Concepción in mid-October? I could endure only so much of this not knowing, but the questions kept coming notwithstanding. And it tortured me that my Pilca Huaca and children knew nothing of my situation. I had to return to them. I had to.

Two days from Valdivia, de Almagro sent two men ahead to find Francisco Villagran to tell him of our approach. As we neared the town on Saturday, January 9, a rider sent to meet us said that Villagran had arrived from the south and all there were awaiting news of what had happened. Juan

Gómez and the Captain embraced each other warmly upon our arrival, and the large crowd of assembled Christians then listened in horror at what had befallen the Governor and our men. There were many head shakings of disbelief and occasional epithets of disgust and oaths of revenge at the wretched Mapuche. When Juan Gómez had finished, he paused a minute and then said, "Captain Villagran, my good and close friend, you will now be our Governor. Long be your reign!" There were loud shouts of approval at this, until the Captain raised his arms to ask for quiet. "Thank you, Juan Gómez, however that is for the Santiago *Cabildo* to decide.[450] In the meantime, we must prepare immediately for our departure to Concepción."

There occurred now a great commotion of preparation. Villagran identified eighty men for the march north, while sixty were to remain here in Valdivia and Villarrica under the command of Captain Ariza to provide protection should the hordes from the north decide to strike here in the south. In a surprise, Captain de Almagro declared himself fit to travel, although Villagran sought, and failed, to dissuade him. It was a brave and courageous decision by Juan Gómez and I told him so, for he was still in a good deal of discomfort due to his wounds. He thanked me for my comments with, "Many thanks, Pedro. But I must avenge the death of our Governor no matter how I feel."[451] And my friend of long standing, Ayar, asked to stay and help me and Gregorio, both of us unable to walk without the use of canes. "No, my friend, your place is with the Governor and the men. They need you more than we do. I shall see you soon, I am sure." That evening, Father Robleda brought us medical cream for our injuries, blessed us in His name, and said he would pray for our good health. On the new day, our men rode off, with expressions of determination and resolve. As they galloped past, we saluted them and yelled out the vengeance they should render upon the despicable unbelievers.

---

[450] Because of the confusion and disruption caused by Tucapel and internal bickering, it took the Santiago *Cabildo* several months finally to appoint Villagran the Governor.

[451] Lobera in his Ch. XLIII, Part III, refers to de Almagro's desire to go despite his injuries.

On January 15 of the new year, shouts from our sentries alerted us to Captain Villalón's approach in the *Santiaguillo*, coming upriver from the sea. In a surprise, two cannon shots rang out in salute, accompanied by white billows of smoke. When he had anchored in the harbor roads, he and his men disembarked and rowed ashore, where he waved and shouted to us his relief that we were alive and safe. He inquired after Villagran, de Almagro, and the men, for Captain de Miranda, left in charge in Concepción by Valdivia, had sent him to see if they might have fled here for safety after Tucapel. When told that they had marched north to Concepción, he was relieved that most of the men were still alive. I could not bear to delay my inquiry and burst out with, "And what of Montesinos, Huenu, and Father del Pozo?" The Captain's face clouded with sadness as he put his hand upon my shoulder. "Pedro. I know they were your friends, especially Captain Montesinos. All were with Valdivia and, as of yet, only burned body parts have been found, none of them identifiable. I am sorry that you, and we, have lost them. Our men experienced our Lord God's apocalypse." So, I thought, Vicente's premonitions had been correct. That is why he asked that I not accompany his command when we left Concepción two months ago. And his and the men's deaths in this fashion were abhorrent. I excused myself and limped back to my tent. I lost myself, Excellency, in pleasant memories of our adventures together through the years, ever since we met in Puná in 1532,[452] and knew I would never have another friend like Vicente. Yet, I consoled myself with the knowledge that his remembrance would live in the years to come through my son, Vicente. Following these quiet moments of personal mourning, I recalled the letter he had given me months before with instructions to open it upon his passing. I took it from my belongings and read his handwritten note: "I hereby bequeath my 120 acres of land awarded me in January of 1544[453] on the eastern boundary of Santiago del Nueva Extremadura to my namesake, Vicente de Mérida de Santiago, for his benefit and enjoyment. So rendered by me this date, October 10 of 1553." At the bottom appeared his signature and below it that of Governor

---

[452] De Mérida refers here to their early years together in the conquest of Peru. See <u>The Adventure Chronicles of *Conquistador* Pedro de Mérida. Volume III: Pizarro.</u>

[453] De Mérida mentions these grants in Part RR of the Fifth Letter.

Valdivia. Such was my son's inheritance from this most extraordinary of men.

I shall return now to my recounting, Sire. When I rejoined the men, Captain Villalón told us what he knew about Tucapel, and I repeat his story now. They learned in Concepción that Captain de Almagro and his men had arrived at the battlefield a day after the tragedy and had found roasted body parts there but no bodies, told them by the few *yanaconas* that accompanied Valdivia and his men as supply carriers when they returned to the township and told their story. But these were conflicting stories about what had happened, and since none of our Christians survived, these accounts were all that we had. He went on to say that there was one report that a swampy marsh slowed the horses and prevented efficient maneuvering or escape, and that the Governor remained with Father del Pozo and Agusto to protect them from the Mapuche hordes. He and the men were surrounded and told to dismount by Lautaro, the scoundrel *toqui* responsible for setting the trap for our Christians. Valdivia tried to talk with him as to surrender terms, even offering to leave Chile, while the warriors built a large fire. Lautaro refused any discussion of terms and decreed death the only just verdict. According to this story, the Indian devils cut pieces of flesh from the arms and legs of the men, roasted them on the fire, and ate them in front of them. Afterwards, they tied the Governor hand and foot and the scoundrels then ate his flesh as he watched them do so. Then, Lautaro ordered him beheaded and had his head hoisted skyward on a long lance to the cheers and singing of the Mapuche.[454] Another version had it that as Valdivia tried to bargain with Lautaro, one of his *caciques*, Pilmaequén, brought his many-headed stone mace down upon the Governor's head, splitting it wide open.[455] In yet one more account, Villalón said that they kept the Governor living for three days and ate him alive by the mouthfuls.[456] Even at the date of this letter to Your Highness, we still do not know completely what happened on

---

[454] Marmolejo tells a similar story to this in his Ch. XV.
[455] Lobera, in his Third Part, Ch. XLII, echoes this version of what transpired.
[456] This grisly tale comes from the account in the *Cabildo de Santiago á la Real Audiencia de Lima*, in Medina, <u>Documentos inéditos</u>, IX.

that terrible Christmas day of 1553.[457] And there was more destruction, for Caupolicán had burned to ground the fortress at Los Confines on the same day. Fortunately, our few men there escaped back to Concepción.[458]

Please forgive a brief personal comment, Your Grace. In the years after the shock of Tucapel, I found myself subject to occasions of despondency, when I remained uncommunicative and undesirous of physical activity, except to stare blankly at nothing in particular. Pilca Huaca and the children knew at these times to leave me undisturbed, until I returned to my normal disposition. In attempting to overcome these withdrawals, I tried to find their cause through long moments of solitary reflection. After many bouts of contemplation on these matters, I understood that the cause of my troubled inner emotion was the many battles I had participated in with Captain Almagro and Captain Valdivia. I shared my situation with de Villarroel and de Morales and found that the pall of battle possessed us even when we did not think about it. Our meetings to talk of our experiences helped us, not to obliterate our feelings, for we still bore those, but to bear more manfully our inner burdens.

I return now to my relation. On January 20, the supply goods for the Valdivia settlement now off-loaded, we said our farewells to Captain Ariza and his men and boarded the *Santiaguillo* for the passage back to Concepción. Having departed the roads and harbor, the Captain recorded in his journal that "we ran W in light SE breezes, then tacked N on the identical parallel of 39°40′S, caught a strong current setting that stood NE, and beat our way towards the town with the aid of blustery westerlie winds." Upon our entry to Concepción harbor and dropping anchor at the roads at the call of full fathom seven, Villalón fired a two cannon salute. Once disembarked, we found all in great fear and consternation and on high alert expecting an attack by the three Mapuche *toquis* at any instant. Gregorio and I, with help from one of the medical men, left to meet de Miranda. We found him directing the strengthening of the fort's

---

[457] De Mérida's observation is still true today.
[458] Garcilaso de la Vega, the Inca historian, tells of the Tucapel disaster in his <u>Royal Commentaries of the Incas</u>, published in 1617. It resides on the web site under "Historical Sources."

walls and he embraced us in welcome and relief that we were alive. I told him of Villagran's and de Almagro's approach and he said a messenger had arrived that morning with news they were two days distant. When the Captains and the men rode in on Thursday, January 28 of 1554, we greeted them with great relief at their safe arrival. Captain Villagran began preparations straight away for a mission of destruction against the Mapuche. He reviewed the physical condition of both of us and ordered our return to Santiago for better care. "And, Pedro," he told me in a personal comment. "I believe your days of combat are over. I need you much more in the Santiago *Cabildo* and ask that you return there, settle down with your family, and begin the next period of your life. I believe the time is right to do so." When I agreed to this without dissent, he gave me a stern military salute and then grasped my hand in a tight grip of warm friendship.

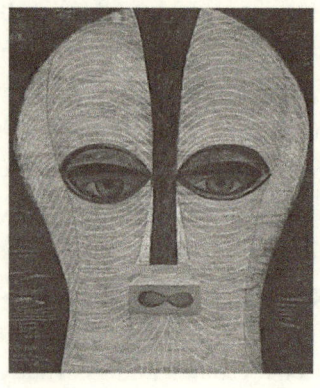

THE AFTERMATH; THE CLOSE OF THE CHILE ADVENTURES

With this, Noble Excellency, I shall draw my account of the Pedro de Valdivia years in Chile to a close. Yet before ending, I beg Your patience so that I might relate notable events from the days after Tucapel down to the date of this correspondence some fourteen years later.

The return to my Pilca Huaca, Vicente, and Inés, caused close embraces and tears of joy. To me, they were all in life that mattered. As to their present circumstances, Pilca Huaca is still the director of the Indian medical facility with forty workers, with Collardis her close assistant. And our Inés, now with sixteen years, has begun a three year assignment training as a physician, the particulars taught to her by several of the physicians who have settled here from Spain. As Your Honor knows, our Vicente is studying law and judicial matters at the University of Salamanca[459] and will return to us in another two years. And I must offer our deepest gratitude and appreciation for the gift Your Grace

---

[459] As noted in the Fifth Letter, the University of Salamanca is the oldest in Spain and the third oldest in the world. King Alfonso X granted it the title of "University" in 1254.

bestowed upon him when he visited to pay our respects and homage to Your Majesty. He will keep it always.[460]

PAINTING: This book's back cover is the Glanzman painting that depicts the later years' lifestyle of Pedro and Pilca Huaca.

Doña Inés de Suarez de Quiroga remains as the Director of the Santiago medical operation, now grown to three levels with seventy-five medical personnel. We dine with her and Rodrigo occasionally and recall our past days of adventure together.[461]

In September of 1552, our Governor Valdivia sent to Your Majesty Gerónimo de Alderete, my close and good friend, to pay the Governor's respects and to tell of his plans for our new land and his accomplishments during the years here. Gerónimo was also to offer his regards to the Governor's wife, Marina Ortiz de Gaete González, and convey Valdivia's request of her to resume their lives together in our land. In mid-1554, word came of the death of the Governor at Tucapel. Doña Marina Ortiz embarked for Chile in September of 1555 and lives today with her sisters and brothers on their estates in Santiago and Concepción. She is respected and loved by all Chileans.[462] As for Gerónimo, he contracted yellow fever in Panamá upon his return here and passed from this life in 1556.[463] It is unfortunate that he would not assume the post of Governor of Chile that Your Excellency bestowed upon him. May my friend rest in peace, dear Lord.

Our priest, Rodrigo González de Marmolejo, the man praised by Governor Valdivia and recommended by him to Your Grace for promotion to bishop,[464] was appointed Bishop of Santiago but died in early October of 1564 before he took office.

---

[460] It is unfortunate that de Mérida does not share what the gift was!
[461] As mentioned previously, she and her husband passed away in 1580 within six months of each other.
[462] Doña Marina passed away in April, 1592.
[463] His death occurred on April 7, 1556.
[464] See Valdivia's Letter III, p. 202,203, in "Historical Sources" on the site.

The wars with the Mapuche still rage on, Sire, and appear to have no end in sight.[465]

As to my personal situation, one of our Spanish physicians contrived a device that permits me to walk, although still with a measure of difficulty. It is a curved piece of thin wood that I wear in my boot that lifts my foot when I walk and prevents me from stumbling or falling. As for my *Cabildo* duties, Governor Villagran appointed me to the position of permanent assistant to the *Cabildo* president, a post I am honored to discharge.

In the February 15 letter to me, Your Noble Highness remarked kindly that my observations concerning matters in Chile from the years 1535 to 1554 have been helpful in understanding better the state of affairs here. Your Eminence requested also that I write of my years in Peru with the Captains Diego de Almagro and Francisco Pizarro and the early days of the Conquest. I feel capable of doing so since Vicente Montesinos and I were recruited by Captain Hernando de Soto,[466] our Extremadura countryman, and joined the Almagro and Pizarro forces in February of 1532. In the first years I knew Captain Almagro but little. However, he asked me to join his expedition to Chile in the years 1535-1537, as I have informed Your Majesty, and during that journey I conversed with him several times about his early years with Pizarro in their voyages of discovery from Panamá City during the years 1524-1532, before my arrival, and am able to share his observations. For the telling of events during these years, I will also rely upon the sea journals of Captain Juan Bautista Pastene for his reflections, since he piloted for the captains on several voyages to the land of Peru. From 1532 to 1535, I have my own recorded documents to draw upon as to what occurred. During my absence to Chile with Almagro from 1535-1537, I will rely upon friends living in Cusco at the time to provide the details of the happenings during those years. And for 1537-1540, I have the personal notations sent me by Father Cristoval de Molina, my close friend from the days with Captain Almagro. And, finally, I will rely upon another Extremaduran

---

[465] As noted previously, the Arauco Wars continued until the late 19th century.
[466] (1500-1542). Born in Badajoz, Extremadura, he was the captain soon famous for the discovery of the Mississippi River.

compatriot from the earliest conquest days, Juan de la Torre y Díaz Chacón,[467] presently the mayor of Arequipa, for the valued information he will provide. With all these ready sources of information, I shall eagerly honor this request from Your Grace with the dispatch of three more letters in the ensuing months.[468]

---

[467] (1500-1590). Another man born in Badajoz, he led a lifetime of distinguished municipal service in Peru.
[468] See The Adventure Chronicles of Conquistador Pedro de Mérida, Volume III: Pizarro.

I Remain, Majesty,   Your Most Humble Servant

Pedro de Merida (signature)

Don Pedro de Mérida

Signed

September 12 1568

Santiago *del Nueva Extremadura*

SO CONCLUDES VOLUME II: VALDIVIA

APPENDICES

FOR VOLUME II

APPENDIX A

A PARTIAL LIST OF THE 150 MEN WHO JOINED CAPTAIN VALDIVIA PRIOR TO REACHING PAPUDO AND MARCHING INLAND TO FOUND THE CAPITAL CITY OF SANTIAGO.

1. Juan Almonacid
2. Alonzo Bustos
3. Juan Alvarez
4. Rodrigo de Araya
5. Francisco de Arteaga
6. Avalos Juan Jufré
7. Lope de Ayala
8. Santiago Azoca
9. Juan Benitez Monge
10. Juan Bohón
11. Juan de Bolaños
12. Juan Cabrera
13. Alonso del Campo
14. Juan Martin de Candia
15. Juan Carmona
16. Alonso Caro her face
17. Luis de Cartagena

18. Francisco Carretero
19. Antonio Carrillo
20. Gaspar de las Casas
21. Martin de Castro
22. Diego de Céspedes
23. Pedro Cisternas
24. Alonso de Cordova
25. Juan Crespo
26. Gabriel de la Cruz
27. Juan Cuevas Bustillos y Teran
28. Juan de Chaves
29. Alonso de Chinchilla
30. Diego Delgado
31. Antonio Diaz de Rivera
32. Bartholomew Diaz
33. Garcia Diaz de Castro
34. Mateo Diez
35. Pedro Dominguez
36. But Esteban del Manzano
37. Juan Fernandez de Alderete
38. Bartolomé Flores
39. Juan Funes
40. John Galaz
41. Francisco Galdames
42. Juan Gallegos
43. Pedro de Gamboa
44. Ruy Garcia
45. Diego Garcia de Caceres
46. Gerardo Gil
47. Juan Godíñez
48. Juan Gomez de Almagro
49. Pedro Gomez
50. Juan Gomez de Yébenes
51. Juan Gonzalez
52. Pedro Gonzalez de Utrera
53. Rodrigo Gonzalez Marmolejo

54. Juan Gutierrez
55. Garcia Hernandez
56. Francisco Hernández Gallego
57. Juan de Herrera
58. Pedro Herrera
59. Anthony Hidalgo
60. Juan de la Higuera
61. Martin de Ibarrola
62. Pascual Jenovés
63. Juan Jimenez
64. Ortún Jimenez de Vertendona
65. Juan Jufré
66. Lope de Landa
67. Francisco Leon
68. Pedro Leon
69. John Wolf
70. Bartolomé Márquez
71. Bernal Martinez
72. Martin Pores
73. Pedro de Miranda
74. Alonso de Monroy
75. Alonso Moreno
76. Salvador de Montoya
77. Bartolomé Muñoz
78. Juan Navarro
79. Juan Negrete
80. Alvar Nunez
81. Diego Núñez
82. Francisco Nunez
83. Lorenzo Nunez
84. Juan Nunez de Castro
85. Diego Olea
86. Juan de Oliva
87. Oribe Sundade
88. Diego de Oro
89. Juan Ortiz Pacheco

90. Martin Ortuño
91. Juan Pacheco
92. Antonio Pastrana
93. Luis de la Peña
94. Alonso Perez
95. Diego Perez
96. Santiago Perez
97. Juan Pinel
98. Francisco Ponce de León
99. Rodrigo de Quiroga
100. Francisco de Rabdona
101. Juan Rasquido
102. Francisco de Riberos
103. Gonzalo de los Rios
104. Francisco Rodriguez
105. Juan Romero
106. Juan Ruíz
107. Gabriel Salazar
108. Alonso de Salguero
109. Alonso Sanchez
110. Rodrigo Sanchez
111. Diego Sanchez Morales
112. Sancho de la Hoz
113. Martin de Solier
114. Ines de Suarez
115. Antonio Tarabajano
116. Luis Ternero
117. Luis de Toledo
118. Hernando de la Torre
119. Antonio de Ulloa
120. Francisco de Vadillo
121. Pedro de Valdivia
122. Juan Valiente
123. Hernando de Vallejo
124. Sebastian Vazquez
125. Marcos Veas

126. Diego de Velasco
127. Jeronimo de Vera
128. Juan de Vera
129. Gaspar de Vergara
130. Francisco de Villagran
131. Pedro de Villagran
132. Gaspar de Villarroel
133. Antonio Zapata
134. Juan Zurbino.
135. Omar Andres Chala Guzman

From Errazuriz, Crescente. *History of Chile: Pedro de Valdivia*. published by Imprenta Cervantes, Santiago de Chile, 1911-1912.

NB: Valdivia says in his Letter I that he arrived in the area of present-day Santiago with 150 men. As we now know, most of these joined him after he left Cusco. The reason the above list does not contain names for the 150 is that those missing have been lost to history.

APPENDIX B

THIS DEPICTS HOW DOÑA INÉS, CISTERNAS, AND THE MEN ARRANGED THEMSELVES FOR THE GUANACO HUNT.

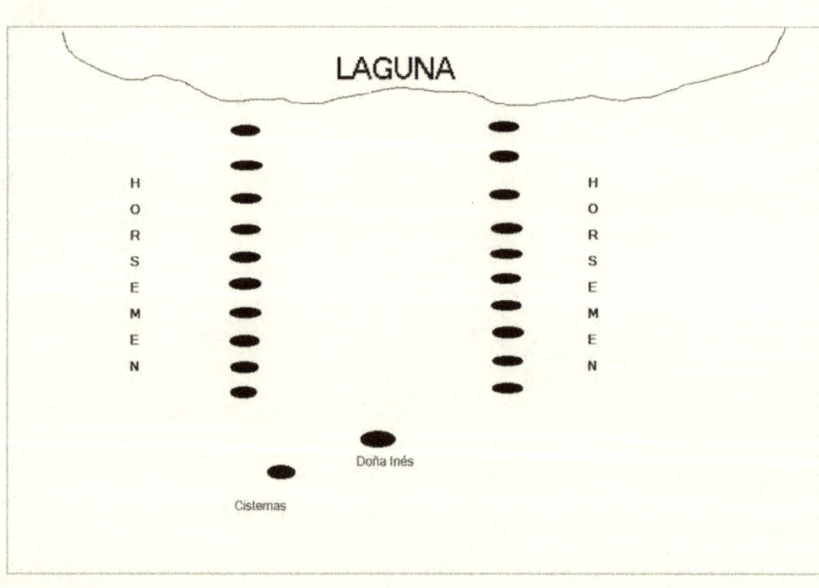

APPENDIX C

BELOW ARE TWO OF PEDRO DE GAMBOA'S DRAWINGS OF SANTIAGO'S TOWN LAYOUT.

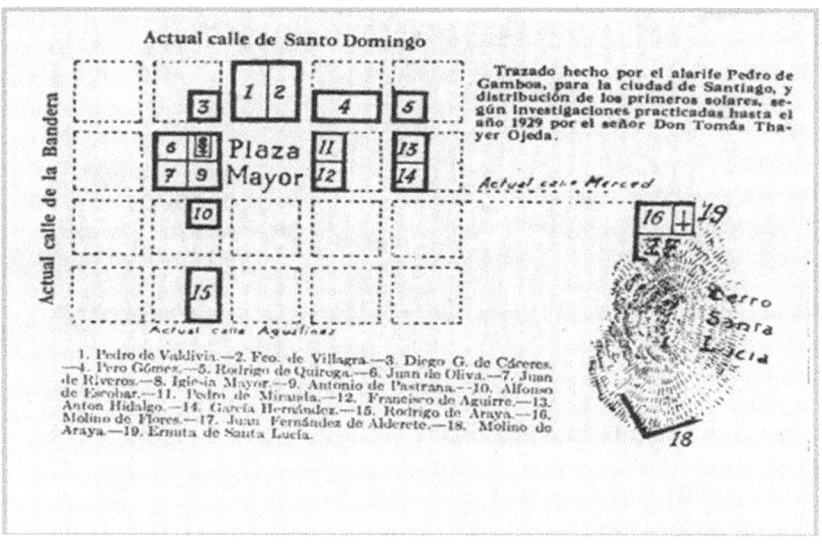

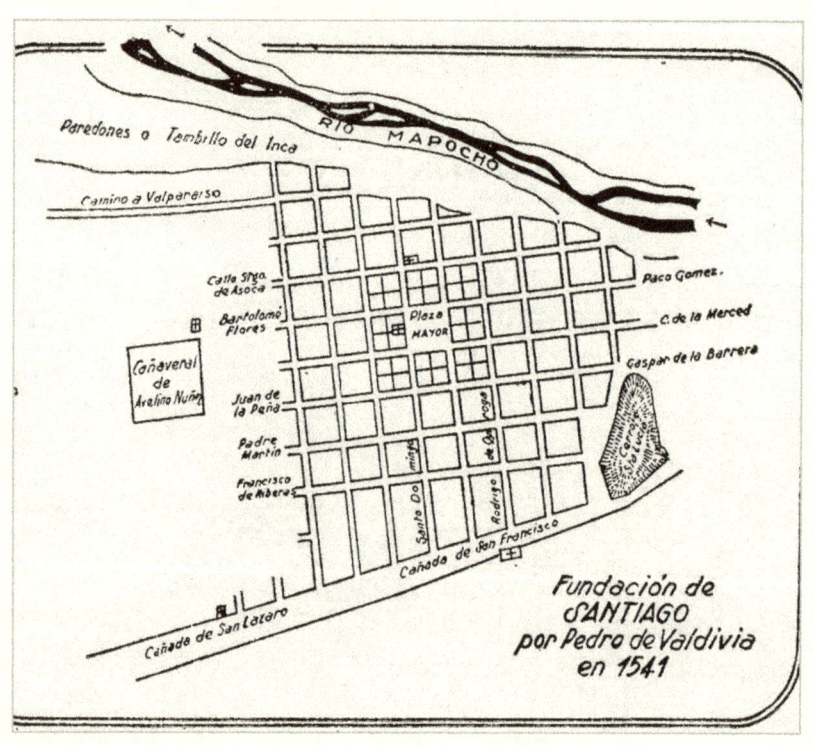

"Courtesy LLILAS Benson Latin American Studies and Collections, The University of Texas at Austin."

APPENDIX D

THE MEDIEVAL CLOCK AND ITS INTRODUCTION TO CHILE IN THE MID-16TH CENTURY.

De Mérida says in Part QQ of the Fifth Letter that the merchant, Lucas Martinez Vegaso, brought a clock to Santiago in September of 1543. In the years after, Valdivia makes several references to clock time in his Letter I (1545) and Letter III (1550). De Mérida also mentions clock time on several occasions.

As for context, during the 15th and 16th centuries, clock making flourished, particularly in the metalworking towns of Nuremberg, Augsburg, and in Blois, France. Some of the early table clocks had only one time-keeping hand, with the dial between the hour markers divided into four equal parts making the clocks readable to the nearest 15 minutes. Other clocks were exhibitions of craftsmanship and skill, incorporating astronomical indicators and musical movements. Eventually, the minute hand entered into common use. During the latter part of the fourteenth century in Europe, the 'chamber' clock brought clocks down to a size to fit into the home. Then, in the fifteenth century, table, or mantel clocks, using springs instead of weights for power, started to appear. Some clocks also started using a balance wheel escapement. Valdivia and de Mérida do not describe the clocks that found their way to Santiago, but that is of no account. The relevant matter is that after the clock's delivery, both began to use hours and minutes frequently to refer to the passage of time.

APPENDIX E

THE CANONICAL HOURS

- Matins (during the night, at midnight with some);
- Lauds or Dawn Prayer (at Dawn, or 3 a.m.)
- Prime or Early Morning Prayer (First Hour = approximately 6 a.m.)
- Terce or Mid-Morning Prayer (Third Hour = approximately 9 a.m.)
- Sext or Midday Prayer (Sixth Hour = approximately 12 noon)
- None or Mid-Afternoon Prayer (Ninth Hour = approximately 3 p.m.)
- Vespers or Evening Prayer ("at the lighting of the lamps", generally at 6 p.m.)
- Compline or Night Prayer (before retiring, generally at 9 p.m.)

APPENDIX F

NAUTICAL TERMS

ABAFT. Toward the stern of a vessel.

AFORE. Forward. The opposite of abaft.

ALFONSINE TABLES. They were a set of astronomical data that enabled calculation of lunar and solar eclipses and the positions of the planets for any given time based on the Ptolemaic theory. Calculated in 1252, they were the best astronomical tables available, until the work of Nicolaus Copernicus superseded them in the 1550's. Please see an image of the Tables in 8J-L. on the site.

AMIDSHIPS. In the center of the ship; either with reference to her length or to her breadth.

ANCHOR. The weight by which, when dropped to the bottom, the vessel is held fast.

ARM. Yard-arm. The extremity of a yard.

ASTROLABE. An astrolabe is an elaborate inclinometer historically used by astronomers and navigators to measure the inclined position in the sky of a celestial body, day or night. The word means "the one that catches the heavenly bodies." It can thus be used to identify stars or planets, to determine local latitudes, to survey, or to triangulate. It was used in classical antiquity, the Islamic Golden Age, the Middle Ages, and the Age of Discovery for all these purposes. Also, called a "ring." See image 7A-D.8,9 on the site.

In order to use the astrolabe, the navigator held the instrument by the ring at the top. This caused it to remain in a vertical plane. The alidade was aligned to point at the object and the altitude was read off the outer degree scale.

If observing a dim object such as a star, the navigator would view the object directly through the alidade. If observing the sun, it was both safer and easier to allow the shadow of one of the alidade's vanes to be cast onto the opposite vane.

ATHWART. Across.

ATHWART-SHIPS: Across the line of the vessel's keel. In opposition to fore-and-aft.

BACK. To back a sail is to throw it aback. To back and fill is to alternately back and fill the sails.

BEAMS. Strong pieces of timber stretching across the ship to support the decks. "On the weather or lee beam," is in a direction to windward or leeward, at right angles to the keel. "On beam ends:" The situation of a vessel when turned over by the winds so that her beams are inclined towards the vertical.

BEAR. An object "bears" when it is in such a direction from the person looking.

BEARING. The horizontal angle between the direction of an object and another object, or between it and that of true north.

BEATING. Going toward the direction of the wind, by alternate tacks.

BETWEEN-DECKS. The space between any two decks of a ship.

BINNACLE. (See COMPASS, MAGNETIC).

BOATSWAIN. (Pronounced bo-s'n). The ship's officer (mate) who has charge of the rigging and calls the crew to duty.

BOW. The rounded part of a vessel, forward.

BOWLINE. (Pronounced bo-lin.). A vessel is said to be "on a bowline" or "on a taut bowline" when she is close-hauled.

BROADSIDE. The entire side of a vessel.

BULK HEAD. Partitions of boards to separate different parts of a vessel.

BULWARKS. The woodwork around a vessel, above her deck, consisting of boards fastened to stanchions and timber-heads.

BUNTLINES. Ropes used for hauling up the body of a sail.

BY. "By the head." Said of a ship when her head is lower in the water than her stern. If her stern is lower, she is "by the stern."

CABIN. The after part of a ship, where the officers live.

CANVAS. The cloth of which sails are made.

CLEW. The lower corner of square sails, and the after corner of a fore-and-aft sail. "To clew up" is to haul up the clew of a sail.

CLOSE-HAULED. Applied to a ship that is sailing with her yards braced up so as to get as much as possible to windward. The same as "on a top bowline," "full and by," and "on the wind."

COMPASS. The instrument that tells the course of a vessel. See image 5QQ-SS.18.

COMPASS, MAGNETIC: Pastene used a magnetic compass to plot his way. Introduced into Europe around 1200 AD, it, along with dead reckoning, determined a ship's forward progress. At the forward edge of the bowl, a black, vertical line was drawn. As the needle always seeks magnetic north, the point on the circle that touched the vertical line indicated the direction in which the ship was heading, as long as the diameter of the bowl that passed through the line was kept parallel to the ship's keel. That was done by keeping the compass in a fixed position in the binnacle, a rectangular box secured to the deck. It was located on the quarter-deck where the captain could watch it. He was then able to give orders to the helmsman as to the course.

COMPASS POINTS:

COMPASS POINT	ABBREVIATION	IN DEGREES
NORTH	N	0
NORTH by EAST	N by E	11 ¼
NORTH NORTHEAST	NNE	22 ½
NORTHEAST by NORTH	NE by N	33 ¾
NORTHEAST	NE	45
NORTHEAST by EAST	NE by E	56 ¼
EAST NORTHEAST	ENE	67 ½
EAST by NORTH	E by N	78 ¾
EAST	E	90
EAST by SOUTH	E by S	101 ¼
EAST SOUTHEAST	ESE	112 ½
SOUTHEAST by EAST	SE by E	123 ¾
SOUTHEAST	SE	135

SOUTHEAST by SOUTH	SE by S	146 ¼
SOUTH SOUTHEAST	SSE	157 ½
SOUTH by EAST	S by E	168 ¾
SOUTH	S	180
SOUTH by WEST	S by W	191 ¼
SOUTH SOUTHWEST	SSW	202 ½
SOUTHWEST by SOUTH	SW by S	213 ¾
SOUTHWEST	SW	225
SOUTHWEST by WEST	SW by W	236 ¼
WEST SOUTHWEST	WSW	247 ½
WEST by SOUTH	W by S	258 ¾
WEST	W	270
WEST by NORTH	W by N	281 ¼
WEST NORTHWEST	WNW	292 ½
NORTHWEST by WEST	NW by W	303 ¾
NORTHWEST	NW	315
NORTHWEST by NORTH	NW by N	326 ¼
NORTH NORTHWEST	NNW	337 ½
NORTH by WEST	N by W	348 ¾
NORTH	N	360

CORPO SANTO ((holy body). See St. Elmos' fire.

DEAD RECKONING. A reckoning kept by calculating one's current position by using a previously determined position and advancing that position based upon known or estimated speeds over elapsed time and course.

DRAUGHT. The depth of water that a ship requires to float.

EVEN-KEEL. The situation of a ship when she sits evenly upon the water, neither end being down more than the other.

FATHOM. One fathom is equal to six feet. Mariners have taken water soundings since Greek times using a lead weight attached to a thin, marked rope. On the Mississippi in Mark Twain's day, they used "twain" for the word "two". Thus, a depth of two feet was called out as, "By the mark, twain."

FULL-AND-BY. Sailing close-hauled upon a wind.

FURL. To roll a sail up on yard or boom securely.

GALLEY. The place where the cooking is done.

GANGWAY. That part of a ship's side, amidships, where people pass on and off the vessel.

GUNWALE. (Pronounced "gun-nel.") The upper rail of a ship.

HALYARDS. Ropes used for raising and lowering sails and yards and flying signal flags.

HAMMOCK. A piece of canvas, hung at each end, in which a seaman sleeps.

HATCH. An opening in the deck to allow passage up and down.

HAUL. Said of a ship when she comes up close upon the wind.

HEAD. The unique figure at the prow of a vessel. Also, the lavatories in the bow.

HEAVE-TO. To put a ship in the position of lying-to. See. Lie-to.

HEEL. The after part of the keel. "To heel" is to lie over on one side.

HELM. The wheel and machinery by which the ship is steered.

HOLD. The inner part of a vessel where the cargo is stored.

JIB. A triangular sail set on a forward stay.

KEEL. The lowest and principal timber of a ship, running fore and aft its entire length and supporting the complete frame.

LABOR. A vessel is said to labor when she rolls and pitches heavily.

LAND HO. The cry used when land is seen.

LATITUDE. Latitude is a geographic coordinate that specifies the north–south position of a point on the Earth's surface. It is an angle which ranges from 0° at the Equator to 90° (North or South) at the poles. Lines of constant latitude, or parallels, run east–west as circles parallel to the equator. Latitude is used together with longitude to specify the precise location of features on the surface of the Earth.

LEE. The side opposite to that from which the wind blows. If a vessel has the wind on her starboard side, that will be the "weather," and the port side will be the "lee" side.

LEEWARD. Any direction away from that whence the wind blows, as opposed to "windward," which means any direction toward the wind.

LIE-TO. To stop the progress of a ship, either by counterbracing the yards or by reducing sail.

LIST. The inclination of a vessel to one side, as a list to port or starboard.

LOG or LOG-BOOK. A journal kept by an officer, in our case, Captain Pastene, in which the situation of the vessel, winds, weather, courses, distances, and everything of importance that occurs is recorded.

LONGBOAT. The small boat to carry passengers to and from shore.

LONGITUDE. Longitude is a geographic coordinate that specifies the east–west position of a point on the Earth's surface. It is an angular measurement, usually expressed in degrees. Meridians (lines running from pole to pole) connect points with the same longitude. The only practical method for determining longitude at the time of the Conquest was a well-known method of timing eclipses. The eclipse timing method is, first, you determine the local time that starts or ends by direct observation. Then you compare your local time for that event against the local time at some distant place. The difference in the two times is the difference in longitude. Neither Pastene nor Ruíz refers to the determination of longitude as they probably were mystified by it. Following the South American coast line in the new land was much easier to do, and that is what they did.

MAST. A spar set upright from the deck to support rigging, yards, and sails.

MASTER. The captain of a sailing ship

MATE. The captain's mate was responsible for fitting out the ship, and making sure it had all the sailing supplies necessary for the voyage. He hoisted and lowered the anchor, docked and undocked the ship, examined the ship daily, notifying the captain if there were problems with the sails, masts, ropes, or pulleys. He executed the orders of the master, and would command in his place if he was sick or absent.

MERIDIAN. A line of longitude.

MESS. Any number of men who eat and lodge together.

MIDSHIPS. The timbers at the broadest part of the vessel.

MIZZEN-MAST. The aftermost mast of a ship.

PARALLEL. A line of latitude.

PERU OR HUMBOLDT CURRENT. This current extends from southern Chile (~45th parallel south) to northern Peru (~4th parallel south) where cold, up welled waters intersect warm tropical waters to form the Equatorial Front. Captains Pastene, Ruíz, and Grijalva knew it as the Peru Current. Its alternative name is taken from that of the German scientist Alexander von Humboldt, who in 1802 took measurements that showed the coldness of the flow in relation to the air above it and the sea around it.

The trade winds are the primary drivers of the Peru/Humboldt Current circulation. Variability in this system is driven by latitudinal shifts between the Intertropical Convergent Zone and the trade winds in the north. Shifts within the South Pacific High at mid-latitudes, as well as cyclonic storms and movement of the Southern Westerlies southward also contribute to system changes. Atmospheric variability off central Chile is enhanced by the aggravation of coastal low pressure systems trapped between the marine boundary layer and the coastal mountains. This is prominent poleward from 27th parallel south to 42nd parallel south.

PORT. The left side of a vessel.

QUARTER-DECK. That part of the upper deck abaft the main mast.

REEF. To reduce a sail by taking in upon its head, if a square sail, and its foot, if a fore-and-aft sail.

RIGGING. The general term for all the ropes of a vessel.

ROAD, ROADS, OR ROADSTEAD. An anchorage some distance from shore.

SAILOR, SEAMAN, MARINER. Names for those who manned sailing ships.

SAILS. Sails are of two kinds: square sails, which hang from yards, their foot lying across the line of the keel; and fore-and-aft sails that set upon gaffs, their foot running with the line of the keel.

SAND OR HOUR GLASS. The nautical half-hour sandglass is a timepiece known since the 14th century (although presumed to be of very ancient use and origin). They were employed to determine the standing time of the watches. Columbus, for example, used them on his voyages in the late 15th century. The British navy kept watch times with them until

1839. Also, they helped determine a ship's speed and distance traveled. (See Speed Measurement.)

SCUD. To drive before a gale, with no sail, or only enough to keep the ship ahead of the sea. Also, low clouds that fly swiftly before the wind.

SCUPPERS. Holes cut in the ship's water-ways for the sea water to run from the decks.

SOLAR ECLIPSE. The story de Mérida tells in the Seventh Letter about how Captain Almagro used a solar eclipse to his advantage was due to the mate's use of the Alfonsine Tables to predict the event.

SOUNDING. See FATHOM.

SPAR. The general term for all masts, yards, booms, and gaffs.

SPEED MEASUREMENT. In Pastene's day, pilots used a shaped piece of wood attached to a line in which knots were spaced, so that the number of knots paid out in half an hour, as measured by a half-hour sand glass, equaled the number of nautical miles per hour the ship was making. Hence comes the word "knots" for speed at sea.

ST. ELMO'S FIRE. St. Elmo's fire (also St. Elmo's light) is a weather phenomenon in which luminous plasma is created by a coronal discharge from a sharp or pointed object in a strong electric field in the atmosphere (such as those generated by thunderstorms or created by a volcanic eruption). St. Elmo's fire is named after St. Erasmus of Formia (also called St. Elmo, one of the two Italian names for St. Erasmus, the other being St. Erasmo), the patron saint of sailors. The occurrence sometimes appeared on ships at sea during thunderstorms and was regarded by sailors with religious awe for its glowing ball of light, accounting for the name. Sailors considered St. Elmo's fire as a good omen (as a sign of the presence of their patron saint). Also known as *corpo santo* (holy body).

STARBOARD. The right side of a ship.

STERN. The after end of a vessel.

STRIKE. To lower a sail.

TACK. To put a ship about, so that having the wind on one side, she is brought about on the other. Also, a ship is on the starboard tack when she has the wind on the starboard side.

TOP. A platform placed over the head of a mast for the convenience of men aloft.

TRADES. The trade winds (also called trades) are the prevailing pattern of easterly surface winds found in the tropics near the Earth's equator. These winds blow predominantly from the northeast in the Northern Hemisphere and from the southeast in the Southern Hemisphere. The trade winds act as the steering flow for tropical cyclones that form over the world's oceans, guiding their path westward.

TRUCK. A circular piece of wood at the head of the highest mast of a ship, with small holes for signal halyards.

WAIST. That part of the upper deck between the quarter-deck and forecastle.

WATCHES: The seamen of a sailing ship were divided into two watches, one the starboard and the other the port. Each watch period varied between the two, so that over two days their total watch times were identical. The time was kept by the 30 minute sand glass. Please see below:

	DAY 1	DAY 2
First watch: 2000 to 0000	starboard	port
Middle watch: 0000 to 0400	port	starboard
Morning watch: 0400 to 0800	starboard	port
Forenoon watch: 0800 to 1200	port	starboard
Afternoon watch: 1200 to 1600	starboard	port

First dog watch: 1600 to 1800	port	starboard
Last dog watch: 1800 to 2000	starboard	port

TOTAL HOURS DAY 1: Starboard = 14; Port = 10
TOTAL HOURS DAY 2: Starboard = 10; Port = 14

WEIGH. To lift up, as to weigh the anchor.

WESTERLIES. The westerlies are the prevailing winds in the middle latitudes (i.e., between 35 and 65 degrees latitude), which blow in areas pole ward of the high pressure area known as the subtropical ridge. These prevailing winds blow from the west to the east, and steer extra-tropical cyclones in this general manner. The winds are predominantly from the southwest in the Northern Hemisphere and from the northwest in the Southern Hemisphere.

WHEEL. The instrument by which the ship is steered.

WHISTLE. This was today's "bosun's whistle" used by a petty officer (boatswain) in charge of rigging, anchors, cables, and watches to communicate with sailors. Ancient Greeks and Romans used flutes.

YARD. A long piece of timber, hung at the center to a mast, to spread square sails upon.

BIBLIOGRAPHY FOR VOLUME II

Alegría, Fernando, <u>Lautaro: Joven Libertador de Arauco</u>. F. S. Crofts & Co., 1946.

Arana, Diego Barros, <u>Historia General de Chile</u>, Linkgua Digital, 2012.

Cruz, Eduardo Agustin, <u>The Grand Araucanian Wars in the Kingdom of Chile, Xlibris, 2010.</u>

De la Vega, Garcilaso ("El Inca"). <u>Royal Commentaries of the Incas</u>, 2 Vol. New York: Burt Franklin, 1968.

De Vivar, Jerónimo, <u>Crónica y relación copiosa y verdadera de los reinos de Chile (Chronicle and abundant and true relation of the kingdoms of Chile)</u>.

On-line: https://web.archive.org/web/20080526101641/http://www.artehistoria.jcyl.es/cronicas/contextos/11498.htm

Diaz Meza, Aurelio (*Leyendas y Episodios Chilenos*. 1929, *Soc. Imp. y Lit. Universo en Santiago de Chile.*

Errazuriz, Crescente, History of Chile: Pedro de Valdivia. *Imprenta Cervantes*, Santiago de Chile, 1911-1912.

Galdames, Luis, The History of Chile. New York: Russell and Russell, 1964.

Lazaeta, Luis Silva, *El Conquistador Francisco de Aguirre*, *La Revista Catolica*, 1907. 7 guys left Cusco.

Lobera, Pedro Mariño, Chronicle of the Kingdom of Chile. Book First.

On-line: http://www.cervantesvirtual.com/obra-visor/cronica-del-reino-de-chile—0/html/feec70e8-82b1-11df-acc7-002185ce6064_1.html

Mackenna, Benjamin Vicuña, *Lautaro Y Sus tres Compañas*, Santiago: *Imprenta de la Librería del Mercurio*, 1876 (Reprint).

Marmolejo, Alonso de Góngora, History of All Thngs that have occurred in the Kingdom of Chile and of those who have ruled (1536-1575). *Instituto de Literatura Chilena*, 1969. Web: http://www.historia.uchile.cl/CDA/fh_complex/0,1393,SCID%253D10200%2526ISID%253D404%2526JNID%253D12,00.html

Medina, Jose Toribio, Collection of Unpublished Documents Concerning the History of Chile (*Documentos inéditos*), 1888-1902.

Ojeda, Tomás Thayer, *Los Conquistadores de Chile*, Vol. 1, *Imprenta Cervantes*, Santiago de Chile, 1908.

Prescott, William H., History of the Conquest of Peru, New York: Hurst & Co., 1895.

Vernon, Ida Stevenson Weldon, Pedro de Valdivia: *Conquistador* of Chile, University of Austin Press, 1946.

CPSIA information can be obtained
at www.ICGtesting.com
Printed in the USA
LVHW090957140120